T0368731

THE
GOLIATH STONE

Charles Cobb

 www.trafford.com
North America & international
toll-free: 1 888 232 4444 (USA & Canada)
fax: 812 355 4082

The Goliath Stone

The Goliath Stone is an action/adventure thriller set in the first world war. It is based on factual occurrences. The protagonist, Lieutenant Miles Armstrong, is a Canadian who enlisted in the Canadian cavalry and later transferred to the Royal Flying Corps. The story starts with Armstrong, who is multi-lingual, being recalled from front line service and seconded to the Foreign Office.

He is told that he will fly to Rumania for the purpose of rescuing the queen of that country from the advancing Germans. Queen Marie, wife of the ineffectual Ferdinand of Rumania is a granddaughter of Queen Victoria and a one time sweetheart of George V of England. Marie was a noted beauty who, relatively, created as much interest in the society pages as the late Diana does in our time.

There is a second motive for the assignment, and that is to assist the Rumanians to recover their national treasures that had been sent to Russia for safe-keeping when the Germans took Bucharest. But now the Tsar has been deposed, Russia is in revolutionary turmoil and Marie wants her country's treasures saved. Armstrong has a third and secret assignment, separate to the others. He is told that in 1907 the Irish crown jewels (the property of the English crown) had been stolen from Dublin castle. The German Kaiser, Wilhelm 11, acquired them and gave them as a gift to Ferdinand, king of Rumania. Armstrong is told that he is to attempt to remove the Irish jewels from the others and get them back to England.

While being briefed in London he meets the lovely Anna-Marie DeCourville and has an affair with her, unaware that she is trying to steal one of the Irish jewels known as the Goliath Stone.

With his mechanic, Sergeant O'Reilly, he flies to Jassy in Rumania, which is the new capital, now that Bucharest has fallen. There he meets Marie and her Canadian lover the fabled Klondike Joe Boyle, now a Colonel in the Canadian army. Armstrong, Boyle and other go to Moscow but arrive as the Bolshevik revolution boils over, forcing them to break into the Kremlin during the fighting and recover the jewels. Armstrong again meets Anna-Marie and promises to give her the Goliath Stone.

Armstrong survives train wrecks, armed attacks, the capture and rescue of Anna-Marie, the theft of 100,000,000.00 dollars in gold bullion, and the bombing of a ship to fly away with Anna-Marie, O'Reilly, the Goliath Stone...and a few bars of gold.

Facts: The recovery of the crown jewels did happen but the gold bullion was never returned to Rumania and the soviets denied all knowledge of it. Boyle was an actual character and his liaison with Queen Marie was a celebrated affair. Most elements of the train journey are based on actual fact, including the royal steam engine kept at instant readiness on an obscure branch line throughout three years of bloody warfare.

THE GOLIATH STONE

The Legend

After David slew Goliath, the giant's head was cut off and exhibited for all Israel to see...with the stone still embedded in the skull. The military commanders of Israel's armies kept the skull as a symbol of the chosen people's invincibility. Due to religious strictures against symbols; graven images; unclean practices and the like, the relic was kept low key and no further mention is made of it in the Bible.

Legend tells us that the stone was removed from the head and found to be a large diamond. It was cut and polished by Hebrew craftsmen into a jewel of exceeding value and beauty. It then became part of the treasure of the royal house of David and passed on through the generations, until the time of the Babylonian conquest of Jerusalem and the execution of King Zedekiah with all of his male offspring. Only his eldest daughter, Tamar was saved and she fled with the prophet Jeremiah to Egypt and safety. They took with them many precious things, including the Goliath Stone.

Tradition has it that Jeremiah and the princess Tamar then left Egypt for the Isles of the North – landing near Belfast, Northern Ireland. Later, Tamar married King Heremon of that country. Of the precious things she brought with her only Jacob's stone, which today sits under the coronation throne in Westminster Abbey, and the Goliath Stone survived to modern times. The Goliath Stone became part of the Irish crown jewels. These jewels were the property of the king of England and were worn by him on ceremonial occasions when in Ireland.

In 1907, a gang of dissolute upper-class hell-raisers, desperate for money to pay debts, stole the Irish crown jewels from Dublin castle and sold them in Paris and Amsterdam. The Goliath Stone disappeared forever... Or did it?

CHAPTER ONE

September 1917. Western front, Amiens sector.
Armstrong thought that if he had to die, he'd rather have done so with another cup of coffee in him. As it was, his pounding head and his boiling stomach kept reminding him of the cheap wine he had drunk last night. And that bastard German was still trying to kill him!

He held the joystick of the Sopwith Pup towards his left groin so that the stubby biplane gently spiraled upwards through the cloud and only the swirling eddies streaming back from the wingtips indicated movement.

He was large for the cockpit of the small plane. His shoulders touched the rim on either side, and the top of his head was above the protection of the visor that sat over the instrument panel. He pushed his goggles off his eyes to let the vaporous slipstream moisten his face and mix with the castor oil thrown off by the Clerget rotary engine. He looked behind him and cursed the jagged line of holes that ran from just behind his seat to the tail – more work for O'Reilly when he got back...if he got back.

That Hun was good. Too bloody good. And in moments the fight would be on again. The cloud he had sought cover in was small, rapidly dissipating, and the British lines were miles to the west. He centered the stick and eased the plane into level flight. He needed a few more seconds in the cloud, a few more seconds to clear his head.

He had been one of a three-plane patrol that swept across the German lines at dawn, and his flight had met with a host of Albatrosses over Cambrai. The fight was amazingly brief. One moment the sky was filled with maltese-crossed machines, spitting machine-gun fire in all directions. The next moment he was all alone...except for the German in the gaily painted Albatross who put the bullet holes in his fuselage.

The two pilots duelled for over five minutes, twisting and turning, diving and soaring, spiraling and spinning. The German countered Armstrong's every maneuver. The Pup was outdated, compared to the Albatross, due for replacement by the highly successful Camel, but the Camel hadn't got to Armstrong's squadron yet, and Armstrong knew he was at a disadvantage in this fight. Only his skill had kept him alive, but the German was good and time was running out. The shuddering impact of bullets striking his airframe had caused Armstrong to seek a few seconds of fragile safety in this cloud.

Armstrong craned his neck, searching for the German as the cloud thinned. Whoever saw the other first would have the edge. His eyes caught a black speck coming from above and he rolled the Pup away from it. The German flashed by, machine guns spitting fire. He missed. Armstrong roared out. "Too soon, you bastard!" He shoved his throttle to full power and, screaming profanities, pushed the joystick forward and took the Pup into a vertical dive. Down through the cloud. Down into clear air. Down to meet the Albatross as it pulled out of its dive. The German, his reflexes and controls rendered sluggish by 'G' forces, was unable to avoid the bullets that stitched a seam of holes the length of his plan, shattering his propeller and caused his unloaded engine to race to destruction.

The Pup, every strut and brace vibrating, pulled out of the dive and Armstrong, after a quick look around for more hostiles, watched the Albatross flutter, erratically spinning, to earth. He saw a figure fall away from the plane and the mushroom of a parachute pop open, a parachute that was denied him in a British plane because the high command thought they were bad for morale. He eased the Pup over to where the German was gently falling, and studied him and his miracle life-saver. The German raised his arm in an ironic salute, confident of his safe arrival on friendly soil. Armstrong grinned and touched his hand to his helmet as he turned westwards toward the allied lines.

Fifteen minutes later the Sopwith Pup bumped down on a grass field, safe behind the front lines, and taxied to where mechanics and fitters were waiting to service it. The propeller clattered to a stop, and Lieutenant Miles Armstrong MC, late of the Calgary Light Horse and now transferred to the Royal Flying Corps, eased his six foot three inch frame out of the cockpit and wearily dropped to the ground.

He pulled his leather helmet off his head as he cleared his throat and spat out the residue of caster oil that fouled his mouth. Next he pulled a stained rag from his pocket and wiped his face. He had a strong face, confident and assured, with heavy brows over ice-blue eyes. His hair was a wiry sandy-red, cut shorter than that of his brother pilots. A firm jaw indicated both obstinacy and resolution. His nose had been broken once but its slightly swollen bridge was in harmony with the toughness of his features, now strained with fatigue lines that aged him beyond his twenty five years.

A soldier detached himself from the waiting ground crew and ambled in an unmilitary way to Armstrong.

With a wide grin, Private William O'Reilly, a sixty three inch graduate of the Dublin slums, thief, drunkard, womanizer, and mechanic of genius, chopped off a flippant salute and said, "Ah Jasus melord, did you let the Heinies put holes in me machine? Couldn't ye have ducked?"

Armstrong smiled at the diminutive Irishman. He enjoyed O'Reilly's cheeky, insubordinate humor, and now his nervous tension eased at the sight of his thin-faced mechanic. O'Reilly was of indeterminate age and had left his native Dublin for the fleshpots of the East End of London. As a consequence, his speech was a riotous Irish-Cockney mixture of expressions and oaths. He had, or so he told Armstrong, enlisted in the army to avoid a lengthy prison sentence for safe-cracking. The sensitive fingers that had served him in civilian life now were applied to the care of aero engines. It was said that O'Reilly's engines ran sweeter than anyone else's.

Armstrong clapped "O'Reilly on the back with a familiarity unusual between officer and ranker, and spoke in the easy clear English of the Canadian west, so different to the strangled 'far back' tones affected by some of the British officer corps.

"I don't think he hit anything important, O'Reilly, but you'd better get the riggers to check the control wires in case of nicks."

"To be sure I will your honor. I'll check the whole bleeding plane personally. Er, did ye get the whoreson that put the holes in your backside then?"

Armstrong looked eastwards "Yeah. I got him!" He turned on his heel and strode off to his quarters.

O'Reilly watched him go, then he and the rest of the ground crew pushed the Pup to its maintenance area.

The pilots were quartered in an old farmhouse that had been abandoned by its owners during one of the earlier

German advances. About fifteen officers slept in its rooms, though the number varied due to cranky aircraft and the Hun in the sun. A nearby barn was used as a mess and the squadron offices were set up in a stable.

The room Armstrong shared with three other pilots was empty, being breakfast time. He wearily took off his Sidcot flying jacket, splashed water over his face from a washstand bowl and soaped off the flying grime. He was pulling on a casual sweater, preparatory to going to the mess for his meal, when the squadron adjutant, Captain Forsythe, walked into the room.

"Ah Armstrong. I hear your flight ran into trouble. Glad to see you're all right. How were things?"

"Well I got an Albatross but I don't know what happened to the rest of my sortie. We got separated."

"Got one eh! Bloody good. Give me a report after you've eaten. The rest of your flight are all right. Swan landed a few minutes before you and Bright's sent a signal from the front lines. He had to put down – plane's all buggered up but he's not too damaged. Did anyone else see the one you got?"

"No, but I got him for sure. I saw him crash."

"Ah. Quite! Well, take a nap this morning if you can. You'll be out again before noon. The General Staff are asking for an all out effort in support of the latest push."

With that he left and Armstrong, grimacing with distaste at the news of yet another "all out effort" went down to the mess. The barn was quiet. Most of the pilots were either patrolling or sprawled on the grass, enjoying precious moments of peace before they took their place in the skies over the lines. A few officers sat at a rude plank and trestle table reading yesterday's newspapers and drinking coffee. The rich smell of frying bacon came from behind a canvas screen that separated the cooking and dining areas. Here and there on the rough frame walls were hung souvenirs of the fighting. A broken propeller, the joystick from a Fokker Tripe, a "picklehaub" cavalry helmet. The furniture was primitive, either benches or bales of hay, and the heavy odor of cattle still permeated the air.

Armstrong acknowledged the nods of his fellows, and an orderly slid a large serving of bacon and eggs in front of him. There was no shortage of food here, not with planes making daily mail runs to the coast. He was contentedly drinking a second cup of coffee when the squadron clerk, Corporal Entwhistle, poke his head in the barn door.

"Lieutenant Armstrong sir. The Major wants to see you as soon as possible, if you please sir."

Armstrong groaned to himself. What the hell did old Stuffy want now? Didn't the man know he needed his meal. "All right Corp, I'm on the way."

The squadron commanding officer, Major Horace Harper – "Stuff" to his pilots – was a short rotund man with no sense of humor and none of the leadership qualities one expected to find in a young and adventurous service. He learned to fly – badly – before the war and had suffered a broken leg when he crashed–landed the day after he had received his wings. He rarely flew operations again but, being a stable "by the book officer", he had quickly risen in rank.

Armstrong knocked at the door and entered. Major Harper was sitting at a battered old desk, a remnant from the farm house. Stuffy, however, was not alone. Sitting on the only other chair in the room was a civilian who looked at Armstrong with sharp inquisitive eyes. The man dressed in clothing more appropriate to the corridors of power in Whitehall than a front-line airfield. Striped city trousers showed under an expensive Burberry raincoat and he held a black homberg hat in his hand, as if unwilling to put it down in the dusty office. He looked well-fed and sleek and projected an aura of power.

Stuffy Harper spoke. "Ah, Armstrong. Here you are. Stand at ease please. Forsythe tells me you got another Hun this morning. That's your eight isn't it? Well done Lieutenant. How did you get him?"

"I got the edge on him and blew out his engine," Armstrong said, omitting the required "sir". He didn't trust Harper and considered him to be more concerned with his own advancement than the welfare of his pilots.

"And the pilot?"

"He parachuted down."

"Ah humph." Stuffy turned to the civilian. "The Germans are using parachutes, cowardly behavior don'tcher know. Thank God our general staff won't hear of our men using the things."

The civilian shot a keen glance at Armstrong. "So the German landed safely?" His voice matched his appearance – sharp and incisive, with an impatient quality.

"I expect so," said Armstrong, eyeing the man with interest. "That's the idea of the bloody things, is it not? To allow the man to escape a damaged plane, not like our brave men who laughingly flame their way into mother earth. Of course, the German will be flying again tomorrow. Maybe I should have shot him on the way down for being such a coward?"

Stuffy's prominent eyes bulged even further from his head. His face went brick red and his mouth flapped like a cod out of water. Armstrong watched with amusement. Stuffy had been known to get so enraged at the antics of his officers that he almost collapsed with apoplexy.

Stuffy finally spluttered, "Don't be so damned impertinent, Lieutenant. You mean to say you'd shoot a defenseless man in a parachute!"

Armstrong, prompted by a mischievous urge to enrage Stuffy more said, "Sure I would, that's my job, isn't it?"

"But, but...Damn and blast it man, it's not cricket. It's not fair. Don't you Canadians have any sense of ethics? God-damn it man, don't you know how to behave like a gentleman."

"I guess not. I just want to kill the bastards. I didn't realize Germans were off limits."

"Say sir when you speak to me, you insolent young puppy. By God I'll, I'll."

Stuffy stopped spluttering, not because he had run out of words, but because the civilian had stopped him with a gesture. Armstrong noted the degree of control the civilian had over Stuffy.

"That will do Major," said the civilian. "What I have to discuss with Lieutenant Armstrong is of more importance right now."

Stuffy's face turned even redder. "But damn it sir, what he has said is probably a court-martial offence."

Armstrong flushed with anger. Contemptuous of Stuffy's authority, he balled his fists and banged them down on the desk as he leaned forward and thrust his face close to the Major's. "Maybe you can have me shot while I'm hanging from a nonexistent parachute," he snarled.

Stuffy began to splutter again but the civilian arose abruptly from his chair.

"Enough! I am not interested in this issue at this time. Perhaps if Armstrong and I cannot reach an agreement, you can take it further. Now, however, I need to be alone with him. Major, please excuse us." The civilian moved to the door. "Come with me, Lieutenant."

It was an order, not a request, delivered in the manner of one accustomed to power and privilege. Armstrong felt resentment at the man's arrogance but followed him outside, leaving a scarlet-faced Stuffy standing at his desk.

The pair walked in silence for a moment. The man had donned his homberg and wore it at a rakish angle. He was almost a foot shorter than Armstrong but he set the pace with quick forceful strides.

The civilian stopped suddenly and faced Armstrong. "Why did you deliberately anger the Major?" He stared at Armstrong with cold gray eyes.

"Because he's a pompous prating ass," said Armstrong. "And I'm not a career officer. I'm only in this war till it's over."

The civilian's eyes locked on Armstrong's as if to search out every thought and weakness. He made a noise, somewhere between a grunt and a snort, that managed to sound both contemptuous and understanding. He began walking again and Armstrong followed. Armstrong was puzzled by the man. He instinctively distrusted and disliked him yet he was excited by the mystery of his presence. The man spoke again.

"You're twenty-five. A graduate of Oxford by way of a Rhodes scholarship. Your family are Americans, from Montana, where you were born. Your father moved to Alberta, Canada when you were three, to a small ranch in the Highwood area. That is where you have spent most of your life. You are a skilled outdoorsman and competed in rodeo when you were in your late adolescence. You are, apparently, highly intelligent. You have a flair for languages, being fluent in German as well as French. You even did well in Latin at Oxford. You joined the Calgary Light Horse at war's outbreak and, despite being considered too big for flying duties, you transferred to the Royal Flying Corps after a year in the trenches. Your previous commanders have spoken highly of your aggressiveness, but less highly of your disciplinary attitudes. Indeed, today is not the first time you have heard the threat of a court-martial. You are also partial to the ladies. A certain Polly Martin from the chorus of Chu-Chin-Chow, has been a constant companion whenever you are in London. Am I accurate so far?"

Armstrong stopped short. "Who in hell are you?" he said truculently, his thoughts racing.

"Ah, do excuse me. Major Harper neglected to introduce me. My name is Gabbert-Smythe. Sir Reginald Gabbert-Smythe of the Foreign office, an undersecretary in an obscure department." He spoke in an off-hand, deprecating manner, but Armstrong sensed that there was nothing obscure about the man or his duties.

"What the devil does the Foreign Office want with me? I'm a pilot, not a diplomat."

"Very obviously you're not a diplomat," agreed Sir Reginald dryly. "But it should interest you to know that I have had a considerable staff searching through thousands of files looking for a suitable candidate. We came up with three. And frankly I would have preferred the other two, both being British and perhaps more amenable to my control. But now I find that one is wounded and the other is in hospital too. Got the pox I'm afraid. These French whores are as much a liability as they are an asset. So, we end up with you Lieutenant. You are the current candidate. It will mean taking you out of from line duty for a while, but only a fool would complain of that. Come, let us walk a little more. This air is somewhat softer than London's."

He resumed pacing and Armstrong, after hesitating a moment as he tried to understand the implications of Gabber-Smythe's statements, followed.

"What exactly do I have to do."

"Ah," said Gabbert-Smythe. "Now, one thing I want you to clearly understand is that your assignment is covered by the Defence of the Realm act. That means should you tell anyone about this and subsequent conversations, I'll have you shot. And I won't need a bloody court-martial to do it either. Clear enough?"

"Well, I guess so!"

"On the other hand, the mission I want you for requires intelligence, resourcefulness, the ability to communicate in several languages, the ability to fly, and the ability to operate on your own. Do you think qualify?"

Armstrong grinned and said, "Obviously you think I do or else you wouldn't be wasting your time with me. What do I have to do, shoot the Kaiser?"

Sir Reginald shot him an impatient look. "No. Nothing as dramatic as that. No, the job is rather more prosaic I'm afraid. But it will transfer you away from Major Harper's wrath. Apart from that, I can't tell you any more until you are away from the western front. Are you interested?"

"Certainly I am."

"Good. Now to brass tacks. First, you are relieved of operational duties immediately. I'll arrange that with Harper. Next get your gear together and make your way to London. I want you to report to me on Monday next at the Foreign Office. Sharp at nine o'clock. That should give you a day or two with dear Polly. Clear enough?"

"Yes it's clear, but what am I to do? When do I find out?"

"When you're in my office next Monday. Oh, and by the way Lieutenant. Now that you're in my employ, as it were, perhaps you could practice calling me "Sir". We English are sticklers for the properties, as you know."

Armstrong grinned again, but a mocking grin this time. "Yes, Sir. All right, Sir."

Sir Reginald nodded, not at all perturbed by Armstrong's tone. "Well, I have to get back. London calls." They turned and walked back to the squadron office. Armstrong was both curious and elated. His curiosity would have to wait until Monday, but for now he enjoyed the euphoria of release from patrolling the deadly skies. He walked in silence until they reached the stable. He saw a large black limousine there with a uniformed driver industriously polishing off the French mud that marred its gleaming sides.

"We'll be leaving shortly," Sir Reginald said to the driver. "I want to be in Calais by this afternoon." He turned to Armstrong. "Till Monday then, Lieutenant."

Armstrong nodded, turned and went to his quarters. "Stuck up bastard could've offered me a ride to the coast," he muttered to himself. "But what the hell. I don't want to be in a car with him for hours either."

As it was, he made better time to London than did Sir Reginald. He packed, changed into his best uniform, collected the necessary travel and movement documents from a subdued Stuffy, and hitched a ride on a BE 2 that was making a mail run to the coast. At Calais a friendly RTO put him on a fast destroyer that was crossing with dispatches. At eight pm the very correct receptionist of the Russel Square Hotel, lifted a disdainful eyebrow as he handed a room key to a rangy RFC Lieutenant with a trace of engine grime behind one ear.

CHAPTER TWO

Armstrong lay back in the bath tub and let the hot soapy water soak away the memory of France and its mud. His eyes closed in contentment as he clamped a cigar in his mouth and blew fragrant smoke into the steamy atmosphere. An empty brandy glass sat on the edge of the bath and the liquor spread its benevolent grace through his stomach. The desperate morning dogfight was from another world, forgotten in the luxury of the bath. He would have to get dressed soon to be at the stage door of the Drury Lane theatre in time to send a message to Polly. He hoped she hadn't any other plans for tonight. As he thought of her, her bright chatter, her perky animated face, her soft smooth skin, his body responded and he decided that he'd better get out of the bath and take his arousal to where it would be appreciated. He smiled as he thought of Polly. He knew he was not her only lover, but they had great fun together when the war permitted, and he wanted tonight to be no exception.

He got out of the tub and stood drying himself before a slim, gold-framed mirror, the cigar still in his mouth. He wiped the fogged glass with a towel and looked at his reflections. The bath-water had softened his red hair so that it flopped over his forehead and he brushed it aside as he stared at the streaked glass. The blue eyes had lost the harshness that had been there in France, the lines of strain had gone, and he looked years younger. He examined his body, a crooked smile on his lips. It was still in good shape. Not quite as heavy as it had been when he played rugby at Oxford – and the skin was a damn sight whiter than when he rode shirtless on his horse in the hot summers of the Alberta foothills. The muscles still stood out with broad shoulders tapered to lean hips. He gently scratched the long red scar that seared across his stomach where an archie fragment had almost eviscerated him.

Armstrong snorted with amusement at his vanity, tossed the towel on the floor, the cigar into the toilet, opened the door, strode naked into his room and almost cannoned into a woman, a very beautiful woman.

She had just struck a match to light the gold-paper wrapped cigarette that she held in a long ebony holder, and the flame burnt out unheeded as she stared wide-eyed at him. Armstrong stood frozen for a split-second then backed into the bathroom his hand frantically reaching for a towel. "I think you've made some kind of mistake," he said as he wrapped it around him and came back into the room.

The women shook her head as if in disbelief. The corner of her mouth lifted as she tried to control an embarrassed smile. She spoke in a clear, French-accented voice. "You. Monsieur, are most evidently not Raoul, yet this is his room and this is his key." She held up a room key and averted her eyes from him, eyes which suppressed a flicker of interest as they flitted across his body.

Armstrong, his poise recovered, grinned as he looked at her. She wore a scarlet gown of a silken material, figure-hugging until it fell in a wide flare to her feet. The rich color of the gown accentuated the whiteness of her shoulders which were bare, except for a double row of pearls that encircled her neck and caressed the cleavage of her breasts. She was small, compared to Armstrong, about five and a half feet, slender waisted, high breasted, sleek hipped. Her dark lustrous hair was swept around her head and fell gently to the nape of her neck, framing a face that Armstrong thought wonderfully attractive. Dark brown eyes flashed under high arched brows. Her nose delicately curved above full sensuous lips. High cheek bones, tinged pink with surprise, curved gently down to a firm, but utterly feminine, jawline.

"Miss, I don't know who Raoul is," he said, "but I assure you this is my room. I just checked in, less than an hour ago. Look, your Raoul must have left earlier, but if you're at a loose end I'd be happy to have a late supper with you."

She shot a glance at him, then said coldly. "Raoul, Monsieur, is my brother. And I am not in the habit of dining with strangers, and certainly not naked ones. Good night." She turned away to leave and Armstrong switched to French.

"The nakedness can be clothed in a matter of minutes Mademoiselle. And as for being a stranger, let me introduce myself. My name is Armstrong. Miles Armstrong. Lieutenant

in the Royal Flying Corps. An officer and a gentleman. A very
hungry officer and gentleman who has just arrived from your
native land."

The woman, paused, as if impressed by his fluent
French, and looked at him in surprise. She hesitated, appeared
to think for a moment, and again there was that brief flicker of
interest as she eyed his almost naked form. Her mouth
twitched with amusement and she replied in the same
language.

"I came to say goodbye to my brother who is to return
to Paris tonight. Apparently I have missed him. Therefore I
have to decide whether or not to return to a dull embassy party
or to go home to bed." She picked up a fur stole that lay on a
chair and casually swung it across her shoulders. "I think I
shall sit in the cocktail lounge downstairs and have a drink to
console me for missing Raoul while I decide. A decision that
should take about five minutes. If by that time, a certain
Lieutenant should present himself – fully clothed of course –
he may ask me again. Au revoir monsieur Lieutenant."

Again she turned to the door. Armstrong watched her,
stirred by the way her hips moved under the silk gown. She
opened the door and turned to look at him. His towel was
beginning to slip, and the corner of her mouth lifted, as if she
was trying to suppress a grin. "Five minutes, mon Lieutenant,"
she murmured. "No more." And the door closed.

Armstrong stood transfixed, staring at the door, then
dismissed all thoughts of Polly, threw the towel into the
bathroom, flung on his clothes and fumbled with buttons and
laces with fingers that moved too slow. As he rushed he
thought about the woman and the apparent stroke of luck that
had caused this opportunity. Who was she? She had the poise
and sophistication of a mature woman, but she looked young,
mid twenties maybe. He skin and complexion looked perfect,
and she moved with the grace of a dancer. He pulled his Sam-
Brown belt across his tunic, cinched it tight with a swift tug,
pulled his hat on over uncombed hair and left the room. His
finger hit the lift button – flour minutes and thirty-five seconds
from the time she had closed the room door.

The cocktail lounge was off the hotel foyer and, as
Armstrong hurried through the arched entrance, he saw her
sitting on a stool at the bar. The stole had slipped from her
shoulders and she held a glass of green liquid in her hand. She
was pensively looking into the drink as if into an augury.

The bar was crowded. Tobacco smoke swirled
overhead mingling with the odors of sweat, alcohol, and the

expensive perfumes worn by the ladies. Almost without exception the men were in uniform, all commissioned officers, with the browns outnumbering the blue about two to one. Armstrong, shouldering through the throng, saw a Major lean over and speak to her. She turned to him abruptly, spoke once, and the Major flushed and backed away. She looked impatiently at the wall clock, set her unfinished drink on the bar and slid from the stool. She saw Armstrong then and an expression of relief came momentarily to her face, to be replaced immediately by the self-assured air she had possessed in his room. She made her way towards him and they met in the middle of the bar. She spoke in her husky French-accented English and he had to strain to hear her words.

"It is good Lieutenant that you were not late. That man was the third I have had to discourage. My God! What is it about you English, have you no finesse?"

Armstrong looked down at her, his eyes revelling in her beauty and the smooth curves of her shoulders.

"I'm a Canadian, mademoiselle, not English. And to me finesse is a word in card games. Where shall we go? But before you answer that, tell me your name."

She smiled at him, her big brown eyes shining with mischief in the dim lights of the bar. "It's Anna-Marie...Anna-Marie DeCourville."

"Then, Anna-Marie, may I have the pleasure of your company at a late supper?"

She laughed and linked her arm in his. "It will be an honor to dine with a gallant aviator," she said. "And what do you say to the Savoy Grill? You see I have already reserved a table there, intending to eat with Raoul. Would that be suitable?"

Armstrong whistled appreciatively. "Ye Gods, Anna-Marie. You must be a woman of some influence. It's almost impossible to get a table there at this time of night."

She shrugged. "Perhaps so, Monsieur."

"Please no more Monsieur. The name is Miles, remember."

She threw back her head and laughed, a free and easy laugh. Then she squeezed his arm. "All right. No more Monsieur or Lieutenant. Miles it shall be. Now, take us to the Savoy, Miles."

She held his arm as they walked through the foyer and waited for the doorman to whistle up a taxi. The night was warm for the time of year and she let the stole slip from her shoulders. The flickering gaslight of the street lamps accentuated her curves and made the shadow of her cleavage infinitely alluring. Armstrong wondered what it would be like to caress that smooth skin, but he sensed that this was a woman that granted favors sparingly, and he knew that to rush her would be foolish. The taxi arrived and eh held the door open for her as she slid to the far side of the seat, then he sat in the opposite corner. He said little as the taxi rattle down Kingsway to the Strand. He felt excited and enthusiastic, partly because of the way they had met, partly because of her beauty, the dress she wore, her expensive perfume, but mainly because he was sitting with such a woman when just a few short hours ago his life expectancy was almost zero. And, at the Savoy, as they were bowed to their table by an obsequious maitre' d, he felt a juvenile exhilaration at the way heads turned to watch them.

Waiters pulled out chairs and they were seated, Armstrong thought, with a deference usually accorded to royalty. He commented on this and Anna-Marie shrugged her shoulders, murmured that the DeCourville's had spent enough money at the Savoy over the years and it was no more than their due. He looked at her, impressed, despite his western disdain for the old country trappings of power.

"Tell me about yourself. What do you do in London? Where is your home in France? And Raoul, has he rejoined his regiment?"

"There's not much to tell about me," she said. "Raoul is only eighteen and works as a diplomatic courier for Papa, so he's constantly in motion. I only wish I could do something as exciting, but I'm afraid I lead a very dull life. Papa used to be strict until the war kept him too busy to worry about me. We have land in France, none of it in German hands, which is fortunate. Sometimes I act as Papa's hostess – poor Mama died before the war, you see – but I don't want to sit and talk about myself. I want to hear about you. Tell me about Canada. Are you from Quebec? You speak French almost like native. Are you on leave from the front? Do you have to go back there? Oh God, I think it is awful the way the killing goes on month after month. And all those poor wounded men one sees at the railway stations." She looked at him and her eyes widened. "That isn't why you're is it? You haven't been wounded have you?"

He smiled at her, pleased by her concern. "No I'm fine – I'm back on a duty rotation."

"A la, that's a relief. It would be a great pity if one so – er – masculine as yourself was injured." She frowned thoughtfully. "Though I do seem to recall a rather vivid scar on your lower stomach. You are lucky Miles."

Armstrong shrugged. "I suppose so, I got his last year. Just a surface cut, not very serious at all. A few stitches and a weekend in Paris to convalesce."

He mouth twitched as she tried to control a smile. "It would have been serious if it had been an inch lower."

He looked at her, surprised by her frankness, then he saw her eyes twinkle in amusement. He grinned but was saved from further comment by the arrival of the wine waiter.

After ordering the wine, Armstrong, with the memory of front line cuisine to erase, ordered a steak garnished with mushrooms and grilled as only the Savoy can grill. Anna-Marie, explaining that she had dined previously at the embassy reception, had a plain salad and toyed with it as Armstrong ate with appetite. And all the time she piled him with questions, seemingly fascinated by his words and his descriptions of the bone-chilling cold of a prairie winter and how the brilliant blue sky accentuated the ground-hugging ice-fog. He told her of the rugged beauty of the Highwood country in the hunting season. He told her of the heat and the dust when he rode the broncs at the new Calgary Stampede. He told her of the grandeur of the Rockies, of panning for gold in the Yukon, of sleeping on the prairie as he herded his fathers cattle. He talked through the last cup of coffee, through the clearing of table. He talked through the main course, through the bottle of wine, through the last cup of coffee, through the clearing of the table. He talked until the candle guttering on the table gave a last flicker and went out. And all the time he was conscious of her dark eyes, either thoughtful and absorbed, or sparkling as he amused her.

Voila," she sighed when the candle went out. "It is time for this mademoiselle to seek her bed. So, mon cheric cowboy, you may now escort me home."

Armstrong stood and reached in his pocket for his wallet but she stopped him with a gesture, picked up the bill and handed it to the waiter.

"Let Papa pay," she said. The waiter pocketed the bill, smiled and bowed.

"Now look here," Armstrong started to protest.

She placed a finger on his lips. "Please Miles, Papa can afford it. He's having a very good war. Come. I'm tired. It's been a long day." She linked her arm through his they left the Savoy. The doorman whistled for a taxi and held the door for them. She entered the cab but this time she did not slide over to the far corner of the seat. Armstrong, encouraged by her nearness, the wine he had consumed, and the intimacy of their meal together, put his arm around her shoulders and let his hand rest upon her smooth skin.

She chuckled – a deep throaty chuckle, and turned her face up to his. He kissed her parted lips, thrilling to the sweet smell of her, the soft warmth of her body, the feel of her skin. His hand slipped lower, almost to the cleavage of her breasts when, to his disappointment, the taxi stopped. Anna-Marie pulled away and he could see her eyes, huge in the dim light as she gently ran her cupped hand along his face.

"Such a strong face," she murmured and she leaned forward to lightly brush her lips to his. "Good night mon ami cowboy," she whispered, then slid to the door as the driver reached behind him and opened it.

Armstrong, all his attention on Anna-Marie, had paid little heed to where the taxi was taking them, and when he looked all he could see was a large building, surrounded by a brick wall, with an ornamental iron gate. On the gate he could see a polished brass crest.

"Welcome to France in England," she said as she swung her feet out and stood on the pavement.

Armstrong caught her by the hand. "Can we..." he began; but she pulled her hand away and shook her head.

"No, Miles. Papa is not that busy with the war. He will have you shot at dawn – or worse."

"Well, can I see you again? Tomorrow?"

Her lips curled into a smile. She leaned into him and gave him another gentle kiss. She spoke in a husky whisper.

"I will be riding in the park at noon. Alone. Perhaps I will see you there?"

"I'll be there with bells on," he promised.

"With bells will be wonderful," she said and laughed as she turned and walked to the gate.

"Hey, where do you get a horse in this town?"

She paused at the gate. "Don't worry. Meet me at the Hyde Park corner of Rotten Row. I'll have a groom with a horse for you." She blew him a kiss and slipped through the gate.

Armstrong watched her until the gravelly voice of the Taxi-driver brought him back to earth.

"Where to now Guv?"

"Oh. Back to the Russel please." And he sat silent with his thoughts as the taxi took him there.

*   *   *   *   *   *   *   *

London was having a rare cloudless day for so late in the year with a brilliant sun high in the blue sky. The sprawling old city was awake and bustling, reveling in the unaccustomed beauty of the day. The park thronged with people, some walking, some picnicking, some standing and some listening to the hoarse-voiced preachers on their soapboxes.

Others were engaged on more serious business. Armstrong grinned at the sight of a pair of lovers trying to vanish into the shrubbery, but he became more somber as he noted the many convalescent servicemen in their hospital blues, their pallid faces and shattered bodies in jarring contrast to the fine day. He felt glad to walk into the less populated area towards Rotten Row, his boots crushing the first brown leaves of autumn, releasing their distinctive odor that told of both decay and rebirth.

There were few riders on the Row despite the fine day. Not many men had the time in this, the fourth year of the war. Armstrong noticed an elderly man standing under the trees, holding a horse by the bridle.

"Lieutenant Armstrong sir? The lady's just up the Row a spell, 'er horse was a bit restless so she's trotting a bit of the ginger out of him. Now this 'ere is Arabella and she's a nice little mare. The lady said you was experienced with horses so you shouldn't have any trouble."

Armstrong thanked the man, then disdaining the stirrup, lightly vaulted in a half roll to the saddle. The mare gave a startle whinny as he took the reins and his feet found the stirrups.

"'Ave a good ride sir." the groom said.

Armstrong calmed the mare and heeled it into a brisk trot. God, it was good to be on horseback again, even on an English saddle. He hadn't been on a horse since the early days in France. The mare's hooves clattered on the hard surface of the Row and he rode easily, the reins held loosely, using his knees to guide the horse. He looked for Anna-Marie and there she was, atop a big gelding, trotting sedately towards him. Today she wore a mauve riding habit, trimmed around the neck with foxfur, and a jaunty bowler was perched on her head. Her cheeks were flushing with riding, almost as flushed as they were last night in his hotel room.

"Hello Miles," she called. "Isn't this a wonderful day." Her eyes flashed with pleasure and excitement as she drew her horse, nose to tail, alongside Armstrong. His pulse raced at the sight of her beauty. She gave a moue with her lips to him in greeting and, before he could respond, she whirled her horse around and said.

"One is not supposed to gallop in the park but there's so few people around no one will mind. So come on cowboy, let's ride." She kicked with her heels and the gelding leapt forward.

Armstrong followed, leaning far over the mare's neck, urging her into a fast gallop. He quickly caught up to Anna-Marie but did not pass her, for he was entranced by the sight of her in front of him. The wind flung back her hair and the absurd bowler bounced off her head to hang behind on its safety strap. She looked back her shoulder with excited eyes.

"Come on Miles," she cried, "I'm beating you."

Armstrong grinned and urged his mare level with her, then he grabbed its mane and slipped from the saddle... His feet hit the blurring ground and with a bound he was back in the saddle. It happened so fast the mare didn't have time to shy at the unusual antics but snorted nervously until he patted its neck with a firm hand.

Anna-Marie yelled with excitement and pulled her racing horse up in a flurry of gavel and sliding hooves. Armstrong pulled up too and trotted sedately back to her.

"Where on earth did you learn to do that?"

Armstrong shrugged and smiled. "Well, us kids used to fool around on the range during roundup time. All the hands got together once a year, you see, and we'd get pretty competitive."

"You crazy fool, you could have killed yourself."

"Not really, it's not as hard as it looks, though I admit it's a damn sight easier with a saddle horn."

"Ah yes. The cowboy saddle for a show-off cowboy." Her eyes laughed as she spoke and he grinned at her a little abashedly. Her expression changed and became serious. She reached out her hand and touched his face. "You could become a problem Miles," she murmured.

He caught her hand and kissed it. She looked at him, for a moment there was a startled flicker in her face, then she caught herself and, in a soft voice said,

"Let's go on."

They rode on, side by side, walking their horses, letting them find their own way. They talked of trivial things and inconsequential matters but under the small talk he was entranced both entranced and intrigued by her. Occasionally the pair met other riders but for all the notice they took of them they might have been alone. Only the irritated grunt of a General officer, riding with his lady, penetrated Armstrong's engrossment in time for him to chop off a hasty salute.

They came to a heavily treed area of the park, where they dismounted and sat amid the fallen leaves. Armstrong pulled his cigarette case from his pocket and offered it to her. She took a cigarette, he gave himself one, then lit them both from a flint lighter that had been made for him by O'Reilly. She took a contended drag at the cigarette as she lay back in the leaves. She looked at him and blew smoke out in a gentle stream.

"A lady is not supposed to smoke in public...no?" she queried. Not waiting for an answer she went on. "But, my dearest Miles, I have never claimed to be a lady." She smiled a slow secretive smile.

Armstrong leaned over and kissed her, a long gentle kiss that she responded to in kind – not yet passionate, but responsive. He absorbed the sensation of her soft lips, her perfume mingling with that of the autumn leaves, the feel of her fur collar against his cheek and the slimness of her waist under his hand. He gently ran his fingertips along her face, feeling the soft texture of her skin. Her eyes flicked open. Dark unfathomable eyes. Eyes that for a moment held no expression. Almost, he thought, as if the mind behind them was making a calculated decision...or taking a calculated risk.

She suddenly reached with both hands and pulled him to her. This time the kiss was not gentle but demanding. Her lips were now hard and hot. Armstrong, inflamed, rolled his body over hers, feeling her tongue against his, erotically questing. He ran his hands between her thighs and she thrust against the pressure. Then, with surprisingly strength, she pushed him away. She looked at him with eyes that smouldered above flushed cheeks.

"I'm not a shop girl, to be bedded in the open air, my friend. Come. My flat is not too far away and one has to seize the moment while this awful war is raging."

Armstrong stood and pulled her upright. She threw her arms around him and kissed him passionately. Her face was hot against his. And when they separated he felt a pang of concern because her eyes were moist with tears.

"Take me home," she whispered in French.

He walked with her to where the horses stood tethered under the trees. He made a step for her with his hands and boosted her into the saddle and watched as she hooked her right leg over the tree of the side saddle, momentarily revealing a well-formed calf. She smiled at him, but said nothing as he turned away and mounted his mare. They trotted in companionable silence through the park, back to the groom. Armstrong thought about Anna-Marie. She was obviously sophisticated and educated, obviously upper-class French, and not the type, one would have thought, to readily make love to a man she had only just met. Yet one could not escape the fact that the war had changed many of the social taboos of the era. And, what the hell. A fellow couldn't refuse a lady...could he?

The horses were returned to the surprised groom, who did not expect to see them back so soon on such a beautiful day. They found a taxi and Anna-Marie gave the driver an address in Kensington area. She had her own small flat there, she told Armstrong, away from the embassy residence, and away from Papa's eagle eye.

As the taxi rattle through the light Sunday afternoon traffic her hand found his and squeezed it tight. She held it until the taxi turned into a small square and stopped outside a two-storied building built of aging yellow brick, fronted by a minute flower garden. The square was quiet, away from the noise of London's traffic and seemingly devoid of any life, except for a large black cat that lay sunning itself in a bed of flattened geraniums. Anna-Marie walked to the door and opened it as he turned from paying the taxi. She looked at him, gave a small smile, raised an eyebrow and mouthed the word. "Come."

He crossed to the open door, his boots loud on the paved path, the noise intruding on the cat's somnolence so that it turned and blinked great yellow eyes at him. He closed the door and stood in a narrow hall. She was on the first step of a staircase and she took his hand to lead him up.

"My flat is on the second floor," she said.

He rested his hand on her waist as she walked up, feeling the movement of her body under his fingertips. He was hot with desire for her, desire to strip her clothes from her, desire to feel her body. Yet with all of his desire, there was a cold spot of caution. Maybe it was the inherent caution of the hunter. Maybe he just couldn't believe his luck. Maybe it was just the damn war.

She stopped outside a door and inserted a key. He nuzzled her neck as she did so and she made a sound that was almost a giggle. Then she flung the door open and said.

"Entrez mon cherie."

The flat was small and rather sparsely furnished, with few of the personal effects that Armstrong would have expected.

"This is my retreat," she explained. "It's where I go when I want some peace and quiet, away from Papa's endless receptions and meetings." She turned to him but held up a restraining hand as he reached for her. "Not yet darling." She wrinkled her nose at him. "I smell of horse, wait here, I won't be long." She went through a door and closed it behind her.

Armstrong lit a cigarette and walked to some books in a small case and examined the titles. A mixed assortment, he thought – a few classics, several romances, some non-fiction. His fingers rested on one book and he raised his eyebrows as he read the title. "Der Judenstaat"? Theodore Herzl's dream. Our girl has wide interests, he muttered to himself. He pulled the book out and began to read Herzl's arguments. Time passed, rather a long time, until a voice said "Miles darling."

He spun around. She stood framed in the open door. The late afternoon sun streamed through the windows behind her and illuminated her with a golden aura. The rays made nonsense of the flimsy gown she wore, revealing her body as if she were naked.

The blood pounded in his head and he strode towards her and pulled her into his arms. She threw her arms around him and they kissed. His senses reeled with her closeness, the heat of her skin beneath the silk gown, the firmness of her loins pressed against him. She pulled herself higher upon him as her legs embraced his waist and aflame with passion he carried her into the bedroom and rolled her onto the bed as he pulled off his clothes.

She lay on top of the covers, her gown loosely wrapped around her, her lustrous hair wreathed around her flushed face. She watched him struggle with his buttons and she chuckled.

"Slow down cherie, there's no hurry, we have all day and night."

Armstrong grinned at her and finished undressing, aware of her dark eyes watching him with mischievous interest. When he finally pulled off his shorts and stood facing her, she clapped her hands and cried.

"Bravo, mon ami. Just as when I first saw you." And she laughed, a totally uninhibited laugh. A laugh that changed to a "Ooh la la" of mock surprise as he embraced her and slid the gown from her body.

Armstrong's senses revelled in her body. He stroked, fondled, nibbled, nuzzled, and nursed her body, marvelling at the feel of her breasts in his hands and the sweetness of her nipples as he kissed and gently teased them with his mouth. Her nipples were like those of a maiden, small and pink and surrounded by a delicate aureole. The breasts, though, were mature, shapely and firm, standing proud from her body. Her skin had a faint olive tinge in the sunlight – sunlight that bathed them both in its gentle autumnal warmth – sunlight, he thought that seemed to transport them back to a time when the world was at peace and the evil of total war was unknown. As he parted her legs and entered her moist, willing body, Armstrong thought of nothing but this exciting woman. She made love with a panting, writhing passion that had her shuddering in orgasm scant seconds before he achieved release. Afterwards they talked and then they slept still holding each other.

The sun sank lower and Anna-Marie stirred, declaring she was hungry, and arose to make an omelette while Armstrong watched her through half-closed eyes. The wrap around her shoulders covered her, yet its silky fabric clung to every curve of her body. They ate in bed, sharing a bottle of wine with the omelette, and afterwards lay in each others arms until the sun dipped below the horizon and the cool night air caused them to cover themselves with the bedclothes.

Armstrong held her to him all night, at times talking then he'd sleep for a while, then he'd wake as she stirred and reached for him and the lovemaking would start again. She made a pot of tea, during the night, claiming that they needed its reviving strength. But the sight of her moving about the room, her body dappled with moonlight, was too much for Armstrong to endure, and the tea, when they drank it, was cold.

He answered her, when gently probing, she talked to him about his family. Did he have brothers and sisters? What was he going to do after the war? What were the duties he had in England? How long did they have together? Natural questions he thought that every girl asks her lover. And he replied to them all...except for the question about his duties in England. He couldn't. He didn't know himself, and he was mindful of Sir Reginald's warning to keep his mouth shut. Finally, as the first graying of dawn appeared over the London rooftops, they slept. They slept with the abandon of the exhausted. They slept in each others arms, flesh upon flesh, limbs entwined. They slept until the crash and clatter of a horse-drawn cart, outside the window, caused Armstrong to sit bolt upright and stare bemused at a clock that sat on the chimney-piece. A clock that said eight thirty.

He looked at the clock, at Anna-Marie, who lay with her eyes squeezed tightly closed and a mutter of protest on her lips. "Shit," he swore. "the Goddamn appointment." He flung himself from the bed and scrambled into his clothes. He felt the stubble on his chin and groaned. He had no toilet gear with him. He was in a hell of a state to visit one of His Majesty's ministers – albeit a junior one. Anna-Marie saved the day on that one. She pulled herself from the bed like a sleepwalker and, with her eyes screwed against the light, walked into the bathroom and came back holding up a dainty ladies razor, which he took from her hand as she collapsed face down on the bed and fell asleep again. He shaved, splashed water over his face and dried off. He dressed, almost as fast as he had the previous night when Anna-Marie waited in the bar, and jammed his hat on his head as he pulled his watch from his pocket. The wall clock was three minutes slow compared to his.

He paused by her and ran his hand down her back to the join of her buttocks. "Darling," he said urgently. "I have to go. May I see you tonight?"

She opened one bleary eye. "You'd better," she mumbled into her pillow. "Just come here as soon as you can. I'll be waiting." She smiled, made a kissing motion with her lips and fell asleep again.

Armstrong kissed her on the buttocks and regretfully sighed as he pulled the covers over her. He left, running down the steep stairs and into the square. He made a firm note of the name on an enamel plate on the side of the house. "St Michael's Square". He found a taxi almost immediately on Kensington High Street and told the driver to take him to the Foreign Office. It was ten minutes past nine.

CHAPTER THREE

T
he taxi stopped outside a building in Whitehall. He got out and the driver said. "That'll be a bob guv. Ta." He took the coins from Armstrong and drove off.

Armstrong ran up the stairs to the entrance, acknowledged the salute of the armed sentry, and entered into a large ornate hall with a porter's cubby-hole immediately to the left of the door. Inside the cubby was a gray-haired pensioner with the ribbons of various wars and conflicts across the breast of his uniform.

"Now then sir," he said, alternately eyeing Armstrong and a brass-bound appointment book before him. "You'll be Lieutenant Armstrong no doubt. Here to see the Under-Secretary. Identification please sir." He held out a large, horny hand that looked as if it had slapped the butts of a thousand rifles from Khandahar to Spion Kop.

Armstrong pulled his identification from his pocket. The porter scrutinized it through wire-rimmed glasses, eyes flickering from it to the tall officer with the Canada flash on his tunic. He put a tick in his book, the snapped his fingers at an assistant porter.

"Take this officer to Sir Reginald. Sharp now, 'e's a bit late."

Any thoughts Armstrong may have had of being in the elegant corridors of power left him as the porter took him past a beautifully curved staircase and through an archway that led to a descending stairway. Immediately the décor changed, from Mid-Victorian Greco-Roman to dingy brick, painted institutional green. The passage ran for a considerable length and half-way along the lighting changed, from bare electric bulbs handing from wires, to softly hissing gaslight, as if the war had halted modernization.

"Not too bright down here sir," commented the porter cheerfully as he stopped outside a door, on which the numeral 010 had been hastily applied in matte white paint that was already peeling away from the varnish underneath. He ushered Armstrong in with a wave of his hand. Armstrong stepped into a small room, hardly better lit than the passage, although there was a grimy slot of a window, high near the ceiling, through which daylight reluctantly entered. A young clerk sat at a desk, tapping at a typewriter.

"Lieutenant Armstrong to see the Under-Secretary," said the porter.

The clerk stood up, gave a nervous nod to Armstrong and opened a door that had been soundproofed by a thick layer of felt. He murmured inaudibly, then turned and motioned to Armstrong to enter.

Armstrong's feet sank into a soft carpet as he walked in towards a desk. He judged it to be an expensive desk, large and leather covered. Behind it sat, also looking expensive, was Sir Reginald Gabbert-Smythe. He eyed Armstrong sourly he approached. "You're late!" A statement, brusquely uttered.

"Yes, sir." Armstrong, thinking of Anna-Marie didn't really give a damn as he sensed the power of the man through the office he had. He judged it to be about twenty five feet square and brightly lit from well designed fixtures. The walls were paneled in light oak, except for one that was covered by a curtain.

"Hmm," Sir Reginal grunted. "All right man, you're here now. Sit down."

Sir Reginald watched with hard slate eyes under heavy lids as Armstrong sat in a chair opposite him. He said nothing while he lit a large cigar. Then he blew out a puff of rich smelling smoke and said. "What do you know about Rumania?"

Armstrong blinked, as the question took him by surprise. He thought for a moment and said. "Not much, I'm afraid. It's in the Eastern Balkans. They have a king of German descent – despite being a Latin race. They entered the war on the allied side last year and the Germans have beaten them... and Bram Stoker wrote a novel about a man eating ba..." He trailed off as the other waved an impatient hand.

"Yes, yes, lot of bloody nonsense." He stood abruptly and walked to the curtained wall. He reached out a well-manicured hand and pulled a hanging sash. The curtain swished open revealing a wall covered with a map of Europe and Asia. He picked up a cane from behind the curtain and used it to emphasize points as he spoke.

"Grand strategy lesson. The front, from Switzerland to the sea at Belgium is at a stalemate and not much chance of breaking it, no matter what Haig says." He wagged his cane at Armstrong, like a school-master admonishing a troublesome pupil. "Not a word of this conversation is to be repeated outside this office, you understand. Haig is the king's favorite and he doesn't like criticism of the good General."

Armstrong shrugged. "Yes sir," and thought that he didn't give a damn for Haig, King George, or Sir bloody patronizing Reginald.

Sir Reginald went on. "Of course, now that the Americans are in the war, the situation will change and, although we know it won't be easy, the end is in sight. That was not the case last year however. The Somme offensive had failed. The Americans were still sitting on the fence and we needed help. So we put pressure on the Russians to start an offensive. It failed miserable and as a result, the Tsar was deposed. We also put pressure on the Rumanians to declare war on the central powers, with the result you know."

Armstrong nodded, and Sir Reginald continued.

"The eastern front is in a state of utter bloody chaos. The Russians under Kerensky seem incapable of further effort. Since the Tsar abdicated, the Russian military effort has gone from bad to worse and if the Bolsheviks get to power they will pull Russia out of the war completely. And frankly, that's what will happen in my opinion. An unpopular view I'm afraid but time will prove me correct."

He stared broodily at the map for a moment then turned and walked back to his desk. He sat and placed his hands in a praying position with the tips of his steepled fingers touching his lower lip while his eyes look unblinkingly at Armstrong, who shifted uneasily in his seat as he wondered what the hell he was in for.

Sir Reginald spoke again but his manner had changed and his voice was almost conversational. "You know, this country's too small to lose manpower at the rate Haig did last year. So we persuaded the Rumanians to come in on our side. And, thanks to Queen Marie being of British descent, we succeeded. The results were disastrous, of course. We, in Salonika, also failed to drive through Bulgaria and, as a consequence, the Rumanians were on their own. So now they're pinned up in the eastern provinces and are negotiating an armistice." He picked up the cane again and slapped it in his hand. Armstrong watched him. He was suspicious of this man. He met too many of this type – power-hungry and ambitious, not caring who they crushed on their way to the top.

Sir Reginald sucked on his cigar then laid it in an ashtray. "Well, to brass tacks," he said. "His Majesty has a high regard for Queen Marie of Rumania. They are first cousins and childhood friends. She is now, of course, in a very perilous position. The kaiser is likely to be vindictive towards her after the armistice is signed but we feel that she is in far greater danger from the Bolsheviks. If they get their hands on her she'll be lucky to survive." He gave a contemptuous snort. "Balkan politics are a mess. Puppet princes and squalid intrigues have plagued the area since the dawn of time. And old hatreds die hard. Therefore, His Majesty has asked us to be prepared to get Queen Marie to safety by whatever means possible." He looked at Armstrong for a long moment. "You Lieutenant, are one of those means. This is your assignment. You will go by ship to the Salonika front where you will pick up a two-seater plane and fly it to Jassy, in Rumania. That is where the Rumanians are making a last stand and the government is there. If the need arises, if other means fail, you will fly Her Majesty to safety, probably to Greece. I have agents monitoring the situation, and you will act under their direction. Understand, Lieutenant, that you will be one of several options and, in the event we find a more orthodox method of securing the queen's safety, you will make yourself generally useful to my staff over there until you're recalled."

Armstrong began to speak but Sir Reginald cut him off with a gesture.

"Save the questions Lieutenant, I'm a busy man. The only reason I'm telling you in person is to impress upon you the importance of the exercise." He tapped on a brass bell that sat on the desk. "My staff here will adequately brief you. One thing more. You will not mention Her Majesty again anywhere until you're talking to my agents in Rumania. This project is code-named "Archives" and your cover is that you are part of a team trying to recover the Rumanian state archives from the Russians. Apparently the fools sent them the Tsar for safe keeping when they realized they were losing the war. Now with the Tsar gone they want them back. All of my staff refer only to Archives. Paper, not people. Understand?"

Armstrong nodded, as the clerk entered in response to the bell.

"Take this officer to Mr. Maitland," Sir Reginald said. He turned to Armstrong. "Maitland is your controller for

"Archives". He'll brief you and arrange your travel. I will see you at a later date."

Armstrong followed the clerk to the door, his mind whirling. They wanted to stick a queen in the cold and dangerous cockpit of a fighter plane. And he had to be the dummy selected for the job. If anything went wrong he'd be the goat of history.

"Armstrong"...The cold arrogant voice. He turned and looked into Sir Reginald's black eyes, hard and merciless under heavy brows. "This town is full of eager ears from every nation on earth. So I repeat: You will not discuss this mission or your destination with anyone except myself or Maitland. Is that clear?"

"Sure it's clear," Armstrong said, trying to control his dislike of the man as he left.

The clerk took him further along the passage as it twisted and turned for a considerable distance, all underground. "This place is a bloody rabbit warren." Armstrong observed.

"Yes sir," the clerk replied. "A lot of important offices have gone underground since the zeppelin raids. We're actually under Downing Street at the moment. I've heard tell that a lot of these passages were built in the days of the Bucks and Corinthians so that the aristocracy could visit each others bedrooms on the QT. Well, here we are then. Mr. Maitland's department." He opened a door and they entered.

Armstrong was surprised by the size of the room. It was larger than he would have expected in this warren, and was brightly lit by bare electric bulbs and from beams of sunlight streaming in through narrow slits of windows high above. He saw a flash of blue sky above the sunken area that surrounded the windows outside, and he felt grateful, the time he had spent in the trenches had left him with a distaste for underground places. The room was filled with busy men at paper-heaped desks. One corner of the room had been partitioned off to make a small office in which a man sat at a desk. The clerk took him to his office.

"Lieutenant Armstrong sir," he said, and left.

Maitland was a large man, with a cheerful face and a Yorkshire accent, only slightly refined to the officialese of government service. "Come in lad," he boomed, as he stood up with hand outstretched in greeting. "Ee, but you're a big fellow aren't you. And you fit in one of those little planes eh! Well, better you than me. The only time I want to fly is when St Peter fits me for a pair of wings." He indicated a chair. "Now sit here man and we'll get to business."

Maitland looked out at his staff as if to see that they were out of earshot, then he turned to Armstrong. "All right, me lad. As you may know, all intelligence work is handled by a department called MI6, foreign intelligence that is. Therefore you'll be working with MI's man out there, a Lieutenant George Hall. Now he's a pretty smart lad, regular army, and he knows the situation there, so you'll be in good hands. His nibs, Sir Reggie, has told you he wants you to fly Queen Marie out of there if necessary, and that's your main assignment."

"Is that the real story?" queried Armstrong. "Does he actually think that one of the crowned heads of Europe is going to entrust her blue-blooded body to an aeroplane? My God, that'll be a first!"

Maitland leaned back in his chair, placed his hands behind his neck, and regarded Armstrong with an amused expression. "Do you think your wee planes are dangerous then?"

Armstrong shrugged. "They probably kill as many men by accident as does the actual fighting."

"Aye, maybe so. But you're a skilled pilot, not like the kids we're rushing through flying training now, and the machine we're got for you is one of the best, a Bristol."

Armstrong's eye's flickered with interest. He had heard of the tough new two-seater's but had never flown one.

Maitland continued. "Let me tell you why this mission is so important to Sir Reginald. I was in the navy, back in '88. Same ship as the King was serving in – Mediterranean fleet. And in Malta there was a sweet young lassie that our George fell very hard for. Very hard indeed. She was the daughter of the Commander-in-Chief, the Duke of Edinburgh. Now the Duke was a proud man and he didn't want his daughter marrying George because he was only the second son of the heir apparent. Thought he could do better for her you see. So he shipped her off and she ended up marrying a German prince, Ferdinand, who latter became King of Rumania. So King George has some very tender memories of his Rumanian cousin. Sir Reginald knows this, as he makes it his business to know everything, so whether or not you do fly her Majesty to safety doesn't really matter as long as Reggie can tell the King that he's prepared for any eventuality. That covers the first item of business." He pulled out a pipe and began filling it from a tobacco container on his desk. Armstrong took out his cigarette case and lit a cigarette. Mailtland made a production of lighting the pipe and kept silent until great puffs of smoke floated over his head.

"The archives are the second item," he began again. "The Russians do have them and we have promised to help get them back. Your involvement with this may be major or minor, as I expect they'll try to get them out of Russian by train and you can't get much of a load on your plane. You see, the Russians are in such a mess that no one can be bothered to sort this problem out and Queen Marie has appealed for our help." He sucked on his pipe for a moment as he watched Armstrong, who was wondering why the hell anyone would bother about state archives in the middle of a war.

"Item three," Maitland quietly said. "And the most important save the queen herself. Along with the archives the Rumanians foolishly sent their crown jewels to Uncle Nicky for safe keeping."

Armstrong, his interest piqued, raised an eyebrow, "Crown jewels?"

"Yes," said Maitland. "Crown jewels. Also all of their gold reserves. You see, the Rumanians didn't become a nation until 1881, but although they are comparatively new monarchy, their crown jewels and state regalia would make Captain Kidd's treasure look anaemic. A lot of inherited swag there of course, plus they got lots of gifts from various rulers trying to curry favor with the new country. Now, among the rulers giving gifts was the kaiser; and thereby hangs a tale."

Maitland paused as a pensioner knocked at the door and entered with a tea-wagon. "Ah, eleven's," he said. "Lieutenant?"

Armstrong came back from a reverie in which glittering gems were cascading from his fingertips. "Er...Oh thanks. Plain please."

The pensioner poured two cups and gave them, together with a plate of biscuits, to the two men. Maitland said nothing until the man hand trundled the tea-trolley away and closed the door behind him. He took and appreciative sip of the tea. "Did you ever hear of the Irish crown jewels then?" he queried in a soft voice.

Armstrong grinned. "I never knew they had any." Maitland smiled. "Well, of course they belonged to the crown, but instead of keeping them locked up in the Tower of London they were kept in Dublin castle and the Viceroy of Ireland had the use of them for ceremonial occasions. They were in the care of a silly old fart called Sir Arthur Vicars who had some very strange men friends, strange in that they preferred the company of men to woman...Do you understand?"

Armstrong shrugged and nodded.

"It was back in '07 that this bunch of dainty fellows held an orgy in the castle, at which Sir attended, not as a participant you know, but the old fool liked the drinking and revelry and didn't really understand what his amusing friends did for their sexual pleasures; naïve do ye see. At any rate, what transpired is that they got the old boy drunk, pinched his keys and stole the jewels."

Armstrong raised his eyebrows. "I never knew about this," he said.

"Well," said Maitland. "It was kept very quiet to the public but there was a rare old fuss made about it in political circles I can tell you. Old Teddy was extremely upset, er King Edward do ye ken. He threatened to hang, draw and quarter the culprits for treason, then shoot them for theft, and put a red-hot poker up their bums for buggery. A substantial reward was offered for the recovery of the jewels but nothing was ever recovered. The culprits were eventually rounded up and punished but not before they'd disposed of the swag on the continent." His pipe had gone out and Armstrong waited while he repacked and relit it.

He pointed the pipe at Armstrong. "Now this is where Kaiser Bill poked his teutonic nose into the business. Very childish man is our Kaiser. He thought it would be a great joke on his insufferable English cousins if he rounded up the jewels himself. Oh not to keep – he's not that stupid. He had his agents offer vast sums for them before they could be broken up in the diamond centers of Amsterdam and Paris, and then when he'd got them he gave them as a gift to the new king of Rumania – King Carol. Currying favor with England's jewels, you see – while he sat back and laughed.

"But surely the Rumanians knew the jewels were stolen properly?" said Armstrong. "They must have done."

"Not at first. And later, when sharp eyes recognized various gems being worn at social functions, well you can hardly imagine an Ambassador clawing a tiara off the head of a Grand Duchess at a state ball, can you? No, things have to be done very diplomatically in those circles to avoid embarrassment. Which is why the Kaiser did it I suppose. You should understand, lady, that there's a mystique about precious stones among the aristocracy. They're a symbol of their God-ordained right to be at the top of the heap."

Maitland stopped talking and gazed at Armstrong with a benevolent smile, rather like a favorite uncle waiting for a nephew to ask a question.

Armstrong asked it. "What the hell has all this to do with me?"

Maitland grinned as he stuck a large finger in his ear and wiggled it vigorously, as if to stir up the mental process. "Well actually laddie, we were kind of hoping you would find a way to stick them in that wee aeroplane of yours."

Armstrong's mouth dropped open and he gaped at Maitland, then he shook his head and said. "Let's get this straight. You're trying to tell me that you've pulled me out of front line duty in the greatest war there's ever been to hijack some damned sparklers for King George?"

Maitland flushed. "Lieutenant," he said stiffly, "the reasons you have been given are good enough for your secondment to us. We need a pilot and you qualify. We need help for our agent and you're multi-lingual. We need resource and guts, well the ribbons on your chest speak for themselves. But do you know what is meant by serendipity?"

"Of course I do," Armstrong said shortly.

Maitland leaned forward and spoke almost pleadingly. "Can't you see the serendipitous pattern beginning to unfold. We'll be transporting the damn jewels from the Russians to the Rumanians. The whole area is in chaos. We don't know from one minute to the next if the Russians are in or out the war. We don't know from one minute to the next if the Rumanians will sign an armistice – so we're saying that, should the opportunity arise, should circumstances permit, should conditions allow, we want to pick out what's ours and bring it back."

Maitland's face lost its look of bluff heartiness, his eyes hooded and became secretive. He pulled the pipe from his mouth and tamped the embers ad he softly spoke.

"Remember this – there's still a big reward for their return, and His Majesty will be very, very pleased with all concerned. To the extent that I'm sure you'll be delighted with your honors."

"I'm a serving officer so I can't accept any reward, but I'm sure that Sir Reginal will make the peerage," sneered Armstrong.

"Aye, maybe so. But the Sir Reginalds of this world are always scheming, why should this one be any different eh! A word of warning. He wants to go far, so don't get in his way. Don't mess up".

"Where is the plane I'll be flying?"

"It's already in Salonika. We shipped it out on a seaplane carrier about three weeks ago. You'll be leaving at one a.m. from Portsmouth. We have a dispatch destroyer sailing for the eastern Med' and we've arranged passage on that.

"Tonight!" said Armstrong appalled. "So soon?" Damn! He had to see Anna-Marie once more.

"Aye, I'm afraid so. The destroyer is set to leave on admiralty business. We're just cadging a ride and it's a grand opportunity to get you there in a hurry. Sorry if you've made any plans for tonight. You'll have to tell Polly that duty calls."

Armstrong's head snapped up. Polly! She was the last person in his thoughts. Anna-Marie, and she only, had been in his mind. Dismay filled him at the thought of not seeing her again. He looked at Maitland and saw a man-of-the-world smirk. "Dammit, does everyone know my business," he snapped.

Maitland shrugged. "Don't take on so, laddie. I'm the man who picked you out of the barrel and started a file on you. So naturally there isn't much about your life that's a secret to me."

Armstrong looked at him and thought, Yes, you don't know about Anna-Marie and I'll be damned if I'll tell you. "So there's definitely no chance of seeing...Polly tonight?"

Maitland shook his head as he looked at the wall clock. "You have to be inboard before midnight and the last train to Portsmouth is the nine-eighteen from Waterloo. But you should be able to manage a couple of hours this afternoon. Which should be enough for a lusty lad like you." He grinned knowingly.

Armstrong stared at him, irritated by his tone but excited at the thought he would have a few hours to spend with Anna-Marie. "Just where the hell is Jassy?"

"In upper Moldavia, hard against the Bessarabian border...Here." He turned to a wall map behind him. "About five hundred miles north-east of Salonika. It's where the government fled to after the fall of Bucharest."

Armstrong studied the map, his lips pursed in thought. "A Bristol doesn't have the endurance to fly that far. Its good for about three hours in level flight.

"Well actually it's not quite 500 miles," said Maitland. "And you'll be using a field near Stavros as your take off point, and that's a little nearer. In any case, read this." He handed Armstrong a buff colored envelope, stuffed with papers. "I think you'll find it explains everything. You'll see they've installed an auxiliary fuel tank."

Maitland sat silent as Armstrong skimmed through the papers. They gave a technical description of the Bristol Type 14 F2B. Armstrong knew of the plane. He knew it was a machine of great strength and maneuverability together with a reasonably high rate of speed. Its virtue was that it could be fought as a single seater, attacking with the front gun but with a sting in the tail from twin Lewis guns operated by the observer. Armstrong saw that the auxiliary fuel tank had been installed under the fuselage in the gap above the lower wing. A manual fuel transfer pump was fitted in the observer's cockpit. The designer calculated that the extra fuel would increase endurance to five hours.

"Not too bad," said Armstrong. "That should do it but how about spare parts? Must have spares – planes wear out too damn quick."

Maitland beamed at him. "All taken care of. A complete set and all necessary tools went on the seaplane carrier."

"I want my own mechanic," said Armstrong forcefully. "Private O'Reilly. He's a great mechanic and I shall need all his skills in that neck of the woods."

Maitland frowned. "Well," he said slowly. "I suppose it would be possible to get him there. Do ye think it's really necessary?"

"Yes I do," said Armstrong. "Those Falcon engines are temperamental – good, mind you, but tricky. And five thousand feet in the air is no place to find out that your mechanic is a dummy."

"All right," Maitland promised. "I'll do what I can to get him there in time. Salonika I mean; obviously we can't get him to Portsmouth by tonight. Now, lets get to business."

For the next few hours Maitland and his staff plied Armstrong with itineraries, documentation, instructions and briefings on the changing conditions in Rumania, Russia, and the Salonika front. He was also given a complete listing of the Irish crown jewels, and Maitland described each piece in detail. The collar and insignia of the Order of Saint Patrick. Necklaces, diamond and emerald brooches. Tiaras and other regalia. Then, last of all, Maitland picked up a photograph.

"Take a look at this one." he said. "This is probably the most valuable piece and for several reasons. Its size, its beauty and, not least, because of its historical value. Here." And he handed Armstrong the photograph.

Armstrong gave a murmur of appreciation. A huge multi-facetted, diamond hung from a gold chain and, even in the uncertain sepia of the photograph, glittered with a cold fire. And then, as he looked at the picture there came a tingling in his spine, as if some primeval sense was trying to whisper a message. He arose from his chair, unaware that Maitland was still speaking, and stared at the jewel while the short hairs on his neck seemed to crawl.

"Will you pay attention, laddie?" Maitland's voice finally penetrated his mind, and he turned to him, startled.

"Now take a look at this picture," said Maitland, and he handed a sheet from a newspaper to Armstrong.

On the sheet was another photograph. An attractive lady was on the arm of a regal looking man and they were reviewing troops. "That's her," said Maitland. "Queen Marie and Ferdinand. This picture was taken when they declared war on Germany so it's not that old. Now take a look at the rock that our Marie has around her neck." He passed Armstrong a magnifying glass.

Armstrong studied the picture. Without a doubt it was the same stone that lay on the soft curve of the lady's bosom. It had the same square-cut shape, the same size and the same chain as on the previous photograph.

"That stone is the most valuable of those taken from Dublin castle and we want it back at all costs. The Irish call it "The Goliath Stone" because legend has it that it's the same stone that David used to slay Goliath. Which is a typical Irish story, I suppose. However, that's beside the point. Which point is that the stone's ours and we want it back. The king is not disposed to allow it to remain in some tin-pot Balkan state. But King George doesn't want any undignified squabbling about it with his former sweetheart, so we'll lose it in the chaos of war. Which is why we use you and your plane. If the king can tell his old flame that the plane carrying her jewels crashed in the mountains somewhere, he's spared her and him the embarrassment of deciding ownership. Do ye understand?"

"What's the value of the stone," said Armstrong, unable to take his eyes from the pictures.

Maitland shook his head. "It's priceless be boy. That's a cliché I know. But how else do you describe a flawlessly cut stone of over 400 carats."

"Ye gods," said Armstrong, startled.

"Aye," said Maitland. "If the legend's true, it means that our Shepard boy, David, buried three ounces of hard rock in yon Goliath's pate." He grinned. "The stone is supposed to be unlucky, you know, legend has it that it's certain death to touch it. But there's similar stories about every exceptional jewel so we won't take too much notice of that. However, it's time for lunch." He stood up, walked to the door, and motioned Armstrong to follow him.

Armstrong shot an impatient glance at the clock and cursed under his breath. The last thing he wanted was to waste time talking over lunch with Maitland. Maitland caught the glance and glance and grinned. "Don't worry laddy, we've cut down on two hour lunches since the war began. You'll be through with us shortly."

He led Armstrong out, along the tunnel and upstairs to a small canteen in which several other civil servants were eating. The two men sat by themselves and Maitland ordered mutton and vegetables for them both, ignoring Armstrong's wince at the mention of sheep meat. True to his word the lunch was short and business-like. Maitland had a secure grasp of Balkan conditions and, despite his impatience to be away, Armstrong found himself absorbed in the intricacies of the eastern front politics.

One hour later they were back in Maitland's office, where a briefcase was waiting for Armstrong. Maitland took it in his big hands and patted it. "Everything that's necessary to your mission is in here; papers, descriptions, maps, and personality profiles of anyone you're liable to meet. The passage out should take about five days, so you'll have plenty of time to familiarize yourself with its contents. One other thing. Money. You'll need it. I suspect that a lot of Slavonic palms will have to be greased. The best currency in the world is gold...English sovereigns. In here, is 5000 pounds worth. Lieutenant Hall will be the best judge of how to dispose of them, so be guided by him. But we expect you to take great care of them. Until you hand them over they'll be on your charge."

He clapped Armstrong on the back, put the brief case on the floor behind his desk and walked to the door. "I'll deliver the case to you on the train at Waterloo. Besides the money, the contents are too sensitive to carry around London all day. Now you take off, but mind you get to Waterloo in plenty of time. I'll se you there."

Armstrong hastily said goodbye and left, through the dark passage and up to the impressive hall. Once outside he flagged a taxi. "St. Michael's Square," he snapped at the driver and settled back in the seat, his mind full of his mission. He stared out of the window at the panorama of London, as he contemplated the history of Rumania. It had been a collection of principalities, all vassals of the Turks, Russians, Hungarians, and Austrians. It became a nation under King Carol, father of the present Ferdinand, and had already been involved in wars with former over-lords. And now it was in its death throes against the greatest enemy of all – Imperial Germany. And he – Miles Armstrong, was going to do his bit to preserve of its heritage.

His thoughts were interrupted as the taxi turned into the square. He paid the driver and hurried to Anna-Marie's door.

Her name, on an embossed card, was in a holder above the doorbell. He pushed the button before he noticed a note pinned to the door. "Miles," it said. "I shall be back later, wait upstairs." He opened the door and went up to her flat. Her door was locked but he, realizing she must have hidden the key, looked under the mat. Drawing a blank there, he ran his fingers around the door frame. He was rewarded by the feel of metal and he unlocked the door and entered, full of anticipation. The anticipation didn't last. A note was prominently placed on the table. He picked it up and read. "Darling. Papa needs me for a cocktail party but I'll leave as soon as I can. Make yourself at home and I'll be there about 8.30."

The note was signed with an "A" followed by a line of scrawled xxxs. Armstrong cursed. "Of all the damn luck. A bloody cocktail party and the train leaves at nine." He screwed up the note and threw it on the floor, then slumped in a chair to think. He checked his watch – two-thirty. He had told Anna that he would most likely be tied up all day and would be there in the evening. Well, the usual hour for cocktail parties was six-thirty so, Papa or no Papa, he was going to gate-crash a party. In the meantime he had some affairs to arrange before he left. He needed to see his tailor and he could write letters at the service club. He left a note on the same table, in case she returned here before him.

*   *   *   *   *   *   *   *   *

"I am very sorry mon Lieutenant, but I assure you there is no cocktail party here, neither is there one at the embassy. Perhaps the Lieutenant has mistaken the night, although I truly have not heard of a party in the near future. You should understand sir, that such events are rare while the war is so intense."

Armstrong sighed with exasperation. Prompt at six pm he had presented himself at the French ambassador's residence and had sent his card to be presented to Anna-Marie – only to be assured there was no party. "It is important that I speak to the Mademoiselle DeCourville. I have only an hour before I leave for overseas. Perhaps you can make enquiries for me and find out where this cocktail party is. Her father is attached to the embassy so I'm sure someone would have the address of it. I must see her before I leave."

The butler studied him thoughtfully. In his eyes was a mixture of compassion and puzzlement. "I am truly sorry mon Lieutenant," he finally said. "I would help if I could, but I know of no Mademoiselle DeCourville or indeed any one of that name. Perhaps this person is with the trade commission and the party is at a..." He shrugged his shoulders in a gallic manner and thrust out his bottom lip as he thought for a suggestion, "A hotel?"

He ushered a downcast Armstrong out of the door and stood watching him as he got into a waiting taxi, then he shook his head as he closed the door.

Armstrong bit his lip as he thought of places she could be. He has assumed that the cocktail party would be on official function, but it was not so. He looked at the driver, who raised and inquisitive eyebrow at him. "Drive around the other embassies," Armstrong said. "Perhaps we will see if something is going on."

Monday night in wartime London was not a good time for parties. Most of the embassies were dark and he sat in the cab in a foul mood as the taxi rattled from one imposing building to the next. The meter kept ticking away and the cockney driver became increasingly cheerful as the charges mounted. Armstrong tried the West-End hotels but they too were suffering a post-weekend hiatus with no evidences of a large group of people. Finally he told the driver to take him back to St. Michael's square.

The square was quiet in the evening dusk and her window was dark. He looked at his watch, almost eight pm. He told the driver to wait and again went up to her flat. His note was untouched. He sat, not bothering to put on the lights, and stared out the window, tensing every time a vehicle's lights flickered at the entrance to the cul-de-sac. He sat, smoking cigarette after cigarette and watched the minutes tick away. Eight thirty, eight forty-five. Finally, as the minute hand remorselessly touched fifty minutes past the hour, he cursed, viciously ground out his cigarette in the ashtray, and left.

"Waterloo station, and step on it," he snarled at the driver.

Waterloo, that Monday night, seemed to reflect the same inertia that Armstrong had found all over London. It was almost deserted, with none of the usual troop trains leaving for the coast. He paid off a very pleased cabbie, got his baggage and went to the Portsmouth platform. The train sat waiting, with steam hissing from the engine. The platform too was empty, save for the ticket collector and an impatiently pacing Maitland.

"God, man, you're cutting it fine," said Maitland as Armstrong came through the gate. "The bloody train leaves in two minutes. Damn it all I've been pacing up and down here in one hell of a stew in case you were late."

"Well I'm here," Armstrong snapped. "So let's get to it." He strode past Maitland.

"I've reserved a compartment in the next carriage," panted Maitland as he struggled to keep up with the younger man. "And there's been a change of plan."

Armstrong stopped and Maitland almost cannoned into him. "We're not leaving tomorrow?" he queried hopefully.

"Oh yes, of course you are. No, the change is that I'm to travel to Portsmouth with you. Sir Reggie thought it better with all this money you see. So I'm to see you to your ship and give it to you there." He grinned as Armstrong glared. "Don't blame me. I'm just following orders." He stopped outside a compartment with a reserved sign on the door. "Ah, here we are then." He looked at his watch. "Well that's cutting it fine I must say. One minute to go."

They boarded the train, Armstrong shoved his baggage up on the rack as Maitland uttered a tired sigh and settled himself in a corner seat, clutching the briefcase to him. Armstrong glanced at him and stepped back down to the platform. He looked at the station clock. Nine-seventeen. He turned to see the ticket collector starting to close the platform gate. The engine gave a snort and steam eddied along, obscuring his vision and as it cleared he saw a female figure struggle with the collector before brushing by him to come running down the platform.

"Anna," he yelled, startling Maitland so that he dropped the briefcase and had to scramble for it.

"Miles," she screamed, and was in his arms in a wild flurry of embraces and tearful kisses.

She felt wonderful there, soft and yielding, with the salt of her tears on his lips, the aroma of her perfume in his senses and her arms around his neck.

"Oh my darling," she sobbed. "I read your note and I thought I would die. Oh that stupid party. If I had known you were leaving so soon I wouldn't have gone to it but I thought we would have such a wonderful night together afterwards."

The engine whistle gave me an earsplitting shriek as the guard yelled and swung his lamp. "Get aboard man," said Maitland in a panic, reaching for him. "Polly will be here when you get back. But, as Armstrong reluctantly pulled away from Anna-Marie and Maitland saw her face for the first time, his jaw dropped open in astonishment.

The train groaned and began to move as great gouts of steam burst from the cylinders. Armstrong, his heart lightened by the few seconds he had been able to hold Anna-Marie, stepped into the compartment, still holding her hand. She walked, keeping level with him as the train slowly moved. She said nothing more but looked at him, her dark eyes moist with tears.

"I'll be back, do you hear me. I'll be back soon. Wait for me."

She nodded her head, unable to speak, as a porter came running to shut the door, severing contact between the lovers. He lowered the window and leaned out as the train gathered speed.

"I'll write," he shouted above the clatter of the train, and said again, "Wait for me!" He watched her until the track curved and she was gone from his sight. He pulled the window up, shutting off the noise of the train and the rushing air. He stood for a moment, collecting his composure, then he turned away from the window...and found himself staring into the wicked muzzle of a Webley 45 revolver, a Webley with the hammer cocked back ready to fire, a Webley held in the large hand of a grim-faced Maitland.

CHAPTER FOUR

T he train rattled and bumped across the maze of track as it felt its way to the main southern line. Slowly it gathered speed as the crew few high-pressure steam to the massive cylinders. But, with all the movement, the Webley wavered not an inch. Maitland held it cocked, his buff Yorkshire face showing both distrust and puzzlement. Armstrong jerked his eyes from the gaping muzzle to Maitland. Did Maitland want the gold?

"I want the answers, good answers, right now," barked Maitland. "That wasn't Polly Martin. What the hell is that woman to you?"

Armstrong spoke slowly, while part of his mind wondered why his own revolver had never looked so menacing. "I never said it was Polly. The lady is a friend. Why is she any concern of yours? I'm a pilot, not a monk."

"Do ye know who the lady is?" queried Maitland, the aim of the gun deviating not an inch from Armstrong's head.

"She's Anna-Marie DeCourville, the daughter of some French big-wig."

"Oh, what a very classy name," sneered Maitland. "Well, laddie, I'll tell you who the lady is. Her real name is Anna Crystal. She's German Jew. And she's also the mistress of the Baron Barreroth.

Armstrong's eyes jerked wide open with surprise. He felt his stomach muscles tense with shock. "Crystal," he said unbelievingly. "Crystal! Jewish? Just what the hell is going on. She's German you say?"

Maitland grunted, "Well actually she's American by naturalization. But she was born in Germany, so we've had our eye on her. Barreroth brought her from the States a year ago, calls her his secretary – if you can believe that. But enough;

just how did you get to know her and what's your involvement with her?"

Armstrong's eyes flickered from the face to the gun and back again. He felt sick dismay as he grappled with her deceit. Oh God, he still had the taste of her on his lips, the scent of her in his nostrils. He slumped back in his seat and told Maitland about the time he had spent with Anna – omitting only the fact that they had slept together. Maitland stared at Armstrong until he finished talking, then his thumb uncocked the revolver and pushed on the safety.

"Well laddie," he said as he slid the weapon into a pocket. "It looks as if we have a blabbermouth somewhere in the department and word of our enterprise got to Barreroth, so he sent his lady to pick your brains. Fortunately you've got damn little of that commodity, so she can't have found out much...could she?"

Armstrong flushed angrily and snapped, "How the hell am I supposed to know enough to damage the mission. I wasn't briefed until today. And in any case, am I supposed to know every German spy in London?"

Maitland wearily rubbed his face and shrugged. "Oh of course not. But bloody hell man, how could you fall for that wrong room ploy. It's so damn obvious."

"Yeah, maybe. But I bet that ten out ten men would have fallen for it on their first night back from the front. Does brother Raoul exist?"

Maitland shook his head and Armstrong swore. Then, "Who is this baron? Is he a German spy too? And why is he such a concern of yours?"

"Maybe we shouldn't make too much of the fact that Anna Crystal is of German descent. I strongly doubt she's working for the Germans, so that's not the reason for their interest in us. The baron first then. He's a banker; but that's rather like saying a battleship is a boat. I mean he's big – Rothschild class. Now he and Sir Reggie are political enemies and the reason they don't get along is Palestine. Barreroth is a strong advocate of the Zionist movement and he's been pressuring the government to make a statement that Palestine will become a homeland for the Jews – well, Sir Reggie is against this policy and has been blocking the baron as much as he can. He has his own pet plans for that area when the Turks are out and the war is over."

"Zionism!" Armstrong's thoughts flashed back to a book title seen just hours ago. "Yes I see now. But what the hell has this to do with Rumania?"

Maitland leaned back, clasped his hands behind his head and stared into space. "I don't know laddie," he murmured. "I wish I did."

The train shrieked and clattered through the night, the red embers from the stack illuminating for an instant the embankments of the right-of-way. Armstrong closed his eyes and tried to remember everything that Anna-Marie and he had talked about. Dammit, he thought caustically. It ain't Anna-Marie, it's just plain Anna! Anna-God damned-Crystal. What kind of name was Crystal. It sounded like the name some immigrant would choose because his ethnic name was too hard for the new world to pronounce.

He thought about their lovemaking, about her standing on Waterloo station with tears on her face. He knew that wasn't acting. She did care for him. The mysterious link between her, the baron, and his mission would be explained in time. When they met again...he knew they would meet again.

The train rolled slowly into Portsmouth harbor station and the two men stepped off as it came to a halt. A porter carried Armstrong's baggage, but Maitland kept the precious briefcase clutched in his hand.

At the exit Armstrong took his baggage and they walked the short distance to the dockyard gate. Maitland showed a pass that had the dockyard police hustling to get them down to the jetty. They boarded the destroyer, introductions were made, then Maitland handed the briefcase to Armstrong.

He offered his hand in an abrupt gesture as he said "good luck son." Armstrong thought that Maitland looked almost sympathetic as he turned and walked down the brow to the jetty.

Thirty minutes later the destroyer slipped its stern spring and its screws began to churn the water. Armstrong, keeping out of the way as the hands secured for sea, stood at the break of the fo'c's'le watching the shore slide away from him. Maitland watched by the light of a street-lamp, and Armstrong raised a hand in farewell. Then he turned and went below to the cabin he had been given.

*   *   *   *   *   *   *

Armstrong groaned, eased his buttocks on the hard seat and stared gloomily out at the rock-strewn cart track, over which bounced the Crossley tender that was driving him to Stavros. The driver beside him handled the lorry with bored competence. Armstrong was glad of the silence for he had

been wrapped in his own thoughts since the army had picked
him up from the docks in Salonika.

He had studied his briefing notes and documents
during the voyage in the destroyer, a voyage both exhilarating
and soothing. The swift dispatch destroyer, unhampered by
fuel restrictions, had romped along at high speed and he spent
hours each day on the upper deck as the ship bounced through
boisterous Biscay or slid through the calmer waters of the
Mediterranean. The hissing, scudding wake, flashing by at
almost thirty knots, had a calming quality and he quickly
recovered from the hurt of Anna's duplicity. He thought much
about his mission. He knew that he was going to one of the
most volatile areas of the war. The balkans, where old hatreds
were lovingly fostered, where the allies of today could become
the enemies of tomorrow. In Greece the allies had been unable
to launch an offensive against the central powers because they
didn't trust Constantine, the Greek king. It was feared that as
soon as they went on the offensive Constantine, a German
sympathizer, would attack their rear. Now that he had been
deposed, however, there were signs that the stagnation was
over, and Armstrong knew that soon a great offensive would
start, probably timed to coincide with the arrival of the
American armies on the western front.

The lorry swayed violently as the wheels dipped in a
deep rut. Armstrong cursed softly as he grabbed the seat to
steady himself. The driver grinned and said. "Won't be long
now sir, another couple of miles and we'll be there"

"Thank God for that, " answered Armstrong and lapsed
into silence again, a silence that lasted until they rolled into a
dusty enclave of tents spread out at one end of a field that
showed no blade of grass on its hard-packed surface. The
Crossley stopped near the tents, and Armstrong jumped stiffly
out and waited for the driver to unload his gear.

He heard the snap of boots behind him and he turned
to face a beaming O'Reilly, whose right hand quivered in the
smartest salute the Irishman had ever bestowed.

"Damned if it isn't O'Reilly." Armstrong's grin of
pleasure matched that of the Irishman. He slapped him on the
back in a most unofficer-like gesture. "My God, I asked for you
to be assigned to me but I didn't expect it to happen this quick.
The brass must have moved for once."

O'Reilly nodded. He was so excited his broque was
almost unintelligible. "Oh Jasus sure your honor. I got pulled
out of the squadron and shipped down to Marseilles before you

could say Cromwell – curse his name – and then to here by fast steamer. I got here last night."

"That's just dandy. Now, where's the plane? Did it get here all right?"

"Sure 'tis melord. It's over in the trees there. A real beauty. I've been stripping it and putting it back together. Let me take your bags melord. They've put you in that tent at the back there."

Armstrong let him take his kit but he kept the briefcase in his hand. "Where's the adjutant?"

"He's in the end tent, the one by the messhall."

Armstrong nodded, turned on his heel and strode to the indicated tent. His eyes flickered around the field, noting the ancient BE 2's that sat around the perimeter; the indolent riggers and mechanics working on the machines. This airfield was in need of a shake-up he thought. It looked as if the base personnel considered the Salonika front to be a backwater in this war. He entered the tent to see a tired looked Captain there, desultorily working his way through a pile of papers.

The Captain looked up at Armstrong. "Ah. Here you are. You'll be the fellow for Jassy. Sit down." He indicated a chair.

Armstrong sat. "Yes sir," he began. "I'm..."

The Captain cut him off with a wave of his hand. "Oh yes, we've had our orders from headquarters already. lots of them. we know all about you Lieutenant. We've had several signals concerning your assignment and apparently they want you to try to get there on Tuesday morning. That should give you a couple of days to get your machine in perfect order. By George, that is a great looking plan. My pilots are absolutely green with envy." He stuck out his hand. "My name's Whitton by the way. Now you're not attached to us, even temporarily. So make yourself at home until Tuesday and if there's anything you need, just ask. I have here a file I've been preparing for you concerning your flight path and other flying conditions. I've had my pilots give me all the information they can collect, so study it and if there's anything else, let me know." He stood up, indicating the meeting was over. Armstrong took the file and handed the briefcase to Whitton.

"Would you mind keeping this in the squadron safe until I leave, sir. It's rather valuable."

"Not at all, old boy," said Whitton. "Glad to be of help. Pick it up when you leave. You have a difficult flight ahead of you, but I don't know if I don't envy you. I think anything would be preferable to this dustbowl."

Armstrong saluted and left. He went to his tent where O'Reilly had placed his bags on an empty cot. He sat, opened the file, and quickly studied the suggested flight plan, then slid the file under a bag and went to look at the Bristol.

The machine stood separate from the other planes and was hidden from casual view by a camouflage netting, draped from surrounding trees. O'Reilly stood on a ladder, bent double, his head deep inside the observer's position. Armstrong stood admiring the Bristol. It was obviously brand new and the smell of newly doped fabric stung his nostrils. It was modern, compared to the antiquated BE 2's, and big for a fighter. The wingspan was over thirty-nine feet, the height over ten feet and it was metal covered from the pilot's cockpit forward to the big Rolls-Roybe Falcon 275 horsepower engine. On the nose was a Vickers machine gun and in the observers cockpit was a twin Lewis, mounted on a scarf ring. Below the fuselage had been added a metal auxiliary fuel tank, a thin boxlike structure that looked as if it had been hastily welded together. He stood on the mainplane to look to look into the pilot's cockpit and study the controls. O'Reilly felt the plane move and pulled his head up.

"What do you say O'Reilly," said Armstrong, "how soon can we fly this beauty?"

"Oh jeeze, melord, ye can take her up first thing in the morning. I've got the auxiliary fuel pump in pieces, but ye don't need that right away."

Armstrong looked at him. "Better be damn sure she's airworthy by first light because you're flying with me as observer."

O'Reilly's eyes widened with surprise. "Me, your honor, but I'm not aircrew. Ye have to be a bloody officer to fly as observer."

"Not this time Irish. Not this time. You're flying by my rules on this mission. So you'd better get acquainted with that twin Lewis eh. Oh, and by the way. We're gone from here Tuesday so everything on top line by then, clear?"

"Oh to be sure melord, breathed O'Reilly, a glint of excitement in his eyes. "And where would we be going to?"

Armstrong winked. "Mind you own God-damned business. I'll tell you when we're aloft. That way you can't run off your Irish mouth in the wrong place."

O'Reilly grinned, not at all disturbed by Armstrong's words. "Aye, it's probably safer that way, especially seeing that it's my arse that's in the plane. But we should pack in some warm clothing. It can get pretty cold in Rumania I hear."

Armstrong jerked in surprise, then recovered as he looked at O'Reilly with suspicion. "Who the hell told you about Rumania?"

"Well, melord, "said O'Reilly, a wicked leer on his face. "It don't take much savvy to find out that yon Whitton has been asking pilots for flying conditions to the north-east and everyone knows that he's been gathering charts of the Balkans and Russia for ye. Also that's a bloody large fuel tank we've had added. I think the whole bleeding squadron knows where you're going."

Armstrong shrugged. "Oh well, whatever you figure out, keep it under your hat. These Greeks are split down the middle between the Huns and us, so I don't want any whispers to get to them. Understand?"

O'Reilly stood up and chopped off a flamboyant salute that almost toppled him off the ladder. "Oh yes, melord; me lips is sealed."

"Keep 'em that way," ordered Armstrong, and he turned back to his tent.

Later that night he dined with the other pilots in the mess tent and listened to tales of their operations against the enemy. He spoke little, only enough for the necessary courtesies of mess life. Any other time, in any other mess, he would have joined the drinking and talk with enthusiasm. But here he felt apart and alien.

A few of the pilots tried to pump him regarding the Bristol, but he sidestepped their questions about the plane and his mission. Presently they gave up on the taciturn Canadian and the evening degenerated into one of drinking and horseplay. Armstrong left the mess as soon as it was polite and sought out his cot. He wanted to be up early to send a full day putting the Bristol through its paces.

He found it hard to go to sleep. The tent was cold an the cot narrow. He lay on his back, thinking of the mission and the strange business of Anna-Marie. He stared at the dim outline of the tent, but what he saw was a pair of dark eyes that had been moist with tears on a smoky train station in London. He licked his lips, remembering the brief moment they had been pressed to hers as the train moved. And remembering the taste of her tears. Tears, unusual reaction for a spy. He lay, smoking cigarette after cigarette, until the raucous sound of singing voices nearing the tent, stirred him to stub out his last cigarette and feign sleep, as the pilots who shared his tent staggered in and sought their own cots.

The next two days were spent in flight testing his machine and practicing aerobatics until he was totally in control and used to its idiosyncrasies. He was delighted with the performance. The big strong fighter was a beauty, rugged but responsive, fast and maneuverable. The gun in its tail also delighted O'Reilly, who blazed away with reckless enthusiasm at whatever clouds, birds, trees or sheep crossed his line of sight as Armstrong jinked the plane about the sky.

It was noon on the Monday when Armstrong finally crabbed the Bristol into a strong cross-breeze and touched down for the last time on the dusty field. He taxied across to the dispersal area, cut the engine and pushed his goggles off his eyes. He swung out of the cockpit and turned to the small Irishman as he too left the plane.

"What do you say O'Reilly. Are we ready to go?"

"Sure are yer honor, she's running like a top. I just want to change the oil before we leave."

"All right. We take off at three a.m., be ready eh!"

"Yes sire, melord," said O'Reilly. He looked at Armstrong with eagerness. "Er...do you think I might get a shot at a Hun then?"

Armstrong grinned. "God, I hope not. This flight is supposed to be secret."

The hours went swiftly. He checked weather reports and his flight plan. He was keyed up, excited by his assignment and the adventures he could encounter in a new land. His restless mood stayed with him through the day, to the extent he joined in a cricket game with the pilots in the evening. Armstrong had been introduced to the game at Oxford, but he played it like a baseball player, slashing at every ball that came at him. His innings lasted less than one over, in which he hit two sixes, two fours, and was clean bowled by the fifth ball. He walked off the sand pitch feeling better and acknowledging the cheers and laughter of the other pilots with a wave of his bat.

Whitton met him as he came off and handed him a signal, it read. "Expect you 0730. Good luck. Hall."

He retired early for a few fitful hours of sleep until the whispered voice of a sentry awoke him.

He dressed hurriedly and left the tent. The Bristol was rolled out ready, and Whitton was standing by it, the briefcase in hand. Armstrong shook Whitton's hand, took the case, and stuffed it beside his seat. O'Reilly was already in the rear cockpit, his head barely visible and resting back as if he were asleep. And, judging by the smell of rum that came to Armstrong, he probably was.

"Switch on," called the duty mechanic, standing by the engine. Armstrong stuck up his hand. "Contact." And the engine roared into life as the mechanic swung the propeller. Armstrong ran it up until the engine was warm then nodded to the mechanic, who pulled the chocks away from the wheels and waved him off. He rolled the plan forward until he was lined up between the yellow oil lamps that indicated the runway. He blipped the engine to check his magnetos, pushed the throttle forward and sped down the lamps. His stomach was taut with apprehension. The plane was heavy, with all the extra stores and fuel in it, and he had never taken off at night before. Swiftly the lamps flashed by, the last lamp approached and Armstrong pulled back on the stick. Sluggishly the Bristol came unstuck from the ground and he released the breath that he had been holding. Behind him the line of lamps shrank and disappeared as he kept the Bristol's nose level, looking for speed, then he pulled back on the stick and sacrificed speed for altitude as he slowly banked and took the machine into a spiraling climb. The Stavros area was not far from the Rhodope mountains – nine thousand feet of them – over which he had to pass. He held the climb to ten thousand feet then leveled out and steadied on a course of north by east. Next stop Jassy!

This was his first night flight and for a while he was awed by the sensation. He flew in a black cocoon of space, illuminated only by the red flame from the engine exhaust. The night was dark, with clouds obscuring the moon, and Armstrong hunched down in the cockpit and flew by instruments. After an hour he judged that he was clear of the mountains and he dropped down to nine thousand feet. Now the cloud was thinning and the moon broke through. He was flying over enemy territory but there was no chance of any reaction from the Bulgarians. He caught the glint of the Maritsa river and later, as they droned on, he picked up the broad outline of the Danube.

And so the hours went by. The engines unfaltering roar was testimony to O'Reilly's skill. O'Reilly himself stirred into life and passed over a flask of hot tea, heavily laced with the rich dark rum that was issued to front line troops. More rivers were sighted, their thin streaks acting as signposts to the flyers. Armstrong felt the thump of the hand pump as O'Reilly moved fuel from the auxiliary tank to the main. He felt the cold night air seep through his flying gear and numb his legs. He felt the touch of O'Reilly's hand on his shoulder and reached for another swig of the potent mix that coursed through his body and stirred his blood into life. And, as the first rays of the sun lit the eastern slopes of the Carpathians, his eyes found the spires of Jassy on the horizon.

His briefing had cautioned him against flying directly over Jassy and announcing the planes presence. He swung the plan to approach the city from the east. He had been told that a prepared field lay approximately five miles from the city so he dropped down to two hundred feet and, as the sun's rays illuminated the ground beneath him he cursed bitterly.

Mist! Mist crawled wraith-like across the land, blanking out contact with the earth.

Armstrong flew the Bristol in a search pattern, back and forth across the eastern edges of Jassy, his eyes anxiously seeking for the field. His eyes also flickered to the fuel gauge. O'Reilly had long ago sucked the last petrol from the auxiliary tank and, if the gauge was accurate, he had less than thirty minutes flying time left.

O'Reilly saw it first and thumped Armstrong on the arm, at the same time letting out a high pitched yell of relief. A bright yellow Very light curved lazily up into the sky, over to starboard. Armstrong swung the Bristol in a tight bank and lost height until he could see the shadowy outline of trees. He roared low, his propeller swirling the mist. There! He saw men, their arms waving frantically. He saw another Very light go shooting up from the group and he crabbed the plane around and headed down the reciprocal of the course he had been flying. He throttled back and the Bristol sank slowly down. There it was, solid ground flash-by beneath. There was no time to think of holes, ruts, trees, bushes, rocks or any other hazards that could smash the plan into match wood and its crew into history. He felt the wheels touch and he cut the throttle as the plane rolled, bumping over the rough grass. The Bristol came to a halt and he sat stiffly, rubbing his frozen legs as the propeller clattered to a stop. Behind him he heard O'Reilly gasping out profane prayers of relief.

The engine made cracking noises as the hot steel began to cool off an, as he released his flying harness, he felt the weight of someone stepping on to the mainplane. He pulled off his goggles to look into the smiling face of a man, a man who stuck out his hand and said.

"Bloody fine landing. Damn glad to see you old chap. I'm George Hall."

CHAPTER FIVE

Armstrong came slowly awake as the late afternoon sun, streaming almost horizontally across the room, beamed in his eyes. He lay quiet for a while, collecting his thoughts. He was on a narrow army-cot, one of two in the room he was to share with Hall. Hall had driven O'Reilly and he to the allied mission headquarters and, after arranging a breakfast, had left them to catch up on sleep.

Armstrong had felt an immediate liking for the affable Englishman, who had been full of apologies for the problems Armstrong had experienced in finding the landing field. He explained that he had been unwilling to fire the very flare at first because he was trying to keep the arrival of the plan secret, but when it became obvious that Armstrong needed help, he had done so.

The landing strip was on a farm, owned by a friend of the queen's and worked by a tenant farmer. Hall told Armstrong that the farmer was loyal to the queen so that the machine would be safe. It was pushed into a barn and left with two French soldiers from the mission to guard it. As Hall explained, Jassy was packed with refugees and soldiers of all nationalities...including German infiltrators.

The room Armstrong occupied was in the allied mission headquarters, to which Hall had driven them from the farm. The headquarters was a long, three story building, near the center of town and it was shared by the French and British missions to Rumania.

Armstrong shook the last traces of sleep from his head and swung his legs out of the cot. As he did so the door opened and Hall entered.

"Ah, the traveller stirs. How do you feel now, old boy? Rested, I hope?"

Hall was shorter than Armstrong by a good four inches
and much slighter of frame. He radiated a nervous energy that
enlivened his lean face and gave a sparkle to his eyes. Floppy
yellow hair hung long on his collar and his face was without the
usual moustache of the career officer.

"Yeah," said Armstrong, rubbing his hand over his
face. "What do we do now."

"Nothing until after dinner, then we have an audience
with her majesty."

"So soon," said Armstrong, startled.

Hall chuckled.   "Don't get in a panic, she's a very
democratic lady and there's almost no ceremony here."

Armstrong stood and began to pull on his trousers.
"Tell me about Jassy and the queen."

Hall sat on his bed, pulled out a cigarette case, and
after offering it to Armstrong, lit up and said.   "Well, the
original population numbered about seventy thousand, but
now, with all the soldiers and refugees, the figure is nearer a
quarter-million. So it was bloody awful here during the winter.
Thousand died of disease and starvation and food is still very
short. God knows what will happen this winter. But one good
thing about the crowds is that there's so much military here no
one will notice another lieutenant with the allied commission.
Tell those who realize you're a pilot that you've been grounded
with a gammy leg. Good story that. The women here love
wounded heroes and you might get your willy wet. I should
warn you about Rumanian women though, particularly those
attached to the court." Hall grinned a reminiscent grin. "The
idea of self control is totally alien to the Rumanian mind, also
the two main preoccupations of this society are sex and
politics. So don't get carried away if a local popsy gets you into
her bed, she'll be fishing for information to give to her husband
or lover – or both."

Armstrong laughed.   "Sounds like a pilot's idea of
heaven. The standing joke on the western front is to plead for
Mata Hari to come and seduce you. I think I shall have to have
a talk to O'Reilly as well. When it comes to women he has the
mentality of a buck rabbit."

"You're an unusual pair," said Hall offhandedly, "A
Canadian with an Irish noncom observer."

"I guess we are," agreed Armstrong. "But I prefer to
have someone with me who can make an engine sing, rather
than an old Etonian who wouldn't know a dipstick from a
dildo. I figured there would be very few qualified mechanics
this far east. Strange thing though, the bosses in London

agreed without any argument. I expect they thought that a mechanic was more expendable than an officer, should I have to take out a certain personage of note. Only two seats in a Bristol you see."

Hall pursed his lips as he thought of the implications of that statement. "Yes, I suppose the poor chap will have to get out with the rest of us when the armistice is signed."

Armstrong looked at the room and his nose twitched with distaste. Two iron cots took up most of the floor space and the sunlight entered through a grimy window. The room smelt of carbolic and old cabbage. Hall noticed Armstrong's expression.

"This room used to be the caretaker's closet but, if it's any consolation, some of the French are sleeping in the coal cellar."

"I think we'll have O'Reilly here tomorrow to do a bit of cleaning," said Armstrong. "I've been in a sourdough's shanty that didn't smell as bad as this."

Hill smiled and said, "I'm afraid the cabbage smell is all pervasive in eastern Europe." He picked up the brief case that Armstrong had carried in after landing. "Now I have to grease various palms with some of these sovereigns. I suggest you get cleaned up ready for the queen."

"How about Ferdinand. Why does no one ever mention him?"

Hill smiled. "There's a saying here. "There's only one man in Rumania, and that's the queen!" With that he left, leaving Armstrong who picked up his toilet gear and went along the passage and found a room with a battered and rust-streaked bath in it. A bath whose taps produced only tepid water, no matter how long he ran them. He grimaced but quickly stripped off and bathed.

Thirty minutes later, dressed ready for his audience with the queen, he came downstairs. He found a kitchen with a large fire blazing in a farmhouse type stove, on top of which was bubbling a cauldron of aromatic stew. Next to the kitchen was a dining room in which were seated two French officers, a Captain and a Lieutenant. They greeted him with cordiality and he introduced himself. His fluent French quickly thawed their reserve as he seated himself and was served a plate of the stew. When Hall found him, and hour later, he had amassed a crowd of the Frenchmen around him and was regaling them with a tale of a student holiday he had taken in Paris. Hall too took a plate of stew and joined in the friendly banter.

"This stew isn't too bad," said Armstrong in a quiet aside to Hill. "I thought we'd be on bully beef and black bread."

"Ah, yes," murmured Hill. "Actually, old boy, we always let the French do the cooking, they seem to be much better at it than us. But never, never, ask what they put in the stew. One of our chaps did once and we had to send him home."

Armstrong grinned and said he'd probably eaten stranger things up the Yukon, and they left the room together.

"Right," said Hill as they entered their room. "All booted and spurred are we, that's good. Now the ticklish matter of weapons. I'm afraid that it's not good manners to carry a pistol into the royal presence so I shall be content with a swagger stick. How about you?"

Armstrong shrugged, rummaged through his kit, and with a flourish he produced a large knife held in a brightly beaded sheave. "Buffalo knife with Indian sheave," he said, and hid it behind him, under the waist band of his trousers.

"Good God, said the startled Hill, "that's almost as big as a Cossack sabre."

"My father gave it to me when I volunteered," said Armstrong proudly. "He also gave me this." With a flourish he produced a long black single action Colt 45, the famed "Peacemaker" model, and spun it around his trigger finger.

With a whistle of appreciation, Hill took the weapon and felt its balance.

"That is a thing of beauty," he said softly, as he stroked the ebony butt. "Nonregulation though."

Armstrong took back the revolver and stowed it away again. "Regulations be damned," he said cheerfully. "I'd sooner have that in my hand than a "Wobbly Webley". I found it useful in France. My dad claimed he bought it in Dodge City before he settled down. But he's a great one for a yarn." He straightened his tunic and ran a brush through his hair. "Right. I'm ready; let's go and meet this queen."

The two officers left the residence and set off at a brisk pace through the narrow winding streets of the old town. Jassy was a small town, typically eastern European, with narrow cobbled streets, many churches, mean peasant dwellings, but with fairly affluent middle-class houses in the center core. The evening dusk had fallen and the streets were deserted. The houses they passed had their shutters closed and Hill explained that there was a curfew at night. Any civilian out after dark probably had a sinister motive. They came to a square, centered in which was a small but solidly built house, with every window beaming out light. Smart sentries stood to attention outside the front entrance, their dress uniforms an elegant contrast to those worn by front line troops. As the two Lieutenants entered the door a worried looking man in a plain civilian lounge suit greeted them and, after assuring himself of their credentials, ushered them into a drawing room.

A bright fire burned in a grate, warming away the chill of an autumn evening. The room was simply furnished with none of the frills one would expect in a royal residence. A single armchair held pride of position by the fireside and a sofa sat along a wall. A few pictures of pastoral scenes were hung and there was a small table beside the armchair. The floor was of polished pine and uncarpeted, save for a rug in front of the fire. Armstrong, prepared for more opulence, thought he'd seen richer furnishings in prairie farmhouses. He mentioned this to Hill.

"You must take into account the fact that Queen Marie left Bucharest in rather a hurry," said Hall. "And she was lucky to get this place, by the time the government had snaffled any dwelling large enough to support a minister and his staff... Ssshh, this'll be her!"

The door swung open again and a lady entered. Hall, with Armstrong immediately following suit, drew himself to attention and gave a slight bow from the waist. She paused for a moment, spoke a few words to the civilian who was anxiously hovering and closed the door in his face.

She turned and crossed to Hall. "Lieutenant. It is always good to see you." Her English was clear, soft and rather high pitched, obviously her native tongue. She turned to Armstrong. "And this is our gallant aviator who wants to carry me off in his winged chariot." She looked at him with clear gray eyes in which there was a trace of mockery. "My God, what is it about Canada that she breeds such tall men. You and Colonel Boyle make a fine pair. Welcome to what is left of my beautiful country, Lieutenant." She offered her hand and gave Armstrong's a firm shake.

Armstrong was entranced. He had heard of the queen's beauty but had been prepared to be disappointed in the flesh – hyperbole about royalty always being suspect. Marie, although obviously in her forties, was still a beauty by any standard. Taller than her illustrious grandmother by several inches, yet with none of Victoria's severity of features, her figure had the slimness and natural grace of an athlete. Soft brown hair, gently waved, was drawn back in a loose bun that rested on the nape of her neck. Her complexion was clear, like that of a girl

half her age. Well defined eyebrows, expressive eyes, slim
nose, gentle lips, firm curving jawline. Armstrong took it all in
with appreciation.

"It's an honor to meet your Majesty," he said, as he
released her hand.

She smiled at him, then walked to the chair and sat
down. "Come over here by the fire gentlemen and relax. I'm
afraid there is a paucity of chairs, conditions being what they
are, but what I have to say won't take long." The two officers
crossed to the fire and stood facing her. She looked at them
and the soft lines of her face became firm.

"Dear Georgie, your King, has been very concerned
about me and has sent many, many messages, telling me to flee
before the Germans capture and punish me. Well I'm terribly
appreciative of his concern but I made a decision years ago. A
decision that Rumania was to become my home. And, no
matter the consequences, here I stay. I shall not voluntarily
leave. And I shall certainly not flee from that strutting
popinjay, cousin Willy. It was mainly through my efforts that
Rumania entered the war on dear England's side and I will
abide by the results of my decision. Therefore, Lieutenant
Armstrong, I am afraid you have had a wasted trip." She
cocked her head to one side and raised an inquisitive eyebrow,
as if to invite comment.

Armstrong smiled, appreciating her resolution. "Never
wasted ma'am. Not if I'm to have the pleasure and privilege of
meeting you. Though I must confess to disappointment that
you won't be my passenger. No fairer lady could ever have sat
in the plane."

Marie eyes sparkled. "Aha, a true gallant. A fitting
companion to my Colonel Boyle."

"Colonel Boyle, ma'am?"

Hall stirred and said, "Colonel Joseph Boyle, of your
Yukon regiment. He's attached to the Allied commission to
Russia. He was here for a short visit a few weeks ago."

"Boyle? Joseph Boyle; surely not Klondike Joe Boyle?"

The Queen burst out laughing. "Is that what they call
him. How wonderful. Just like a Jack London character. How
do you know him, Lieutenant."

"If it's the same person, ma'am, I met him briefly in the
Yukon when I was trying to get a poke to help me through
Oxford."

Hill grinned. "It sounds like the same person. He
wears rather a splendid uniform, had it tailored in Saville Row.

All of his insignia is pure gold from his own mines. Wonderful fellow – absolute dynamo of energy."

Marie clapped her hands, and the civilian who had been hovering outside the door, entered. "Wine for my guests," she ordered, then she looked at Armstrong with inquisitive eyes. "How is it that you know of my Colonel Boyle. Is he such a famous man?"

"Among the men of the Yukon, yes ma'am."

"Then sit down here on this footstool and tell me all about him."

For an hour Armstrong, his big frame awkwardly poised on a small footstool at the queens side, told her of the far north and of the men who had made legends there. The wine came and was drunk. Hill, almost ignored, retired to the sofa and sat there, sipping the wine and watching the pair by the fireside. The flickering fire illuminated the queen's face and its amber glow made her look a young girl as she listened with absorbed attention. Armstrong, for his part, forgot he was talking to the granddaughter of the most powerful woman the world had ever known. The ambience of the warm room, the rich wine, her level gray eyes fixed upon him, created a feeling of such ease he was startled when the queen laid a gentle hand on his sleeve to cut off the flow of reminiscence.

"Thank you my dear," she said. "You have quite taken my mind off my poor country's troubles. But now it is time I retired for the night." The queen stood, and the two men scrambled to their feet. She walked to the door, which swung quietly open, as if the civilian had been waiting out there all this time. She turned and looked at Armstrong. "You ride of course?" And when Armstrong answered in the affirmative. "Good, I shall send for you shortly and we'll ride together. Goodnight gentlemen."

The queen left and the two officers picked up their hats from the hall and went out into the night.

The moon had risen and was casting its eerie light on the old town. Hall was silent for a while then he said. "You certainly made an impression there. I think her Majesty was quite taken with you. Better be careful, old boy. From what I remember of Boyle he won't take kindly to some young stud queering his pitch."

Armstrong smiled. "She's a lovely lady all right. But royalty is a bit too rich for my blood. I prefer the plebes to the patricians. Less chance of having your neck stretched or whatever method they use in this country."

Despite his words, Armstrong felt stirred by his image of the queen. Her warmth and charm made a deep impression upon him and he resolved to help her in any way he could. He sensed that she was a desperately lonely woman. He knew from his studies that many of her ministers were opposed to her. And her husband, the king, was a weak character who would just as soon be on the German side.

The two officers walked in silence, Armstrong, because he was thinking of the queen. Hall because he was uneasy over the absence of patrols. They turned into a long narrow street with the buildings all darkened and shuttered.
Softly on the night air came the sound of a gentle whistle, evidently a signal, because there soon came the clatter of boots, many boots. From out of the dark doorways came men armed with cudgels.

Hall uttered a yell of warning as he swung his swagger stick in a vicious slash to the head of one of the assailants. Just how many attackers there were Armstrong never knew. He was too busy fighting for his life to count. There was no time to draw his knife. It was gutter fighting —fists, elbows, knees, boots, flailing, gouging, biting. In a sense it was lucky that there were so many of them for they got in each other's way and the brawny Canadian was at his best in such a melee. He did not know if Hall was still in the fight and there was no time to think about him. He realized his opponents were German when his fist smashed into the face of an attacker and the man sobbed a German curse. Armstrong went down. He rolled to his side, pulled the buffalo knife from his waistband and sprang to his feet with the agility of a cat. By this time he was howling mad, his eyes dilated in fury, his teeth bared and snarling defiance. He slashed the big blade across the face of an attacker, slicing down towards the throat. The man screamed – a high pitched scream, and slapped his hands to his face. The blood, black in the moonlight, streamed between his fingers and fell splashing to the ground. The scream unnerved the attackers and they broke and fled, all but one who stood, clear in the moonlight, and pulled a Luger pistol from his belt. He pointed it at the frozen Armstrong and yelled "Die Englander." But, before he could pull the trigger, a figure arose from the ground behind him and lunged. Armstrong saw a thin black spike appear in the center of the German's chest. The man coughed softly, dropped the pistol and clasped both hands to the spike as he slowly sank forward.

Armstrong saw Hall, bleeding from a blow to his head and staggering slightly as he pulled a sword stick from the

German. He wiped it on the dead man's clothing and flourished it to Armstrong before slipping it back into his swagger stick.

"Not quite as deadly looking as your weapon, old boy," he murmured. "But just as effective in a pinch, eh what!"

Armstrong bent and picked up the Luger. "Are you all right?" he queried.

"A bit bruised about the noggin, but otherwise fine, and you?"

Armstrong shrugged. "Slightly battered but otherwise all right, but this one isn't." He was feeling the pulse of the man he had slashed. "Dead, I'm afraid. Pity really, I would have liked to ask a few questions. What do we do about the bodies?"

"Nothing old boy," said Hall, searching through the dead men's pockets. "Just leave them there. If the bloody Rumanian patrols hadn't been bribed to be conspicuously absent there wouldn't be any dead bodies. To hell with them. Let the Rumanians clean them up. Perhaps they'll think twice about whose side they're on."

The two limped off leaving an empty street, empty except for the two dead Germans.

"What was the idea of the attack do you think?" asked Armstrong.

Hall shrugged. "Oh, probably wanted to capture us and screw some information out of us. We are always observed; particularly if we visit the queen."

They reached their residence and thankfully climbed the steps towards the sentry, who regarded their disheveled appearance with stolid interest.

Hall stopped before the stairs. "I'm going to report the attack to the OIC. You might as well go and get cleaned up." He looked at Armstrong with approval. "You're a good man in a fight old boy. Don't ever get mad at me will you?"

Armstrong started to climb the stairs then he stopped and said to Hall. "Do you know what really got me mad? It was when that Hun bastard called me an Englander. Now that really is fighting talk. I can see I've a lot of educating to do around here." He grinned at Hall, who laughed.

Armstrong gave him a mock salute and went to his room. He wearily stripped off his clothing, grimacing with disgust at the bloodstains that soiled his shirt cuffs. He washed and fell into bed. He was deep in a dreamless sleep by the time Hall came to the room.

CHAPTER SIX

Armstrong awoke with a start, lifted his arm to see the time on his wrist watch, and groaned as a twinge of pain shot through his muscles. He rubbed the shoulder which had taken the impact of a cudgel during last night's brawl. Six a.m. and dawn was easing its fresh light through the window. He lay still, thinking over yesterday's events and he shivered momentarily at the memory of a slashed neck streaming blood. He reached to the bedside chair, shook a cigarette from a packet and lit it with O'Reilly's lighter, then lay back again, sucking the fragrant smoke into his lungs. The slight noise he made aroused Hall. The Englishman lifted his head from his cot and regarded Armstrong with a bleary eye.

"What's your problem, old boy?" he muttered, as he wiped a hand across his face. "Can't sleep? Guilty conscience? It's a little early to be showing our handsome faces on the streets of this great metropolis."

"I've had all the sleep I need and I'm thinking of what I have to do around here," grunted Armstrong.

Hall stared at him for a moment, then he sighed and sat up. "Toss me one of your fags old chap," he said. "Must have a smoke while I tell you the plans."

Armstrong flipped a cigarette across the room to him. "There isn't a lot we can do here," Hall said, "until Boyle arrives, and he's somewhere in Russia with a trainload of food. As soon as he gets here and the train is unloaded we take it back to Moscow to liberate the Rumanian's swag."

"The Bristol. Where does that fit in?" Armstrong asked.

"Nowhere at the moment. The Queen doesn't want to fly off with you and you can't load too much bullion in a small plane. I think we'll keep it for an emergency, and leave a couple of soldiers on guard. O'Reilly went back to the farm yesterday afternoon to service it. What do you think of leaving him there as well, to keep an eye on things?"

Armstrong thought for a brief moment, then shook his head. "No. I think we'll need O'Reilly's skills with us. He's a good man for – er – unusual projects."

"All right then," Hall agreed. "We'll plan on that. In the mean time let's keep our eyes and ears open and keep out of trouble if we can. But, obviously, something has got out about your arrival because the huns are interested in you."

Armstrong shrugged and agreed. He arose from the bed and bathed. After getting dressed and having a cup of ersatz coffee, he announced to Hall his intention of going to the farm to check on the Bristol and O'Reilly. Hall arranged for a pair of soldiers to accompany him, so within the hour, Armstrong and two corporals had driven the few miles to the farm.

The farm lay basking in the morning sun. There was little of the normal noise one would expect. No cattle were to be seen and but one solitary pig grunted its way through a trough of swill. This close to Jassy, the farm had been stripped of most of its livestock during last winter's famine. The open tourer stopped outside the barn which held the Bristol, and Armstrong entered. The guards were sitting or lying on the straw, smoking cigarettes. They scrambled for rifles as Armstrong entered, then relaxed when they recognized him.

Armstrong shook his head, "A lot of damn good these men are," he said to the corporals. "We could have been anyone: Bolsheviks, Germans, Spies. And this barn is full of petrol and straw – great combination to be smoking near. Get ride of them."

One of the corporals barked out orders to the men and Armstrong was again amazed at the amazing argot that the British tommy acquires whenever he is in a foreign land, which is a mixture of pigeon English, local expressions and universally understood blasphemous curses. The French soldiers sheepishly got their equipment and began the march back to Jassy and barracks.

Meanwhile Armstrong went and found O'Reilly in the farmhouse kitchen, smoking an after breakfast "tickler" cigarette while he talked to the farmer's wife in a vile mixture of French-Irish English. He jumped to his feet as Armstrong entered.

"Ah, 'tis yourself melord. I beg to inform yer honor thet the Bristol is in tiptop shape and ready at a moment's notice."

"Okay O'Reilly, cut the crap. I've just come from the barn where I found the guard sitting on their asses with no one keeping a lookout."

O'Reilly gasped with injured innocence. "Oh to be sure, 'tis a terrible lot they are. I've told them to sharpen up but it don't do much good. They're all bloody bolshy inclined."

Armstrong grunted. He looked at the farmer's wife, a plump comely woman in her late thirties. He looked at O'Reilly. There was a sly air about the two of them.

"What have you been up to, O'Reilly?"

O'Reilly grinned and shrugged. "Well, you see sir. Her husband got called up this last spring and she's been very lonely. I just cheered her up a little."

Armstrong glanced at the wife, who caught his look and curtsied, blushing as she did so. "By the look of her you cheered her up a lot. Well, the good times are over. Get your kit, we need you in Jassy."

They drove back to Jassy, leaving the two corporals to guard the Bristol. Back at allied mission headquarters he showed O'Reilly the room he and Hall shared and told him to clean it up and find himself somewhere to sleep. As O'Reilly went off to find cleaning materials, a messenger came from the lobby to tell Armstrong that there was an officer of the Household Guards to see him. He went downstairs to meet a rail-thin subaltern, elegantly dressed in a uniform that seemed to have all the colors of the rainbow, who bowed as he handed him an envelope embossed with the royal coat of arms.

The note inside had been scrawled in a flowing hand. It was from the Queen, requesting him to appear for lunch at noon and be prepared to ride.

"Her Majesty is most kind," said Armstrong in French to the officer. "Please inform her I shall be honored to accept." The man bowed and left.

Armstrong spent the time until noon writing a report about the flight into Jassy and concluded it with a description of last night's attack, then he set off alone to walk the cobbled streets to the Royal residence. This time, not giving a damn for protocol, he retained his side arm. Having to fight for his life when under Rumanian protection had left him bloody-minded enough to shove his colt up the nose of anyone who didn't like it.

He was received by the same secretary and the man, after a disapproving look at the holstered Colt, ushered him into the room in which he had first met the Queen. A buffet table was set along the far wall and the room was full of people dressed in all styles. The war had come hard to the gilded upper crust of Rumanian society, and the hurried exodus from Bucharest to Jassy had left little time to gather wardrobes.

Marie was in the midst of a group, chatting gaily, a glass of wine in one hand and a sandwich in the other. She was wearing a black riding outfit and a tasseled bowler was jauntily perched on her lustrous hair. Seeing Armstrong she put the sandwich down and stretched a hand out in greeting.

"My dear Lieutenant, I'm so glad you could attend us at such short notice." She said as Armstrong crossed to her and bowed. She raised her voice and addressed the room at large. "Everyone. This is Lieutenant Armstrong, one of our Canadian allies. We are honored to have such men willing to rally to our cause."

The room gave mixed acknowledgement of Armstrong's presence, a few stiff nods from the few uniformed officers there and speculative glances from the predominately female members of the group. Marie squeezed Armstrong's hand.

"Help yourself to the buffet, Lieutenant. We shall be riding shortly." She left him and went back to her group.

Armstrong went to the table. He eyed the array of sandwiches and cold preserves and realized that austerity was here. The sandwiches were small and thinly laced with preserved meats. The talk, that had died at his entrance, arose again in a variety of tongues. Armstrong picked out German, French, Rumanian, Russian and one that he thought to be Hungarian. He filled a plate with sandwiches and caviar when he felt a touch on his sleeve. He turned to face a tall slim woman. She was blonde, attractive, fair complexioned. She looked to be in her early thirties and the tight fitting riding clothes she wore accentuated her breasts and gave her an air of sexual vitality. Her eyes, staring in frank curiosity, were a startling blue.

"Dear Marie spoke your name so fast I wasn't sure I heard it correctly. How do you do. I am the Countess Von Hess-Steiner." Her voice matched her appearance. Hard yet alluring, like a tempered blade.

Armstrong bowed formally, deftly balancing the plate of sandwiches. "Lieutenant Armstrong, Royal Flying Corps, Countess," he said. "Now attached to the allied military mission here." Her eyes widened with interest. "My God, an aviator. What are you flying here? Are we to get aeroplanes?"

Armstrong smiled at her. "No ma'am. You see, I've been grounded as a result of a wound and I am seconded here until I'm fit to fly again."

Her voice deepened, almost to a purr. "Ah. We have a wounded hero. How pleasant for us ladies. You must come to my house tonight Lieutenant. I am giving a small party to help forget the stupid war."

Armstrong thought she could be a very exciting woman and he felt a surge of interest in her. "That sounds very pleasant Countess. Is your husband away at the front?"

She threw back her head and laughed. "Yes, that is it exactly. Only it's the wrong front. Ernst was on business in Germany when the war started in 1914, and of course he immediately joined his regiment. As a good Prussian should."

Armstrong's eyebrows rose in surprise and this seemed to amuse the Countess, for she smiled, a slow secretive smile as she reached out her jeweled hand to his arm.

"You see Lieutenant, Rumania is a country of divided loyalties. I am a true patriot, as dear Marie can attest. But my beloved Ernst is also a true patriot. So I am alone these past two years. Silly, is it not?"

Her eyes flashed at Armstrong – bold eyes, inviting eyes. Armstrong smiled at her. He thought she was damn dangerous. He thought it unlikely she spent much time alone.

He heard Marie's voice behind him and he turned. From her expression she was less than happy to find him talking with the countess.

"It's time we went to the horses," she said.

Armstrong, a little surprised at the sudden end to his lunch, nodded to the countess then took a quick bite of a sandwich as he followed the queen.

Outside the house was an open car with two officers of her household guard. Marie was leaning forward to tell the driver to proceed when the countess came running out.

"Oh do forgive me, your Majesty," she said, rather breathlessly, "but I changed my mind. I do think I will go with you after all."

Marie smiled, a grim little smile. "Of course my dear, you are always welcome company." But she looked at Armstrong and one eyebrow elevated a millimeter.

Armstrong kept his face impassive, unwilling to appear interested in the conflict between the two women. The countess settled herself between the guardsmen and the car started off.

"Are you skilled at riding?" the countess asked Armstrong.

Armstrong shrugged. "I've yet to meet the horse I couldn't ride."

"Oh la la," the countess said teasingly, she turned and spoke to the two guardsmen, who looked superciliously at Armstrong.

Marie was silent during the short ride to the stables and upon arrival everyone was too busy putting on saddles and tack to talk. Only one old man tended the horses – in sharp contrast to the opulence of prewar days.

Armstrong tugged at his saddle girth and patted his horse on the neck. He'd been given a tall rangy horse that looked quite old but the horses the others were riding were not much better. Except for the queen's which was a young hunter. She smiled when she saw Armstrong admire the horse.

"This is one beauty I couldn't leave in Bucharest. His father was my dear Wheatland, a really great horse."

Armstrong swung into his saddle as the rest of the party mounted, except for the countess who stood demurely, waiting for someone to help her mount. And the person she had her eyes on was Armstrong. The queen looked at her and murmured resignedly.

"Marthe, my dear. You were born on a horse. Do come." She wheeled her horse and trotted off.

Armstrong grinned at the countess, shrugged and followed Marie. The countess's lips went thin with temper and she angrily waved off one of the guardsmen who had dismounted to help her. She swiftly mounted her horse and followed after the queen and Armstrong, catching up with them after a short canter.

The three of them rode in silence for a while, keeping several yards ahead of the escorting guardsmen. Armstrong rode between the two women. He thought they made a damned attractive pair. Marie possessed a serene beauty that was in marked contrast to the sensual good looks of the countess and he supposed he was a lucky man to be in their company. He could, after all, be over the western front, dodging hostile planes.

The air was cool, hinting of the coming winter and the queen suddenly said, "Enough of the dawdling, my friends, let's gallop and warm up."

She looked at Armstrong as she dug her spurs in and her eyes sent a message when her horse leaped forward. Armstrong and the countess followed suit but their horses were unable to match the queen's and they dropped behind. Armstrong's horse was slightly faster than the countess's and she called out for him to slow down and wait for her but he affected not to hear and leaning forward over his horses neck, he urged it on, ignoring its laboring lungs. Marie took a path that led into a small wood, forcing her to slow down, and Armstrong had nearly caught up when she wheeled and took a small trail that was almost obscured by the underbrush. As she did so she turned her head to Armstrong and indicated he should follow her.   Armstrong, interested by her air of conspiracy, followed her.

He slowed his horse to a walk, fearing its tough old frame would collapse from the strain of the gallop. He heard the clatter of hooves fading away as the countess and the guardsmen passed on the main trail. Armstrong found the queen waiting for him a few yards further on. She sat on her horse, her cheeks flushed with the wind and her eyes sparkling.

"Thank you for understanding, Lieutenant," she said. "I have to talk to you for a few moments privately and my dear Marthe has very inquisitive ears. I'm sorry I made your horse run."

Armstrong smiled as he slipped from his saddle and slapped the horse's heaving flanks. "Probably made the poor nag's day, your Majesty. Hasn't had much excitement lately by the look of him."

She looked at him. "You may call me Marie when we're alone. I'm not very fond of all this stuffy court protocol. And especially so after meeting Colonel Boyle. My God, what a breath of fresh air that man is to me."

Armstrong stroked her horse's nose with a gentle hand. He nodded. "It'll be a pleasure Ma-am – er – Marie. I'm not too fond of fancy ceremonies myself."

She leaned forward and took his hand. Her face was just inches from his and her gray eyes studied him intently.

"Miles," she said. "I may call you Miles?"

Armstrong, surprised, murmured "Of course."

She spoke quickly. "We don't have much time, so listen carefully. I have received a wireless signal from Colonel Boyle this morning and he expects to be here early tomorrow morning. As soon as the train is unloaded he's returning into Russia to recover our national treasures. I don't want him to go, but he's determined to do this thing. And my dear Joseph is a very obstinate man." Her hand squeezed his for emphasis. "I want you to go with him. I feel that you two are birds of a feather, and if anyone can help him it's you."

Armstrong started to say it was already arranged for him to return with Boyle but there came the sound of hooves returning and she put her hand over his mouth.

"You must be careful yourself but I want you to particularly careful of my Joseph. He's not a well man and he doesn't know the meaning of relaxation. I've known him to almost collapse with fatigue. Please look after him for me."

Armstrong nodded. "Yes I will your...er, Marie."
He grinned at her, "Foolish me though that you had got me in the woods alone for other reasons."

Marie tapped him on his shoulder with her riding crop. "Lieutenant," she said, a wicked glint in her eye, "if I were ten years younger I doubt we would be coming out of these woods for quite a few hours yet. But alas, I think we had better rejoin our companions." She straightened up, pulled her horse around and kneed it forward, away from the copse and Armstrong.

He watched her ride away, admiring the way she sat the horse. By the time he caught up with her again she had met with the countess and the guardsmen. As he rejoined them she said, in a voice that gave no indication of their previous short rendezvous.

"Ah the good Lieutenant has found us. I'm sorry we made your horse run. The poor thing looks as if it would prefer to have someone lighter on its back."

The countess moved her horse close to Armstrong, looking at him with her big blue eyes as she softly murmured in English. "Possibly the Lieutenant should find something more capable of bearing his weight?" Her lips twisted in a smile as she spoke.

Armstrong glanced sharply at her and her eyes lost their innocence and momentarily flashed an invitation. He grinned and shrugged. She flushed and pursed her lips to prevent the smile from spreading.

The queen watched them as she sense the atmosphere between the two.

"Perhaps we should ride on for a while. The day is so lovely and fresh we can all benefit from it." She spurred her horse forward.

Little was said for the rest of the ride. The queen rode, bracketed by Armstrong and the countess, seemingly intent only upon the exercise of horsemanship. She threw the occasional remark to one or the other of her consorts, rather like a schoolteacher on an outing with pupils. They arrived back at the stable, she dismounted, patted her horse lovingly on the neck before allowing the groom to lead it away, then turned and extended her hand to Armstrong.

"Thank you Lieutenant for your company," she said formally. "From here it is but a short distance to your headquarters and it will not be necessary to ride back with me." As he bowed over her hand, she murmured. "Remember! Look after my Colonel Boyle for me." Then, so softly he wasn't sure if he heard her correctly. "And keep away from that woman. She's dangerous!"

Armstrong watched her leave, then began to unsaddle his horse. The countess stood by Armstrong as he expertly stripped the tack from the horse.

"How is it that an airman is such an accomplished horseman?" she said.

Armstrong grinned. "Ex-cavalry ma'am," he said. "Lots of us applied for transfer to the flying corps. There's not a lot of use for cavalry on the western front."

She moved closer to him. So close he caught the bouquet of her perfume. "Please Miles, call me Marthe." She flashed her blue eyes at him and slipped a pasteboard calling card in his hand. "This is where you will find me. Please come to my party." She kept her eyes fixed upon him as she raised a hand to beckon the two guardsmen and, like well trained dogs they hurried to her and escorted her away.

The old groom nodded his head at the departing countess and leered and as he said something in Rumanian and, although the words were not understandable, the meaning was clear. Armstrong winked at him and left the stable to return to the allied mission. And maybe to get a better meal than the one he had at the queen's lunch.

CHAPTER SEVEN

Hall sat on his cot watching with a sardonic eye as O'Reilly fussed around Armstrong with a clothes brush, making sure that his uniform was spotless.

"I really think that I should forbid this, er, assignation, old boy. You know it's a stone cold certainty that the bitch is a German agent. And don't go telling me that you're going out of a sense of duty – you have the air of a warthog on heat."

Armstrong grinned at him and lifted an eyebrow. He spoke to O'Reilly in a voice dripping with self-righteousness. "I have never heard such an example of selfish whining. Just because you have never had the opportunity to meet with the upper classes you would seek to deny me that privilege. What think ye, O'Reilly? Is Lieutenant Hall suffering an attack of sour grapes?"

O'Reilly's intelligent eyes glittered from one to the other. "Well melord," he said. "What Lieutenant Hall fails to realize is that us colonials know how to keep our lips buttoned while we're unbuttoning our flies. Not like the fooking English, begging your grace's pardon."

Hall shook his head at the laughing Armstrong and the grinning O'Reilly. "Two days with you two and nine centuries of military discipline and tradition have gone for a Burton." He stood and strapped on his revolver, "I'm off tonight to the lines to check on the situation there, so I won't be around to hold your hand if there's any trouble. You're on your own, old boy, so keep your powder dry and don't shoot until you see the whites of her thighs."

He left, Armstrong gave a final twitch to his Sam-Brown belt. "Perhaps we should take Lieutenant Hall seriously," he said to O'Reilly. "I think it might be a good idea

if you use your lurking skills and keep an eye out for me about
midnight. The street here can be dangerous when it's dark."

O'Reilly's eyes glittered again, with pleasure. "It
sounds like we could be having a broth of a time, melord, oi
tink oi'll be having me shillelagh wit me."

Armstrong hesitated over the colt, then he shook his
head and shoved the less cumbersome buffalo knife in his
waistband.

"I suspect trouble, if any, will come when I leave the
party, so I want you to meet me with the Colt in case I need it. I
don't want to wear it there in case I scare them off. If they try
anything I want to get one of them to find out what's going on."
He grinned. "Well, I'm off then. To do my bit of spying for
King and country. And should I happen to get some fanny in
the process, well...c'est la guerre!"

Armstrong strode at a fast pace through the cobbled
streets of the Balkan town. Dusk was making shadows in the
deep doorways and narrow lanes. Few people walked the
streets but here and there he caught the whispers of men as
they lounged in the dark spaces while the occasional peasant
woman scurried by with a pitifully small bag of food for her
family. The Rumanian patrols he passes studiously ignored
him, and he realized they had no further interest in the war;
they had the appearance of marking time until they could go
home. He had no fear for his safety this early in the evening.
Even if he had, he would still have gone to the countess. He
thought about his motives as he walked. One he had no doubt
about. Sex. The countess radiated it, her lean body had
vibrated with energy and he thought that making love to her
would be like trying to screw a catherine wheel – with a
burning fuse. He had other motives. As a boy on the prairie he
had thrown rocks at a hornets nest to see what would happen
and tonight he would be doing something similar. Also, he
thought, it was his duty to try to find out if she was a German
spy. Duty could be a very good thing, sometimes. He thought
of Anna Silver and wondered where she was and what she was
doing. He felt a twinge of conscience when he remembered
their lovemaking, but thought too of her deceit and pushed her
from his mind. Armstrong hummed a tune to himself as he
walked.

The countess had managed to find a larger house than
her queen. It was a long brick built building, two stories high,
situated on a street close to the town square. There were no
grounds and the front door directly faced the street. Heavy
curtains covered the windows, emitting only the faintest light

and serving to muffle the music Armstrong heard as he tugged at a massively knobbed bell pull. The door was swung open almost immediately by a burly footman, and Armstrong thought the man had been waiting for him. The man said nothing but indicated by a nod of the head for Armstrong to follow him.

They ascended stairs to the first floor and the footman ushered Armstrong into a softly lit room. The party, as such, was not well attended. A small group of Rumanian senior officers sat around a table talking quietly. A quartet of civilians at another table played cards and the countess was the only woman present. She leaned on the piano listening to a young subaltern, no doubt an aide to one of the senior officers, play Viennese waltz tunes. Her face was bored and sulky until she saw Armstrong; then she smiled a slow seductive smile and walked to him, her hands outstretched in greeting.

"Why, here is our young Canadian pilot. How nice of you to join us." She spoke in French to the room at large. "May I introduce Lieutenant Armstrong!" She waved her arm to include the occupants of the room and quietly said to him. "I won't bother to introduce you to all these people. Such a bore trying to remember names, God knows, life in this damned village is boring enough. If you want to talk to anyone just ask their name. But, I rather think I don't want to share you with anyone at the moment. Come. Sit there by the fire while I get you some wine."

She went to a drinks cabinet, while Armstrong, role playing, shot a shy and ingenuous grin at the room at large. He received a few stiff nods in return from the Rumanian officers and a concerted stare from the civilian card players. Civilians, Armstrong noted, who looked young enough to be in uniform – civilians who wore their hair cut short, military style – civilians who wore ill-fitting suits. Armstrong returned their stares with a bland smile that concealed the surge of adrenalin that shot through him at the sight of them. He accepted a glass from the returning Countess.

He looked at her appreciatively. Her ivory silk gown caressed her slim body, accentuating the curve of her breasts, and her exotic perfume did wonderful things to Armstrong's senses. She sat beside him on the sofa and raised her glass.

"To beloved allies," she murmured.

Armstrong clinked his glass against hers. "I'll drink to that, Countess," he said, "But your friends don't seem particularly pleased to see me."

The Countess impatiently shrugged her shoulders. "Oh, don't worry about them. They're here every night, like flies around a jam pot. They're probably jealous of a handsome new face. You see, there aren't many women here in Jassy, except for the local peasants. I sometimes feel like Penelope beating off hordes of suitors while she waits for Ulysses to return. Ah, my poor Ernst." She soulfully looked at Armstrong and he was intrigued to see moisture in her eyes. Armstrong composed his face into an expression of concern at her sadness, but inwardly, he was filled with cynical amusement. This dame could teach Polly a thing or two about acting, he thought. "Yes, war is terrible," he murmured, taking her hand in his. He was surprised to find it damp with perspiration. She gripped his hand with a wiry strength and squeezed it.

"I want to talk to you," she whispered. "God knows it's dull seeing the same people day after day. In a little while I will get rid of these boors, then we'll be by ourselves." Her eyes flashed a message as her fingers caressed his palm.

"Who are the civilians Countess? They all look to be of military age. I would have thought that in view of Rumania's desperate situation, they'd be in uniform!"

She dismissed his question with a wave of her hand. "Oh, they're either bureaucrats or unfit for service. Ignore them. And please Miles, call me Marthe. Tell me about your home."

For the next half hour he talked to her about the Canadian West and his life before the war. While he talked he watched the others in the room, disguising his interest under an air of absorption in the countess. The civilians, who appeared to be playing whist, spoke very little and their communication to each other consisted of gestures and grunted mono-syllables. The young aide-de-camp, realizing that he had lost the attention of the Countess, closed the piano and flounced from the room. A servant entered and served coffee. Immediately after the coffee, the Rumanian officers stood, made their farewells to the Countess, bowed distantly to Armstrong and departed. The countess stood, clapped her hands and spoke rapidly to the whist players in Rumanian. They rose from their chairs and, one by one, kissed her hand, bowed formally to Armstrong and left the room. The countess left the room with them to see them to the door but Armstrong, who had heard the front door open and close when the officers left, was amused to note that the same thing did not happen with the civilians. He stood and stretched his legs, glad of the pressure of his hunting knife in its concealed sheave.

He stood with his back to the fire, conscious of its dying warmth against his trouser legs. The lamp at the car table guttered and went out and, accentuated by the gloom, his shadow flickered enormously against the far wall. There came the click of the door opening as the Countess returned.

"Oo," she said teasingly. "The lamp has gone out, shall I call a servant to refill it?"

Armstrong grinned at her, his craggy face made devilish by the red embers of the firelight. "Not on my account sweetheart."

He seized her roughly, deliberately coarse in manner and word. If there was going to be a crisis tonight he thought he'd take control of events right away. But she matched his aggression.

She threw her arms around him and pressed her mouth to his, her body so tight against him he could feel her heat through the silk dress. Her tongue penetrated his mouth and he tasted the wine she had drunk. Her lips, hard and urgent, writhed against his as she held her hips against his body.

She broke away with a gasp and stepped back from him. She raised her hands to run them through her hair, pulling out the pins and clasps that had held it carefully coiffured. She shook her head so that her hair fell softly to her waist. Armstrong was reminded of the sensual preening of a cat.

She smiled at him, a twisted smile that did not reach her eyes. Greedy eyes that smoldered with desire. She reached out her hand, lightly brushing it against his loins before she grasped his hand. She jerked her head towards the door and Armstrong followed. As they passed the table she picked up a bottle of champagne and glasses.

The hallway was dimly lit by a small oil lamp in a wall sconce and by its light they went upstairs to the second floor. Armstrong, every sense alert, one hand held by the countess, the other under his tunic on the haft of his knife, watched the shadows of doors as they passed, ready to strike. He knew she would betray him sooner or later but, considering her passion, he thought it would be later.

Her room was lit by a soft stream of moonlight. She released his hand and went to a small table that stood beside a double bed and put the champagne bottle on it. He closed the door and leaned against it. His hand found a key that he turned, feeling the heavy ward thump home. A match scraped and the countess lit a tall candle on the bedside table. She

crossed to the window and swished the curtains shut as
Armstrong eyed the room. The furnishings were ornate, in
contrast to the Spartan simplicity of the queens house. The bed
was overhung by a richly brocaded canopy, the sheets looked to
be satin, and he was sure the rub beneath his feet was Persian.
The countess must have had plenty of warning to bring these
comforts from Bucharest.

She slipped into his arms and kissed him. His hands
behind her began to unhook her dress, hook by hook, his large
fingers fumbling with the tiny fasteners. She never took her
mouth from him as this hands traveled down her back, the
dress slowly gaping open, inch by inch, until it was open to the
cleft of her buttocks and he slid his hands across and caressed
them.

She pulled away from him, her face flushed with
passion, and pulled impatiently at his sam-brown belt. "Get
this off, my dear, while I pour the drinks, life is so much more
fun with champagne don't you think?" She swayed away to the
table as her dress slipped from her shoulders and she stepped
out of it.

Armstrong, all qualms forgotten, pulled off his tunic as
his eyes lustfully followed her. She wore no underwear, the
only thing she wore under the dress was a slim gold chain
around her waist, for the eyes of a lover only. His hands
paused on his underpants as he saw her front side in the
dresser mirror. Her jutting breasts stood out proud as she
poured champagne into the glasses and he thought they had
been rouged...And then, he saw something the countess
thought she had hidden from him by her back. In the mirror
he saw her finger in a glass...stirring it!

Now Armstrong was no wine connoisseur, but he did
know there was no reason anyone to stir champagne. She
turned to him, her face as innocent as the Lady of Lourdes, the
loaded glass held out invitingly.

Armstrong took the glass from her with one hand and
with the other he swept her legs from under her so that she fell
with a thump to the carpet. She shrieked with surprise as her
rear hit the floor.

Armstrong dropped on top of her, the impact of his
weight driving the air out of her lungs with a woosh. Holding
the glass in one hand he caught her nose with the other and
pinched it tight, causing her mouth to open as she gasped for
air. He poured the entire glassful into her mouth as she
choked and fought beneath him. He knelt over her, holding
her down by the shoulders, knees on either side of her chest.

In a voice made hoarse by fury she screamed curses at him in an eclectic variety of languages.

Armstrong heard the sound of footsteps hurrying along the passage and then a loud knocking on the door as a muffled voice shouted a question. He jumped off her, pushed the dressing table across the door, and started to pull on his clothes. The countess staggered to her feet and, still cursing she began to throw objects at him, starting with the champagne bottle. Evidently the drug was beginning to work because her aim was poor.

The door, fortunately of heavy construction, shook as a large weight was smashed against it. Simultaneously there was a crash at the window and the curtains billowed inwards.

Armstrong swung around, still naked to the waist, knife in hand, eyes red with anger and alarm. The curtains waved and gyrated then ripped off the hangers as the person wrapped in them desperately tried to free himself from their smothering embrace. Armstrong sprang to the curtains, knife raised ready to strike; then relaxed as an unmistakable voice said.

"Goddamn the fooking bejasus curtains. Melord, help me out of this fooking mess. I'm all tangled up."

Armstrong bent over and slit the wringgling fabric to reveal the scarlet face of O'Reilly. As he did so there was a splintering blow at the door as a panel split wide open and a hand holding a Mauser automatic came through. O'Reilly thrust the Colt into Armstrong's hand and the heavy gun bucked twice in his hand as he put two quick shots through the door. The Mauser fell to the floor, a squeal of pain was heard, and the hand was withdrawn.

As O'Reilly struggled to his feet Armstrong stared at him. O'Reilly had prepared well for the night. He wore black trousers, black sweater, black plimsols on his feet, and a black balaclava masking most of his head.

"For Gawds sake melord, let's get the fook out of here! The place is crawling with Huns. Come on, the drain pipe's are easy to climb." His eyes opened wide and he nudged Armstrong. "Jasus, look at her ladyship."

Armstrong swung around, pulling on his shirt as he did so. The countess was still on her feet. But her eyes had lost their hatred. They were glazed orbs, starting vacantly into space. She swayed and crumpled to the carpet, emitting a most unladylike snore.

O'Reilly gazed appreciatively at her naked body as he dragged Armstrong towards the window. "That is one wild woman melord," he said, "But you certainly showed her a thing or two."

"Wait a minute," roared Armstrong, "I'm not leaving without my boots." He ran across the room as someone outside the door began pumping high powered rifle bullets through it. He grabbed his boots and, snapping off a couple more shots at the door, he ran to O'Reilly at the window and scrambled through. He dropped the boots to the ground as he started down the pipe. O'Reilly followed, his nimble feet moving with assurance.

"Do you mean to tell me that you were behind that curtain watching me?" gasped Armstrong as he slid past the second floor.

"To be sure melord," returned O'Reilly. "You asked me to keep an eye out, didn't you?"

Armstrong did not have a chance to consider the ramifications of this answer for, as they neared the ground, the front door of the house burst open and four armed civilians, one with a bloodstained shoulder, poured out. They yelled with satisfaction at the sight of the two men still above them, confident of taking them prisoner.

There came a voice. Loud above the yells of the Germans. The type of voice that had given orders from Waterloo to the Marne.

"SQUAD... PRESENT... AIM!"

The four swung around, to stare astounded at the sight of ten Lee Enfield rifle pointing at them from close range. Ten rifles held unwavingly by ten Tommies, ranked in two rows of five, the front row kneeling in traditional style. Four guns were dropped instantly before the menace of the rifles. Three and a half pairs of arms shot skywards with alacrity. The voice spoke again. This time it had reverted to its traditional far back drawl." I would advise you to get down from there, old boy. You really do look a twit. And as for you Huns...RAUS."

The four Germans, abandoning their weapons, scurried back inside the building. Armstrong reached the ground and thankfully pulled on his boots as he hobbled over to Hall.

"Thanks for your help, pal," he said with a grin. "I guess I owe you."

Hall beamed smugly at him as the Tommies gathered up the German's small arms. "Couldn't leave my colonial colleague entrapped by the scarlet woman, could I. Especially since old Boyle is due in momentarily."

Even as he spoke there came the wail of a train whistle, repeated again and again.

78   Charles W. Cobb

CHAPTER EIGHT

Hall smiled as the whistle shrieked in staccato bursts.

"Sounds like Boyle is in fine fettle and letting the whole world know he's arrived. We'd better get these men down there before a mob gathers. The town is full of rumors about this train and the food it's supposed to be bringing. Right you men. Fall in. Double march." Hall led his squad, running through the cobbled streets, in the direction of the station.

Armstrong, pulled on his tunic as he ran. "bit of a surprise Lieutenant Hall and his soldiers being there!" He called to O'Reilly, whose short legs were pumping to keep up.

"Not really, melord," gasped O'Reilly. "You see, he came in as I was leaving, all tarted up in my black. He'd heard the train was due so he cancelled his trip to the front. He decided to bring the troopers here first, just in case like."

Armstrong groaned. "I suppose the whole bloody garrison was outside listening."

"Oh no squire. You see, we had to leave a couple of the lads on guard at the mission, and then there's the two out guarding the plane, they don't know about it. Yet. And there's no need to embarrass yourself about it all. All the lads thought you were doing a fine thing. In fact we were having bets on your stamina. To be sure though, that Countess is a noisy bitch when she's on heat. Jasus. We could hear her down in the street."

"O'Reilly, shut up," roared Armstrong, "God-dammit, you unscrupulous sod, you probably sold tickets."

"Ah no melord," said O'Reilly sadly, as they came to the station approach. "There wasn't time you see." He looked slyly at Armstrong. "Perhaps your lordship could do it again and we could organize a money-making venture?"

Armstrong was spared the indignity of a reply as the pair ran into the station. Already, despite the curfew, people were beginning to crowd onto the platform. They were raggedly dressed and their faces, in the yellow guttering oil lights of the station, were drawn and pallid. Hall had spaced his squad along the puffing monster that still gave out periodic blasts of steam through its whistle. It was not a long train, five cars only were connected to the engine. Four of them were cattle cars, now loaded with crates and boxes. The fifth however, was a behemoth of a coach, with woodwork lavishly enameled in glistening royal blue paint. The gold Romanoff eagle on the door seemed to sneer at the people gathering on the platform and, below the eagle, in crimson characters, was the number 451.

Armstrong whistled in appreciation and went to Hall. "That, Mr. Hall, is one hell of a car! Old Pullman would gnash his teeth in envy if he could see it."

Hall nodded and said. "This magnificent example of the coach builders art, Mr. Armstrong, belongs to the Dowager Empress Mother, Marie Feodorovna. Our man Boyle acquired it when the old lady went to live in the Crimea – after Nicholas abdicated. Ah, here he is now."

Armstrong almost expected to see the Tsar, but the ma in the open carriage door was far more imposing than the late ruler of Russia. He stood over six feet tall, and his broad shoulders made the wide door seem small. He wore the uniform of a British Colonel, but the material was of exceptional quality. His insignia and uniform buttons were obviously of gold and across the sleeves at the shoulders was sewn, again in gold braid, the word "Yukon". The face too was larger than life. Dark piercing eyes looked from under jutting brows, a heavy jaw was softened by a wide generous mouth. Black bushy hair, streaked with gray, poked out from under his uniform hat as if it resented confinement, and in his large hands he carried a highly polished swagger stick.

He saw Hall and his mouth split in a grin as he jumped down the steps from the carriage. "Lieutenant Hall! Damn glad to see you man, and your guards too." His voice matched his appearance, self-assured and commanding. Hall saluted Boyle, then motioned to Armstrong. "This is Lieutenant Armstrong, Royal Flying Corps. He's seconded to us to help where necessary."

Boyle looked at Armstrong, momentarily he seemed nonplused at having to look up to someone, but his eyes caught the Canada flash on Armstrong's sleeve and he thrust out his hand, disdaining the military protocol of salutes. "Looks like the high command has finally got some sense. With two

Canadians here we'll really be a match for the enemy. Where are you from, son?"

"Alberta, sir," said Armstrong and he nodded at the Yukon shoulder flash. "Though I spent some time up there in '12 trying to get a stake for university."

Boyle's face brightened and his large hand slapped Armstrong's back. "Well it's damn good to have you here then. We need self-starters around here. If the Queen – God bless her – had more men like us this country wouldn't be in the mess it's in now. As it is, she's surrounded by self-seeking sycophants who are crapping their pants because they think they've picked the wrong side." With supreme self-confidence Boyle gazed around the station platform, now flooded with people, all trying to get near the food train.

"Look at them," he said scornfully. "The government knows I'm bringing in provisions, yet they are incapable of organizing distribution. Well, I suppose I'd better do something or there'll be a riot."

He left the two Lieutenants and pushed his way through the excited crowds until he reached a bench that had been placed on the platform for waiting travelers. He sprang on to the bench and, spreading his arms out in an appealing gesture, he began to harangue the crowd in a commanding voice. Boyle used very few words of the native language, most of his orders were plain blunt English. The forceful manner of his delivery however, together with his arm gestures, left the people in no doubt of his meaning and they began to move back from the provision cars. Armstrong was intrigued at the way Boyle used his powerful personality to control the impatient crowd, and he noted that they did not resent the man but submitted to his authority with good humored resignation.

"Boyle is well liked and trusted here," said Hall "If Ferdinand were to cash in his chips, Boyle could be King tomorrow as far as the people are concerned. And the Queen too, I bet." He grinned a sly grin. "Imagine that. A sourdough King! That would be one for the history books."

Armstrong looked at Hall, unsure if he was patronizing Boyle. "He built a damn good empire up in the Klondike, that I know and I bet he'd be a sight better ruler than some of the imperial, chorus-line nancy's I've seen prancing around Europe with their fancy spiked helmets and tight pants."

"Too true, old boy," agreed Hall hastily. "The man is a marvel at organization. Ah. Here come some of our trusty Rumanian troops to help out."

A contingent of soldiers appeared, led by an officer who made a great show of saluting Boyle. Boyle returned the salute with grave ceremony and, after a short discussion, the Rumanians began to unload and distribute the provisions to the waiting crowds. Hall and Armstrong, now that order had been established, withdrew their squad to march them back to allied mission headquarters.

Armstrong lay on his back in his cot, a cigarette smoldering in his mouth, moodily staring into the dark night. His hand nursed a glass of vodka, vodka from a bottle that had magically appeared from under O'Reilly's tunic when they reached the mission. It seemed that when all eyes were on Boyle, he had slipped into the carriage to get a little treat for his officers, as he slyly put it. Across the room he could hear Hall's breathing in deep sleep. From outside came the click of steel tipped boots as a sentry paced. Despite the eventful day and evening Armstrong was finding it difficult to sleep. He couldn't clear his mind of the swirling thoughts that intruded, thought that involved the ambiguous nature of his mission. This complicated little backwater of the war in which he found himself. The Countess and her motives. The Queen. Boyle. Russia. Armstrong thought he wouldn't like Russia. Too damn far from anywhere and too damn Eastern for a prairie pilot. Also there kept coming to his memory dark lustrous eyes, soft brown hair, and a tear-stained face, last seen on a smoky railway station in London. He cursed to himself, angrily stubbed out the cigarette and thought "to hell with everything" as he gulped down the vodka, rolled onto his side and sought sleep.

Boyle appeared at the mission after breakfast. Hall had already gone out and Armstrong was sitting on his bed smoking. He stood up, but Boyle waved a dismissive hand and sat heavily on Hall's bed. He appeared to Armstrong to have lost the energy he had shown last night.

"Are you all right, sir," said Armstrong.

Boyle looked at him and shrugged. "As all right as anyone can be after attending a meeting of the general staff of the Rumanian army. Damnation it to hell," he burst out. "If I could have had a free hand in Russia and had not been side tracked by so many self-serving, goddamned hide-bound brass hats, I could have had an army out there facing those Huns." His eyes blazed under the heavy brows. "Do you know I went to Russia to organize their railroads, if you could call them that. And in a few short months I had the entire rail system running smooth as clock-work. I had the ear of Kerensky too.

He was willing to give me authority to rush a whole corps to this front but certain people in the British diplomatic corps got their noses out of joint and I was told it was none of my business and would I kindly keep playing with my trains."

Boyle continued to express his bitterness towards those in charge of allied liaison. Armstrong listened but said nothing. He thought perhaps Boyle was a little touched on the subject. After all, if a man was doing a good job why would anyone want to stop him.

"Hall will be back soon. Do you want to see him?" queried Armstrong.

"No. Thank you, I'll catch him later" said Boyle. "I want to report to the Queen as soon as possible." He grinned suddenly and his face lost its weary look. He clapped Armstrong on the shoulder. "You're a good man Lieutenant. Walk me to the door." Armstrong stood and went with Boyle down the stairs to the hall. Boyle lowered his voice to a whisper, or as close to a whisper as his booming voice would allow. "Be ready to leave soon. I want you with me in Russia." With that he left, striding impatiently, his swagger stick raised in farewell.

Armstrong spent the rest of the day with O'Reilly at his side exploring Jassy. Hall was still away, no doubt sticking his thin nose into someone's business. Armstrong watched the civilians as he strolled. They seemed to cling together in groups, rarely did one see a solitary Rumanian. Mostly male, they gathered in crowded restaurants, if one could so call the shabby establishments, drinking countless cups of ersatz coffee and arguing about the war. Despite the cool autumnal day, many of them sat in the public squares and parks, smoking cheap cigarettes as they watched passersby with the wary interest of people who have nothing else to do.

Armstrong noted the soldiers also. Rumanians who looked bewildered and demoralized; and Russians, unkempt and uncaring, swaggering through the crowds, some with red armbands prominently displayed, some bargaining with civilians, selling food they had pillaged from the countryside to the hungry populace. O'Reilly snorted with contempt when he saw none of the soldiers, either through indifference or Bolshevik conviction, saluted his officer.

"Shabby looking bunch, eh?" Armstrong said over his shoulder.

"Aye, that they are," said O'Reilly. "I've seen better fooking fighters in Ballybunion on a race day. But where are all the women, guvner?   Seems to be damn few colleens around!"

Armstrong shrugged his shoulders.   "You must remember, O'Reilly, that this is not Paris or London.   These people were under Turkish domination for centuries, so they still follow some of the old traditions like keeping their young women under seclusion. Among the peasant class, that is."

"Seclusion is it, muttered O'Reilly to himself.   "Not if you're a fooking officer with a bejasus hot-knickered countess after your body."

*   *   *   *   *   *   *

Hall returned later that evening.   The two officers decided to eat in the mission, rather than chance the fare in Jassy's restaurants and, as they cleaned up prior to the meal, Hall told Armstrong of his thoughts.

"Absolutely no doubt about it, old boy," he said as O'Reilly fussed around Armstrong, brushing off his uniform with extravagant gestures he had probably copied from a Biograph film. "The countess and her establishment are the center of the German spy network in this town. I've a maid of hers on the payroll, and she tells me that the countess gets a regular letter from old Ernst. I'd dearly love to get a look at that correspondence."

"Can't the maid get at the letters?" queried Armstrong.

"No. She's too scared and the countess is too careful. They're brought in by the armistice negotiators and she locks them in her safe immediately after she's read them."

"Ah, to be sure that'll be the tin box she keeps in her bedroom," interjected O'Reilly.

"You've seen it!" said a startled Hall.

O'Reilly grinned and his small black eyes gleamed mischievously. "Well sir, you must understand now that there were times that I had to avert me eyes from his lordships going's on, as any gentleman would. From my position behind the curtains you understand. Well, as I was gazing to the bed, I happened to notice the safe in a corner of the room, under a table. It's covered by a cloth which melord dislodged during his – ah – exercises."

"Damn your prying eyes," muttered Armstrong grimly.

"You called it a tin box," said Hall, swiftly motioning Armstrong to silence with a wave of his hand. "What do you mean by that?"

O'Reilly pursed his lips in a gesture of contempt. "It was a Bausch and Linder 1870, single key model. It should take a flashman about five minutes to open it...wiv his eyes closed."

"How, in the name of the great Harry do you know these things," roared Hall.

"Don't even ask," groaned Armstrong. "Not unless you want to hear a load of Irish blarney." He caught O'Reilly by the collar of his tunic and pulled him towards him. "Listen to me you little Mick, are you trying to tell us that you can open that safe if we get you in the room."

O'Reilly eyes bugged out with the pressure of his collar being pulled tight and Armstrong released him.

"Jasus, melord," O'Reilly gasped. "But surely. I can have that wee box open in no time. When do you want me to do it. Tonight when she's asleep?"

Armstrong turned to Hall. "What do you think...can it be done?"

Hall shook his head as he considered. "No," he said slowly. "I think they will be too much on guard after last night. The maid told me they now have armed guards outside the building."

O'Reilly grinned. "Now sirs, tis evident that ye have never seen the boyos picking pockets at Dublin races." He leaned in towards them, his eyes glittering excitedly, and neither of the officers thought it strange that they should listen so carefully to a ranker.

"Now every race-goer knows that he has to keep his hand on his wallet all the time, eh? So we have to get them aroused enough to forget the purse's. And what better way to an Irishman than a good old donnybrook." He laughed at the look on their faces. "Ye organize a fight and I'll nip up the ivy and have that safe open in two ticks, your honors."

"By god, that'll work," said Armstrong. "Let's do it."

Hall looked from one to the other doubtfully and then smiled as their enthusiasm aroused him too.

"All right then," he said laughing. "God, what a couple of rogues. I go then and see if I can find some volunteers to have a brawl. Right after dinner, before any of the countess' retainers go to bed."

Armstrong looked at O'Reilly. "Listen to me carefully," he said. "It's important that this operation be carried out in secrecy. That means I don't want the Countess to find she's missing items of jewelry or money. Understand?" O'Reilly nodded his head. "One other thing. If you can disguise the theft of the letters, do so. Take a selection of paper and put it where you take the letters from. If she doesn't notice we've stolen her letters, so much the better."

It was almost two hours later. Armstrong and Hall waited in a doorway opposite the countess' house. It was dark, with fast scudding clouds obscuring the moon. Across the road Armstrong could see the shapes of two men as they lounged against the entrance steps, occasionally stamping their feet to keep warm.

"Not very disciplined, are they?" whispered Hall, as one of the sentries lit a cigarette.

"Shh," hissed Armstrong as the noise of voices raised in song came to their ears. "Here they come."

Four soldiers came down the road. British Tommies with caps on the backs of their heads, arms around each others shoulders, singing raucously about the misadventures of a Liverpool whore named Maggie Mae.

Armstrong nodded approvingly as he checked his watch. At any moment now another four soldiers, almost the total strength of the British contingent, should come from the other direction and the two groups would stage a brawl outside the Countess's front door.

Hall caught Armstrong's arm. "Oh shit," he gasped. "That's torn it. Look. Bloody Russians."

Along the road, heading towards them came a group of Russians. All of them with red arm-bands. All of them far drunker than the Tommies. And several ladies of the night were with them.

The ladies proved be a heaven sent opportunity for the Tommies. Immediately they tried to separate them from the Russians and within seconds the street was a cacophony of screams, curses, blows and angry shouts. The piercing screams of the ladies added to the confusion, as with a clatter of steel-tipped boots, the remainder of the British soldiers arrived and joined in the melee. Armstrong, despite his years in the army and his experiences as a sourdough, was amazed at the rich variety of profanity uttered by the soldiers. They seemed to regard the whole affair as an opportunity to express, at full lung power, their command of swearing in the dialects and languages of every nation the flag of empire had waved upon. Hindi and Egyptian pre-eminent, but all laced upon the foundation of gutter English.

Armstrong jabbed Hall with his elbow and nodded across the road as lights sprung up all over the ground floor of the house. He caught his breath as he saw the slim figure of the countess, her neck craned over the backs of her retainers,

interestedly watching the brawl.   Behind her, in a blur of
movement, a black figure shot up the side of the building,
paused momentarily outside a window, and was gone.

It was unfortunate that the Russians were too drunk to
offer great resistance to eight well trained and enthusiastic
Tommies, because they broke and ran. The British, still yelling
outlandish and lurid oaths started to follow them but, realizing
that their orders intended them to stay outside the house
making as much noise as possible, began to fight each other.

After a few minutes, a sergeant, specially coached to be
at his parade-ground loudest, arrived on the scene and
commenced to restore order.   He lined the troops up and
berated them continuously for their behavior. Typically he
overacted with his commands and orders but it didn't matter to
the viewers. Armstrong was amused to note that the countess
had watched the fight with avid interest. But, now that order
had been restored, he saw her return to the house.

A minute dragged slowly; a minute in which Armstrong
shook his watch twice, convinced it had stopped; a minute in
which Hall muttered, time and time again, the words, "Come
on. Come on;" a minute in which the Sergeant finally had the
men lined up and marched away; a minute, which ended with a
light coming on in the room into which O'Reilly had
disappeared.

"Shit. That's torn it," said Armstrong, fumbling with
the cover of his service holster. "Stand by to bust in. No, on
second thoughts you go and bring back the troops before they
get too far away."

Hall nodded and sped away.   Armstrong remained,
tensed and alert, drawn colt in hand. The curtains fluttered in
the night breeze and she saw a slim hand pull the window shut.
A hand, the fingers of which glittered with jewelry. It could
only belong to the Countess.

"Goddammit O'Reilly, where in hell are you?" he
muttered.

"Well sure and bejasus tis myself here right beside you
melord," came a softly accented voice.

The hair rose on Armstrong's head as he jumped with
surprise. "Hell's damnation you little sod, how the devil did
you get back here?" He caught O'Reilly by the shoulder as he
peered at the Irishman. "How did you get out?"

Even in the dark O'Reilly's eyes glittered. He laid a
finger alongside his nose and said, "Practice makes perfect,
squire."

Armstrong heard the clatter of boots and caught O'Reilly by the arm and said. "All right, never mind the blarney, let's get out of here," and they ran until they reached Hall and the returning soldiers.

Hall called out. "Thank God he's safe. Did he get anything?"

Armstrong looked at O'Reilly and grinned. "I guess I was so damn relieved to see him I forgot to ask. Did you, O'Reilly, get anything?"

O'Reilly gave a proud nod of his head and patted the front of his black jersey, "I emptied out the whole fooking lot melords, and left a pile of paper in its place, they were wrapped in a piece of cloth so I did the same with the paper."

"Good man," sang out the delighted Hall. He turned to the Sergeant and his squad. "Well done, all of you, a good night's work. Right take them back sergeant. I'll get the mess sergeant to send you all a tot of rum." The men, big smiles across their battered faces, marched back to their quarters. The three followed.

The two officers sat until the early hours of the morning going through the letters. There were a great many, all written in a arrogant, sweeping hand, and every now and then Hall would murmur or grunt with surprise and make notes. O'Reilly kept them plied with the Vodka he had acquired the night before.

Hall tossed the last letter aside and looked at Armstrong. "Not a bad night's haul I'd say. Damn good show O'Reilly."

O'Reilly gave a cheeky grin in answer. Armstrong ignored them both, his concentration absolute on a letter in his hand. He read and reread a particular paragraph, gnawing at his bottom lip as excitement rose within him.

"Listen to this you two." IIe raised his head and looked at them. His eye caught O'Reilly's and he paused for a moment considering. Then he spoke, slowly and carefully. "Understand this, O'Reilly. What I am about to tell you is privileged information. The only reason I'm not sending you out of the room at this time is because I think we'll need you and your skills before this assignment is over, so you might as well know what's going on now. But I warn you. You open that gabby Irish mouth of yours about anything that's said in this room and you'll face a firing squad of one – me! Understand."

O'Reilly grinned, not at all bothered by Armstrong's threats. "Oh jasus, yes melord. Me lips is closed as tight as a mother superior's knickers."

Armstrong raised an interrogative eyebrow at Hall, who slowly nodded assent. "Okay then. In most respects it seems that our Ernst is a typical Hun husband. Full of wind and piss and dogmatic instructions to his hausfrau. And to show her what an important man he is, he tells her of various snippets of information that have come his way. Listen here." He read slowly as he translated. "Well, darling, this will amuse you. Ferdinand's English wife has been agitating her ambassador to Moscow to arrange for the return of Rumania's jewels and gold that was sent to the Tsar for safe keeping. Poor woman. What she does not know is that we told the Bolshevik Lenin, when we allowed him to travel through Germany to Russia, that if he can organize a revolution and take Russia out of the war we will give him all the Rumanian jewels and their money too – about ten million pounds." Armstrong looked up. "That, gentlemen, is over forty million dollars! And here's the nub of it. According to our Ernst, Lenin is to attempt a coup in early November. That gives us one month – give or take a couple of days."

CHAPTER NINE

By noon they would be in Moscow. Armstrong found it hard to believe they had come so far without incident. Every stop they made for water or fuel had been an opportunity for something to go wrong. But the Russian soldiers at the stations, apathetically sitting or lying on their kits, had treated the Rumanian-flagged train with total indifference. Armstrong thought they looked whipped, waiting only for orders to disband and go home.

Now the train was running through countryside that looked much the same as that of northern Alberta. Rolling hills, heavily forested, stretched to the horizon and every now and then the train trundled by swampland, gleaming blackly in the dawn light. The first snows of the season had fallen, dusting the trees with white. He looked out the grimy window at the passing landscape and lit a cigarette as he watched the sun creep above the horizon.

Car 451 was a great way to travel. The bulletproof steel-walled car contained a dining room cum observation lounge. A combined stateroom and bedroom suite, complete with a bath – now occupied by Boyle. A kitchen, generating plant, lavatory and five double berth rooms. These rooms had been furnished in a suitable manner for the retainers of the Dowager-Empress of all the Russia's. Now Armstrong and Hall each had a room, and O'Reilly, together with two Royal Engineer corporals, Brewer and Streat, shared another. The train comprised three cars. The car next to 451 had a platoon of Rumanian soldiers, officered by two very junior subalterns. The third car was empty, for the archives. The Rumanians were from the queen's Royal Guards, handpicked for their loyalty. The Rumanian brass had been incensed that a foreign Colonel was to be in charge of the mission to recover their national treasure and had accordingly sent the subalterns, rather than more experienced officers. Despite their opposition, the queen had been adamant. This was to be an allied effort, and she believed a disinterested third party would be better accepted by the Russians.

And then there was Ivan. Ivan was not his name but it had been given to him because his true name was too difficult for western tongues to pronounce. He was a grizzled old bear of a man whose life had been spent as a Romanoff retainer. He came with car 451 and acted as cook and servant and he combined a facility to make appetizing meals with an implacable hatred of the revolutionaries who had toppled his royal master. He had taken an instant liking to O'Reilly and had invited him to his kitchen where the two conversed in their versions of French.

The journey across the southern Ukraine had been uneventful so far but Boyle, Hall and Armstrong kept watch through the night – Russia was no place to be careless. This morning, the sixth of their journey, Armstrong had paced the luxurious car during the darkness while Boyle and Hall slept. The center of the lounge was dominated by a huge enameled stove, richly decorated with a painting of a hunting scene of dogs and horsemen chasing a wolf around the firebox. The stove was supposedly for use when there was no steam heat from the engine, but last night Ivan had lit it and the embers still glowed through the glass door of the firebox.

Armstrong sighed with boredom, opened the firebox door, flipped his cigarette in and walked through car 451 to the forward door that opened to the tender. He climbed the steel ladder to the top of the tender, made his way across the logs to the footplate and dropped down beside O'Reilly, who shared footplate duty with the two sappers.

O'Reilly grunted an acknowledgement of Armstrong's presence, "Nothing to report melord," he said. "but there seems to be more bonfires than at Paddy O'Grady's wake. See, there's another over there on the horizon."

Armstrong took O'Reilly's binoculars and studied the flames. He saw tongues of fire leap up in the dawn sky from buildings and said, "That's no bonfire O'Reilly, that's burning buildings. We'll be seeing more of that as the country moves closer to civil war."

"Civil war?"

"Yeah, that's what Colonel Boyle thinks. Me too."

They stood in silence for some minutes watching the fire as it lit up the skyline, bright against the gray morning, while behind them the Rumanian crew kept the engine firebox fueled with logs. O'Reilly shifted to a comfortable position as he took the binoculars back from Armstrong and said.

"What about these fooking Bolsheviks then? Are they something to look out for in Russia or are they a flash in the pan?"

"Damned if I know, O'Reilly. I studied them some when I was at Oxford. Read Marx, you know, and attended a couple of meetings out of curiosity; so I'd say that Russia is fertile ground for the system. The place is ripe for change, that's for sure."

"So you think these Bolsheviks are going to rebel against the government. Where does that leave us?"

Armstrong grinned. "Out of Russia I hope. That's if we can get this mission finished in a hurry." He slapped O'Reilly on the back. "We'll be in Moscow by noon so keep your wits about you. I'm going back for breakfast. I'll send your relief up as soon as he's eaten." He climbed back over the tender to car 451 to find everyone awake and ready to eat.

They sat around a small table after breakfast, Boyle, Hall, Armstrong, and the two Rumanian subalterns, as Boyle briefed them on the mission. He stared at each of his officers with piercing eyes beneath jutting brows, so fierce looking Armstrong wondered if the man had a special brush to make them stick out. He began to speak and Hall whispered the occasional translation to the Rumanians.

"All right now, listen carefully," he began. "I don't know what kind of reception we'll have in Moscow, or indeed if there'll be any government left by the time we get there. But, before we left, the Kerensky government had agreed to let all the Rumanian archives and various state treasures be returned to the proper owners, and has signed a protocol to that effect. Of course, when the Rumanian government sent them to Russia for safe keeping the idea that the Tsar would be deposed was unthinkable. Put not your trust in princes, eh? Still, here we are assigned to recover them and by God we'll do just that. Now the Rumanian Ambassador is a M. DiAmanti and he has arranged for transportation of all materials from the Kremlin to the train. Also there is a M. Guerin with the legation and he will be working directly with us. The object is to get the material loaded on the train and get it safely back to Rumania before the Germans force an armistice and kick us all out. Any questions?"

Armstrong and Hall shook their heads and the Rumanians looked on uncomprehending. Then Armstrong

spoke as a thought occurred to him. "What's to stop the
Germans from taking all the "material" when we get it back to
Rumania?"

Boyle shrugged. "Her Majesty tells me that the state
jewels and archives are protected under the terms of the
armistice. As for the gold reserves, no doubt the Germans will
insist upon reparations but that's not our problem. The fact of
the matter is that they will be safer in Rumania, even in its
present state, than left here to the mercy of revolutionaries."

"That's true I suppose," said Armstrong slowly, "but
I'm opposed to taking several millions in gold for the Hun to
get his greedy hands on. That could be constructed as giving
aid and comfort to the enemy."

Boyle raised his head, glared at Armstrong and spoke
with glacial emphasis. "In this matter we are all servants of
her Majesty and we will obey her commands. Those commands
are to recover her nation's treasures. That is what we will do.
Is that clear?"

"Well of course it's clear," said Armstrong sharply.
"My briefing is from the Foreign office and that's their
instructions too. But my comments on the bullion are valid."

Boyle inclined his head slightly, as if unwilling to agree
to anything that would deprive his beloved Marie of her
possessions. "With regard to the bullion, I don't think the
problem will arise," he said finally. "My information is that the
Kerensky government has not consented to the release of it,
pending settlement of loans to the Rumanians. So we'll have to
wait and see what occurs. Now I want us all to be armed and
prepared for any eventuality, the other ranks too. I'm not sure
what reception we'll get in Moscow, so let's all keep on our
toes. All right!"

The meeting broke up and Armstrong thought he'd
better make preparations for Moscow. He got O'Reilly to pack
his kit, then stood by him as the Irishman gave a final polish to
his flying boots.

"Bit of a Tartar for a militia man isn't he, melord?"
observed O'Reilly, his inquisitive eyes flicking to Boyle, who
was standing outside his sleeping berth, giving orders to Ivan.

Armstrong grinned. "He's in love, that's why, so be
careful what you say about the Rumanians."

"Oh to be sure I will melord. 'Tis the soul of discretion
I'll be. Even if I am a republican at heart."

Armstrong looked at him thoughtfully. Then he spoke
so softly O'Reilly had to strain to hear him. "One more thing –
there may come a time when Colonel Boyle's requirements are

radically different to mine. Should that time come you will take orders from me and only me. Is that clear?"

O'Reilly slyly cocked his head and stared at Armstrong. His whole demeanor showed his love of intrigue. His face lost its inquisitive look and became cunning. His hand polished faster as he absorbed the import of Armstrong's words. "You're the boss squire," he hissed. "Anything you say."

Armstrong nodded then walked to the windows and stood studying the scene as the outskirts of Moscow began sliding by. For the most part the buildings were crude wooden plank houses of the type known as 'isbars' with the cracks between the planks packed with clay, much like the early settler cabins of his native west. They were built low to the ground and huddled together for protection against the savage Russian winter. Few people were to be seen; only the occasional child gathering firewood watched the train pass with incurious eyes. He looked at his watch, almost noon. He opened the window and leaned out, eyes watering in the bitter wind. There! In the distance he could see the spires of Kremlin, the winding course of the Moscow river and the more comfortable houses of the middle classes.

"Almost there!" he called out as he pulled his head back in.

"Oh jolly good," said Hall. "I think I'm getting jail fever from being on this train too long. It'll be a relief to stand without rocking from side to side."

"Right," said Boyle, rubbing his hands together. "This is where we earn our keep." He looked at his lieutenants, his eyes intense with purpose, and again Armstrong was impressed with the power of command that exuded from the man. Boyle had obviously prepared for this moment. His uniform had been well pressed and his gold insignia glittered. "I want a standing guard put on this train as soon as we pull into the station. We will be entering the 'Riazansky' station, which is not too far from the Kremlin." He looked at the two Rumanian subalterns. "You two will ensure that no unauthorized person enters the train or in any way interferes with it. The guard will be armed and bayonets will be fixed." He waited impatiently while Hall translated to the Rumanians and continued as soon as they nodded their understanding. "This carriage will be our headquarters for the duration of the mission. If we get separated for any reason then check back here. For the rest of it no one knows what will happen so let's keep on our toes, keep alert and be prepared to use our initiative." He grinned at them as he said. "And God bless us all said Tiny Tim."

The train lurched and rattled as it went over sets of points and the engineer released a shrill whistle as he began to slow. All the company stood to the windows, watching as the train finally rolled into the station. Riazansky station was old and cavernous, with steel vaulted girders rising to a glass roof that reluctantly allowed light to enter through the soot and dirt of years of neglect. Here, crowds were immense, but they were not the crowds that the travelers had seen in other cities. These crowds were frightened, seeking any train that would take them away from a city that was threatening to boil over into bloody revolution. Families stood surrounded by baggage. Ragged-uniformed soldiers thronged everywhere, some with red arm-bands, all carrying rifles. Here, an orator was haranguing a group. There, soldiers were looting baggage. All stopped to watch the train with Rumanian flags go by. The civilians with hope and the soldiers with interest.

The platform at which the train came to a stop was however, almost deserted. The Rumanian officials in Moscow had evidently arranged this, for there were several armed soldiers at the platform entrance. A small group of well-dressed civilians stood waiting by 451 as Boyle and party stepped off.

Armstrong stood with Hall behind Boyle as the big Colonel advanced upon the civilians with a smile on his face and both arms outstretched in greeting.

"M. Guerin. It's always a great pleasure to see you. How are you sir?"

Guerin, a small stout man wearing a thick walrus moustache, didn't understand English but he didn't need Hall's translation to appreciate Boyle's words. He beamed with pleasure as he embraced Boyle. Boyle politely disentangled himself and introduced Hall and Armstrong. Armstrong's facility with languages had helped him to understand more and more conversational Rumanian, and he replied to Guerin's greeting in the man's own language.

Guerin had arranged for the party to stay at the English Club, a large early nineteenth century building on Tverskaya street. Upon his assurance that the train and contents were safe under the control of his guards, Boyle consented to them all attending a small luncheon at the Rumanian consulate.

Boyle looked at his two Lieutenants. "Gentlemen," he said. "Let us be on our toes. The sooner we're out of this country the better. Maybe we can talk M. Guerin into moving material tomorrow. In the mean time let's have a couple of drinks and look over the situation."

The party left the station, the way being cleared by a squad of armed guards. Guerin explaining that the guards were seconded from the household troops and loyal to the Kerensky regime.

"What's your evaluation of the situation here, sir," asked Hall when they were settled into a large car and moving through the streets.

Guerin shrugged his shoulders and grimaced. "There is much unrest, you understand. Keresky is rapidly losing control and seems unable to prevent the anti-war factions from persuading the army to lay down its arms. There is much talk of moving the government to Moscow away from the Bolshevik influences in Petrograd. Petrograd being their stronghold you see. But I fear that it's a case of too little too late. Kerensky wants to lead a slow and cautious evolution into a modern state. But the time has passed for being slow and cautious and the Bolshevik dogma of armed insurrection appeals to an army that has been too long betrayed and slaughtered by incompetent Generals in a war they've ceased to believe in." He sighed. "I fear there will yet be much blood shed in Mother Russia."

Armstrong listened with interest, at the same time watching the streets, observing the life of the city. The cafes which seemed to be full, the boulevards crowded with bewildered looking peasants in ragged clothes alongside elegant women in furs. It was a city of paradox. Troops of Cossacks rode by on their wiry ponies while red arm-banded soldiers howled vodka-inflamed jeers at them. Beggars held out entreating palms while sleek well-fed bourgeoisie sat and conducted business in the café's. He thought Moscow to be an unhealthy place to be in and that it could boil over at any moment. He thought the sooner they finish their mission and got out the better.

*   *   *   *   *   *   *   *

Armstrong leaned back in an overstuffed armchair and sipped at a vodka as he talked over the day's events with Boyle and Hall. They were in the lounge of the National Hotel which, being nearer to the Kremlin than their rooms in the English Club, had become their unofficial headquarters for the last three weeks. The trio had found the English Club inconvenient for planning business because of the large throngs of reporters and writers that had gathered there to witness the end of an era. In this ornate old hotel they found the privacy they needed.

They had worked hard since their arrival in Moscow. With Guerin's help they had persuaded a reluctant Kremlin garrison to release the Rumanian archives, and trucks had run in a steady stream between the Kremlin and the train. Books, ledgers, manuscripts, documents, files and paper of all description had been packed aboard the train in the second car, leaving the third one free for the bullion.

Boyle looked at his two Lieutenants and took a good pull at his drink. His deep voice rumbled. "Today was the last of the archives. Now we have to get the expensive stuff out of their hands and Guerin tells me that Rossolovski, the garrison commander, is getting panic-stricken over the news from Petrograd, and he's scared of doing anything wrong. So I guess I'm going to have to use some of the Boyle persuasive powers on him. Goddamned Russian bastard won't know what hit him by the time I'm finished."

Armstrong thought he was beginning to show his age. The strong face was grayer and the lines seemed to be etched deeper.

"Why don't you take a day off tomorrow and get some rest sir," he said. "You've been pushing yourself without a break since we arrived. You've finally got the Russians to release the archives and the state jewelry will be released any day now. We need you in good health you know sir."

Boyle shrugged his shoulders. "I wish I could young fellow," he said. "But I don't think we have time for such a luxury. The damned government is almost non-existent. Kerensky can't be found, and no one wants to approve the release of such valuables. The only way to get action is to bully whatever petty bureaucrats we can. I still have some influence here because of my work with the railroads, so I guess I'll keep my nose to the grindstone for as long as it takes. Now tonight we've been invited to a reception at the consulate and M. Guerin tells me that there will be people there to help us."

"Ah", said Hall brightening. "Action at last. I've been getting a little cheesed off with all this work and no dollies."

Armstrong grinned to himself at Hall's remark and privately agreed with him. The last few days in the Byzantine and tortuous old city had been spent in hard work with little chance for relaxation, while Boyle had done most of the negotiating with M. Guerin's Russian contacts.

"We've definitely established the whereabouts of the jewels?" queried Hall.

Boyle looked at him and nodded. When he spoke it was in a whisper. "Yesterday, while you were moving the last of the archives, Lieutenant Armstrong and I were taken by M. Guerin to the cellars of the Grand Kremlin Palace where a Major of the Preobrashensky Guards unlocked a vault and showed us the boxes containing the crown jewels. They were still sealed and untouched from the day they arrived in Moscow. They're well guarded by loyal troops, and also the Kremlin has been occupied and refortified by additional loyal troops and cadets. They intend to make the Kremlin their headquarters in the event of an armed uprising. Our problem is therefore compounded by these extra troops, and we have to find someone with enough authority to persuade the different factions to let us take what's ours."

Armstrong grinned. "And if we can't," he said, winking at Hall, "maybe we should think about applying O'Reilly rules to the task."

Hall laughed and Boyle looked perplexed but before he could ask the meaning of the remark a doorman approached to tell him that a car had arrived for them. Boyle stood and straightened his jacket. "All right," he said, beaming at his two Lieutenants. "Let's see if we can get some action." As they left the hotel Armstrong checked the date on a calendar behind the reception desk. It was November the fifth. The day the English call Guy Fawkes day, after the man who tried to blow up parliament.

The Rumanian consulate had the baroque look of most official Moscow buildings. It was large enough for an embassy, indeed it had been so before the Tsar moved his capital to St Petersburg. Smartly uniformed guards snapped to attention as the trio strode through the door and entered an ornate reception hall, glittering with light from huge chandeliers.

Armstrong was surprised by the large, elegantly dressed, crowd. It seemed as if Guerin had invited all of the important people in Moscow to the reception. He raised an eyebrow at Hall who smiled and murmured out the side of his mouth.

"Looks like the grand ball before Waterloo ploy, eh!"

Armstrong smiled as Guerin greeted them and introduced various persons. "I don't think the Russians have anyone like the Duke of Wellington to lead them out of the crap-hole they've fallen into," he murmured in Hall's ear in between uttering stilted Russian phrases. He was very interested in the event and its contrast with the chaotic state of Russia. The male guests were equally divided between middle-

aged well-fed bourgeoisie, and a military contingent wearing
an astonishing variety of garishly decorated uniforms. The
women wore their brightest and most daring gowns. The air
was heavy with their perfume, and Armstrong met with many a
bold-eyed invitation and suggestively pressed hand as he
circulated. Drinks were forced upon him as the party
abandoned itself to a desperate gaiety. Drinking was heavy,
and waiters rushing with trays of champagne and vodka were
hard pressed to cope. He thought that most of the guests knew
they were at the end of an epoch.

"Lieutenant!" Armstrong heard Boyle's voice above the
din and he saw the Colonel standing in a doorway at the far end
of the room. He disengaged himself from a well-endowed
muscovite matron who had been rubbing her legs against his
and pushed his way through to Boyle.

"In here," grunted Boyle as Armstrong got to him. "A
quick meeting with some people who can help us. Let's get it
over with and back to the party before anyone gets curious."

It was a small ante room off the reception hall and Hall
was already there with Guerin and a Russian officer.

"Lieutenant, I want you to meet Captain Count Aleksi
Tolstoi of the First Smolensk Guards. Count, this is Lieutenant
Armstrong of the Royal Flying Corps.

Armstrong shook the Russian's hands. He was
impressed by his air of alertness and efficiency. Tolstoi was a
tall thin man in his early thirties, swarthy of complexion but
clean shaven except for a thin moustache. He looked from
Boyle to Armstrong and murmured a pleasantry about the size
of Canadian men. As he listened to Tolstoi, part of Armstrong's
mind wondered how the devil did the man get into the skintight
uniform he wore with such panache. His eyes though, were
alive with curiosity and a zest for living. Armstrong thought he
looked to be a good man to have around if things got tough.
Tolstoi seemed genuinely glad to meet him.

"Count Tolstoi?" he queried with raised eyebrow.

"A distant relation," said Tolstoi with a smile.

"Count Tolstoi has orders from Kerensky himself to
assist us in every way possible to return to Rumania that which
is rightfully hers," said Boyle, a pleased and somewhat relieved
smile on his face.

"That's very good news, said Armstrong, speaking in a
courteous and diplomatic French. "I'm sure we shall bring this
mission to a rapid conclusion with such capable men on our
side."

Tolstoi inclined his head in acknowledgement of Armstrong's use of the court language.

"Gentlemen," said Boyle. "I don't want to spend too much time away from the reception but the Count has told me that he has information from various sources that the pot is just about ready to boil over. He means the revolution is ready to start, so I don't want to waste any more time. I suggest we meet at 0900 hours tomorrow at the English Club, and from there we'll make an official call on the Kremlin. All clear on that?" The commanding eyes flashed from one to the other as Hall translated for Tolstoi. All nodded their understanding, and Boyle said, "Let's not upset the party. You two lieutenants get back there and circulate, and keep smiling."

Hall nudged Armstrong's elbow as they returned to the reception and said. "I say old boy, I've found a little popsyvich here who wants me to protect her from the Bolsheviks. The protection may take me all night so don't wait up for me." He made off with an anticipatory look on his face.

Armstrong grinned to himself and pushed through the crowd to the buffet table. All seemed happy to pat him on the back or shake his hand as if taking courage from the uniform of an ally.

The buffet table showed little sign of the privation that three years of war had caused. It was loaded with meat delicacies, cold cuts, cheeses of all types, fish dishes, bowls of black caviar and elegantly sculptured jellied desserts. Waiters stood with open bottles of wine ready to pour. He filled a plate with food, took a glass of wine and turned to watch the party. He saw Hall talking to a worldly looking blonde and he wished him well. He saw Tolstoi, eyes flashing, surrounded by women. He saw Boyle talking quietly to a group of businessmen. He saw Guerin and a woman slipping out the door. And against a wall – alone – her enormous dark eyes locked upon him, he saw Anna Crystal!

CHAPTER TEN

Armstrong stood frozen, the food forgotten, as his brain tried to comprehend the evidence of his eyes. His stomach tightened. Blood soared to his head and pounded in his ears. Anna? My god it was Anna! Standing there dressed in a sleek clinging gown of silken lace. Anna, staring at him from across the room, her eyes unblinking, as if willing him to come to her. Armstrong took a quick look around the room, no one seemed to be watching him. He casually dropped his plate on to the table and eased his way through the crowd.

She watched him come, the crowd parting to let him through, some of them glancing curiously at the tall airman with the staring eyes and, just before he got to her, she nodded her head and slipped out through a door.

Armstrong reached the door and stood by it for a second as he again looked around the room. Some new arrivals to the reception causing a flurry of interest and, while attention was distracted, he pushed through the door. For a heart stopping moment he thought he had lost her, for the door led onto a small, murkily lit passage, empty for its length. Then hearing a soft hsst, he saw her, half into the doorway of a room along the passage, her one visible eyes fixed upon him, like a child playing hide and seek.

He walked towards her, his thoughts racing as his mind searched for reasons why she was here. She edged backward into the room and he followed her to a small, sparsely furnished office, lit only by the dim light of the passage. She moved back until she stood against a desk, her arms behind her, the palms of her hands on the desk top. He walked to her, saying nothing, feeling stunned, until he stood close, looking down at her. She stared up at him and her eyes had an imploring looking them, as if she was afraid of him.

Armstrong swallowed, his throat harsh and dry. He wished he'd brought his drink with him.

"Miss Anna Crystal, I believe. This is a long way from London!" He was surprised that his voice sounded normal.

Anna flung her arms around his neck and pulled his lips to hers. Armstrong, excitement rising, cast aside all he knew about her and clasped her to him, eagerly he returned her kiss. He knew she could be a German spy, that she was the mistress of Baron Barreroth, that she had lied to him, but he didn't give a damn. For the taste of her was on his lips. Her body was hot under his hands. Her skin was soft against his face. Her kiss was passionate and imploring, as if to ask forgiveness for her duplicity. His kiss was at once joyous and demanding, serving notice that she was his, no matter the cost.

He broke from her and gently stroked her face, feeling moisture on his fingertips, in the uncertain light he saw her eyes glisten with tears.

"We have much to talk about Anna," he whispered. "Or is it still Anna-Marie?"

She shook her head and flushed. "So you know," she said in clear unaccented English. She hesitated, bit her lip, and gave a gallic shrug. "To you my darling it's plain Anna."

"We have a lot of talking to do."

"Oh, not here. Can you leave? Are you attached to that formidable looking Colonel I saw you come in with?"

"Not so attached that I can't leave him here."

She looked up at him, pulled his face to hers and gave him a kiss that just fluttered over his lips and said "When I saw you it was wonderful. I hoped you would be here."

Armstrong laughed, feeling a swoop of joy that defied all logic and distrust. "I think I've got a case of shellshock," he said "I'm not sure this is really happening."

She stroked his face. "I'm real, my darling. As you'll find out. Come let's get out of this crowd. I have a car waiting. I'll meet you outside. Give me five minutes. All right?"

He reluctantly took his hands from her waist and said. "Five minutes only. One second more and I'll call out the Imperial cossacks to find you."

She smiled at him as she walked to the door. "That wouldn't do any good, darling," she said. "I can ride better than they."

Armstrong grinned as he followed her out. He hung back so that they wouldn't enter the hall together and he watched her walk away with that lithe grace he remembered so well. By the time he entered the hall she was not to be seen and he sought out Boyle, who looked as if he was settling down to make a long night of it.

"I've had enough of this high society stuff," he told Boyle. "I'm off to the club and some sack time."

Boyle nodded his head and patted him on the back. "That's the style my boy," he said. "Quit while your head is in one piece. There isn't a hell of a lot to be done here now, but I'm glad you met Tolstoi. I shall stay for a while longer because I'm hoping that Rossolovski will come over from the Kremlin. He was invited. Maybe a little-face-to-face persuasion can pressure him to release the "archives", I hope."

Armstrong smiled, said "Goodnight sir," and left the reception. He stood at the top of the entrance steps and breathed the crisp November air to clear his head and lungs from the hothouse atmosphere inside. He saw a limousine roll forward to the foot of the steps.

He ran down the steps to the car. A chauffeur got out and opened the door for him. He slide in beside Anna, who was now wrapped in a white fur coat. She shook her head, making a hush sign with a finger, nodding towards the driver. The car was a big Citreon with no divider between the chauffeur and the passengers. So they sat, not close, but holding hands, looking at each other until the Citreon stopped outside the Hotel Billo on Great Lubianka.

Inside, the rode up several floors in a clanking vibrating elevator that was almost as old as the operator. The elevator stopped and the operator slid the doors open with a crash. His bleary eyes looked at Armstrong with interest and Anna with approval. He cackled a lecherous remark as the pair left the elevator but Armstrong was too engrossed in Anna to attempt a translation.

Anna's room typified Tsarist Russia. Originally decorated in opulent bad taste, it was now weary and worn, with threadbare carpets and faded décor. Gilt trim flaked off the bed and furnishings, and the room was lit by softly hissing gaslight.

Anna smiled and said, "Not quite the Savoy but the only accommodation available, and that took a lot of Papa's influence."

The mention of a nonexistent papa caused Armstrong to tighten up. He looked sharply at her as she walked away and casually tossed her coat on a chair. She took a pair of cigarettes from a box on a table, lit them from a lighter, and walked back to Armstrong, placing one in his mouth. He slowly drew on the cigarette and unblinkingly stared at her.

"It's explanation time I think," he said slowly.

She looked at his set face and laughed. "Oh Miles. It's not that serious. Come, let's sit here at this table and tell all. All of our deepest secrets. All of our hidden thoughts." Mockingly she fluttered her eyes at him. "All of our suppressed desires too."

Despite himself, Armstrong grinned at her banter and sat opposite her. "Okay," he said. "It's your nickel. But I want all. No bullshit, if you'll pardon the expression."

She put her elbows on the table and rested her head in her cupped hands, causing her lips to pucker at him. The smoke from her cigarette lazily curled around her face. He thought she looked wonderful. He thought that maybe he was in love with her. He thought it would be wonderful to be with her in that bed.

She spoke first. "How did you know it was plain Anna and not Anna-Marie?"

"The man I was with, in the carriage at Waterloo. He recognized you."

"And what did this clever man tell you?"

Armstrong looked into her deep brown eyes, and marveled at the clearness of them even as he spoke. "He told me you were Anna Crystal...a German Jew. And that you were the mistress of the Baron Barreroth."

A subtle hardness crept into her eyes. "And who is this know-all gossip?" she said.

Armstrong shrugged. "A man in the Foreign office."

"I did not see him at the train. Would this tattler be Sir Reginald Gabbert-Smythe?"

"Oh, you know him do you?"

"No. I know of him. Was it he?"

"No. It was one of his assistants. When he saw you and realized who you were he pulled a gun on me. He thought I had betrayed my er mission."

"Ah. The great and mysterious mission. To recover England's lost heritage. Her priceless jewels. Hah!"

Her voice harsh and derisive, startled Armstrong both by the passion with which it was expressed and by the extent of her knowledge.

'Whoa back lady," he said, alarmed. "I didn't say anything about jewels."

"Oh my darling, you don't have to. I knew all about the plan long before you were involved. I know that a certain self-

seeking bureaucrat thinks that if he can recover certain items
he will help his career."

"You'd better tell me the whole story," said Armstrong.

"All right," she said. "But talking is thirsty business."
She leaned back and pulled a shawl off the bedside table to
expose an ice bucket with a champagne bottle in it. "Pour
while I talk."

Armstrong picked up the bottle. "You were expecting
someone?" he said.

She impatiently waved her hand. "You, of course. I
expected you to be at that reception. We secret agents are well-
informed you know."

He eased the cork out and poured the golden bubbling
liquid. She told her story in a offhand, almost flippant manner.
Whether from bravado or nervousness he wasn't sure.

"In the first place, mon cherie, my French accent is
legitimate, if I choose to use it, my mother being French. My
father was German that is true. He died soon after we arrived
in New York. DeCourville was my mother's maiden name
which I use when I think it necessary." She sipped from her
glass. "Ah," she said, forcing a stage accent. "There's nothing
quite like champagne when one is being interrogated by a
jealous lovaire." She looked at Armstrong's set face, rolled her
eyes, and said. "Back to business. Papa Barreroth is an uncle
from my mother side. It's true he has several mistresses, but
I'm not one of them. I call him Papa because all of his
intimates call him that. He was very good to us after daddy
died. He is now my employer. I am his confidential secretary.
Confidential you understand because this is not a woman's job
and his associates wouldn't understand." She took another sip
of champagne. "So, because I am always in close proximity to
him the story arose that I was his floozy. I've never let that
bother me because, in a way, the story helped my position. I
find one is more acceptable in business at the Barreroth level
as a mistress than as a secretary. Women," she said, a bitter
edge to her voice, "have no head for business, especially if one
is attractive ."

"Why did you come to my room?" Armstrong asked
quietly.

"Papa Barreroth is a Zionist. Both he and Baron
Rothschild have been pressuring the Foreign Secretary, Lord
Balfour, to allow the establishment of a Jewish state in
Palestine when the war is over. Gabbert-Smythe is opposed to
this and actively campaigns against it. So, when a little bird
told papa that he had gone to the front and selected a pilot,

there was much interest , you see, and Papa asked me if I could find out anything about you. Well it started as a bit of a lark and I thought I would beard you in your den, as it were. I didn't plan on falling in love with you."

"What little bird?"

Anna spread her arms and shrugged, "Oh pooff. The Barreroths and Rothschilds of this world have many agents you know. There are no secrets when money is in circulation. I don't know, someone on Gabbert-Smythe's staff I expect. What does it matter."

"Why are you here? How did you get here?"

Anna grinned and said, "Do you want all of my secrets?

Armstrong glared at her and she flung up her arms in surrender. "Okay, okay, I'll tell all. How did I get here? Harwich to the Hook of Holland. Holland through Denmark through the Baltic to Petrograd and from there to Moscow. Am I alone? No, I came with some tough agents of Papa's. We are supposed to be a mission investigating the possibility of loans to the Kerensky regime. Which is a laugh. Papa didn't make his money making stupid loans. But as a cover story pretty good, eh? We're all Zionists actually."

Armstrong looked at her thoughtfully. This was a new Anna. He had sensed steel in her in London but this self-assured woman had brains as well as steel.

"How did you know I was going to be at that reception?"

"Oh God. All of Moscow knows of the Rumanian train with the English officers. As soon as I heard, I said my darling Miles could be there. So I went, uninvited of course, and I was right. When I saw you come in, so big and so strong my knees went weak." She leaned over the table and kissed him.

Armstrong gently pushed her away. "Dammit woman don't distract me, there's more I have to know. Now you keep your body over that side of the table until I'm finished asking questions. Now here's the big one. What do you want here? What are you doing in Russia?"

She looked at him wide eyed. "Why darling, haven't you figured it out. We want the Goliath Stone."

Armstrong said nothing for a moment. He stared at her, his eyes lost their warmth and became steel-gray; hiding the fact that his thoughts were chaotic. The carefully kept secret of his mission was known, it seemed, and the woman he loved was part of some scheme to prevent its success.

Finally he spoke. "Why?"

Anna looked at him and gnawed her lip as she thought, then she shrugged her shoulders. "All right. I shall tell all. We, and by "we" I mean the Zionist organization, are going to take Jews from every nation and of every variety and we're going to put them down in the midst of a desert and surround them with people who are going to resent them being there. Mainly the Arab's but also the colonial powers. That means these Jewish serfs and peasants, shopkeepers, tradesmen, people of every stripe and personality are going to have to fight. A sad statement but true. However, at first we're not going to get the self-reliant Jews of Whitechapel or the Bronx, but the poor and illiterate of Europe. The persecuted and the fearful. Jews escaping the pogroms of Russia. Jews who are second class citizens of every nation. And we're going to say to them. This is your land forever, now fight for it."

She twirled the champagne glass between her fingers, and looked down at the table for a moment. When she raised her eyes up and looked at him, they were damp. "You see," she quietly said. "We're the outcasts of the nations. No matter how many centuries we have lived in a country, we are aliens, and we have to take all of these aliens from scores of different countries and make a nation of them. To make a nation we need ideals, money, pride, patriotism, passion, and symbols. And what better symbol can there be than the stone used by David to slay Goliath? The stone that led to the creation of the first nation of Israel." She gripped his hand with fervent strength, and her voice rang clear, with none of her former flippancy. "You've seen the Tommies marching to the troop trains. Young fresh faced boys, probably scared out of their wits. But the bands are playing tunes that their fathers and grandfathers marched to. Leading them are flags with battle honors, bravely flying before them. They hear the bands and see the flags and their backs go straight, their chests stick out and they're ready to fight to the death."

"We have nothing like that. Not yet. But we will. I don't know if the legend of the Goliath Stone is true, but when we have it and put it in a shrine for the youth of Zion to see it will be a symbol of their heritage. A symbol of their warrior past. Israel will rise again." She fell silent, her hands still clasping Armstrong's.

He studied her face, wanting to believe her, but not entirely convinced he had the whole story. He was stirred by her words, but he sensed there was something more, something she hadn't told him. She'd lied to him in London, was she lying now? "Whose idea is it to take the stone and what are the chances of the creation of a Zionist state."

Anna leaned back in her chair. "We're going to set up a shrine, probably at Masada. You know what happened at Masada, where the zealots killed themselves rather than submit to Roman rule. And this shrine will be a symbol of the new nation. Something to bind us all together. We'll put the stone there, on show, like the crown jewels of England in the Tower of London. And as for there being a Jewish state, well it's happening right now. Papa told me before I left that on November the second, Lord Balfour, the Foreign Secretary, was going to issue a statement saying that the Jews can have Palestine after the British have finished kicking the Turks out. And Balfour did just that, three days ago."

She jumped to her feet again, flushed and triumphant and Armstrong stood too. He pulled her towards him, wrapped his arms around her and kissed her lips that were hot with excitement and passion. To hell with it, he thought. I don't know all of it yet, but I will before I make a fool of myself. He pulled his lips from hers, long moments later and said.

"If I get the chance the stone is yours."

"Do you mean that, really mean that."

"It means nothing to me Anna. I'd rather you have it than have old George stick it in a vault."

"Will you get into trouble? Am I causing you to do something unpatriotic?"

"Hell no, to both questions. I went to war for Canada and jolly old England, not her jewels. And I'm sure we can always blame the Russians. Of course, it all depends on chance. First we have to get the jewels from the Russians, then next we have to pry loose what we want from Boyle. And Boyle's a tough nut to crack. Also I like the guy and I'm already having problems with loyalties. You see, my assignment from Gabbert-Smythe is to recover that portion of the jewels that can be recognized as coming from the Irish collection. Hall and I have to arrange that, and it'll be over Boyle's objections. All he can think of is giving his sweetheart her jewels." He saw the look of puzzlement on Anna's face and briefly explained the Boyle and Queen Marie connection.

Anna's eyes sparkled as she listened and then she said. "Oh, this is too wonderful. Here we have the destiny of nations being decided by lovers and not by stuffy old men and treaties. Perhaps that is the way all things should be decided. In the bedroom, not the battlefield, eh my cherie?"

Armstrong said nothing as he pulled her into his arms and kissed her. His hangs started to unhook the back of her dress and she gave a shiver as his fingers caressed her bare skin. His last thought before passion drove all coherence from his mind was of another pair of lovers whose bedroom antics had decided the fate of nations... Helen of Troy and Paris.

She moaned with pleasure, pushed away from him and whispered, "Take off your clothes," and as he stripped, she walked around the room, turning the two gas lights down to a faint glimmer. Then she stood by the dresser, unhooking her gown. It fell from her in soft folds to the floor. She stepped out of it and walked towards him, slipping out of her petticoat as she did so. Except for a pair of white satin stockings, that was all the clothing she had worn. Armstrong stood waiting, saying nothing, his breath deep and rasping, unwilling to move towards her in case his eyes missed something. She reached him and languorously slid her arms around his neck and eased her body high upon his. Her nipples were so hard with anticipation they felt like acorn points as they rubbed against his chest. She pulled herself up his tall frame, opened her legs wide and wrapped them around his waist as she allowed herself to ease down onto his manhood and take him into her moist willing body. Armstrong cupped his hands under her buttocks and held her tightly to him.

He stood, firm as a rock as she flung her body back, her hands tightly clasped behind his neck. Her loins forced against his, as if by force she could take even more of him inside her. Her eyes were closed, and her breathing was hoarse and heavy. Her perfume rose off her heated body and inflamed him even more. Her buttocks were alternatively silky soft and hard as steel and she pumped her loins upon him. Her satin-covered legs felt slick around his hips, her teeth were clenched tight in her open mouth as her body arched in climax, and long drawn out moan of ecstasy escaped from her as she shuddered against him.

Armstrong exploded inside her, pulsating so long he thought he would never stop. His knees turned weak and he sank to a kneeling position still holding her tightly to him and murmured soft endearments as her sweat-soaked body collapsed against his.

It was long minutes before they stirred. Her body, once so hard and demanding now lay against him, soft and yielding. Her face was buried in his neck and he felt a trickle of moisture run down his chest from her open mouth. She breathed deeply, almost asleep. He was reluctant to move, to spoil the moment, but the threadbare carpet was hard on his knees so he moved his hands from her buttocks to her waist and let himself slip from her. She gave a small whimper of displeasure as she stirred but Armstrong stood and laid her in the bed and pulled the covers over her. He walked around to the other side of the bed and got in beside her. She immediately nestled her body to his with her head on his chest, her hair in his mouth, her loins pressed to his thighs and her slim legs, satin stockings now around her ankles, sprawled across his. Armstrong lay on his back and looked into the darkness. He felt as if his backbone had been pumped dry. He felt a great feeling of calm. He felt full of love for the woman in his arms. He felt it was going to be one hell of a relationship from here on. He felt he needed a cigarette. He looked at Anna, so soft and vulnerable he couldn't disturb her. He fell asleep.

THE PLANE WAS BEHIND HIM, RIGHT ON HIS TAIL. FLAME RED. MENACING. SPITTING FIRE FROM BOTH MACHINE GUNS. HE SCREAMED WITH TERROR AND SWUNG HIS PUP AROUND IN A TIGHT DIVING TURN. NO GOOD – THE BASTARD WAS TURNING INSIDE HIM AND RIDDLIN HIS PLANE WITH BULLETS. PIECES WERE FLYING OFF THE ENGINE. FIRE. ...MY GOD THE PLANE WAS ON FIRE!

Armstrong sat bolt upright in bed and stared about in bewilderment. His breathing was harsh, rapid, and sweat poured off him. The morning light filtered through the curtains as Anna sat up beside him, blinking at him. The bedcovers had fallen away from her and, even in his confused state, he registered the thought that she looked wonderful.

"Darling, darling, what on earth is the matter?" She knelt in the bed and put her arms around him, pulling his head into her breasts and stroking his sweat-soaked hair.

Armstrong sucked air through clenched teeth as he tried to recover his senses. "My God," he muttered. "I haven't had that dream since I left the Western Front."

Anna held him tightly, crooning endearments to him and gradually his heart stopped racing with fear and he began to respond to her naked body pressed so tightly against him. Until he heard again the sound that had penetrated his sleep-drugged consciousness and initiated the nightmare... The rhythmical pounding rattle of a machine-gun burst.

CHAPTER ELEVEN

A rmstrong, adrenalin pumping, was out the bed in an instant, running to the window. He yanked the curtains aside, spilling brilliant sunshine into the room. The machine-gun burst had sounded close, and by the length of the burst, fired by an amateur – A Maxim was better fired in short bursts to avoid jamming. He threw the window up and, heedless of his nakedness, leaned out.

A squad of soldiers ran east along the street, their faces contorted with panic as they fired rifles behind them without pausing to aim. By their uniforms there were regular army troops, and were commanded by a junior officer of the Imperial Guard. Armstrong, uncaring of the cold, watched him shouting orders, trying to control his fleeing men. Again came the rattle of the machine gun and the officer and two of his men collapsed. Armstrong hung out the window to see an armored car with a crudely painted red star on its side. Behind it, yelling in triumph, came a rabble of men – soldiers and civilians – all wearing red armbands. The car was primitive, compared to those he had seen on the western front, but the heavy machine gun on top wasn't at all primitive.

He realized Anna was standing beside him, a blanket around her shoulders, her eyes puffed from sleep.

"The revolution," she breathed, "My God it's started!"

"You're damn right it's started," agreed Armstrong. "And I'm in the wrong place." He pulled her to him roughly and kissed her as the blanket fell away. "I have to go, my love. Get dressed. I'm not leaving you here alone." He let go of her and scrambled into his uniform. Anna did not move for a moment then she slowly crossed to the washstand and poured water into the basin for her toilet.

Armstrong struggled with the buttons of his trousers. "There's no time for that, girl. For God's sake get some clothes on. I'm not leaving you here alone! I'm taking you to the English Club where you'll be safe."

She tossed her head as she dried her face. "I'm not alone and I'm not going with you." Even as she spoke there came a heavy rap on the door and an excited male voice called her name. Not bothering with her wrap, she crossed to the door, opened it a crack so that only her head could be seen, and spoke in a tongue Armstrong did not understand. She closed it again, turned the key in the lock and began pulling on warm underwear. Armstrong fastened his Sam Browne belt with a slap, exasperated by her calmness.

"Listen to me," he snapped. "This is dangerous, you understand? God knows what these revolutionaries will do before things settle down, and I want you safe somewhere. They won't touch the foreign legations."

She reached up and kissed him. Her face was still damp from her washing. "No, you listen to me my darling," she said. "I came here to get the Goliath Stone, and what better time than when the country is in chaos. You go and do what you have to do and I will do likewise. Don't worry about me. I have my men to look after me." Armstrong started to speak but she put her fingers on his lips. "Darling, it's better this way. If I can get the stone without your involvement so much the better for you, don't you see?"

"Bugger the stone," he grunted. "It's you I'm worried about. How many in your crowd? Can they fight?"

She was pulling a day dress over her head as he spoke and her face was red when it emerged. "Of course they can fight, or do you think Jewish boys are good only as shopkeepers? And as for me, mister. Watch." She opened a dresser drawer and there was a Luger parabellum in her hand. In one sweeping movement she aimed and fired. The china pitcher on the washstand exploded in a mess of waterborne fragments.

She looked at him, one eyebrow raised, the pistol smoking in her hand, her dress bunched up around her thighs and, despite his ringing ears, Armstrong grinned. "You sure know how to make a point, my dear."

"Don't you forget it soldier. This is no ordinary girl."

He pulled her to him. "I know you're no ordinary girl," he said, kissing her repeatedly between words. "That's for damn sure. I wouldn't be so crazy about you if you were. But I can't hang around my love. I have to get to the rest of my party. Now you take care of yourself. I'll see you as soon as I can."

She clung to him for a brief moment, then pushed him away. "I'll be fine, don't worry about me. I'll find you when I need you or as soon as I can. Now go."

Armstrong paused at the door and looked at her. She pursed her lips in a kiss to him. Her eyes flashed, her hair was disheveled and her cheeks flushed with excitement as she struggle with the fasteners of her dress. He thought she was one hell of a girl. He left, and ran down the stairs to the lobby. The hotel staff had disappeared when the fighting started. He paused at the hotel entrance to check the street, then stepped out towards the English Club.

He regretted that he hadn't taken his Colt or his buffalo knife to the reception last night, without them he felt exposed as he strode along, warily watching for more of the revolutionaries. The fighting had moved eastwards and he broke into a run, then slowed to a fast walk, concerned about attracting attention.

Occasionally he heard the harsh drumming of a machine-gun and every now and then there was the sharp crack of a low caliber cannon. He passed the slumped body of the Guards officer, his open eyes staring into eternity. "God rest you fellow" he thought as his nostrils wrinkled with distaste from the well-remembered smell of blood.

Armstrong was surprised to find some of the streets were almost as busy as a normal day, with people walking to work or standing in groups discussing the eventful day. Once in a while a truck, loaded with revolutionary soldiers, would hurtle by, with the soldiers shouting exhortations to the crowds to join them in the fight for the workers paradise. Armstrong kept out of sight as much as possible, standing in doorways when the trucks went by. Once a troop of Cossacks, galloped along, one of them holding his sword aloft, with the head of a Bolshevik impaled upon it.

Now the English Club was in sight and, as he relaxed, three soldiers burst from the doorway of a café, drunk from liquor they had looted, and yelling revolutionary phrases. They let out a roar at the sight of Armstrong and surrounded him, menacing him with their ferociously long bayonets.

"I am an English officer in liaison to your government. Get out of my way." Armstrong brusquely ordered in his primitive Russian, hoping by his manner to awe them into obedience. It was effective, for two of them lowered their bayonets and blinked uncertainly but the third sneered and pushed his weapon close to Armstrong's throat. Armstrong's temped snapped. He brushed the bayonet aside with his left arm and smashed his right fist into the face of the Russian, landing full in the mouth. Armstrong felt the man's jaw snap as he went down.

His rifle clattered to the ground. Armstrong kicked it aside with an air of contempt as he drew himself to his full height and bellowed orders at the remaining soldiers. He allowed his face to become red with anger as they sprang to attention, their eyes wide with bewilderment. Armstrong berated them and told them what their commanders would do to them for insulting a foreign officer. It didn't matter that they only understood one word in ten, his manner was overpowering to their vodka-soaked minds.

"Get this carrion off the streets," Armstrong finally commanded, indicating the fallen Russian with a not-too-gentle kick. Then he turned and strutted away.

It was thirty yards to the nearest corner. Thirty long paces and Armstrong felt each pace would be forever engraved on his memory. His spine felt like ice as he waited for the crashing impact of a bullet. He forced a swagger as the corner neared and then at last he reached it. He resisted the impulse to look back at the Russians, realizing that it might only take a fractional eye contact to break the fragile hold his actions had placed upon them.

His shoulders slumped as he breathed in relief, then he sprinted the remaining yards to the English Club, where he immediately bumped into Hill who was nervously pacing.

"Thank God you're here." He grabbed Armstrong by the arm. "They tell me it's absolute chaos on the streets. Apparently this chappy Lenin has ordered his Bolsheviks to rise up all over the country. Boyle's trying to telephone to Petrograd to clarify the situation, but it looks as if the Kerensky people have all gone into hiding. All foreign officers have been advised to stick close to base until the situation clears up. How did you make out?" And, as Armstrong stared at him with raised eyebrow, Hill flushed and said. "I mean, did you have any trouble getting here?"

Armstrong ran his hand over his unshaven face. "A bit, but nothing I couldn't handle. Now I'd better get cleaned up and ready for whatever the day holds. Tell Boyle I'm back." Fifteen minutes later, bathed, shaved and armed, he returned to the foyer, now crowded with allied officers and diplomats. Boyle was both visible and audible in the crush as his big voice boomed over the crowd and Armstrong pushed his way through to him.

Boyle gripped him by the arm. "Thank God you're safe lad. I heard that they were shooting officers of any type on sight out there. Now stick by me for a moment." He began to issue orders for the security and defense of the club should the revolution get out of hand. Armstrong was amused to see that Boyle's power of command was such his orders were obeyed without question, regardless of the service or rank of those so detailed. He turned eventually to Armstrong. "Now I want Hill to remain here with me and I want you to get the train, and make sure that it's secure. Keep everything on top line and the guards on their toes until things settle down. Hill will maintain contact between us."

"How long do you think the emergency will last?"

Boyle grunted, his eyes darting around the crowd as they moved to his orders. "Damned if I know. I hope the Kerenskiites can re-establish order, but I doubt it. We'll just have to wait and see, damn it all. All we needed was one more day. Now get on with you lad and look after yourself."

Armstrong left. He strode through the streets towards Riazansky station, moving with the natural awareness of the hunter, nerves tense, hand on the Cold in his service holster. He heard the sound of small arms fire from the vicinity of the Kremlin, so he took a side street. He arrived at the station and pushed his way through a crowd that had doubled in size and anxiety since the last time he was there.

The train lay silent at the platform, with wood smoke curling lazily from the chimneys of the stoves used for heating and cooking. The engine fires had long since been allowed to die. The platform was well guarded, thanks to the two Rumanian subalterns, who upon hearing the firing had roused their men and double the sentries at the gate. The subalterns, looking relieved at the sight of him, plied him with questions about the firing, causing him to spend a few moments telling them what he knew and praising them for alertness.

O'Reilly greeted him with a grin that threatened to split his face wide open. "Holy mother of God," he said. "It sounds like Saturday night at the Ballybunnion races out there. What's happening melord?"

"Revolution is what's happening," said Armstrong, noting with approval that O'Reilly carried a Lee-Enfield and had a bandolier of ammunition slung from his shoulder. He boarded the car, acknowledging the salutes of Brewer and Streat, also armed. "Good. You all seem to have your wits about you and are ready for action, well done! As far as I'm concerned this train is allied territory and if any damned Bolshevik tries to take it you can put a bullet up his ass. That's "arse" to you men."

The Corporals, well used by now to Armstrong's manner, looked pleased as they assured him they were ready for the Bolsheviks should they come. Ten minutes later Armstrong was sitting down to an English style breakfast of bacon, eggs, fried kidneys and sausages, served by a beaming Ivan. It seemed the giant Russian and O'Reilly had formed an unholy alliance to plunder food and supplies for the mission, and O'Reilly had been teaching Ivan the subtleties of English cooking.

Armstrong finished his meal, lit a cigarette, and took a deep drag of the fragrant smoke. He felt great. Anna was here and in love with him. This tinpot revolution would add to the confusion and likely help him fulfill the mission given to him by Gabbert-Smythe. He watched the smoke drift lazily to the roof of 451 as the thought about the Goliath Stone. What he had told Anna was the truth. He'd volunteered to fight for Canada and the old country. That meant killing Germans until they had had enough. This business of the King's jewels was a side issue of little interest to him. The hell with it, he decided stubbing out his cigarette. If I can separate the Goliath Stone from the other jewelery it's hers.

"O'Reilly," he roared, and O'Reilly stepped back into the car from the platform.

"Yessir, melord. 'tis I myself, ready for orders."

"Sit down here and listen to me carefully. Keep your voice down and if anyone asks you what we're talking about, I'm giving you messages for Colonel Boyle. Clear?"

"'Tis so, 'tis so."

"I told you that there may come a time when Colonel Boyle's orders and mine will be in conflict."

O'Reilly's eyes became alive with interest. "Ah that you did sir."

"What I am about to tell you is confidential information. That means if you tell anyone else I will have your balls for breakfast."

O'Reilly grinned. "Me lips are sealed. Saint Patrick himself won't get a word from me."

Armstrong groaned "God help me, you've more flannel on your tongue than a train load of army blankets. Just shut up and listen."

O'Reilly adopted his impression of an intelligent expression and Armstrong said, "What is our mission here in Russia?"

"Why 'tis to take back the Rumanian stuff they sent to Russia for safekeeping."

"Right, and part of that "stuff" is the Rumanian crown jewels."

At the mention of jewels, O'Reilly demeanor changed entirely. His eyes seemed to light up and he looked like a ferret about to pounce. "Jewels your honor," he breathed.

"Yes jewels," said Armstrong testily. "These jewels are the property of the Rumanians, of Queen Marie and Boyle will also have your balls if anything should happen to them. They all go back to her." He paused, then said with heavy emphasis, "With a few exceptions."

"Exceptions, melord?"

"Yes. Some of them belong to King George. He wants them back."

"Our King George?"

"The very chap."

"Jasus. How did Queen Marie get them."

Armstrong decided not to tell him they were originally known as the Irish crown jewels, in case he got any nationalistic feelings. "They were stolen by agents of the Kaiser before the war. It's a long story and not important. What is important is that they get lost as we travel back to Jassy. Now Lieutenant Hill is the expert on the stones and he'll decide what we set aside. We're doing it without Colonel Boyle's knowledge because he hasn't been cleared by London to be told. So, as far as he's concerned, the missing stones are still in the Kremlin or the Russians stole them.

"What's my part in this, squire?"

"At the moment, God knows. All I want you to do is to be on top line for whatever we have to do."

"Aye sir, 'tis ready I am for King George and his sparklers. As a loyal subject like myself should be."

Armstrong suppressed a groan at O'Reilly's flannel. "Remember O'Reilly, no blabbing that Irish mouth of yours. Now send in the corporals – I want to talk to them."

O'Reilly went to the carriage door and called to the two men. When they came in, the stretched his short inches to their fullest and said, "Corporals Streat and Brewer reporting, sah." And he stood by the side of the table in a unconscious parody of a senior NCO parading defaulters.

Armstrong looked at the corporals standing to attention before him and raised an eyebrow as if to apologize for the behaviour of O'Reilly. The corporals grinned as Armstrong studied them thoughtfully. Brewer was a red-faced, square built Yorkshirman, while Speaker was a slightly built Cockney with intelligent dark eyes. Armstrong had got to know them well during the six days across Russia, and eh knew them to be capable men, selected to help train a foreign army in military engineering.

He briefed them about the current situation and what the mission hoped to accomplish in view of the revolution. He concluded by saying, "You men are to stay with the train at all times. The Rumanian officers are in charge of security, but they're only subalterns and they need the experience of professionals like you to steady them. Keep the Rumanian flag flying and if any damned Bolsheviks try to take the train, shoot them! Is that clear?"

"Yes sir," chorused the men in unison.

"Carry on," he ordered. The men saluted him and left to check on the Rumanian sentries. Armstrong stood in thought for a moment, then he unclipped his holster flap, pulled his Colt revolver and checked the action. He pushed it back again, leaving the flap loose for speed and, not for the first time, thought he should get out his father's holster, it being handier for quick use of the gun.

"O'Reilly, bring your rifle and follow me," he said, and they left the carriage. "I'm going to inspect conditions around the station," he told the subaltern on duty at the platform gate.

Riazansky station was an ant's nest of scurrying humanity. Businessmen who had suddenly decided to take their families on a vacation to their dacha's. Aristocrats nervously aware of the power of a revolutionary mob. High-ranking army officers who had decided that the front line troops were due for inspection. Sleek looking politicians trying to fade into obscurity. And children everywhere – sleeping, crying, playing, fighting, vandalizing children. Their mother or nurses tried to keep order as their fathers endeavored to get seats on a fast train to anywhere. Many were the envious looks directed at the train with the Rumanian flags drooping from its carriages, the train guarded by alert sentries.

Armstrong pushed his way through the crowds, aware of their panic and fear. He could smell it at the ticket wickets, as men in expensive astrakhan overcoats waved wads of roubles at overworked clerks. He could see it in the down-cast faces of army officers as they gathered in groups to talk. He

could see it in the eyes of the women as they sat on their
baggage, waiting for deliverance from the mob now rampaging
through the streets of Moscow. He drew O'Reilly to him to
speak.

"This is no flash in the pan," he said. "I think we have
ourselves a grand slam revolution here, and these people know
it. What do you say, O'Reilly?"

O'Reilly's sharp eyes flashed from scene to scene and
his ratface looked even slyer than normal as he answered.

"Aye melord, 'tis the real thing to be sure. And I think a
real revolution is a grand opportunity for gentlemen
adventurers such as ourselves."

*   *   *   *   *   *   *

Armstrong sat in a chair, looking through the windows of car
451. Four days had passed since the revolt had broken out.
Four days of bitter fighting during which the government
forces had been forced to seek the protection of the Fortress
Kremlin. Four days in which the blood of hundreds had been
spilled. The fighting had been ferocious, Russian against
Russian, with the Bolsheviks slowly gaining the advantage. He
was sure his mission was a failure. The commandant of the
Kremlin had refused to release the jewels before the revolt
broke out, now he couldn't. Armstrong did not believe the new
rulers of Russia would honor the protocol either.

He lit a cigarette and closed his eyes. Boyle was away
trying to negotiate with the Bolshevik leader in Moscow, a Mr.
Muralov. Hall was away too, checking with his network of
agents to see if he could break the impasse.

Armstrong could hear O'Reilly talking to Ivan in the
kitchen, but could not make out the words. He smiled to
himself and wondered how the two understood each other.

He thought of Anna. He had tried to return to the
Hotel Billo the day after the fighting had started but Boyle had
wanted everyone to stay by the train in case the reds had
attacked. Boyle, had thought anything could happen in the
first wild excesses of a revolution. Other days had been spent
with the members of Mr. Guerin's staff, trying to hammer out a
plan should the Bolsheviks succeed. Armstrong was not overly
concerned about Anna. She was match for any red and capable
of looking after herself. He had no doubt she would find him
when she needed him.

He stubbed out the cigarette as O'Reilly entered the
lounge. O'Reilly came to where he was sitting and stood

waiting in front of him. Armstrong raised an eyebrow in query.

"Could I bother your lordship with a little story?" asked O'Reilly, eyes glittering with excitement.

Armstrong smiled. "I've no doubt you will, whether I want you to or not."

"Oh, I'm sure ye will be enthralled with this story," said O'Reilly. As he spoke Armstrong saw that Ivan had left the kitchen too and was watching with an anxious expression on his face. O'Reilly squatted down on a footstool in front of Armstrong and began to talk. "It's like this, guv'ner. I was telling Ivan here about the secret tunnels in Dublin Castle, and he says to me that he knows of some like that in the Kremlin. He says that when he was a lad he used to be a companion and whipping boy for some Grand Duke's son, and they used to slip out the Kremlin by one of these tunnels when the son felt like a bit of skirt, incognito like."

Armstrong sat bolt upright and stared at the two, as O'Reilly smugly smiled and nodded his head. "Sainted Mary above, you see that point melord. 'Tis a sharp man ye are."

"Where are these tunnels? Are they still there?" Armstrong asked Ivan.

Ivan shrugged and nodded his head. "It is many years since I and the young prince used the tunnels," he said in his slow French. "It is possible they still usable."

Armstrong took him by the arm and led him to the table. He took from his briefcase a map of the inner city and laid it out. "Show me," he said.

Ivan bent over the map, his forehead creased in thought. Then he put a finger on the map. "Here, from crypt in St. Saviour's cathedral, along the side of the riverbed, to the cellars of the Grand Kremlin Palace."

"Where in the cellars?" queried Armstrong.

Ivan pursed his lips as he thought how to describe the tunnel's exit and Armstrong took a blank sheet of paper and drew a plan of the cellar to which he had been taken by the Preobrashinsky Major. "Here are the stairs down from the main foyer. Here is the room which interests us. Here above are narrow slits of windows. Here..." He stopped talking because Ivan, smiling in comprehension, stabbed his finger at the drawing.

"Here," he rumbled, "In wine cellar. There is a trap-door to tunnel."

Armstrong raised his head, excitement rising in him. "I think we have enough here to do some serious planning. I'll talk to the others and see what they think. In the meantime keep this under your hat."

*   *   *   *

The elegant lounge of car 451 was heavy with tobacco smoke and full of men as Armstrong stood facing them. He began to speak. "You've been called to this meeting because we feel the situation here has deteriorated to the extent that the mission is in danger of failure. Colonel Boyle is in agreement with me and with the plan I have to propose to you. He regrets not being here, but he is again meeting with the Bolsheviks leaders to try to get them to honor the protocol for the release of the Rumanian archives; but, frankly speaking, he has little hope of success."

He paused and looked at the men facing him. Guerin for the Rumanians, Tolstoi for the Russians, Hall for the British, while behind them, at his invitation, sat Ivan with O'Reilly, Brewer and Streat. Guerin had a look of despair on his face, while Tolstoi appeared bored. The revolt had been a shock to the aristocratic Russian, and he told Armstrong that he was sure his days were numbered. He believed that this revolution would follow the path of the French one, with all members of aristocratic families facing death.

Armstrong spoke again. "The plan is this. The fighting has continued for four days and with all the anti-Bolsheviks now resisting in the Kremlin, it could be many more days before the situation finalizes. Therefore we, Colonel Boyle and I, think it's time for another solution and that is to take the law into our own hands." He looked at them and his eyes glittered with amusement. "We have discovered the existence of certain tunnels into the Kremlin.

"I have discussed this knowledge with some of your and together we have drawn a pretty fair map of the cellars of the Kremlin and I have to tell you that I think it's very feasible to enter the Kremlin and remove the archives without the knowledge of the occupants."

Tolstoi shifted uneasily in his seat. "As you know," he said. "I am duty-bound to help Rumania recover what is hers and indeed my sympathies are with her. Also I feel we all have a bond of friendship. But I have to say that I do not want any violence offered to the defenders of the Kremlin. I feel that they have enough troubles without an attack from within."

Hall answered him. "Lieutenant Armstrong and I have discussed this and we feel that there is every chance of removing Rumania's archives without the defenders being aware of it."

"Yes," said Armstrong, "We think there are two points at which we can abandon the mission if necessary. The first is at the cathedral. If we cannot enter there we cancel the plan. The second is when we enter the wine cellar. If the passage outside is occupied we will not force an entry. And, of course, the whole cellar are must be deserted for the operation to succeed. The idea is to get in and get out, without raising an alarm." He looked at Tolstoi.

Tolstoi gravely nodded his head. "That is acceptable," he said. "And I can help you with the cathedral. I still have some influence with the priests there. They are the enemies of the Bolsheviks, of course, and my name will gain us entry to their crypts."

Armstrong looked at Guerin. "You are the senior Rumanian official here. It's your decision now. Do we try, or do we fold our tents and slink away back to Jassy without that we've came for?"

Guerin's black eyes shot form man to man in the room. His forehead was beaded with moisture as he thought about the problem, then he set his jaw firmly as he nodded. "Yes," he said. "I think it is worth a try. Any other solution increases the possibility of never seeing our treasures again. Gentleman, you have Rumania's blessing."

Armstrong clapped his hands as O'Reilly cheered and the sappers shook each others hands. "All right then," he said. "Action tomorrow night at dusk. It's too late to start tonight so we'll spend the time preparing." He turned to Tolstoi. "Count, if you would clear our entry into the cathedral, I feel that is all we should ask of you at this time because I don't want to cause trouble between you and the new rulers of Russia."

Tolstoi shook hands with Hall and Guerin then Armstrong walked with him to the door. Tolstoi stood for a moment looking out over the city, before he turned back to Armstrong and said. "The night sky is red with fires and the streets are red with blood. Do not add your blood to that already split, my friend." He walked off into the night.

Guerin left also and Armstrong and Hall sat down for some planning after they sent the men gathering tools they might need. When they were alone, Hall told Armstrong that there would be another person going on the mission, a Mr. Smith, from the embassy. This Mr. Smith had arrived just recently and, by an astonishing stroke of luck, he happened to be an expert in the matters of jewelry. Armstrong grinned.

"Do I discern the long arm of Sir Reginald in this amazing coincidence?"

Hall elevated an eyebrow.   "I do declare you're beginning to think like a politician."

"Yeah," said Armstrong.   "Well I hope not.   It's politicians that have caused all this mess."

CHAPTER TWELVE

T he night air was cold, a harbinger of the severe winter to come. Armstrong pulled his greatcoat collar tighter round his neck and turned to the others. He thought they looked an efficient bunch of desperados as they huddled below the low walls of the cathedral grounds. Two sappers and two Rumanian soldiers with their pickaxes and shovels, Ivan carrying ropes, O'Reilly with tools and oil lamps, Hall dressed in old clothes, and he himself wearing the train engineer's overalls. Tolstoi was, as ever, resplendent in immaculate uniform. The idea of being in a situation that called for him to wear working clothing had never entered his head. They were waiting for Boyle and this Mr. Smith from the embassy in Petrograd. Boyle was to meet the man from the train and bring him to the group.

"Damn it, they're late, muttered Hall.

But, even as he spoke, two shadowy shapes loomed out of the night; Boyle and Mr. Smith. "Sorry, but the train was late," said Boyle. "But here is Mr. Smith."

Armstrong stuck out his hand in greeting but froze in shocked amazement...Mr. "Smith" was Sir Reginald Gabbert-Smythe".

"What the.." Armstrong began, but Sir Reginald stuck his finger to his lips and Armstrong fell silent, his thoughts whirling. "Smith" was dressed in plain but heavy clothes as would benefit a lowly clerk, but his face had the same arrogant look he remembered so well and the eyes seemed to regard him with sardonic dislike. Shit, he thought. What the hell was going to happen to his and Anna's plans?

"All right," said Boyle, "I'm leaving you to it, good luck and look after Mr. Smith. And remember, if you're discovered, get the hell out as fast as you can."

As he spoke a soft hiss came from the direction of the cathedral and Tolstoi started forward to meet a man dressed in the flowing robes of a priest of the Orthodox Church. Tolstoi nodded at the priest before turning to Armstrong. "This is the priest, Lieutenant. Father Gregori."

Armstrong held out his hand to the priest who, after a slight hesitation, as if unused to such familiarity, took it in a cold dry hand. In the dim light Armstrong could see his thin, ascetic features framed by a wispy beard that reached down to his waist-line.

"Thank you, Father, for your assistance in this matter," he said.

Father Gregori's eyebrows raised at Armstrong's clumsy Russian and Tolstoi hastily spoke. The priest's manner changed at the sound of Tolstoi's voice and he allowed the Russian to kiss his hand. Then, with an imperious toss of his head, he lead the way into the cathedral.

"I think you scared him a little, my friend, with your barbaric accent," murmured Tolstoi as they crossed the cloister grounds and entered the cathedral through a small door concealed behind a buttress. "He was having second thoughts about allowing such an heretic to penetrate these walls. Fortunately for us his love for the Tsar and Holy Russia is greater than his distaste for the western branches of the faith."

Armstrong shrugged his shoulders. "Tell the old boy I'll convert if it'll make him any happier. I never thought I'd survive this war anyway, and it doesn't make a damn bit of difference who says the last words over me."

The priest did not take them into the great nave of the cathedral, but allowed Ivan to lead the party through dimly lit passages and down a few stairs until they stood before a door set deep into a stone wall. The priest spoke to Tolstoi who turned to the party and said, "It is now time to light our lamps."

Matches flared, and four hurricane lamps flickered into life. The priest produced a large key, gave it to Tolstoi, indicated the door with his hand, gave a cursory nod of the head to Armstrong and left. As the slap of his sandals receded, Tolstoi, with a glance at the others, inserted the key. The key turned a short distance then grated to a halt.

"Let me have a look at it sir," said O'Reilly, holding a lamp to the lock. "Blimy, it's full of rust." He turned to Brewer. "Let's have some of that paraffin." Brewer brought the can and, using a pencil as a spill, they carefully trickled oil into the lock.

O'Reilly inserted a screwdriver into the ring of the key and began to lever it back and forth. Rust grated as the key was forced against the wards. After several minutes of this there came a solid clunk. He looked around in triumph and heaved at the door. Slowly, creaking on its hinges, the door opened.

Holding lanterns before them, they entered the crypt and stood in silence. The crypt was probably older than the structure above it and stank of age and rot. Wooden coffins were irregularly stacked on stone sarcophagi and leaning against the walls, stone walls that wept with moisture.

Streat broke the silence. "Strewth. This is a fucking sight worse than my dugout on the western front." He stared in fascinated horror at an aged coffin that had split from the weight of others piled upon it, a fragment of yellow bone showing through the crack.

Hall stirred and murmured, "Do try to remember that this is a house of God, there's a good chap."

"Yessir, sorry, sir," said Streat, winking at Brewer.

"Father Gregori said this crypt is no longer in use for interments, not since the middle of the last century," said Tolstoi. "These are the remains of priests of the faith, old forgotten men. Mon Dieu, what is life eh."

"It's all we've got," said Armstrong, intolerant of Russian melancholy and unsettled by the presence of Sir Reginald. "So let's find this passage and get on with the job. Here, Ivan!"

Ivan stumped forward on his stiff old legs. He took a lamp from Streat and began examining the floor. The others watched as he moved the lamp to and fro across a corner of the crypt, causing his shadow to dance grotesquely across the coffins.

Presently he gave a grunt of satisfaction and stooped over. The others crowded around him as he pointed at an iron ring set in the floor, just visible through hard-packed dust.

"Sappers to the fore," said Hall.

The men inserted a pickaxe into the ring and levered up. Reluctantly, squealing as the detritus of ages fell away from its edges, a large flagstone swung up and stood vertical. A heavy iron counterweight hung from the stone, keeping it upright. The lantern light revealed a shaft with iron bars cemented into the wall, forming rungs that led down into darkness.

Armstrong grimaced with distaste at the rank odor coming up the shaft. He shrugged his shoulders and stripped off his greatcoat. "Leave your coats here men," he said. All except Tolstoi, pulled off their coats and stacked them on one of the few dry coffins. He turned to Tolstoi, holding out his hand, "Thanks for your assistance, Count," he said. "This is where you turn a blind eye." Tolstoi smiled, shook hands with him and Hall, waved at the others and left.

Lantern in hand, Armstrong began to climb down. Five rungs were in the stone of the cathedral foundation, then there were more set into brick. As Armstrong reached these he realized he had left the shaft and was in a tunnel. Seven rungs in the brick. Twelve in all. Twelve feet under the charnel house.

He stood on the tunnel floor holding his lantern high, examining his surroundings, then he pulled out his pocket compass and checked it. The sewer ran roughly northeast to southwest. He was on an eighteen-inch wide ledge that ran along the side of the tunnel. Below the ledge was a trough filled with black, stagnant water. The walls of the tunnel were of aged yellow brick, crumbling in the moist air.

Holding the lantern, he moved along the ledge to make room for the others as they descended. There came a soft plop from the water and he watched with revulsion as he saw an enormous black rat swim slowly away from the intruders.

"Holy bejasus," yelled O'Reilly, his eyes wide with horror as he hung from the rungs. "That fooking thing is bigger than a Kilkenny cat. Squire; shoot the booger!" Armstrong swung to him and hissed in a whisper, "Quiet, dammit. This is a military operation, not a God-damned carnival. We don't know if there are air shafts that carry sound to the surface, so keep your mouth shut until we're certain. Where's Ivan?" The large Russian blinked at him in the lamplight and Armstrong had Ivan squeeze past the others to take the lead.

Armstrong counted paces as they walked eastwards, they flickering lanterns only dimly cutting through the gloom and by their uncertain light he thought the tunnel looked old and fragile. God help us if it collapses he thought. For the first one hundred paces it was easy going, with the ledge firm and level. Then the passage opened out into a large circular area with a domed roof. Here the trough widened into a pool that filled the whole area. Ivan turned to Armstrong.

"River Moscva," he boomed in his gruff voice, "Outside here, through underwater grating. Very deep. We go around."

The ledge continued around the domed area until it came to another tunnel, smaller than the first, with the flow of water drying out to a trickle. Ivan entered this tunnel without hesitation, the rest followed. This tunnel was older then the other and there were sections where the brick facing had crumbled away allowing the black Moscow earth to spill out, creating an obstacle for them to scramble over.

Armstrong kept counting. Five hundred paces. Six hundred paces. He almost reached one thousand when Ivan stopped and raised his lantern to show a row of iron rungs, similar to those at St. Saviours.

"We go up there?" queried Armstrong, as the others came to a stop.

Ivan shook his head, "Blagoveshchenski Cathedral," he said and walked about ten yards further on. Here another tunnel went off at right angles, reduced in height to five feet. Ivan grinned at Armstrong. "We bend here," he said, slapping his massive waist. Doubled over, they entered the new tunnel.

This time Armstrong counted fifty paces before Ivan stopped again. Here, another shaft led up to a stone trapdoor, counter-balanced the same way as in the cathedral.

"Great Kremlin Palace," Ivan growled.

Armstrong turned to the others, all of them sweat streaked and doubled over, "We're at the palace. I think it better if you all moved back until Ivan and I have got the trapdoor open. No sense in all of us blundering into a bad situation." He looked at Ivan. "All right, my Russian bear, let's see what's above us, eh."

Ivan grinned and climbed up to the door. He braced his legs against the rungs and heaved. His head was bent over as his shoulders exerted pressure against the door, and Armstrong watched with fascination as, grunting with effort and face red with strain, Ivan exerted all of his strength.

Slowly the stone slab moved. It crept up an inch, two inches, then stopped. Ivan released his breath and relaxed to ease his muscles before trying again.

"Wait Ivan," whispered Armstrong. The counter-weight was wedged into a recess in the opposite wall, and it now protruded enough for him to get a grip on it. He scaled the rungs until his head was against Ivan's thighs, turned, leaned over to grasp the arm of the counterweight with both hands, then swung his legs over until they were braced against the opposite wall. The arm on which the weight sat was about two inches in diameter and he felt that rust of ages crumble away beneath his gloves. "I hope the damn thing hasn't rusted through," he thought, then bracing himself, he signaled to Ivan as he threw his full strength at the weight. The veins stood out on his neck like chords as his legs rammed against the shaft wall. Through his shoulders he could feel Ivan's legs become rigid as the two men forced their full power against the door.

Slowly, slowly the rod began to move towards him, moving fraction by fraction until, with a cry, Ivan thrust his arms straight and the door flew open with an echoing crash. The counterweight shot forward, Armstrong's feet slipped, his legs thrashed wildly until they found the rungs again and he was able to recover his balance. He snatched at the rungs and scrambled up until he stood breathless at the top, his stomach tight with apprehension. Had the noise alarmed the defenders of the Kremlin? He felt Ivan's arm on his shoulder steadying him. The only illumination was a shaft of yellow light from the lanterns below.

"Get up here with some light," he hissed down the hole but O'Reilly was already climbing with a lantern. Armstrong grasped it and held it up to see. They were in a storeroom of sorts with crates and boxes stacked all around in no apparent system. One large box lay on its side with ledger type books spilling out. He realized that it must have been sitting on the door and had toppled, causing the crash as the trap opened.

The rest of the party came up as Ivan and Armstrong explored. Ivan broke into a string of Russian, too fast for Armstrong to follow but Hall listened as he brushed off dust from his clothes, his eyes fixed intently on Ivan.

"He remembers this place now," Hall said, when Ivan finished. "It is very close to the strong room, around the passage from it. He says this place was used by the domestic staff for the storage of household accounts."

"Yeah, judging by the dust it looks as if they haven't had an audit since Peter the Great, which is good," said Armstrong. "Here's the door."

The door was built of heavy timber, with a sizable lock. Armstrong bent to put his eye to the keyhole. "I see some light," he said. "Looks like a passage outside, the door's locked of course. O'Reilly, get to work."

A voice murmured in his ear. "Now I know why you insisted on O'Reilly being with you."

Armstrong turned to Sir Richard. "What the hell are you doing here?" he hissed.

Sir Reginald's eyes looked at him balefully. "Maitland told me of your involvement with Anna Crystal, so I had her watched and found she was off to Russia. That is why I'm here.

Do you really think I'd allow you two to romp around Russian without supervision?"

Armstrong had no time to reply as O'Reilly pulled a pick from a pocket, inserted it into the lock, made a twisting motion with his wrist, and the lock clicked open. "Abracadabra," he grinned, "the boyo has magic fingers."

Armstrong turned to the others. "Better douse the lanterns, or at least turn them right down. I'm going out to reconnoiter. Keep the door closed until I get back."

"Shall I go with you melord," said O'Reilly.

"No," answered Armstrong. "I'll do this on my own. If I get caught I need you to lock this door again before they find out how I got in here."

He eased the door open, stuck out his head, looked both ways, and slipped out, closing the door behind him. The long passage was illuminated by a single oil lamp guttering away in a niche in the wall. The passage was high and the top of it must have been above ground level, for there were gratings set into half moon apertures above his head and he thought he could see moonlight. All was silent. Evidently the noise of the box overturning had alarmed no one.

He checked his compass – the passage ran north-south. He decided to check the north first. Pressing his body against the wall to avoid casting a shadow he crept along. Once he heard voices and tensed but they from above, through the gratings as a patrol walked the Kremlin grounds. He came to a corner and dropped to his knees to peer around it.

The blood coursed through his veins in exhilaration. Damnit, Ivan was right. The passage opened up to the chamber in front of the vault that held the jewels. The vault to which they had been taken by the Preobrashinsky Major. And the chamber was unguarded! The fighting for the Kremlin had drawn all men from the non-essential it seemed.

Armstrong ran soundlessly on his toes to the foot of the stairs at the far end of the chamber. He remembered they led up to the foyer at the north entrance to the Great Kremlin Palace and silently crept up. At the top he eased his head up until it was at floor level. By the light filtering through the windows he could see that the foyer was full of soldiers, wounded soldiers, lying in rows, sleeping, moaning, coughing. He tensed as he saw movement but it was only an orderly bending over a patient. Silently he crept down again to the deserted chamber and crossed to the door of the vault. This was a far different door than the one at the ledger room. This one was sheaved in steel plate and had two modern locks. He

examined them feeling daunted. They seemed to be very
modern and very difficult to open. Time for the expert. Time
for O'Reilly. Quickly he returned to the ledger room.

"All right," he began, "this is the way it is. First I want
O'Reilly with me to open some locks. When the door is open
I'll send for you all. Come in pairs and quietly. When we're all
there I want you two sappers to start opening boxes and
Lieutenant Hall and Mr. er, Smith to identify the artifacts.
After that we move the stuff here."

"Is it all clear then?" queried Hall.

"At the moment yes, and as long as we keep quiet, the
chances are good for being undisturbed." Armstrong turned to
Sir Reginald. "You're, the only one not wearing rubber soled
footwear, and those boots will make too much noise on the
stone floor outside."

"Smith's" eyes glittered with amusement. "I shall
remove them and creep like a co-respondent."

Armstrong grinned, despite his dislike of the man.
"Thank you. Now, O'Reilly, follow me."

The two left the ledger room and crept to the chamber.
They stopped outside the steel door where O'Reilly eased his
haversack from his shoulders. He took out a bullseye torch
and examined the locks. He had taped off most of the lens so
that only a thin beam shone, with no spill over.

"Holy mother of God," he said thoughtfully. "This top
one here is just a plain tumbler type. I can open that booger in
a couple of ticks, but the other is a bit trickier. I'll have ta make
a key for that, melord." As he was speaking he inserted a pick
into the top lock and within seconds Armstrong heard the
tumblers snick open.

"How long for the other lock?"

"Well melord, it's like this," said O'Reilly as eh reached
in his haversack and brought out a handful of blank keys. "If
one of these blanks fits in the hole I can cut it in five-ten
minutes. If they don't it's a drilling job."

"Well don't hang around, try them."

Armstrong watched as O'Reilly fitted key after key. He
wondered what his Majesty's provost marshals would have to
say if they saw the man's collection. He wondered how the hell
he had ended up burglarizing the Kremlin. He wondered
where Anna was. He kept an ear cocked for movement from
the foyer above as O'Reilly gave a grunt of satisfaction, kissed a
blank key and smeared engineers blueing on its surface. "I
think we may have it, melord," he whispered. "This one's the
beauty! Hang on me sweety." This last to the key as he

inserted it into the hole and gently eased it to and fro, making tiny vibratory motions with his hand.

Slowly he removed it, taking care not to scratch the coating any more than necessary. "Ah yes," he breathed as he examined the key. "We have enough to go on, squire." He looked at Armstrong, "but I think we'd better but it back in the other room. I can clamp it there."

Armstrong nodded in agreement and they returned to the ledger room. The others crowded around while O'Reilly took a clamp from his bag and secured the key to the upright trapdoor. They watched, lanterns held to throw maximum light, as O'Reilly unrolled a canvas pouch, selected a needlepoint file and rasped away at the blank.

Armstrong checked his watch. Midnight already. Dawn at six. Six hours to get everything from here to the train. Six hours before the Bolsheviks resumed their onslaught. Tolstoi was confident the defenders could hold out until help arrived from the Ukraine. He had told Armstrong the only way the Bolsheviks could win the siege was if they would use artillery and they wouldn't do that. Not against that Kremlin. It meant too much to all the Russian people. Armstrong wasn't so sure. Three years of war had convinced him there was infamy that mankind would not sink to. The file rasped on. All eyes were on O'Reilly as the little man carefully cut crenellations in the flat surface. Armstrong resisting the impulse to look at his watch, slipped out into the passage to check for noise. All was quiet as, alone in the darkness, he leaned back against the door and thought about Sir Reginald and Anna and cursed. It seemed that the man was determined to get his hands on the jewels and was no longer content to allow a third party to recover them. It was going to be even more difficult to give Anna the Goliath Stone.

He returned to the vault as O'Reilly unclamped the key and gently rubbed it with fine emery cloth to remove any burrs.

"We'll try again sir," he said as he held the key at arms length to examine it critically. "There will be a few minor touches but I think I've got the outline of the booger just fine."

"Good man," said Armstrong, and to the others. "Right, same as before, wait here until I return. Now, O'Reilly, let's see how good you are."

He opened the door again, listened intently for a moment then he and O'Reilly went stealthily to the vault. O'Reilly fitted the key while Armstrong held the bulls-eye. The key did not turn. O'Reilly removed it and renewed the blueing. Then he inserted the key, removed and examined it and made a couple of passes with the file. Twice more he repeated his actions. Twice more the key failed to turn. Armstrong, all senses tensed for sounds of a patrol, daren't say a word in case he broke the man's concentration. The third time O'Reilly, after a final rub with emery cloth, inserted the key and, softly whistling to himself, turned his wrist. With a smooth snick the wards activated and O'Reilly, with a grin of triumph, swung open the door of the vault.

"Good man, you damned thief," exulted Armstrong and pounded him on the back.

"Tis a result of me higher education," said O'Reilly smugly.

They entered, shining the bulls-eye lantern. Armstrong thought the vault looked the same as when the Preobrashinsky Major had shown it to Boyle and he. The crates containing the crown jewels were still stacked, pyramid fashion, in the center and ammunition boxes were piled against a wall. He looked at the crates and thought of Anna. Anna! What was she doing? Did she really think her ragtag collection of Jews could have got at these jewels?

He broke from his revelry. "O'Reilly. Slip back and bring the others. Send them in two at a time, space them out so that they're not in a bunch."

"Right, melord," and he was gone, his black dressed body as silent as a thuggee assassin on the prowl.

Armstrong found a lamp hanging from a chain but he decided not to light it until they were all here and the door could be kept closed. The sappers and Rumanians were the first to come. He briefly flashed his torch as he told them to stand in silence. This was the most dangerous part of the mission, he thought, when the men were in the open between rooms. Again the door opened, this time it was Hall with Sir Reginald carrying his boots and looking highly amused by the whole thing. Then it was O'Reilly and Ivan, with O'Reilly nodding to Armstrong to indicate that all was still clear outside. Armstrong breathed a sigh of relief as he told O'Reilly to close the door.

"Let's get to work," he said as he lit the lamp. "You sappers start prying open these crates, but don't break any boards. We want them to look untouched when we leave. Mr. Smith and George, would you please check the contents as they are opened. O'Reilly, stand by the door and keep listening. As little noise as possible gentlemen. Ivan, come with me."

He walked to the back of the vault to check the rest of the contents and was surprised to find that there was an alcove large enough to turn the vault into an ell shaped room. Here, behind the ell, were stacked wicker baskets, the size of picnic hampers, each one encircled by a leather strap, sealed at the join with wax and embossed with the seal of imperial Russia. The top baskets were thick with dust and cobwebs. He pulled at a strap to find it so rotted with age it crumbled in his hands. He looked at Ivan, shrugged, opened the lid of the hamper and shone his light on the contents. Wine in dusty old bottles.

Ivan nudged him, pointing at the seal. "Alexander. The first one," he said, his eyes wide.

Armstrong nodded agreement as he recalled his Russian history...Alexander. First Tsar of that name. Ruled for the first quarter of the nineteenth century. This wine had been here for a hundred years, give or take a few. Well he didn't care about the wine but these wicker hampers would be great for packing the jewelry. He thought for a moment, then told Ivan to empty out the bottom hampers, putting the dust laden top ones aside.

He winced as he heard a screech of nails reluctantly losing their grip on wood, and hurried back to the crates. The first crate was already open, revealing the contents. It was lines with heavy brown paper and filled with straw. Armstrong caught his breath at the sight of velvet wrapped packages nestling in the straw. Hall reached into the straw, gently picked up a package and unwrapped it to reveal a tiara, its diamonds glittering cold yellow fire in the lamplight.

Armstrong took the tiara from him and turned it, admiring the way the lamplight flashed from the diamond studded spines of gold fanning out from the headpiece. He was surprised by the weight of it, for it looked so airy.

"Well, damn it, we've done it," he grinned. "Here we are with Marie's knickknacks and Rumania's pride." He looked at each man, noting their expressions as they gazed at the tiara. Avarice and awe. Desire and envy. Appreciation and calculation. The thought crossed his mind that there were others to worry about besides the Bolsheviks and Jews. It was a long way back to Rumania. He sighed. "Okay gentleman, I estimate we have two hours to remove this lot, so let's get to work. O'Reilly, slip out the door and see if you can hear us opening boxes."

O'Reilly nodded, carefully opened the door and left the vault, closing the door behind him.

Immediately the sappers started opening crates. The noise in the enclosed vault seemed incredibly loud and Armstrong only endured it for moments before he ordered them to stop. He opened the door a crack as they fell silent. "How was it?" he whispered to O'Reilly as the man came back in.

"Just a faint murmur came through. That's a nice solid door that is. I don't think anyone can hear us, melord."

"What's the point of opening all the crates, old boy?" queried Hall. "Couldn't we take them as is?

"I think we have a better idea George. Come back here." Armstrong walked to the back of the vault where Ivan was busy unpacking wine baskets. "We transfer everything to these wicker baskets, leaving empty crates here in the middle. If they inspect the vault daily as we understand maybe they'll see the crates and not check too closely. Give us a bit more time to get out of Moscow."

"Damn good idea, let's do it," agreed Hall.

And so the work proceeded. Crates were opened, the contents checked and placed in the wicker hampers as they became available. Every now and then "Smith" would give a grunt of satisfaction, hold a piece of jewelry up to the light, check its description against a list, and put it into a separate hamper. Armstrong assumed it was the same as the list that had been given to him in London by Maitland.

Time went by. The men, already dirty from their passage through the sewer, became dust-streaked and hot in the airless vault. Armstrong tried to avoid checking his watch too frequently, but as the hour of dawn crept closer, his impatience became almost impossible to control. He wanted the work to go faster, but it was essential they be meticulous in the sorting of the jewels. It must be done now. Here. With Boyle at close quarters on the train, it would be extremely difficult to separate the Irish jewels from the rest of the collection.

As each wicker hamper became full, O'Reilly and he picked it up and carried it through the passage to the ledger room. Each time they crept through the night they listened for sounds of the battle, but there was not the constant sound of sniping that there had been on other nights. Armstrong wondered if the Red guards were husbanding their strength for an all-out assault.

He watched Sir Reginald all the time, eager for the sight of the Goliath Stone and curious to see how the man behaved when he saw it. Crate after crate was emptied, hamper after hamper filled. He paired Hall with O'Reilly because he was afraid he would miss seeing the stone if he was out of the vault. Thirty hampers left the vault. Thirty hampers filled with precious gems, brooches, crowns, tiaras, ornate medals, exquisitely crafted Faberge eggs, ceremonial swords, all of the artifacts deemed necessary for the pomp of royalty...but no Goliath Stone. He gnawed his lips in frustration and anxiety. What if Queen Marie had kept the stone in Rumania? Obviously it was one of her favorite pieces. She had worn it in the photograph of the inspection. Sir Reginald now sorted the last crate.

He watched as the man unwrapped and examined the contents. This crate was filed with personal, rather than state jewelry. Piece after piece was unwrapped, examined and rewrapped. All went into the thirty-first hamper and none to the hamper reserved for the Irish jewels. Armstrong watched, keeping his emotions under icy control. Sir Reginald reached to the bottom and pulled out a blue velvet pouch. The pouch had a silk string pulling it closed and he loosed it, to let the contents spill into his hand.

The men gasped as Sir Reginald slowly held up a jewel that flashed as if the fires of hell were burning within. He held it, swinging from his hand on a thin gold chain. A plain chain, as if the craftsman who had designed the setting had seen that the stone needed no other adornment. All fell silent as they gazed at its beauty, except for a faint whistle of appreciation from O'Reilly. Its square-cut shape seemed to fill the vault with shimmering flames as it caught the light from the lamp and amplified it to a kaleidoscope of color.

Armstrong stared, fascinated by the size and beauty of the diamond. God Damn. The Goliath Stone! A queens bauble and the symbol of an emerging nation. He thought of Anna and fantasized the chain over her head, saw the stone sit between her breasts, saw the expression of joy on her face. Then, as he stared, there came to him a feeling, an intense feeling, such as he had never experienced before. It was as if the stone had transmitted a signal to him, stirring his subconscious into an awareness of ancient mysteries. He shivered as he forced himself to the present.

"Never mind gawking at it, let's get the damn thing stowed away and get the hell out of here," he said, his voice a harsh croak. "Time is running out and we've lots to do. Sappers, see what's in the ammunition boxes."

Hall grinned at him as Sir Reginald slipped the stone back in its pouch. "That little beauty seems to have aroused your baser passions, old boy," he murmured.

"Fooking right, me too, sir," said O'Reilly, "In fact it's given me a hard on."

The company chuckled, with the exception of Sir Reginald, who looked puzzled and queried Armstrong.

"Hard on?"

"You don't want to know," answered Armstrong. "O'Reilly keep your mind out of the gutter."

"Well, I think that's the last of it," said Hall, carefully closing the hamper.

"The entire collection, or just what we're interested in?" Armstrong queried.

"According to my list that's every one of the jolly old Rumanian crown jewels."

"Right then. O'Reilly, let's get this hamper into the other room, the rest of you clear up here. Don't move back until we tell you it's clear," said Armstrong as he bent to lift the hamper."

"These here ammunition boxes sir," said Corporal Streat. "You want us to check them?" Streat lifted one of the boxes. His face went red with exertion and his eyes went wide with surprise. "Gawd blimey the bastard's heavy," he exclaimed and dropped it.

The box burst open on impact, spilling several bars out about the size of a small brick. Bars that glinted yellow in sympathy with the lamplight.

"Great God Almighty," breathed Armstrong. "I didn't realize the gold reserves were here too."

Hall picked up one of the bars, slid his fingers over its slick surface and felt the insignia of the grand seal of Rumania "This is Rumanian gold all right. But what's it doing here? They told us it's stored in the State Bank!"

Sir Reginald took the bar from Hall to examine it then he looked at the boxes. "No," he said. He pursed his lips in thought as he did a quick count of the boxes. "About a hundred boxes, and it looks like we have six bars to a box." He gave the bar back to Hall, pulled a notebook and pencil from a pocket and did some calculations. "Hm," he mused, staring at his figures. "This little lot is worth about two million pounds or eight million dollars. The Rumanian gold reserves sent to Russia totaled twenty five million pounds, so this is only a tenth of the total." He looked up at the rest and his eyes twinkled with malice. "It looks very much as if the Tsar decided to take a tithe from the Rumanians, seeing that they were not in any position to complain."

"Well, old boy," said Hall to Armstrong. "What the devil do we do now?"

"Do?" said Armstrong, the fire of recklessness in his veins. "Do?" I say we go for broke. Let's take the whole damned lot. What do you say?" He stooped, picked up one of the bars, tossed it high and caught it in his large hand. He stood grinning at them, his eyes ablaze with excitement.

They all stared at him, as they considered the logistics of moving more than hampers of jewels. Sir Reginald broke the silence first.

"It is Rumanian property. Personally I don't care what you do, for you have been given the right to act in this matter. I feel I should warned you that you may have a lot of trouble getting it out of the country. My God, do you think the Reds will allow the train to pass if they get wind of the content?"

Armstrong looked at Hall. "Lieutenant Hal" he said, "Let's hear from you. What do you think, George? Do we do it?"

Hall scratched his head as he looked at Armstrong effortlessly holding the heavy bar over his head. Then he shrugged his shoulders, smiled and said, "I think we should try our luck. As the Bishop said with his hand on the actress's knee. Yes. Let's "go for broke" as you put it."

O'Reilly smacked one fist into the other in jubilation. The sappers let out a muffled whoop and Armstrong flung the bar into the air again.

"All right then," he said, catching the bar and handing it to Streat. "As before. Patch up that box and we start moving as soon as we get the hamper over there. O'Reilly!"

O'Reilly and Armstrong picked up the hamper and left. All was still in the chamber and passage. The night sky through the gratings was as black as ever. What little moonlight there had been seemed to have gone. Armstrong snatched a look at his luminous watch dial. Two more hours to dawn.

They entered the ledger room and dumped the hamper with the others. Armstrong gripped O'Reilly by the arm. "Slip to the stars and check the activity in the foyer. I want to be sure all's quiet when we start moving the gold. Understand?"

O'Reilly's eyes flitted from the hamper to Armstrong's face. "Aye, melord," he whispered. "'Tis full of understanding I am." And he touched a finger to the side of his nose as he went out the door.

Armstrong quickly lifted the last hamper's lid, picked up the velvet wrapped stone from where Hall had so casually tossed it and trilled with excitement as he felt its massive shape through the soft pile of the cloth. Hurriedly he thrust it through the boiler suit into his trouser pocket and closed the hamper. He was fastening it when he felt a draft and swung around to see O'Reilly opening the door.

"All clear melord," he chirped.   "Not a dicky birdstirring anywhere."

"Then let's get to work," snapped Armstrong.

Sir Reginald volunteered to be lookout and he sat on the stairs watching and listening for activity as the rest worked. To Armstrong, the next one and a half hours seemed madly surrealistic, like the demented flickering of a biograph screen as they scurried between the vault and the ledger room, carrying the heavy boxes of gold. Six gold bricks to a box. Two men to a box. One hundred boxes, each weighing about 180 pounds. Over thirty times each pair of men staggered between the vault and the ledger room. It occurred to him that this was one of those serendipitous occasions spoken of by Maitland, when all the fates were on their side and one had only to grasp the moment and all would be well. Sweat poured from them, rope handles cut into their hands, knees strained, and backs protested as they all worked like the subterranean dwarfs of a Grimm fairy tale.   While above them, a demoralized and apprehensive garrison slept an uneasy sleep.

Armstrong stood panting by the door of the vault as the sappers carried the final box through.   Ivan and Hall were trying to stack the empty crates on top of the remaining wicker hampers to maintain the appearance of bulk. He took a look at the window aperture. Yes, there was a definite graying. Dawn was here. "That's enough. We're out of time. Leave it. Get to the ledger room."   They left and Armstrong stood while O'Reilly operated both locks.   He now was in a fever of impatience. My God, he thought. We've done it. The worst part is over.

Snick went the lock. Swiftly they ran through the passage, soundless on their plimsoled feet. Hall stood waiting at the ledger room, holding the door his face tense with anxiety. Armstrong could clearly see the sweat streaked dirt on Hall's face in the light from the grating as he followed O'Reilly through the door, shut it behind him, and stood looking at the company. The ledger room seemed packed, wall-to-wall with hampers and boxes. Phase one was over.

As they stood, all of them grinning like Cheshire cats, confident in their luck, there came a sound they had all heard too many times before: the booming, shuddering shattering crash of a high explosive shell burst.

CHAPTER THIRTEEN

"**M**y God" said Gabbert-Smythe. "They're actually shelling their own Kremlim." His face was ashen and his features shocked from their usual hardness.

Armstrong shrugged. "The better for us" he said, "We don't have to worry about a little noise.

And so the work went on. He and Hall tied the boxes to a rope and lowered them down to the tunnel. After a minute Gabbert-Smythe recovered his composure and helped. The shelling was spasmodic, as if the reds were telling the defenders that they could smash walls if they had to. There was a pause as the men below cleared away the build-up of boxes. "Time for a break I guess," said Armstrong and brought out his cigarettes. The lantern light was low enough that the fire of his lighter caused him to blink. He watched their faces as they lit up. Hall, beaded with sweat and dirt. Gabbert-Smythe, drawn and haggard, and all of them covered in the fine dust that had drifted down from the vibration of the shelling. He thought they all looked a mess and he wondered how they would get through the streets to the train. They might have to wait until midnight, though they'd all be hungry by that time.

He thought that the attack on the Kremlin provided ideal conditions for taking the jewels and gold. He thought he would like a beer.

He finished his cigarette and ground it out on the floor as O'Reilly appeared through the hole. "Let's have yer, squire," he said. "Time to move the rest of the booty, we're all clear down here."

It took another hour before the last of the boxes went down the hole, while outside the battle raged. The noise filtered to the ledger room, rifles fired, machine guns rattled and every now and then came the crash of a medium sized field gun. Armstrong could hear the screams of the wounded coming from the foyer and he shut his mind to the scenes that must be taking place there.

The last box went down the hole and they left the room, pulling the trapdoor shut behind them. Armstrong climbed down to the pile of boxes and grinned at a panting Hall who sat, his head hanging as he rested.

"That's phase two complete without incident. What do you say to that Hall, old boy, old boy, old boy?"

Hall lifted his head and winced, as tender muscles told him he wasn't the laboring type. "From here to the crypt, phase three, from the crypt to the train, phase four. Save your crowing until we've completed phase four, old boy, you damned Canuck."

Armstrong squatted on his heels and eyed the men. They looked dirty and exhausted and, if his own stomach was any indication, they were bloody hungry. "Right," he said, "Here's the plan. We move this material to the domed area, away from this tunnel. We leave it there until tonight, when we'll come back and take it to the train. That will give us chance for rest and food, and if the Kremlin should fall, we have at least got the stuff half way to St. Saviours."

The company groaned at the thought of the toil ahead of them but set to work. The hours went by. They carried boxes and hampers along the tunnel to the domed area, setting the boxes two deep in a line on the ledge so that they had just enough room to walk around them to the crypt. Armstrong carried the last box and, as he set it down, the exhausted party cheered. He stood, arched his aching back, then stretched out a hand to Brewer. "Pick axe," he said, and stood waiting as Brewer, with a frown of puzzlement, got him one. Armstrong took it and, taking a lantern, he retraced his steps along the tunnel to the Kremlin. Hall, nodded his head in comprehension and followed him. Armstrong stopped by a section of tunnel where the bricks had already started to fall down. He examined it and said to Hall.

"What do you think?"

"I think this is a good place, too," said Hall.

Armstrong braced himself, swung the pickaxe into the tunnel face and wrenched out a whole section of the old brick. With a hiss and a rumble, black earth fell into the tunnel. Armstrong swung again and again, thudding the heavy implement deep into the wall and roof. Brewer came and tried to take the pickaxe away to do the job himself, feeling it was not proper for an officer to work while rankers stood and watched, but Armstrong shook him off and continued his attack on the tunnel, until it was closed off from floor to roof with broken brick and earth.

Armstrong dropped the pickaxe and rubbed his sore hands together as he nodded at the party. The dirt and the yellow lamplight made his craggy face look satanic. "Let's get the hell out of here," he said. The party moved off, leaving behind two lamps for when they returned. Armstrong, checked his watch, and found it was well past noon. Time had flown while they were in the subterranean depths of Moscow as they struggled to move the jewels and gold from the Palace.

Armstrong waited as the men climbed through the trapdoor and stood upright in the crypt. Taking Hall by the arm he walked away from the men and spoke in a low tone.

"I don't think we will serve a useful purpose by leaving a guard. This crypt had been untouched for years and a guard, until we can get the stuff out tonight, will create problems. Frankly I feel that if we leave a guard on the gold we should also leave an officer to keep a guard on the guard. So you understand me?"

Hal smiled, a tired smile that split the dust on his face into black lines. "All I want to do at this moment is fall into a hot bath and then into a soft bed for a few hours. I'm with you, old boy. Let's lock the place up and head back to the club. What!"

"I'm afraid that is unacceptable to me," said Sir Reginald brusquely. "I've gone through too much to let these valuables sit here unguarded. I shall stay here with them and perhaps one of your men too can stay."

Armstrong was appalled by the statement, for he would be number one suspect if Sir Reginald went snooping and found the Goliath Stone missing. He stammered an objection but the man was adamant so it was agreed to leave Sir Reginald with one of the Rumanian soldiers. No one had thought to bring food but O'Reilly, with a rueful grin produced a bottle of the Tsar's wine he had taken from the store in the castle. They then left, promising to return as soon as possible.

They emerged from the crypt and made their way through the cathedral. It was deserted, except for the main nave, where a few worshippers huddled as if for shelter against the fury that was raging over Moscow. Unseen, the men reached the door through which they had entered the cathedral so many hours before, and brushing themselves off, slipped over the wall.

The streets were packed with people, some going to the Kremlin to see the final assault, others leaving the city. They looked shocked, some weeping at the sacrilege being committed to their beloved Russia. Armstrong was thankful that the chaos of the streets meant the filthy appearance of his men went unnoticed as they made their way down Prechistenski Boulevard. It also looked as if all of the Red Guards were at the Kremlin for the final moments, because none of them were seen as the party reached their destinations – the officers to the English club and the rankers to the train and the comforts of car 451.

*   *   *   *   *

Armstrong groaned as the shaking increased. What the hell was going on. He shrugged off the hand and buried his head in the pillow. The shaking began again and he raised his head, focusing his eyes with an effort. It was Hall. Damn Hall, with his ever present grin.

"Time to wake up, old boy, for the hour of our lurking is nigh. Time for us to slink through the streets. Time to be afoot for the great game, as Sherlock would say. Hop to it laddie, it's swag time. Eh what?"

"For God's sake Hall, you bloody chirper," Armstrong muttered. "Why must you be so cheerful? What's the damn time? Why did I have to get saddled with a man who wakes up so damn cheerful? Bloody, bloody limey."

He sat up in bed rubbing his head as Hall watched him with amusement.

"Well, well," said Hall. "I do believe the bloody colonial is starting to learn the King's English. Look here, old boy, from all accounts the Kremlin has surrendered, so we don't have much time left to bring the boodle in. So, up you get."

Armstrong, grunting an acknowledgement, dragged himself off the bed and sluiced water over his face from the washstand bowl. While he dried, Hall told him of Boyle's plan for the night.

"He wants us to get the boxes out of the crypt to the cathedral wall. Apparently he's acquired two lorries, and as soon as we give him the word, he'll have them at the wall with the Rumanians, who will load. Then it's hey-ho for the train and full speed out of Moscow."

Armstrong rubbed the rough towel over his face, then said, "Sounds like a reasonable plan. Only problem is that there's nothing reasonable about this country. We can but try though." And hope like hell that Sir bastard Reginald hasn't found out that something's missing, he thought.

Outside, the sky was still red with the fires from the Kremlin, although the sound of firing had ceased. The snow, once so white, was now gray with falling ash. Moscow lay silent, as if shocked at the shelling. If any people moved at all they were at the Kremlin. The mighty fortress, the very symbol of Russia, had fallen. Now was the time to count losses. Now was the time to bury the dead. Armstrong stood outside the club for a moment, sniffed the air, redolent with the reek of high explosives, and thought that now was a damn good time for all non-Bolsheviks to be conspicuous by their absence.

He dressed as before, boiler suit over cavalry trousers, with a greatcoat on top to conceal his garb from casual inspection. He pulled his hat tighter on his head against the rising wind and patted his clothing as he waited for Hall, who was having a hurried conference with Boyle. He felt the Goliath Stone bulging in his trouser pocket and he gripped the velvet-covered rock, wishing that its face could warm his chilled fingers. He would have to find a good hiding place when he got back to the train and car 451.

They skirted the Kremlin by walking down Prechistenski Boulevard to the cathedral, their boots crunching on the hard packed snow and the shards of glass from hotel and store windows. The walk was uneventful, save for a moment when they had just reached the cathedral wall and heard the rhythmic pounding of many feet in step.

Armstrong and Hall scrambled over the wall and stood panting as a squad of Bolsheviks marched by. When all was quiet again Armstrong pursed his lips and whistled a soft warbling note. Immediately there came an answering whistle and men loomed out of the darkness.

"All 'ere sir," said Streat's voice in a husky whisper, "and we've brought a couple of the Rumanian soldiers to help wiv the 'umping."

"Good," said Armstrong. O'Reilly?"

"I'm here melord, all ready to do me bit for king and country."

"Right then. Let's move it."

The party left the shadow of the cathedral wall and crossed to the door. The only difference from the party of the previous night was the addition of the Rumanian privates and of course, Tolstoi was absent. Father Gregori had kept his word for the door was not locked. Tonight the cathedral was in total darkness, and the officers used shaded torches to light their way to the crypt. This time the key turned easily and they entered, again Ivan pulled the trapdoor open. Armstrong took a lantern but, as he stood on the first rung, he stopped puzzled by something he had seen, or smelled.

Armstrong climbed down the ladder, stood for a moment holding the lantern high, then cautiously walked. He estimated that he had gone about a hundred yards along the ledge and was expecting to see the gleam from the pool in the domed area, but it seemed to be just black up there. He took a few more paces then suddenly halted and cursed bitterly. Now he knew what he had smelled. The heavy, rank odor of freshly disturbed earth. Now he could see why there had been no glimmer from the pool. In front of him was a solid wall of black Moscow earth, spilling over the ledge into the sewer and blocking it from bottom to top.

"My God," breathed Hall from behind him, "That's torn it. Now what do we do?"

"How did this happen, any ideas?"

"There was on hell of an explosion about an hour before we met sir," said Streat.

Hall snapped his fingers. "That's it. When Colonel Boyle woke me he told me that an ammunition tender had blown up in Alexander Gardens, either hit by a shell or mishandled. The shock must have caved the roof in."

Armstrong sank to his knees, looking at the wall of earth in front of him. He was sure it was massive fall. It had the look of totality. He thought back to a time on the western front when he had seen a whole section of trench blown up by a mine. Blown so deep by tunnellers that there was no question of trying to dig for survivors. Blown so deep that a whole ridge had disappeared forever. Were Sir Reginald and the soldier buried under that lot or were they still safe in the domed area?

"Start digging, sir?" O'Reilly's voice, subdued, atonal.

"What with," said Armstrong testily. "The shovels are back at the train." He looked at Hall. "Conference time, I think. George. Get to Colonel Boyle and set up an immediate meeting in the train, and he'd better bring the Rumanian boss with him. This is a disaster and we'd better have everyone there. The rest of us will go directly there."

Quietly, unhappily, the men left the tunnel but as Armstrong made to follow them he hesitated, still troubled by something he had seen. Without saying anything to the others he turned and went back to the crypt. Five minutes later, his face set in a grim scowl, he left the cathedral.

Boyle and Hall arrived at the train an hour later to find Armstrong at the table eating a sandwich from a stack that had been prepared by Ivan. O'Reilly and Ivan were in the kitchen smoking cigarettes. The other men were either on guard or asleep. Boyle looked as if his normal ebullience had deserted him. He took off his hat, tossed it on the table and heavily sat in one of the stuffed armchairs.

"Sit down George," he growled. "Let's talk this out and see what's the best solution. If those poor bastards are still alive we've got to get them out of there in a hurry, without the Russians knowing about it."

"There is only one solution," said Hall. "Dig!"

Boyle grimaced. That solution did not appeal. He raised a bushy eyebrow at Armstrong, who shrugged and said.

"The trouble with digging, of course, is time. Give us time and we can dig through to China. But we don't have that luxury, we have to be quick. The longer it takes, the more chance of discovery. We can't go slinking around much longer without someone finding us out. And I don't think the Bolsheviks will be amused by our efforts."

O'Reilly poked his head out of the kitchen. "What you need, melord, is a squad of Irishmen. Nothing like a few of the boyo's for digging ye know."

"O'Reilly, if you can't say something constructive, keep your mouth shut," snapped Armstrong.

O'Reilly sniffed and withdrew back to the kitchen.

"I do have a suggestion," continued Armstrong. "I don't know how feasible it is, but if it works it could be a fast way to retrieve the situation." He hesitated and Boyle said. "Out with it man. Any idea at this time is valuable."

"I've been talking to Ivan, about that domed area where the bullion is. I asked him if he knew where the outlet to the river was and if he'd ever seen it. Well, he has. Apparently it's not too deep, and on a dry year when the river level drops, he's seen the top of a grating. It comes out under the Kamenni bridge. I wondered if we could get a boat and try and gain entrance that way. Once in, it would be an easy matter to haul the boxes out by ropes."

Hall shuddered. "Dammit it, Miles. Do you realize how cold Moscow is? Why there's bloody great chunks of ice on it."

Boyle lifted his hand to silence Hall. "Let's think this out." He buried his face in his hands and sat hunched at the table. Watching him, Armstrong felt a twinge of affection for the man and sensed the power that had made him a legend on the Klondike. Boyle, the epitome of the brash, hustling North-American entrepreneur. Sailor, gold-digger, fight-promoter who had gone from singing for his supper on the street of Dawson city to the lover of a queen. Hall pulled out his cigarettes, offered one to Armstrong and tossed one to O'Reilly who had left the kitchen and was standing behind them, eyeing Boyle with interest. As they lit up and inhaled the smoke Boyle slowly sat erect. His black eyes glittered with excitement.

He looked at Armstrong. "Lieutenant. I think your suggestion is very possible. I have already been approached by the Bolshevik district commander, one Mr. Muralov, to reorganize the rail traffic in Moscow after the revolution. He has given me full authority over the district because the Reds are a rabble at the moment. I told him I'd make a start right away and devote full time to it after I return from my Rumanian assignment. The point is, I also control the river traffic. All we need is a steam power craft with a winch and we can pull that grating out in a jiffy." He looked quizzically at Armstrong. "Some hardy man will have to dive in and secure a wire to the grating of course."

Armstrong grunted. "My idea. My Job."

Boyle nodded acknowledgement but O'Reilly coughed indignantly and said. "Excuse me sirs, but it's a well known fact that us Irish are experts at getting through steel bars. Jasus, the bloody English have tried to lock us up for years without success."

Hall gave a theatrical groan and murmured, "I really think we're going to have to shoot this man for sedition and insubordination."

Armstrong smiled. Don't worry about it. I'll drown the little bastard instead. All right O'Reilly. You asked for it. You're going in with me."

O'Reilly, looking furtively pleased, nodded his head. Armstrong thought he would have to keep a sharp eye on the man or more "archives" would go missing during the transfer.

Boyle slapped the table and rose to his feet. "All right then," he said. Keep on top line and don't wander away. I'm going to Muralov's office to check the situation."

"Will you be safe sir?" said Hall.

"Oh hell, yes," answered Boyle. "He's given me an escort. I have to pick them up at the station office."

With that he left, leaving Armstrong and Hall at the table. They smoked cigarettes and drank the rich coffee that Ivan set for them. Hall was talkative, reminiscing of the days when he first joined M15 after being invalided home from

Ypres in '15, but he eventually grew tired of Armstrong's monosyllabic answers and went to bed.

Armstrong cocked his head and listened for a moment to the faint voices through the kitchen door, Ivan's deep rumble and O'Reilly's high pitched burr. He smiled to himself. It sounded as if O'Reilly was indoctrinating the other into the game of blackjack, which the English called pontoon. Neither could understand the other too well but he was sure that O'Reilly would manage to teach Ivan enough to win a few roubles from him.

He stood to his feet with sudden resolve. Screw the revolution! He was going to see Anna. He went to his room and stood for a moment holding the Goliath Stone in his hand. Should he take it to Anna? No. Not Yet. Not until he trusted her for sure. He pulled his knife and went to the wall. They were paneled with light oak in two foot square sections and he had noticed that a section of paneling over the bed had a slight gap between it and the next section. He inserted the knife and levered the panel out. It popped out easily, the glue that held it as dry as dust. Behind it the frame made a perfect receptacle for the stone. He laid it in the frame and gently forced the panel back into position. No one was going to find that on a casual search.

He pulled on his greatcoat and loosened the flap of his revolver holster so that it was ready for quick use. He also picked up his buffalo knife, tucked it in his waistband and then selected the Colonel's swagger stick, a thick piece of cane, tightly bound with heavy leather, which Boyle, in his hurry to get to Muralov's, had forgotten. Armed with fire, steel and cudgel, he felt ready for anyone.

Brewer was on guard at the platform gate and he eyed Armstrong with curiosity as he saluted. "All quiet here, sir but it sounds as if hell's breaking loose over by the Kremlin."

"I'm not going near there, Brewer," said Armstrong. "Keep a sharp watch and if there's any trouble Lieutenant Hall is on the train. I should be back in an hour."

From Riazansky station to the Hotel Billo on Great Lubianka it was not necessary to pass near the Kremlin, it being west of both points, but Armstrong walked briskly, his hand on the open holster and his eyes constantly alert. The hotel, as he approached was also quiet with a deserted foyer, except for a clerk leaning over the reservation desk. The gaslights in the foyer were out and the only illumination came from oil lamps.

The man looked up at his approach. His sallow face was framed by a scruffy black beard and hard black eyes stared above a great beak of a nose. Armstrong was conscious of a scrutiny, surely too intense for an obsequious desk clerk. As he reached the man, Armstrong realized that he did not know what Anna had used to register, but he thought, it would probably have been DeCourville.

The man looked at him suspiciously and spoke in Russian too fast for Armstrong to follow. Armstrong replied in his halting Russian.

"Miss DeCourvill. Tell her Lieutenant Armstrong is here."

The man suddenly barked an order. From a room behind the desk there came the clatter of boots and three Red Guards burst through the door brandishing rifles. Armstrong cursed, his hand flashed down to his holster and before anyone had time to react, he had his Colt pressed firmly into one of the clerk's generous nostrils, his thumb holding back the hammer.

"Tell them to drop their guns," he crisply ordered. "Or I'll scramble your brains."

In his excitement he spoke in English, but the gun in his hand spoke a universal language. The three guards had come to swift halt at the sight of it and were blinking uncertainty at the clerk. They were street rabble and Armstrong felt confident of his ability to handle them.

"Is this any way to treat an ally of the Russian state?" Armstrong now said in carefully enunciated Russian. "Tell them to drop their rifles."

The clerk's eyes crossed as he looked in horror at the weapon in his nostril. It was cold and huge and smelt of death, and the man holding it was a giant with ice in his eyes. He gasped an order, then screamed it when the men were too confused to instantly obey. Their rifles hit the floor with a clatter.

"That's better," said Armstrong, keeping the gun securely lodged. He spoke slowly, hoping that his Russian would be understood. "Now, I am an allied officer, and I resent treatment like this from scum like you. I gave you a polite request and I expect to be answered in kind. I don't give one Goddamn about your politics and I'm not an enemy of your revolution. All I want to know is where is Miss Anna DeCourville?"

"We do not know," the clerk gasped, his eyes glazing like a rabbit mesmerized by a snake. "She has escaped."

"What do you mean, escaped?"

"She is member of a party that was offering aid to the pig Kerensky and, as such, is regarded as an enemy of the revolution. We are here to arrest her and her party should they return. When your excellency came and asked for her we naturally assumed you were in her party. We did not wish to offend you comrade, er excellency." Sweat dripped from his forehead and slid down the Colt barrel.

"Listen to me, you little shit," Armstrong said, his face red with fury. "This lady is a British subject and is not affected by your revolutionary law. If any harm should come to her I will personally find you and blow your fucking head off. Do you understand me?"

"Da," gasped the man.

"When did she leave?"

"We do not know, excellency. They had all cleared out when we came here today."

Armstrong eyed him, feeling the rage boil off him, leaving him sick with disappointment. Anna was gone. She could be anywhere. She knew where he was, therefore it was up to her. She must find him. He jerked his head to the three Reds. "Go. Back to the room."

They hesitated then left, daunted by the fire in his eyes, then he contemptuously flung the clerk to the floor and, without looking back, strode out of the hotel and back to the station.

Boyle was there. Also a sleepy-face Hall and a withdrawn Tolstoi. Boyle's steel wire hair was struck out at all angles from his habit of impatiently running his fingers through. "I thought I told you to stay by the train," he snapped.

Armstrong shrugged off his greatcoat. "I'm sorry sir," he said. "I thought it was advice and not an order."

Boyle grunted, dismissed the subject with an impatient wave of his hand, "I've good news. Lieutenant Tolstoi has found us a river barge for tomorrow."

"And even better news," interrupted Hall, "Is that there is a grand ceremony tomorrow to honor the Bolshevik dead. They're digging a bloody grave right now by the Kremlin wall in Grand Square. The brotherhood grave they call it. Hundreds of Reds all buried together."

"It should mean that we can try for the archives without interruption," said Boyle. "Everybody will be at the ceremony. They're organizing a grand parade right now."

"Looks like I'm to get wet then," said Armstrong cheerfully.

150 Charles W. Cobb

"You ever been in ice water?" asked Boyle. Armstrong shook his head. "Well I have," said Boyle. "When one of my dredgers capsized on the Yukon, and believe me, son, it's an experience you'll never forget. I hope you're just as cheerful tomorrow." He slapped the table and stood up. "I've been invited by comrade Muralov to attend the ceremony at the Kremlin, and I think it incumbent on me to be there. Both as a gesture of goodwill to the new regime and to keep attention away from you people and your task. Get some sleep. Lieutenant Tolstoi will take you to the barge at first light. I will meet you there to make sure all is well, then I'll leave you to it. Good luck to us all. With God's grace we'll be out of Moscow tomorrow night."

He left and Armstrong turned to Hall and Tolstoi, "I'm the officer of the guard. You two head for the bunk-house, as we say on the range."

Hall nodded but Tolstoi shook his head. "I shall not sleep here tonight," he said in his careful English. He hesitated. "There is a lady, you understand? Now this craft I have obtained is at present tied up in the river. All the crew will be attending the ceremony tomorrow except for the captain. He is a man who is a capitalist first and a Bolshevik second. In other words, if we give him a hundred roubles he will forget all about reporting the use of his boat to the authorities. I will meet you at the Kanenni bridge. Seven a.m." He bowed and left.

Hall stood up, yawned, "Lucky bastard, I think," he said and went to his room, leaving Armstrong alone in the lounge. He waited until he heard snores coming from Ivan then he went to his compartment and searched his kit for a single shot derringer that his father has also given him. It had been a kind of a joke, for use if he was captured but now he carefully taped the gun under his shirt to his stomach. Then he went back to the stove. Presently, his greatcoat wrapped around him as the fire in the big stove guttered down, he slept.

*   *   *   *   *

It was cold on the river. A breeze funneled directly between the riverbanks with a cutting edge that penetrated the thickest clothing. Armstrong stood on the deck and cursed the oncoming Moscow winter as he watched the captain ease his boat under the Kanenni bridge close to the north bank of the river. The captain was a squat man with powerful shoulders and a button-nosed Slav face. He was wearing a variety of coats, one top of the other, that had the effect of making his seem as wide as he was tall. Tolstoi had been correct. The only crew on the boat were the men supplied by Boyle's mission. Brewer stoked and controlled the ancient steam engine while the others, including Ivan, were on deck ready to handle wires.

With steam hissing from its stack the boat's bows nudged the embankment under the bridge. Street threw a line up to the embankment where some of the Rumanian contingent were waiting and they secured it to a post. The captain allowed the Moscva current to swing the craft alongside, port side to, then he turned to Tolstoi and spoke in rapid-fire Russian. Tolstoi replied, the captain shrugged his shoulders and went into the deckhouse.

"I have told him that it would be better for him if he is ignorant of our problems." Tolstoi said, "so he is going to sleep there until we are finished."

"Can we trust him to mind his own business and not get curious. Do you think he'll go running to the bolshys later on?" queried Hall.

"Trust him? Probably not," said Tolstoi. "But I will watch the door and keep him in there and once the archives are on the train, who cares?"

Ivan walked the deck with a boathook, probing with it over the side, feeling along the heavy stone buttress of the bridge. The boat was typical of river barges in that it had a very low freeboard, with only a couple of feet to the waterline. Exactly in the center of the span, the hook went further under the water, and Ivan's face split into a wide grin. He excitedly turned to Armstrong and nodded his head.

"Good man," enthused Armstrong. He took the hook from Ivan and began to probe for himself. He hung over the side feeling, the hook an extension of his senses. "I'd say we have a hole about six feet long, about three feet under the water and, yes, I feel a grating." He vigorously swung the hook from side to side. "I feel bars about six inches apart." He probed some more. "There's bars both vertical and horizontal." He looked up at Hall, excited, uncaring of the freezing water on his hands. "I'd say we have an ingress, old boy."

Hall slapped him on the back then called an order to Streat and O'Reilly, who came dragging a mooring wire from the winch. To the eye of the wire they had shackled a spring hook and this they lashed with yarn to the boathook, leaving the spring hook protruding. Armstrong probed again. He shed his hands under water, the better to control the device and, gritting his teeth against the cold, he tried to snag one of the bars. He felt the hook rasp against metal. With an unspoken prayer on his lips he yanked back hard and felt it snap over the bar.

"I've got it," he yelled. He let the boathook drop and said, "O'Reilly, cut it free."

O'Reilly leaned over and cut the lashing that held the wire to the boathook, then he and Streat fed the wire through a fairlead back to the winch.

"'Tis all ready, sir," he called and Armstrong pointed his finger up and slowly rotated it. "Wind in, slowly."

Streat strained at the handle of the steam valve and it swung wide open. With a rush of steam the winch whirled into action, snaking the loose mooring wire along the deck until it tightened with a jerk. The winch screamed as it tried to turn. The boat heeled to port as tension came on the wire. The wire hummed as it snapped the bar taut. Black oil seeped from the heart of the rope, squeezed out by the tension. Before Armstrong could give another order there came a rumbling noise and an incredible rusty piece of junk metal shot up out of the water and, pulled by the wire, jammed itself in the fairlead. It was the grating.

"Shut that goddamned steam off," roared Armstrong, but a wild eyed and confused Streat was already winding the valve shut. The silence after the noise of the steam seemed almost solid. The barge captain poked his head out of his deckhouse, looked at Armstrong, looked at the winch operator, shrugged his shoulders and disappeared again.

"What happened," asked a startled Hall.

"The bloody fool opened the valve wide – put full pressure on immediately," grunted Armstrong, kicking at the grating."

"Er, begging your lordship pardon," said O'Reilly. "But that bloody valve is as stiff as a priest on a Saturday night. Poor old Streat there didn't mean to open the valve that fast."

Hall nodded his head. "All right, let's forget it, no harm done."

Armstrong smiled, a little embarrassed. "Sorry Streat," he said. Now ease up the wire and dump this grating."

The wire was eased until the hook could be unclipped, the grating remaining jammed in the fairlead. A couple of blows with a heavy hammer were sufficient to dislodge it however, and it sank to the bottom of the river. Armstrong watched it slip under the surface then, with a shiver, he began to prepare. He stripped off his outerwear and wrapped it securely in a watertight package as O'Reilly did the same. Ivan stood watching, an anxious look on his face. Tunnel is this long," and he held his arm out wide, "Maybe just little longer, maybe one more arm."

Armstrong laughed and said, "I'm damn glad you're not an octopus."

This drew a chuckle from the men, as Armstrong took the end of a half inch line an tied it around his waist, picked up the oilskin-wrapped package that he had prepared, secured it to the rope around his waist, took several deep breaths, nodded to Hall and dropped himself over the side into the water.

The cold shock almost drove all the air from his body but he steeled himself to ignore its fiery bite and propelled himself down until he could feel the arched outline of the entrance. With a kick of his feet he started along the passage. Immediately the light from the surface disappeared and he was in total blackness. The cold seemed to squeeze his chest in a vise, trying to force the air from his lungs. He fought down a feeling of panic and tried to keep himself oriented as he swam with strong strokes of his arm. Once, twice his heels kicked against the arch of the roof. Then the roof was no more and he thrust up to the surface and expelled his tortured lungs in a great gasp. He could breath. He was in. And there was light! A lamp was still burning.

The musty air of the dome tasted sweet to him and he swam, toward the ledge upon which they had stacked the boxes. Behind him, on the surface, anxious men slowly paid out the line as he moved forward. He heard the plop of something falling in the black water and he shuddered with revulsion as he remembered the giant rat. The cold was tearing at him, dragging the life from his body as he forced his arms to move. God, he didn't think the area was this big. Maybe he was swimming in circles. He thrust the thought from him and concentrated on making his strokes even. One hand slapped against brick. He reached upward to feel the flat surface of the ledge and, beyond it, the outline of a box.

He grabbed the ledge with both hands and tried to force his body up. "The cold, the damned cold," he moaned to himself as his frozen hands slipped on the bricks. Then a hand grabbed his and pulled him to safety.

He lay for a moment, his lungs heaving as he stared at the haggard face of Sir Reginald Gabbert-Smythe.

"My God," he gasped. "You're still here. I thought you were buried." He pulled the package from his waist and forced his numb fingers to draw his knife from its sheave. The cold water had shrunk the knots to hard pebbles, impossible for his fingers. He slashed at the oilskin and opened it while his teeth chattered so violently his whole body shook. Desperately he tore at the wrapping. It suddenly burst open and Armstrong got the precious sweaters out and pulled them on as Sir Reginald explained that when the cave-in had occurred he had realized that he was powerless to get out by himself and had waited for rescue.

Armstrong felt a jerk at the rope around his waist as the crew wondered if he was all right. He pulled it, once, twice, three times and got an answering pull in return. "Where's the other guy," he said.

Sir Reginald shook his head. "I'm afraid he's under the cave-in. There was the explosion, a rumble, and the poor fellow ran for it. I heard a scream and no more."

Armstrong eyed him. There had been a strange note in Sir Reginald's voice and he thought that the man had been buried for too long.

A much cursing and spluttering O'Reilly was plucked from the water and laid on a row of boxes a larger oilskin wrapped package trailing behind him.

"Oh dear Jesus, I'm fooking cold," he moaned.

Armstrong pulled the package to the ledge and slashed at the lashing with his knife, inside were dry clothes and a large bottle of vodka. The three men drank heavily from the bottle then scrambled into the clothes. Armstrong pulled a balaclava helmet over his head, woolen socks over his bare feet, heavy serge trousers, battledress tunic under a greatcoat and made sure O'Reilly did the same. With all the rush to put warm clothing on he did not omit to tug at the rope that brought O'Reilly in and the surplus snaked back out. The rope was to be used as a traveler between the boat and them. As they finished dressing there were another three tugs on the line, and they hauled it in. It had four, three-quarter inch lines, tied to the bight.

"This is what we are going to do," said Armstrong to Sir Reginald. "We're going to tie the ropes to the boxes to the lines and let the others pull them out. Then they pull us out. Do you want to out or wait 'till we're finished?"

"Oh," Sir Reginald quickly said. "I'll wait with you men. I've been here for twenty four hours, I can bear a few more."

Armstrong nodded acceptance as his hand under his clothes loosened the derringer and he slipped in into a side pocket. They removed the lines and secured them around four of the jewelry hampers. Each hamper was tossed into the water and then Armstrong tugged on the line. He waited, biting his lip, hoping that the hampers did not foul anything as they were pulled through to the barge. He thought of them sliding along the mud at the bottom of the pool then being hauled up to the deck of the barge. The guide line also was pulled back, sliding through Armstrong's hands as he waited for the signal that would tell of success. It came. Three big tugs. He and O'Reilly let out a whoop of joy and pulled the line back again.

And so the work proceeded. All of the hampers seemed to reach the surface all right, although when it came to the one containing the Irish jewels, Armstrong, taking an opportunity when Sir Reginald's back was turned, gave it a kick, which split the wicker framework. He hoped that when the Goliath Stone was missed it would be assumed it had been lost when the hamper was damaged. Thirty hampers made the journey through to the barge, and when the last had gone beneath the surface Armstrong turned to the gold.

These boxes were much heavier. At first the weight did not seem to be a problem. The men, instead of each handling and tying a hamper, now had to work together, lashing each box and tossing it into the water, tugging the guide line as soon as four were in. It took longer for the boxes to reach the boat because the crew was now using the winch. But the lines kept coming back empty, proof that the boxes had reached the boat. Four times there were only three lines returning, indicating a problem but they continued to use what they had. Then, after a while, there would be four lines again.

The men worked unceasingly, the cold forgotten except for the freezing wet line that snaked through their fingers. Box after box slipped into the cold black water. The air got fouler. One lamp guttered and went out, its oil used up by the long use it had during Sir Reginald's entombment. The other couldn't last much longer. They tried to work fast, dragging boxes from the ledge as quickly as they could get the lines returned. Some of the boxes were half-buried under the debris that came from the tunnel collapse and they pulled them out. The oil lamp wick began to burn with a thin blue line, instead of a bright yellow fan of flame. Armstrong made sure he had the torch in a handy pocket for when the oil was finally gone. More boxes went. He had lost all track of time and count of boxes. He only knew that there were more and more and more.

The lamp went out with no warning, no final guttering. One minute a thin blue flame, the next – nothing.

"Holy mother of God," muttered O'Reilly. "'Tis blacker than Rafferty's arsehole."

Armstrong pulled out the torch, switched it on, and wedged it in a crevice in the brickwork. By its uncertain light they tied and watched the last of the boxes sink into the water.

He gave the surface crew enough time to pull the boxes through, then pulled a series of rapid tugs at the line. Back came the answer. Four long slow tugs. He took the torch from the crevice, turned to O'Reilly, and said "are you ready?" O'Reilly gave a nervous nod. Armstrong eyed Sir Reginald, "ready?"

"Almost," Sir Reginald replied in a conversational tone, "except for one more thing. Where's the Goliath Stone?" As he spoke he pulled an automatic pistol from his pocket and pointed it at the two.

"What do you mean?" said Armstrong, moving to shield O'Reilly.

"Don't equivocate to me, you colonial scum. I know it's missing and you're the one who took it for that Jewish slut. You damned thief."

"I'm a thief am I," snarled Armstrong. "Well you listen to this you bastard. I know where the Rumanian soldier is and I know what you've stashed in the coffin with him. You murdered the man and put his body in the crypt with a few select items of jewelry, no doubt planning to claim he had fled with the jewels while you slept. You want the stone as much as I do, except I wouldn't murder to get it."

Sir Reginald eyes widened with shock as Armstrong spoke. "How did you know?"

"You disturbed too much dust, I noticed," grunted Armstrong as one hand slipped into his pocket.

Sir Reginald stood thinking. His face feral, like the pistol wavering between Armstrong and a silent O'Reilly. Then as his thoughts reached a resolution the pistol suddenly steadied. Armstrong's hand moved. There came a sharp crack, amplified by the enclosed dome. Sir Reginald's right eye disappeared and he fell backwards into the water, to float for a moment before slipping beneath the surface.

"All you could, boss," said O'Reilly quietly.

"You didn't have much to say," said Armstrong as he stood watching bubbles seep up.

"Nah," said O'Reilly. "I knew you were pissed about something and then I was you palm that wee gun so I wasn't worried. Did he really kill that Rumanian?"

"Yeah," said Armstrong. "Then he put the body on top of one of those skeletons. He must have thought he had it made. He's stolen enough jewelry to keep him in clover, got a patsy soldier to disappear and take the blame and he's free and clear. Only trouble was he didn't reckon on getting trapped in here and I'd already taken the Goliath Stone."

O'Reilly shrugged. "O'kay, I don't have any problem with the shooting. But what do we tell them outside?"

"We tell them that there's no one here. They must have been buried under the tunnel collapse, all right?"

"What can we do about the swag that's in the coffin with the Rumanian?" said O'Reilly.

"We can do nothing," snapped Armstrong. "If we're caught and they discover a body where there shouldn't be one the whole operation goes for a burton."

"Ah yes," agreed O'Reilly in a soft voice. "But that's only if I get caught. And I ain't been caught yet."

Armstrong shook his head and said nothing more. He knew that O'Reilly would go his own way if he got the chance and he wasn't in any position to threaten him with military law.

"Let's get to hell out of here," he said finally as he reached for the guide rope and tied it around himself. "Grab hold of me," he said, tugging at the rope. Immediately they were jerked into the water and were hauled rapidly down through the tunnel and out to clean, icy air. Willing hands hauled them into the barge to lay spluttering on the deck. Armstrong was astonished to find it was still daylight and the light hurt his eyes. A bottle was trust into his hands and he raised it to his shivering lips to pour fiery vodka down his throat.

"Let's have yer then," came the voice of Streat and he and O'Reilly were pulled to their feet and their wet clothing stripped from them. Their bodies were rubbed with rough towels until they glowed with restored circulation. They then were hustled into the deckhouse, crowded already with the captain and a blanket-wrapped Hall, where dry clothing awaited.

As they entered the captain stood, and went to get the barge under way.

"What happened to Smith and the soldier?" Asked Hall.

Armstrong shook his head. "They must have heard the roof caving in and tried to run for it," he said soberly. "They're totally gone, buried under a ton of Moscow earth."

Hall gave a weak smile and reached for the vodka bottle. "Hell of a way to go," he said and took a great swig.

"What happened to you," said Armstrong, suddenly aware of the strained face of the shivering Hall.

"He went in a couple of times when the boxes got jammed, sir," said Streat.

"Three times, actually old boy," said Hall in a weary voice. "And I'm never ever going to get wet again."

Armstrong gave his an appreciative slap on the back with one hand and took back the vodka bottle with the other.

"Well done, George," he said. "The things we do for king and country, eh!"

"Great suffering Saint Patrick," said O'Reilly as he pulled on clothing. "Me balls are so shrunk they'll have me singing soprano in the choir when I get back to Ballybunnion."

Armstrong laughed, and as he did so there came the chug of the one-lung steam engine, and the deck vibrated as the barge pulled away from the bridge. The vodka filled him with warmth as he donned dry clothing.

The barge ran upstream for another ten minutes, then pulled in to the north bank to where the embankment was prepared for river traffic, and there tied up. Within minutes two lorries trundled up full of Rumanian soldiers and, under the control of the Rumanian subalterns, they transferred the hampers and boxes. Boyle also swept up in a car loaded with beaming consular officials and their congratulations were mixed with shock at the fate of "Smith" and the soldier. Armstrong, feeling tired, cold and in need of a bath, brushed off the comments and requested that the car get him, Hall and O'Reilly to a hot bath as soon as possible.

Boyle stroke his chin, "Well," he said. "I think you're right boy. Time for the details later. I'll take you two to the English club right now. Ivan here will get a bath for O'Reilly on the train."

And so, one of the longest days Armstrong had ever experienced wound to its close, as he lay in a red-hot bath, washing away the stink of goose grease, stagnant water, and the memory of a one-eyed murderer sliding beneath the black waters.

And while he soaked, in the warmth and security of the English Club, a few hundred yards to the south of him thousands of voices were raised in mournful song, as five hundred

Bolsheviks were laid to rest in a communal grave, close to the great wall of the Kremlin in Grand Square. The Grand Square of the Tsars, that would be renamed as Red Square.

CHAPTER FOURTEEN

A rmstrong watched as the great engine, steam hissing from every cylinder, crashed its steel buffers into car 451 and was coupled.

"All right," he yelled, eager to be away, "let's get a move on. You all know what to do, so get to it."

The Rumanians swarmed over the engine, strapping their flags to the front and sides, guards took up positions on the footplate, the firemen threw more coal in the firebox and the allied contingent boarded. Armstrong, swinging aboard last, thought there was almost a carnival atmosphere as the train started moving. Even the morning sun, raising itself over the rooftops to cast its light over the station, seemed brighter than normal.

With a grin on his face Armstrong looked at the others standing at the windows of the car. "Away at last," he said.

Hall slapped him on the back. "Too right, old boy, now it's heigh-ho for Jassy. Full speed ahead and damn the torpedoes, eh?"

"Yeah," growled Boyle. "I think we'll be lucky to get there without incident, so keep on your toes and get your men to do the same. Remember this train is Rumanian territory and let no one board without permission." He stood moodily looking out a window as the platform slowly receded. Armstrong, watching him, felt a pang of compassion for the older man, so obviously anxious to return to his beloved Marie.

It was almost the middle of December. Over three weeks had elapsed since they had taken the jewels and gold from the Kremlin. They had been weeks of frustration. Firstly, fighting had started near the station, and the Rumanians had been unwilling to load the archives under those conditions, and had taken them to a Red Cross warehouse. Then Hall, as a result of the cold waters of the Moscva, had come down with pneumonia, and even now was barely recovered. His sickness hadn't been helped by his insistence on taking the Irish jewels to the British consul for shipment home. To date, nothing had been said about the fact that the Goliath Stone was missing.

The main cause of the delay had been Comrade Muralov, the district commander. Muralov knew the Rumanians had loaded their archives, but he kept finding reasons for nothing to happen. The safety of the mission could not be guaranteed. The protocol agreed upon with the Kerensky government needed to be ratified by the Bolsheviks. The rails had been torn up. Fuel was lacking. Always there were excuses, and the mission had to wait, while the chances of the gold loss being discovered increased every day.

Oddly enough, Boyle had been part of the problem too. Daily he put his organizational skills to work sorting out the tangle of Russian transport. Due to his efforts, supplies were again moving to the front, and food into the cities. Muralov appreciated his work so much he had refused to release him to return to Rumania, and he found himself spending more time in Petrograd than Moscow.

Then, two nights ago, Armstrong had been in the bar of the English Club, moodily nursing a whiskey after a day of fruitlessly searching for Anna, when Boyle had entered.

Armstrong looked at him with alarm. Boyle's face was drawn, and he seemed to sway as he stood for a moment before crossing to Armstrong.

"Good God, sir," said Armstrong, "this has to stop. You're working yourself into the grave." He took Boyle by the arm and led him to a chair.

Boyle shook his head as he sat. "I'm not particularly tired, son. I'm furious and shocked and have been for the last twenty-four hours. I've experienced at first hand what murdering swines the Bolsheviks are."

He went on to relate how, coming back on a train from Minsk, he had seen a mob of soldiers pull their own commander-in-chief, General Dukhonin, from the train and murder him, tossing him from bayonet to bayonet, then firing so many bullets into his body he was unrecognizable as a man.

Boyle had been appalled at the ruthless act and, as soon as he had arrived in Moscow, had stormed into Muralov's office and told him that he, Boyle, was ashamed to be working for men that would allow such a thing to happen, and unless he gave immediate clearance for the train to leave he would never again work for the Bolsheviks.

Boyle had grinned then and said, "That scared the hell out of him and he gave us permission on condition I return immediately after we drop off the archives in Jassy. I told him he had a deal, but I regard a promise to these bastards as no promise."

The next two days had been a hectic rush of loading and preparing the train. The archives, packed into Red Cross boxes, had been loaded into the cars – the jewels in a spare stateroom in 451, and the gold into the third and last car.

And now they were rolling. For the men in 451, relief at leaving Moscow was apparent. O'Reilly's thin voice could be heard in the galley, singing off key and giving the lie the belief that all Irishmen were natural tenors. The two sappers, rifles to hand, stood either side at windows, big grins on their faces. Hall flopped down in an armchair and lit a cigarette with a nonchalant flourish. Boyle's shoulders, normally so rigidly square, slumped as tension left them. Armstrong himself, watched Riazanski station recede with mixed emotions. He was relieved at the successful transfer of the Rumanian assets and the fact that no one had yet realized they were missing from the Kremlin. But Anna was still in Moscow, unseen since the fighting had started.

He took his case from a pocket and began to feel for a cigarette, but before he could light it, he lost balance and had to grab for a handhold as the train brakes were slammed on. "What the hell," he said, staring at the others. He looked at Boyle who nodded his head towards the engine. Understanding, Armstrong strode towards the forward door that led through the guard carriage to the fire-box, but before he reached it it flung open and the Rumanian subaltern on footplate duty stood there.

"Red light," he said. "We had to stop."

Armstrong, following through the door and over the fire-box, was filled with anger and apprehension. Rail traffic was minimal, and there should be no reason for a signal to against them.

As he dropped down to the footplate he saw there was a group of soldiers standing on the rails ahead of them, by the signal that had stopped the train. His anger continued to rise as he swung down to the track and walked towards the party. Behind him he heard the crunch of feet on the gravel bed as others of his men followed him.

He halted before the group and stood with arms akimbo, "Who's in charge here?" he snapped.

A man stepped forward. Short and swarthy with deep set sly eyes over a heavy moustache. He smirked apologetically and shrugged his shoulders.

"Please to forgive my English, is not so good, but I am the people's representative here."

"Why have you stopped us?" demanded Armstrong, and when the man again shrugged, indicating that he didn't understand, he cursed and slowly repeated the question in Russian. Before the man could answer Hall arrived and shot off the same question in his rapid-fire fluent Russian.

The dialogue was too fast for Armstrong for follow accurately but he caught the gist of it and it was apparent the man wanted them to return to the station. Hall, raising his hands to stop the man in mid-sentence, turned to Armstrong and translated.

"It seems they want to couple us to several more cars and haul them to Kiev, which is on our way. What do you think?"

By this time Boyle had reached the party and he caught Hall's remark. "Tell them that this train is Rumanian territory and we're not under his jurisdiction."

Hall did so and the man answered with an ingratiating smile on his face.

"He says he knows that, but the station master has requested our assistance," said Hall, then as the man spoke again. "Aha! Here's the carrot. He tells me that if we assist the authorities in this matter it will mean much to those who will control our journey back to Jassy."

"In other words if we don't agree we won't get to Jassy," said Boyle, slapping his swagger stick against his leg. "All right. Tell him we'll be glad to assist. But it has to be done immediately. Tell him these supplies are urgently needed."

Hall translated to the man, who expressed gratitude. Armstrong watching him noted a flash of triumph in his eyes and he wondered how authentic was the request to take the extra cars to Kiev.

Armstrong and the others boarded the train again as it reversed back to the station. It was switched to a different platform where four cars were waiting, packed with passengers. It took an hour to couple the cars, an hour which crawled by for the men of the Rumanian mission. While the coupling was being done, Armstrong paced the platform, looking for anything out of place. Here and there he saw men, young fit men, who seemed to be of military age, yet were in civilian clothes, and he thought he would have to watch them.

Finally all cars were coupled, the commissar
approached Armstrong, bowed again and indicated that the
train could now leave. Armstrong nodding to him, raised his
arm and waved his hand in a circular motion to the driver who
immediately fed steam to the cylinders. With a whoosh the
great driving wheels spun then gripped, to start the train on its
journey across a continent. Armstrong walked towards the
open door of 451 to board himself, glancing at windows as he
passed them.

It was in the last window before his carriage that he
saw Anna! She stood at the window, dress in peasant clothes, a
scarf covering her hair, looking at him, a wry smile on her face.
He faltered in his step, but her eyes widened with alarm and
she slightly shook her head to tell him not to greet her.

Armstrong ran for his door, feeling elated with relief.
Anna was on the train and soon he would be with her again.
Somehow, when it was dark, he was going to get to her –
although it wouldn't be easy the way the four cars were
crowded.

He removed his sidearm and belt, tossing them on a
chair. He smiled with pleasure and surprise as he noticed
Tolstoi standing to one side in deep conversation with Boyle.
Today was full of surprises. Tolstoi had not been seen since the
removal of the archives from the Kremlin, and Armstrong had
wondered if he had survived the blood-letting of the revolution.
He crossed to them.

"Count," he said, I'm glad to see you safe. How are
things in the new Russian Army?"

Tolstoi shook Armstrong's hand with warmth. "Things
in the new Russian army are in a very delicate state. So far, I
haven't been led to the wall. In fact, General Muralov has
reaffirmed my assignment as liaison to this mission, and I was
able to board when you returned to Riazanski station."

Boyle cut in before Armstrong's reply. "The Count has
some disquieting news for us I'm afraid. George! He called to
Hall. "Come over here. The Count has some news for us."

The four settled themselves around the table as the
other ranks discreetly moved out of earshot. Boyle waved his
hand at the count. "It's your story."

The count looked at them, his eyes somber. Watching
him, Armstrong thought that if the Tsar had had an iota of this
man's intelligence, the war would have run a far different
course. "Firstly gentlemen," Tolstoi began in his stilted
English, "please to forget the title. With the Reds in Command
it is better if I am simply called Captain. Now, to what you call

the meat of the matter. In the ranks of the Smolensk Guards, there are men who are still loyal to Holy Russia and who trust me, so periodically I receive whispers of information. One of these whispers tell me that there are "comrades" who have suspicions that this train contains more than Red Cross supplies and, unknown to Muralov – the revolution is still very fragmented you understand – they plan to stop us and plunder us."

"Where and when?" snapped Armstrong, alarmed more for Anna than for the prospect of losing the archives.

Tolstoi shrugged. "Alas, dear fellow, that I can not answer. We must all be on the qui-vivre throughout our travels."

"Oh well," said Hall, his eyes alive at the prospect of action. "Let us grid our loins and put one up the spout – as the Bishop said to the actress!"

Boyle looked at Hall and said, "If you can be serious for a moment, I suggest you make sure everyone is on top line to repel boarders."

"Aye aye skipper," said Hall, "Miles, old chap, let us round up our faithful lads and prime them in case we have to fight our way through."

The two Lieutenants gathered their men and told them the situation. The Rumanian subalterns were also briefed and within minutes all were ready. Hall climbed to the footplate to watch the right of way and Armstrong again strapped on his side-arm. O'Reilly went into the kitchen and Armstrong thought nothing of it until he heard Boyle gasp and utter an amazed blasphemy.

O'Reilly, a proud smirk on his face, was carrying a Hotchkiss machine gun. A big gun, its heavy barrel encased in a cooling tube, ugly and deadly looking. A gun that looked almost as big as himself.

"Where the did you get that?' burst out Armstrong.

"Well guv," said O'Reilly slyly. "It's like this. I was walking a walk, for me health's sake you know, at the station and I see these fine looking wagons on a siding so I did a little investigating like. And there they were. A whole bunch of them – sent over from England to help the Roosians fight the war. So I thought that seeing as how we were in the same war, I'd borrow one."

"That's a damn good man you've got there," said Boyle.

"Did you get panniers?" said Armstrong.

O'Reilly put a long-suffering look on his face. "Now would a man drink whiskey and forget his Guinness? I've got spare panniers and a box of 303, melord. Where shall we put the beastie?"

"Up on the coal tender would be a good place," said Boyle. "Leave it ready by the door there, and if we get stopped we can have it out in a moment."

The train rattled its way through the eastern outskirts of the city. The engineers kept the speed very slow in case of damaged track. It was by no means unknown, in these years of deprivation, for a peasant to remove a sleeper from under a rail. A heavily tarred baulk would provide many hours of heat in an Isbar. The rude dwellings of the Narods had lost the look of crude poverty and neglect that had been apparent when the party had first entered Moscow. Now a thick layer of snow was upon every home, covering the blemishes and giving them a look of pastoral innocence. Despite the peaceful outlook Armstrong could not relax. Were they on their way at last? Would there be another attempt to return them to the station? He wanted to go to Anna, but he couldn't leave 451 until he was sure that the train would not be stopped by force.

Ninety minutes later the attempt was made. The men in 451 were at ease, their senses lulled by the slow clacking of the wheels. With a screech of steam and a lurching as brakes were applied the train stopped. Grabbing for holds as they lost balance the men looked at each other questioningly. "Action stations gentlemen," said Boyle, excitement gleaming in his eyes.

The forward door to the footplate burst open and Hall shoved his head through and yelled. "Tree across the track and about a hundred men around it." Then he was gone, back to the footplate.

Boyle unclipped the leather flap of his service holster, pulled a Webley from it and broke the action to check the load. It was purely reflex because he had already done so before but this time, when he reholstered the gun, he left the flap tucked in behind his belt. He cocked a bushy eyebrow at Armstrong. "What do you say, son? Time for action?"

Armstrong grinned, slipped his Colt from its holster, and spun it around his finger before reholstering. "Let's show them some sourdough law," he said.

Boyle checked that the rest were in position. Streat and Brewer at the windows, rifles in hand. O'Reilly already disappearing through the door to the firebox, the Hotchkiss over his shoulder. Ivan with an antique pistol strapped around him and a Cossack sword in his hand. Tolstoi, grim faced and pistol in hand. "Order of the day," Boyle rapped. "No damned

Bolshevik son-of-a-bitch enters this train without my permission. Understood?"

To a chorus of enthusiastic "yes, sirs" Armstrong opened the door as the train stopped and he and Boyle dropped out to the track. Here, 50 odd miles from Moscow, the countryside was serene, with hardly a sound to mar the silence. The sun was almost at its noon zenith and there was enough strength in it to make the snow glisten. Here the land was flat, with no embankment for the track, and Armstrong could see that, fifty feet ahead of the engine, there were points and a branch line. Across the track ahead of the points, there was a large fir, and behind it was a mob of men.

Boyle and Armstrong strode to the barricade, their boots crunching on the gravel of the rail bed. As they passed the footplate Hall started to climb down to join them but Boyle stopped him with a growl and said, "Stay there, George. If we get into trouble, you're in charge. Run the log off the track and don't stop."

Hall, looking disappointed, nodded and got back on the footplate. The pair continued towards the barricade. As they neared, it became obvious this was a rabble. Few rifles were to be seen and most of the mob seemed to armed with clubs. Two men stepped over the log and stood waiting for them. One, evidently the leader, wore a fur-trimmed coat in contrast to the rags of his comrades, and had a pistol in a canvas holster strapped around him. The other, carrying a rifle, had stripes sown to the rough serge of his coat, indicating nco rank. All of the men, however, wore the red armband of revolution.

The leader, a tall thin man with a luxuriant black moustache spoke rapidly, an arrogant sneer on his lips.

Boyle cut him short. "This is a Rumanian train and is under the protection of General Muralov. Who the hell gave you authority to stop it?" he roared.

Armstrong grinned as the leader stepped back a pace and the nco uneasily shuffled his feet. The leader started to speak again and again Boyle cut him short. "We don't answer to anyone except government officials, so get the hell out of our way." Typical Boyle style, thought Armstrong. Attack, browbeat, and keep them off balance.

The leader flushed with anger at the tone and thrust his face into Boyle's. He spoke loudly and emphasized his words with a prodding finger.

"What's the bastard saying?" asked Boyle, staring unblinking into the eyes of the leader.

Armstrong, watching the man closely, thought he was dangerous, but the mob he had been able to raise was illdisciplined and would probably break if he went down. "He tell us we have to divert to the branch line for inspection – say's its orders from Moscow."

Boyle shot a startled look at Armstrong. "I don't believe it. I think Moscow would have had regular troops here if they wanted to do that. This fellow's working for himself or someone other than Moscow." He turned back to the leader. In icy, measured words he said, "Move that damn log and let us pass."

The man drew himself up and spoke in slow, accented English. "You will do as you are told or you will all be shot. Do you understand me, you English pig?"

A split second elapsed as Boyle mine reached an understanding of the man's words, then his fist shout out and caught the leader full in the face. A face that dissolved in a blur of blood as the man's nose almost met the back of his neck. The man howled in agony and shot backwards, going head over tail over the log. Armstrong dived at Boyle and pulled him to the ground, at the same time yelling for O'Reilly to open fire.

With a stuttering roar the Hotchkiss sent a stream of bullets over the heads of the mob. Instantly they broke, some fling themselves to the ground, and others madly scrambling across the fields towards the trees.

Armstrong rolled over the log and seized the nco, who had fallen behind, and shoved his Colt into the gut of the man. "Tell your men to move the log or I will blow your stomach out through your asshole. Understand?"

The nco gulped and blinked his eyes, he gasped garlic-tainted breath out as he stared up at the tall foreigner with the ice-cold eyes. He looked his leader, but all he could see was the man's legs, sticking up in the air above the log. The rest of his men were either lying flat or running for the woods as O'Reilly continued to stitch short bursts of fire into the air.

Armstrong cocked the Colt to help the man wake up his mind, at the same time calling out for O'Reilly to cease fire. After a last despairing look around, the nco croaked an order. The mob muttered. Armstrong shoved harder with his gun. This time the nco screamed out his orders and repeated them several times, saying the same thing over and over again. The mob stirred by the urgency of his voice, swarmed over the log and, after moving the still comatose leader, they rolled it off the track.

"Tell them to leave their rifles by the track and move about forty yards away," suggested Boyle, his own revolver flourishing and his nostrils flared like an old warhorse.

Armstrong repeated the order and the nco had his men move back from their rifles, but it wasn't enough to suit Armstrong. "You all set O'Reilly?" he called.

O'Reilly, the Hotchkiss perched on the dome of the engine safety valve, yelled ""Tis ready Oi am melord."

"Put a burst over their heads."

With a whoop of joy O'Reilly squeezed the trigger and sent a stream of bullets whistling over the heads of the mob. With one accord they turned and ran, floundering across the snow covered field, leaving their leader, who had revived enough to get to his knees and was holding snow to his nose. The nco looked at Armstrong with terrified eyes and Armstrong, jerking his head in the direction of the fleeing mob, let the man go. He babbled thanks and ran, ignoring his leader.

Boyle and Armstrong stood waiting as the train drew level with then, windows bristling with the rifles of the Rumanians and British. A cheer was given as the pair boarded and the train gathered way.

Boyle grinned at Armstrong. "I guess we made our position understood."

Armstrong looked back at the leader, just staggering to his feet, and shock his head and said, "I wonder if we should have taken that man with us and worked on him. There's something fishy about him. As far as I could tell, his Russian was the real thing, but his English had a German, not a Slavic accent." He turned to Hall, who had joined them. "It's a pity we didn't have you there too, George. Maybe you could have told us if he was a Russian or not."

The train clattered on across the central Russian plain. Hall reported that the quality of coal that had been supplied in Moscow was so poor the engineer was finding it difficult to keep up steam. As a consequence their speed dropped to little better than thirty miles per hour.

After the incident with the mob the party settled down to routine. The next stop was to be the town of Bryansk, some two hundred miles away, and Armstrong thought that now would be a good time to inspect the rest of the train. And see Anna.

He crossed from 451 through the archive car to the gold car, and after checking with the Rumanian guards, he went through the door to the rest of the train.

The shunters at Moscow had not bothered to connect the between carriages walkway and tunnel so Armstrong had to cross the gap to open the door. He stepped through and stood for a moment taking in the sight. In contrast to the luxury of 451 and the well-ordered carriage holding the Rumanians this was a hive of stinking humanity. Slatted wooden seats were on either side of a small center passage. Each seat jammed with passengers, their baggage, their livestock, their pets, their smell. As he opened the door he heard a babbling cacophony of noise but that stopped instantly and all eyes swung to him. He saw Anna immediately, but after a startled glance at him, she demurely lowered her head.

Armstrong pushed his way through along the aisle, examining the passengers. They seemed to consist mainly of peasants and petty-bourgeois, but there was the occasional well- dressed family fleeing the chaos of the revolution. All, however, avoided eye contact, unwilling to draw the attention of the tall foreigner to them. The remaining coaches were all interconnected, so he crossed to each without difficulty. He reached the end of the last one and turned to retrace his steps. He was sure of himself now. Here and there among the passengers he had seen young men, a rare sight in wartime. There were eight in all, and separate from each other. They could be deserters of course, but he thought it more likely they were Anna's men.

As he reentered Anna's carriage he saw her stand and come toward him, her eyes downcast. He swayed with the movement of the train as she neared him and stumbled slightly so that she cannoned into him. She gasped with surprise and an embarrassed shyness that Armstrong thought a masterpiece of acting. He held her for a moment as if to steady her, and she murmured a thank you, before slipping by him towards the toilet. Armstrong left the car, his palm crushing the note that her deft fingers had pressed there. Closing the door behind him he stood for a moment before crossing to the gold car and read it. "Darling," it said, "I'm alone. I need your help, but we have to be careful. We're all in danger."

He held the note for a moment then let it slip away in the air stream. If she was alone, who were the men he had seen? He wondered if Boyle would agree to her coming to 451. He rapped on the door and was admitted by the sentry. Later, when they were at lunch, he told Boyle and Hall that he thought there were suspicious characters in the other cars, and they must be on guard at all times.

Onward crawled the train. Mile upon mile the wheels clacked their rhythm and, as the sun settled on the horizon the lights of Bryansk could be seen ahead. Flickering lights that looked like fires. O'Reilly was on duty on the footplate and he quickly got to the door and yelled.

"Trouble ahead."

Both Armstrong and Boyle scrambled to the footplate and stood watching as the town neared. Over the noise of the engine Armstrong heard the popping noise of rifle fire. "Hell," he yelled. "Looks like there's a full scale battle going on." He looked at Boyle. "I think the revolution's still with us."

Boyle nodded and struck his head out of the cab the better to see. There came the clang and howl of a ricocheting bullet and he quickly pulled his head back. "The bastards are shooting at us," he roared, and as the train continued to slow, he ordered the engineer to go to full speed.

Grimly the man opened the throttle wide. Slowly the train gathered speed. Frantically the fireman threw coal into the firebox. Streams of tracer curved over them as they entered the station approach. Tracer going both ways. It looked like they were in the middle of a battle between the Reds and the Whites, and both sides regarded the train as an intrusion in their war and commenced to shoot hell out of it as it ran between the warring sides. Armstrong, crouching down, cold in hand, hoped that Anna was safe. Some of those bullets were hitting the carriages. The engineer, trying to draw attention to the train's neutrality, grabbed the whistle as the station appeared and held on, the earsplitting scream of the steam drowning the noise of gunfire as the engine worked up to top speed. The buildings of the station flashed by and Armstrong saw troops, shielded from their enemies by the trains bulk, stand up from concealment to shoot at the train. He emptied his gun at all he could see, uncaring if they were Red or White and not really aiming to hit but to make them get their heads down.

Then they through and running past the town, with the sound of the battle dwindling behind them. Armstrong, after conferring with Boyle, went to the footplate and talked to the engineer then returned to Boyle.

"There's a town about thirty miles south of Bryansk named Trubchevsk. The engineer thinks we'll be able to refuel there," he said.

"As long as we don't find ourselves in the middle of a fight again," said Boyle.

Armstrong returned to the footplate and stood waiting. The train lost the speed that the engineer had got out of it when running through Bryansk and settled down to barely twenty five miles per hour. It seemed the high speed run had strained ancient joints and unions, and matter how much coal the fireman threw on, the pressure gauge sat in the lower half of its scale as steam seemed to spout everywhere. Now the fireman had to go to the back of his tender to get coal. Armstrong thought that if the engine had been efficient they would have got to Kiev before refueling.

An hour went by and ahead of them was a red patch in the darkness of the sky. Armstrong bit his lip. It looked as if there was trouble at Trubchevsk as well. Turning to Brewer he told him to alert the rest then he looked at the engineer and made a winding up motion with his hands. The engineer shrugged and indicated that his valves were wide open.

Slowly the town appeared. A small town on the Desna river, hardly more than a siding. What an American would call a whistle stop. Armstrong hung out the side of the cab and watched. The train ran through the last curve before the town and now he could see the source of the glare in the sky. A large building was on fire with flames and sparks shooting high. As the train neared the station he could see that there was people around the building fighting the fire. Just ordinary people. No arm-bands or rifles.

The train eased to a stop and Armstrong jumped down to the platform. The building was adjacent to the station, and as he stood, watching a man detached himself from the firefighters and came running to him. The man spoke in a spate of Russian too fast for Armstrong to follow, but now both Hall and Boyle were with him and Hall translated.

"This old boy is the town mayor and he wants us to get the passengers to help fight the fire. Apparently it's a warehouse for their vodka distillery. What do you think?"

Boyle's heavy voice said, "Tell him if he'll get us fuel for the engine we'll fight his fire."

The man's face lit up as Hall spoke. With much vigorous head nodding he indicated willingness.

"Ask him if there's any soldiers or Reds around," said Armstrong.

The man looked at Armstrong and impatiently shook his head, his hands in the air, as if to query the importance of such a question when precious vodka was in danger of being lost. "Nyet, nyet, nyet," he said, and launched into an explanation.

"He say's the fire started by accident. There's been no soldiers around for days."

"All right then," said Boyle. To Hall he ordered. "You and Tolstoi get every able-bodied man off the train. Leave one guard on our car and four of the Rumanians to guard the archives. Bring the rest." To Armstrong "Come on lad. Let's take a look."

They ran, with the mayor, to the blaze. Armstrong heard a voice behind him pant. "Bejasus now, would I be after hearing right. A vodka distillery is it."

Armstrong groaned to himself. One more thing to worry about.

The fire was being confined to the upper part of the warehouse, with the roof well ablaze. A large hand pump was being operated by several men strongly enough to send a stream of water to the roof. The major, however, was more concerned about the contents than the building. Men were already running in and out of the warehouse carrying crates and as the men from the train appeared a human chain was formed. Crate after crate was passed from hand to hand until a small mountain began to rise in the yard of the warehouse. Crates that clinked merrily as bottles jiggled together. Occasionally an open bottle would appear making its way along the line and mouths would snatch a hasty gulp before the next crate could come.

The mountain grew. The fire grew. Now the top floor was well alight. Still the crates came. Now bottles began to make their way back against the flow, in case someone had missed his share. As the mountain grew so the stream of water grew less, for surely the men at the pump had to drink too. Armstrong, his ears ringing from liquor, his face black from smoke was in the center of the line. Grab and pass. Grab and pass. He knew that Boyle was inside the warehouse for he could hear his bellows of encouragement. O'Reilly he couldn't see but he thought the little mick was the one organizing the bottle flow. The man ahead of him collapsed in the snow a peaceful smile on his face. The gap was closed.

The work was hot. The fire was hot. Vodka was cold. Vodka was free. Now the line seemed to lack co-ordination. A gap of several seconds would elapse before the next crate came. Once a crate was dropped and the bottles smashed. As the raw liquor spread into the snow a groan ran through the crowd. Not a groan of agony or fear but a groan of sorrow, as if a dear friend had been lost.

The roof fell into the top the top floor in a great show of sparks. Men came running out of the ground floor carrying the last of the vodka. Boyle among them. Good old teetotal Boyle, probably the only sober man on site. Armstrong grinned at the sight of Boyle, normally so smartly dressed, in a soot stained uniform and with one of his bushy eyebrows singed to a stubble.

Boyle pulled a silver whistle from a pocket and lustily blew it. With all eyes upon him he jumped upon a crate and bellowed. "All right then. We've saved your vodka, now let's load the train." This was hastily translated by Hall and Tolstoi, and with a great cheer the crowd surged towards the station. The mayor led the procession, almost dancing as his short legs tried to keep up with Boyle.

Armstrong straightened his aching back and noted that the mayor had left the town constable to guard the vodka. He also noted a small figure disappearing in the direction of the train with one of the crates in its arms. He thought it would be a good idea to check O'Reilly's kit when he was back on the train.

He started to follow the others to the train but as he passed out of the circle of light made by the fire he tensed, for he saw someone standing in the shadow. His hand edged to his holster but stopped as the person stepped forward and he saw it was Anna.

He reached for her. The dark evening, the vodka, the moment, gave him a feeling of recklessness. Pulling her close he kissed her. God, even with the ragged peasant clothes she felt wonderful. She clung to him for a moment then pushed away, pulling her cloak tightly around herself.

"Careful, my darling," she whispered. "We mustn't be seen together. For your sake, as well as mine. Come." She drew him with her, back into the shadows.

Again they kissed, their arms around each other, then he held her away and said. "All right, my love, tell me about it. Where have you been? How did you get on this train?"

She looked at him and the rising moon caught her eyes and made them enormous. She shuddered. "The Bolsheviks came for us. They knew us to be agents of the great capitalist Barreroth, you see, so we had to disappear. We knew you were ready to leave – there are no secrets in Moscow you know – so we split up for safety reasons. The others have already left for Kiev."

"Don't you have about eight men with you on the train."

She frowned. "No, it was impossible to travel as a party. I have only one man with me. He's the middle-aged man sitting two rows down from me."

Armstrong looked at her as he thought of the men he had seen on the train. Was she lying? What had she to gain if she was. The gold? Did she want all of the jewels and the gold and not just the Goliath Stone? He looked down at her as he held her close, and her eyes looked back unblinkingly. He dismissed the suspicion and drew her lips to his again. But he resolved to have another look at the eight men.

Slowly, reluctantly, she pulled away. "You must go or you'll be missed, my darling," she said. "Where is the stone? Is it safe?"

"About as safe as anything can be in this country," he said. "I have it hidden away but it's difficult to get at with all the people in the car."

"Could you get it to me before Kiev?" she asked. "We are in contact with some White Russians there, and they could get me to Sweden and a boat home. Then all I will have to do is to wait for you to return to me."

"I'll try," he promised. He grinned, "It's a pity I don't have it on me – then all I would have to do is to drop it down the front of this dress." He touched the rough fabric of her dress.

She shivered. "Oh, God," she whispered, "I picked up these old rags in the market. All but one of my dresses were left in the hotel. I ran out the back as the Reds came in the front. I'm on the train with just one carpet bag."

Armstrong saw how drawn she looked and he came to a decision. "We're moving you. Let's get your bag and I'm going to put you in our car."

Anna grasped his arm. "You can't do that," she gasped. "You'll get into trouble. And I'm trying to avoid looking conspicuous. I will be noticed if I move."

"I don't really give a damn about getting into trouble," said Armstrong. "And I think we can get you into our car while everyone is busy loading fuel." He smiled at her. "My mind is made up, so it's no good arguing with me."

He took her by the arm and walked her to 451. The work of loading fuel was well in progress. Three lines of men and women were passing logs up to the tender – apparently there was no coal – and already the tender was more than half full. The crowd was in high good humor, with so much singing and talking going on it sounded – as O'Reilly would say – like Saturday night in Ballybunnion. Armstrong saw Hall, his thin face flushed and his hat on the back of his head, cheerfully atop the tender giving orders for the stowage of the logs. Boyle was standing with the mayor, each talking at the top of their voice, trying to be heard over the row of the crowd and neither understanding what the other was saying. Tolstoi, Armstrong noted with approval, was with the Rumanian guards that had been left on duty, making sure that no one boarded the Rumanian cars.

Armstrong kept his body between Anna and the crowd as he reached the door of 451 and pushed her up the steps ahead of him. A surprised Brewer, guarding the room with the jewels in, was told to relax, and Ivan was asked to move Armstrong's gear in with Hall so that Anna could have the spare room.

Ivan's leathery old face split into a wide grin as he bowed to Anna and ushered her into the warmth and comfort of 451. Armstrong left her in Ivan's care and went to find Boyle.

Boyle was still with the mayor and Armstrong said, "There's something I have to ask you, sir," and as Boyle raised an inquiring eyebrow, "I know one of the passengers on the first coach. She is the niece of the Baron Barreroth and she was in Petrograd to study the possibility of the Baron loaning money to the Kerensky government."

"Woman?" Boyle gasped. "A woman in finance? Someone's pulling your leg son."

"No it's a fact," said Armstrong. "She's actually his niece and he trusts her judgment. She wasn't here by herself, you know, she had a team of his banking officials with her. However, the revolution has put a stop to the loan idea and I guess the Bolsheviks want to question her about the Baron's support for Kerensky, so she's on the run. The point is, she's on her own back there, and I would like to move her into one of our staterooms where she will be safer. I'm sure the Baron will be grateful to you."

Boyle scratched his head. "And how do you know this lady?"

"Oh I met her at a reception in London," Armstrong said guilelessly. "I remember her telling me she was off to Petrograd for old Barreroth, but I never dreamed we'd meet again. She came to Moscow and attended that party at the Rumanian consulate."

"She's English?"

"Yes, sir, though her mother's French I understand."

"Well I suppose we should make room for her. Though I'm not too happy about having a woman in the car – not that I've anything against women, you understand – I've married some of them myself. But it'll mean I can't walk around without checking that my fly is done up, and we'll have to watch the language. Oh hell. You'd better get her moved." He grinned. "Maybe the Baron will be grateful enough to give me a loan after the war."

Armstrong said, "Thank you sir," and walked through the crowd of onlookers, many of them waiting for someone to tire of the loading so that they could take their place. He stood for a moment watching, and he saw one of the young men from the passenger cars. The man had a sullen look on his face and, although most of the workers had shed their outer coats as they warmed to the job, this one hadn't, and his fur hat was pulled low over his eyes. Armstrong watched him for a while. There was something about him that was familiar. He wasn't with Anna's gang so that wasn't the answer. He shook his head and walked away. It would come to him.

Within an hour the tender was loaded to the top. The mayor embraced everyone in sight, telling them that a Russian winter would have been dreadful to stand without the solace of vodka, and assuring them of his, and the town's, eternal friendship. The passengers were embarked. O'Reilly was, with difficulty, restrained from climbing on to the tender to serenade the crowd, for it was felt that even eternal friendship would not have been able to stand that. Twenty cases of vodka were ceremoniously given to Boyle and stowed in 451 and with a roar and a whoosh of steam the train pulled away from the station.

As Armstrong boarded 451, Ivan came up to him and told him that Anna's bag had been collected from the passenger car. Armstrong thanked him, then looked at the rest of the bleary crew. In a few words he told them of Anna's presence and as he spoke she opened the door of her room and came out. She had changed from the peasant dress to her day dress and as Boyle saw her his eyes widened.

"This is Miss Anna-Marie DeCourville," said Armstrong. "Anna, I'd like you to meet the officer commanding. Colonel Boyle."

"My God, Armstrong," Boyle breathed. "Here I was, expecting a much older person." He looked at her with evident approval. "Well, it wasn't such a bad idea after all, to get you away from that crowded car I mean."

Anna smiled dazzlingly and held out her hand. "Colonel Boyle. I am delighted to meet you and I'm so grateful you found room for me." She fluttered her eyes at him and he beamed as he took her hand in his. "I have been terrified since the fighting started and those awful Bolsheviks have been trying to arrest me. But I shall feel quite safe with you, and I shall tell my uncle, the Baron, what a help you have been."

Armstrong could see that Boyle was reluctant to loose her hand and he quickly introduced her to the others, then said. "Miss DeCourville is exhausted and will want to rest."

"Of course," said Boyle. "We'll talk more after you've rested. But one thing I must insist on and that is do not leave your room while we're in a station."

Anna smiled at him. "Colonel, I haven't slept for two days and I don't think you will see me for the next twelve hours." She went back into her room.

Boyle, watching her go, said to Armstrong, "I never expected her to be so young and, er, attractive. You're not shooting me a line, are you? pretty girl like that on a financial mission?"

Armstrong smiled with an easy conscience. After all, most of what he said was true. "No sir. She's the Baron's niece all right. And I believe the Jews have a tradition of using family members in their business dealings."

"Hmm," said Boyle and he walked to his room. "I'm going to bed. The mayor told me there's a siding about five mile downline and I've told the driver to pull in there for the night. I don't like to travel in the dark, it's too easy to derail a train." He stopped at his door and looked at Armstrong. "Set normal watches and call me if there's a problem."

And so, through the long winter night, the train sat on a lonely siding, with only the gentle hissing of steam to break the silence of the great Russian plain.

CHAPTER FIFTEEN

U ndisturbed, the train sat on the siding with most of its
passengers sleeping off the effects of the free vodka.
Outside, on the track, a sentry's boots crunched the
gravel of the rail-bed as he kept a lonely vigil around the three
Rumanian cars. Armstrong remained on watch, sitting in a
chair by the lounge stove and occasionally making rounds to
check on the sentry and the engineers.

He had switched off the lights, except for a single lamp
above his head. The stove fire was not really necessary because
the car was heated by steam from the engine, but Armstrong
liked its cheerful glow and kept tossing in logs to keep it
burning. He picked up one of the logs and hefted it in his hand.
It was soft pine, only a couple of inches in diameter and,
prompted by childhood memories, he pulled his knife and
began to whittle the log, paring off long slivers that fell into the
grate.

He slid the sharp blade along the wood, with a light,
delicate touch, hearing the whisper of the slivers, smelling the
pine odor released by his knife, and was so engrossed he didn't
hear the click of a door opening.

"What are you doing?" Anna's voice.

Armstrong swung around. She moved into the dim
light and he looked at her with real pleasure. Her eyes were
puffed and her hair tousled from sleep but he thought she
looked adorable. He grinned. "Passing the time thinking and
whittling," he said. "Why are you awake? I thought you'd sleep
for hours yet."

She sat on a chair beside him, and leaned forward to
catch the heat from the fire. "I thought so too, but I woke up
and here I am. What are you doing?"

Armstrong held up the piece of wood and looked at it critically. "Not sure yet, probably a boat. My whittlings usually end up as some form of boat."

"And shall we sail away in it together?"

"Ah. It will be too small for us, I'm afraid." He sliced off more wood. Anna leaned her head on his shoulder watching. Armstrong looked down at her and said in a quiet voice. "My mother always told me that a guilty conscience meant a sleepless night."

"What do you mean?" she asked, pulling the robe tight around her.

He looked around. All the suite doors were closed. "There's more to the Goliath Stone than you've told me, isn't there?" His voice was soft, not accusatory.

She sat thinking as the leaping flames, visible through the glass door, highlighted her cheekbones but left her eyes in mysterious darkness. She shrugged as if reaching a decision and said, "you know the legend of the stone?"

Only that it's supposed to be the stone that David used to slay Goliath."

She rubbed her hands across her face and in a quiet voice said. "We're told that David took five stones from a brook and hurled one of them at Goliath and killed him. David then cut off Goliath's head and held it high for the Philistines to see. After that there's no further mention of it in scripture. However, oral legends have it that the head of Goliath was carried before the armies of Israel whenever they went into battle, with the stone still embedded in the skull. I suppose the reason the scribes never mentioned this is because the priests were always railing against unclean practices. Then, as time went by the stone was found to be a diamond. How or why, we don't know. Maybe one of those old kings switched it to inspire his people, I expect the Jews believed it to be a miracle, after all, it was the age of miracles."

The diamond was then cut by Hebrew craftsmen to the shape it is now and became part of the treasures of the royal house of David. Now here comes the interesting part. The Babylonian conquest." She looked at Armstrong. "If I'm telling you something you already know, tell me and I'll skip past if."

Armstrong nodded without speaking and Anna continued. "The Babylonians were incensed at King Zedekiah for resisting them so they put him and all of his household to death – with the exception of a daughter – the Princess Tamar – who fled, with the Prophet Jeremiah, into Egypt. They took with them as many of the Precious relics of Israel as they could carry, and there must have been a lot because Jeremiah is supposed to have taken the ark of the covenant with him as well. However, eventually God told Jeremiah to flee Egypt also, so he took Tamar and his scribe, Baruch...

"I understood that Jeremiah died in Egypt," interrupted Armstrong.

"According to some scholars, yes, but that belief has no basis in the Bible or in Jewish secular history," said Anna.

Armstrong shrugged acceptance and Anna continued. "The legend has it that Jeremiah, his scribe, and Tamar, fled Egypt be sea and eventually landed in Ireland. In Irish history the names of people who came from Egypt are Ollam Fodhla, which means learned prophet, Simon Brug – secretary, and Tamar Tephi – beautiful palm. Ancient Irish poetry praises her royal birth, a tells of the way her life was saved, both in Jerusalem and Egypt. Old Jeremiah, however, still had all of the precious things he had taken from Herusalem. Some believe they're with him still, interred in a burial barrow, although the only two things that we know of in this day and age are the Goliath Stone and Jacob's Stone. Jacob's Stone, the one he rested his head on when he had the dream about the ladder full of angels, is now in Westminster Abbey, sitting under the coronation throne. Tamar married King Heremon of Ireland and I suppose the Goliath Stone has been in the possession of British Royalty ever since."

"All right," said Armstrong. "Let's take it that the Stone is the real thing, because I don't know who the hell is going to prove or disprove the story. Is it worth risking your life for?"

She smiled, "It seems Jeremiah thought so. I'm sure he could have traveled faster unencumbered. But that's not the full answer." Her face became serious. "Have you ever heard of Urim and Thummim?"

Armstrong shook his head. "No. Who are they?"

"They're not people, my dear. They were devices supposedly used by the ancient prophets to receive revelation or help in translating unknown tongues, they are mentioned in several places in the early books of the Bible. Another name for them is Seer Stones, and not only did they use them for prophecy but the also gave power to the person in control of them.... We believe that the Goliath Stone is one of these. Papa Barreroth has studied the subject extensively and he's convinced the reason Jeremiah took the stone with him is because it's a seer stone. That is why he wants the stone, to give that power to the new nation that will arise when the Jews return to Palestine."

Armstrong thoughtfully drew his knife across the wood, with delicate strokes. "Do you believe what he believes?" he asked, watching her face.

She shook her head "I'm not sure what I believe. I've always thought of myself as a hardheaded girl, with a lot of healthy skepticism about things of this nature. But Papa is totally convinced. He points out that the stone came into the possession of the Kings of Britain and they came to dominate world affairs, and gain a great empire. Let's say I'm sufficiently motivated to do my best to recover the stone." She leaned her head against his shoulder. "And, my dear, you have done that for me."

"How were you planning to get it if I hadn't appeared?"

"Well, we had a plan but the revolution breaking out when it did ruined that. We had bribed an officer in the Preobrashinsky Guards to admit us to the Kremlin and to dope the guards."

"Hell," said Armstrong, startled. "It's lucky for you the fighting started when it did. A plan like that. God, you could have spent the rest of your days in Siberia."

The fire flared up as a log split with the heat and the flickering flames lit her face as she turned to him. "We're not fools you know. We knew the chances were slim but we believed the rewards justified taking a chance. We want that stone, it's very important to us."

"If it's important to you it's important to me," said Armstrong. He held up the carving and critically examined it. It had become a miniature canoe, about six inches long and two inches wide in the middle. He grinned, offered it to Anna and said. "A Canoe for my lady. Keep it as a token of safe voyages."

Anna took the model and smiled.

Armstrong said. "The Russians and Rumanians certainly aren't interested in the stone, beyond its value as a diamond, but I think the Germans are. There's been altogether too much interference from them. In Jassy, before we left, they were prying, and I'm sure that the man who tried to stop us outside Moscow was German."

Anna looked startled. "I can't think why they should be," she said. "After all, it was the Kaiser who gave it away to the Rumanians."

"That's true," said Armstrong, "but maybe he didn't find out about the legend until after he gave the stone away. After all, the man isn't exactly a genius at what he does, is he?

Even I, find all this international intrigue very confusing." He grinned and yawned. "Time I took another walk around." He bent over and kissed the top of her head. "You'd better get back to bed, Anna my love. The dawn will be here in three hours and then we move again."

She stood and said. "Thank you for the little boat. It looks something like a Viking ship. I shall keep it and dream of sailing on conquering voyages with my lover by my side." She kissed him and went to her room.

Armstrong watched her go, then pulled on his greatcoat and went outside. As he walked around the train, checking the sentries, and thinking over Anna's story, the thought came to him that the Vikings had also used their ships as funeral pyres.

CHAPTER SIXTEEN

T hey left the siding and rolled onto the main track at first light. Armstrong slept as soon as the train was moving, until the afternoon and, after his toilet, went into the lounge to find Anna being entertained by Boyle, Tolstoi, and Hall. Armstrong sat with them, as Ivan brought coffee, and watched her as she was obviously changing Boyle's views on women in business.

All day the train rumbled without incident through forest and plain, and Armstrong felt relaxed, although the baffling familiarity of the man in Trubchevsk still bothered him. Again, for the second night, they pulled into a spur line and rested. Armstrong behaved to Anna as if she was only a friend, so that the others would not suspect they were lovers and she took her cue from him. He made no attempt to be with her in her room at night, strong though the urge was. The landscape began to change the further south they got. The snow grew thin on the ground then appeared only in patches.

At noon on the third day they were running flat out trying to make up time. The firebox seemed to prefer the logs over coal and the steam pressure crept higher. Armstrong was waiting lunch, after spending the morning on duty, when the brakes were applied. Brewer scrambling back from the footplate, called out. "Signals against us and we're approaching a village!"

Armstrong joined Hall on the Footplate and watched as the train crept around a curve to the village. He cursed, as the village came into view, because a barricade had been erected across the track, and there seemed to be a company of soldiers waiting for them. They looked nothing like the rabble that had tried to stop them outside Moscow. These were disciplined soldiers, well armed and smartly dressed, drawn up in three ranks. Their officers were at the barrier eyeing the approaching train with interest.

Armstrong went back to report to Boyle. "Soldiers," he said. "Probably a company. Regular troops with officers. I can't tell yet if they're Reds or Whites."

Boyle, who was casually dressed in shirt sleeves, said, "Keep them talking while I smarten up." He turned to Tolstoi. "stay out of sight until I call you, we don't want to let them see we have a Russian officer with us until we know what side they support." He went to his stateroom, calling for Ivan to help him.

The train stopped just short of the barrier and Armstrong stepped down to the crudely cut planks of a level crossing. He motioned to Hall to come with him, while behind him he heard O'Reilly hurriedly set up the Hotchkiss on the tender.

Two officers stood waiting for them, and now Armstrong saw the red arm-band of the Bolsheviks. At least he assumed they were officers, for they wore no badges of rank. Hall picked the one who seemed to be the senior and saluted him.

The man looked a typical Ukrainian. His head was pumpkin shaped above a short, powerful body. His face, with deep set eyes above a squat nose, showed the strain and wear of three years of war. From under the plain cap with a red star on it, down the left side of his face, ran a jagged scar. His hair and his moustache were beginning to gray. Armstrong thought he looked tough and capable. This one would not tremble at the sight of a gun.

"We are on official business for the Rumanian Government and have travel approval from General Muralov,' Hall brusquely said.

The man nodded his head and answered. "Yes. So much is obvious by the flags on the engine. This however, is Russian soil, not Rumanian, and General Muralov is in Moscow and not here."

"What do you want?" said Armstrong

"Are you the senior officer?" The voice was deep and rasping.

"No. He's in the train," said Hall.

The man looked at them both. His eyes had the mildly interested look of someone watching animals in a zoo.

"Then I suggest you take me to him."

Hall looked at Armstrong, who jerked his head towards the car and Hall left.

"He will find out if the Colonel is ready to receive you," said Armstrong.

The man nodded and studied Armstrong. He leaned forward the better to see the name on his shoulders. "CAR-NAR-DA," he said, making each syllable a separate word. "What is that? Why are you not Rumanian?"

Armstrong, only partly understanding the man, shrugged his shoulders. Any explanation in his fractured Russian would only cause confusion. Hall came back, stopped in front of the leader and said.

"The Colonel will meet with you. Your name and rank please."

The man grinned, a grin that pulled towards the scar so that his whole face seemed to be a ghastly slash. "Name?" he rumbled. "My name is Kaminski and as for rank, before the revolution I was sergeant. Now?" He shrugged. "I'm a comrade of the revolution. All these men here will do what I say or they are shot. What rank does that make me?"

Armstrong looked at the soldiers. "He's got a company there," he muttered to Hall. "Call him a Captain."

Kaminski had sharp ears. "Captain!" He Snorted. "what rank is your officer – Colonel you said? So I too will be a Colonel. Tell your Colonel that Colonel Kaminski wishes to have conversation with him."

Hall looked at Armstrong who was having trouble suppressing a smile. "Follow me sir," he said to Kaminski and walked towards the open door of 451.

Kaminski growled an order to the man with him and he went to stand with the soldiers then, with Armstrong, he followed Hall. As they walked he said. "They all big like you in Car-nard-a?"

"Every one of us," said Armstrong cheerfully.

"Hmmm," Kaminski grunted.

Boyle was waiting just outside the door and, as Kaminski came to the steps, he briefly touched his swagger stick to his hat. "You want to see me," he said in English.

Kaminski halted and stared at Boyle. Boyle was indeed a sight to stare at. He had donned his best uniform, gold insignia glittering, medals swinging, cavalry pants atop burnished boots.

"I have orders to inspect your train for enemies of the revolution," said Kaminski, visibly impressed by the splendor of Boyle.

"This car is the property of the Republic of Canada and as such has extraterritorial rights which make it the territory of the republic and an attempt to forcibly enter will be regarded as an act of war," said Boyle haughtily. He stood waiting while Hall, a stunned expression on his face, translated to Kaminski. "Also tell him that the Republic of Canada is the ally of Rumania, therefore the cars with the Rumanian flags on them are under my protection."

Kaminski looked up at Boyle, looked at Armstrong and evidently decided that war with a nation that produced such giants would not be a good idea. He talked to Hall, while Boyle and Armstrong stood waiting. The conversation went on for a few minutes then Hall turned to Boyle and said.

"What Colonel Kaminski really wants is to get a ride for himself and his company into Kiev. I have told him that the end four cars were attached to us and we are hauling them as a courtesy. His reply is that he's sure you would have no objection to squeezing the passengers into three cars and letting him have the last one. What do you think?"

Boyle looked at Kaminski. "Tell this Colonel I wish to discuss it with my staff," he said to Hall. "Invite him in and get Ivan to give him a drink while he's waiting, then you two come with me."

Kaminski was ushered in with great ceremony and seated in one of the late Tsar's armchairs. If he thought there was something odd about the Republic of Canada using chairs embossed with imperial eagles he gave no sign.

Boyle took the two Lieutenants into his stateroom. It was already occupied by Tolstoi and Streat who were at the windows, weapons in hand, ready should it come to a fight. Boyle turned to his two Lieutenants. But before he could speak both Armstrong and Hall said, almost in unison, "Republic of Canada?"

Boyle grinned. "It's a lot easier to say than trying to explain that the King of England is also King of Canada. IIe might find that difficult to understand. Hell, some of us Canadians find it difficult. But to the matter in hand – do we give him a car?"

Hall shrugged his shoulders and Armstrong said. "Yeah. The fellow looks meaner than a gut-shot grizzly. It'll be a tough fight if we refuse, and it's better to have him where we know than standing on our rights and putting his back up. Would be nice to have a few pounds of gun cotton though. We could put it on the hitch and blow it if they get to be trouble."

Boyle looked at Hall, "George?"

"I agree."

"Then it's done," said Boyle.   "George, inform this
Kaminski that we'll move the passengers and he's welcome to
the last passenger car."

It took an hour to get the barricade removed, the
complaining passengers relocated and the troops loaded.
During that hour Boyle brought Kaminski back for a drink.
He, Armstrong, and Hall plied the Ukrainian with Vodka while
Tolstoi kept a low profile in the archive car. Kaminski had the
true Russian capacity for drink. He would insist all glasses be
filled, jump to his feet, propose a toast, drain his glass with one
gulp and instantly refill it. Armstrong groaned, feeling his
head swimming, but he was determined to keep pace with
Kaminski. He was impressed by Boyle. Good old teetotal
Boyle; drinking vodka; submerging his principles for the cause.
King, country and Queen Marie. And dammit, he looked the
least affected of the four. Hall was beaming at all as he slipped
lower and lower in his chair. The toasts went on and on.
Toasts to the revolution. To the Republic of Canada. To the
mother Russia. To the war. To the allies. To Rumania. To
friendship. Kaminski was on his feet, proposing yet another
toast, when one of his men appeared at the door to tell him that
all was ready to proceed.

Boyle stood immediately, and without any wavering or
slurring of words, gravely thanked Kaminski for his company
as he escorted him to the door. Kaminski seemed reluctant to
leave the comfort of 451 for the car with his men but Boyle gave
him no opportunity to stay, firmly escorting him to the door,
and watching as he walked the length of the train to his men.
Boyle grunted with satisfaction when he saw Kaminski stumble
once, then he faced the engine and, in his big booming voice,
yelled. "Roll this son of a bitch." O'Reilly came scrambling
down from the firebox with his Hotchkiss. The engineer
cracked the throttle lever to feed steam to the pistons, slowly
the train began to move.

Boyle got back in 451 and looked at his two
Lieutenants. Hall, jacket undone, blearily regarded him from
deep in an armchair. Armstrong seemed all right, but surely
the train wasn't swaying that much. Boyle stretched his arms
to ease his muscles. He grinned at his Lieutenants. "I'm going
to have a nap. By the look of you two I suggest a spell on the
footplate. Nothing like cold air rushing over one's face to blow
away the fog. See you gentleman at dinner." He strode off to
his quarters without a waver.

Armstrong, looking at the befuddled Hall, laughed and said. "I think I'd better take first spell up front. You'll fall off, the state you're in."

Hall's head fell forward and immediately he was asleep. Armstrong told Ivan to wake Hall in a couple of hours and pour some coffee into him. He then climbed to the footplate and stood there with Streat, watching the steppes roll by. The Ukraine, he thought, looked like Saskatchewan prairie with its level, almost treeless plains. He wondered if they had gophers here.

Onward rolled the train, the fireman fed logs to the firebox, the fire burned fiercely, but steam pressure was weak. The engineer kept watching his pressure gauge and told Armstrong that maybe they should try to get another engine in Kiev. Armstrong hoped they would be able to reach there by nightfall. He also hoped that the civil war brewing between the Reds and the Whites would hold off until they cleared Kiev.

He was relieved by a sorry looking Hall, who groaned in agony as the cold air cut through his vodka-induced headache. Armstrong left him there and returned to the car. He sat warming himself by the enameled stove as he thought of Anna and the stone hidden in the wall. He wondered what her thoughts would be if she knew how close she was to the object of her quest. It would not be easy to retrieve the stone. Car 451, because of the crown jewels, was guarded the whole time, and if he went with her into her room, someone would talk.

When Ivan woke him with a cup of coffee it was late afternoon. Car 451 was very quiet. Brewer sat by a window, rifle in hand, having been relieved on the footplate by Streat. Tolstoi was stretched out on the sofa, his eyes closed, and Anna was in the kitchen, talking to Ivan and O'Reilly. Boyle was still in his stateroom. It all seemed very peaceful with the train slowly trundling along through the fast fading light. He thought of home. To the ranch on a Sunday afternoon in winter. His mother would be placidly knitting by the fireplace while his father, sitting opposite her, slowly rubbed oil on the butt of one of his beloved hunting rifles.

He shook his head. Let yesterday and tomorrow take care of themselves. He stood, pulled on his greatcoat, and went to relieve Hall.

Armstrong leaned out of the engine cab and strained his eyes for a sight of Kiev. The cold air removed the last traces of his hangover. He thought if he stayed in Russia much longer his liver would be pickled. Two bouts of heavy drinking in three days was too much. The drinking during the fire had been spontaneous, a natural result of the event and peoples gratitude for their help. But today! If Boyle's idea had been to get Kaminski drunk enough to loosen his mouth it hadn't worked. Rule number one, he thought: Don't try to outdrink a Russian.

He thought about Kiev. It would be a tough town to get through without incident. Strategically situated on the high right bank of the Dnieper river it was one of the oldest cities in Russia. It had attracted many industries – railway shops, foundries, machine plants – all requiring a strong labour force. He thought that the place would be a natural for both Reds and Whites to seek control.

From Kiev to Jassy was about three hundred miles as the crow flies but nearer four hundred over the ground by rail – And much of that distance was over old, neglected track. During the journey from Jassy to Moscow the engineer had been very cautious, frequently stopping to examine the track ahead. Now, two months later, God knows what shape it was in. True, all factions of the revolution seemed to appreciate that the rails were essential to whoever won the fight, but both revolution and war were due to a failure of logic and, sooner or later, later some idiot would tear up a section of track. Armstrong was sure that a crisis would come in Kiev.

The train trundled through the outskirts of the city. Kiev had a pall of smoke hanging over it, whether from burning buildings or from normal industry output he didn't know.

Brewer called out, "One of the Russians is coming, sir."

Armstrong turned, as one of Kaminski's men climbed down the tender ladder. He must have been sent over the tops of the cars, because Kaminski had no way of entering the Rumanian part of the train. The man dropped down to the footplate and, seeing Armstrong, drew himself to attention and said, "Comrade Kaminski requests that you stop the train to let him off before Kiev station."

Armstrong eyed him thoughtfully. Evidently Kaminski was reluctant to arrive at a station that might be in the hands of the Whites. He nodded, said "Wait," and sent Brewer with a report to Boyle. Brewer returned a few minutes later with approval, and Armstrong sent the Russian back to Kaminski, telling him to signal when he wanted to get off.

Ten minutes later they ran through a long cutting, sheltered by high banks, and Brewer reported that the comrades were waving a flag, red of course, from their car. The train drew to a stop and Armstrong jumped down to the track and watched as Kaminski and troops detrained. Boyle, always cautious, had put his troops on alert, and Armstrong grinned as he heard O'Reilly crooning to his beloved Hotchkiss from the top of the tender.

Boyle came to the door as Kaminski approached, flashing his ferocious smile. "Thank you Colonel," said Kaminski. "I leave you now, but maybe I soon ride in big car like this one eh!" and he slapped the side of 451.

Boyle, not understanding a word, unsmilingly saluted, and Kaminski turned to Armstrong. "Goodby, Car-nar-dar," he said. "You look like damn good man in a fight." He thumped a stubby thumb repeatedly against this own chest. "Me too." He laughed, a raucous contemptuous laugh, turned and strode back to his men.

Armstrong watched him go, then looked at Boyle, shrugged his shoulders, and ran for the engine as the engineer eased open his throttle lever.

The arrival at Kiev was anti-climatic. All seemed normal, even to the extent of having a uniformed station master waiting at their platform as they drew in. The civilian passengers from Moscow were detrained and the four cars they had traveled in were unhitched. After talking to the stationmaster, who told them that Kiev had been relatively quiet, with fighting only in the industrial areas, Boyle, Hall and Tolstoi went off to find the allied mission for Kiev, leaving Armstrong in charge of the train and contents.

Armstrong went with them to the station exit and watched as they walked towards a boulevard lined with chestnut trees, dimly seen by flickering gaslights. He turned and went back to the train. He had a sense of excitement because he would be alone for a while with Anna. Maybe he should pass her that damned stone and not have it on his mind any more.

The platform was almost empty now. The passengers had left, only the armed sentries over the precious cargo remained on the platform. The engineer and fireman were drawing the firebox fir preparatory to doing sorely needed maintenance. O'Reilly had stowed the Hotchkiss away, and was now in the kitchen, talking to Ivan, and Brewer and Streat were guarding the gold car. As Armstrong walked along the platform a shunting engine came puffing up and the four passenger cars were removed.

He boarded car 451 to find Anna sitting in the Dowager Empress's favorite sofa, a worried look on her face. She rose as he entered and was in his arms. He kissed her, reveling in her closeness as she pressed against him.

"This is Kiev," he said. "What happens now?"

She opened her eyes wide and shrugged her shoulders in a gesture that was very French. "I don't know. The other members of our party were supposed to meet me here, but no one came. I've sent Gustav, the man with me, to look for them. God, I hope nothing has happened to them."

He indicated the empty car and said. "We're about as alone as we shall ever be. Do you want me to give you the stone now?"

She thought for a moment then shook her head. "No. If the others are not here then it would be foolish for me to take it. If I should be arrested with it on me it's gone forever. I'll leave it with you, darling, until we know something for sure."

Armstrong grinned at her and pulled her to him again. "Well, if there's nothing else we can do at this time what say we retire to your chamber for a little wooing."

She fluttered her eyes at him and said, "Why, Miles, you have the makings of a roue. It is not yet dark and you wish to bed me. Heaven protest a poor girl from men like you." She flung her arms around his neck and kissed him with passion, then she pulled her head back to look at him through narrowed eyes and was suddenly serious. "What kind of man are you? I don't flatter myself that you're risking imprisonment by stealing your country's jewels just for love of me. I don't think you're the type to risk everything for love of a girl. What makes you tick Mr. Armstrong." She down and patted the sofa beside her in invitation.

He shrugged as he sat beside her. "As I told you before, my dear, the jewels mean nothing to me. Let me say, though, that doesn't make me unpatriotic. I love my country and think there's no place like it on earth; and England is part of it, like family, you know. I've spent enough time there to convince me it's worth fighting for. But jewels! I don't give a tinkers cuss if George wears jewels or chicken eggs in his crown. My main reason for being here was to fly the queen of Rumania to safety. This expedition is an unimportant side issue of the war, so I can't get excited about baubles while men are dying in their thousands over a few yards of trenches in France. You feel that the stone will be an important symbol for your new state and you think that it also has some mystical power. All right, that's all the reason I need. Have I made myself clear?"

She looked at him her eyes wide and serious, then she leaned to him and kissed him again. She reluctantly drew away as O'Reilly opened the kitchen door, and said, "Oh, you're so sure of yourself. No wonder I love you, you oversized cowboy."

She looked at him, one eyebrow raised. "I bet you have women all over the place, like a sailor with a girl in every port. Who have you been with since we met in London?"

"No one," he lied, thinking uneasily of the Countess. MY GOD!.. The Countess! Jumping to his feet he strode to the window and stood thinking furiously as Anna watched him surprised. The thought of the Countess had triggered a memory. That man – the one he had noticed at the vodka fire – the one with the sullen face – one of the eight that had boarded at Moscow. He had been at the Countess's soiree in Jassy. One of the card players. The one who had sat with his back to him. He had only looked at Armstrong once, but Armstrong was sure of himself. One of the Goddammed Germans in the Countess's stable. What the hell was he doing on this train. The others! The rest of the men he had noted. They must be her agents too. Armstrong cursed out loud because he hadn't paid enough attention to the men when he had the chance in Jassy.

Anna jumped to her feet, ran to him and caught him by the arm. "Darling, what is it. What's the problem. You look shell-shocked. Was it something I said?"

He looked at her, almost looked through her, then he shook his head impatiently. "No love, it's nothing to do with you. Just something I've remembered. Excuse me for a while, will you? I've got to see the guards. O'Reilly," he roared. "come with me."

He left Anna standing, stiff with surprise, and walked to the platform, being joined by O'Reilly, curious over the abrupt summons.

"Ye called, melord?"

"Yes," he snapped. "You remember the men I asked you to keep an eye on. The single young men that boarded with the civilians in Moscow."

"Sure do, but there's been no chance to do much about it since then. Though I watched them leave the train when we got to Kiev. What's the trouble, squire?"

"I'm damn sure I've recognized one of them as one of the Germans we met at the countess's."

"Sweet Jasus almighty. Are you sure?"

"I think so. No, I'm sure. Yes, the more I think about it the surer I get."

"Well, what's he doing here."

"No doubt that bitch has gotten wind of our cargo and wants to screw up the operation."

"You mean she's after the gold for Kaiser Bill?"

"Keep your voice down man. No, no one knows of the gold except us. But the jewel transfer was arranged in Jassy." Armstrong said, his thought racing as he considered the woman and her possible motives. "I think she's after the jewels. Think of it! Here we are, an Anglo mission to recover Rumanian crown jewels. If she can hijack them it'll be a smack in the eye for us and a great propaganda boost for the Huns. Also they're easy to move, not like the gold, and I wouldn't put it past her to keep them for herself and bloody Ernst. She could be wanting to feather her nest, you know. She's smart enough to know that the Germans can't win now that America's in the war."

"So what's our plan, Squire?"

"Stay on the alert. I'm going to caution the Rumanians but I want you to prowl around the station. Get some old clothes on and spy out the land. Keep a low profile, but let me know immediately if you see anything suspicious. You'd better get a Webley from the armory, but keep it tucked out of sight unless you need it. If you think there's cause and you want to raise the alarm, fire a couple of shots. I'm going to put everyone on full alert. God, what a place. If it isn't the Reds or Whites after our loot it's the Huns. We'll have to keep our wits about us all right."

"Well, we'll just have shoot the bastards if they try anything, eh melord? Maybe I should get the Hotchkiss set up?"

Armstrong grinned at the Irishman's enthusiasm for his beloved weapon. "No," he said. I want that kept hidden until we have to use it. But keep it loaded and handy."

O'Reilly went to get ready, and Armstrong strode down the platform to the gold car and, after taking two soldiers to boost the guard on 451, told the subalterns to prepare the rest of their men for an attack. He told the engineers to forget maintenance and to raise steam for immediate need, then he returned to 451 with the two men and put them with Brewer and Streat.

Anna watched the bustle as he placed the men at windows and inspected their rifles. Finally, as O'Reilly, wearing an old coat of Ivan's over his burglary black, slipped out, she spoke.

"What is the matter? Why all the fuss?"

He sat beside her, took her hand in his, and told her of the Countess Von Hesse-Steiner – omitting, of course, certain details. He told her that he thought the Countess was plotting take the crown jewels, and her men had been among the passengers.

"Do you think her Germans will attack this train?"

"I think it's a very real possibility. She's evidently infiltrated enough of her men into the country. It's a pity I thought the men I had noted in Moscow were your crowd. It would have been easier to kick them off the train there."

"If they are all Germans why haven't they made a move before this. I mean, they had plenty of opportunity at the vodka warehouse fire."

"Who can be sure? Probably because they want to be nearer to Rumania before they make their move. Even Kiev is a long way from the border. No, we'll stay on full alert and if nothing happens here then we can expect trouble nearer to Jassy. Still, forewarned is forearmed eh?"

She frowned as she thought about this development. He had an almost irresistible impulse to hold her tightly to him. But the men were eyeing her with interest so he refrained. Fortunately Ivan came shuffling up to tell Anna that her bath was ready for her. Anna gave a moan of pleasure. "this is going to be heavenly," she whispered. "Ivan told me that when Colonel Boyle was away I could use the suite bath." Armstrong walked with her as she gathered fresh underwear from her room and went through the suite to the bathroom. "Oh my God," she breathed as she looked at Marie Feodorovna's luxuriously appointed bath, now brimming with scented water. "This is going to be wonderful."

"Need any help?" said Armstrong, leering at her.

"No," she hissed. "Not with all these men around. God and do your inspections or whatever soldiers do." She pushed him out, closed the door and he heard the very definite snick of the bolt going across.

Regretfully he turned away, growled an order to the men to keep their eyes to the outside of the train and went on to the platform. It was dark now, with a cold wind fitfully gusting. A pair of Rumanian sentries were pacing the platform, and from the track side of the train he could hear the crunch of boots on gravel as sentries paced there too. He walked past the engine and stood looking along the track. Kiev station was open construction and it would be easy for an attacking force to come from this direction, he thought. Later, after midnight, when an attack would be more probably, he'd increase the guards.

Armstrong paced the platform, a strong sense of foreboding putting his nerves on edge. Dammit, where the hell were Boyle and Hall. The station was quiet, closed down, with no sign of the men who had greeted them on their arrival. Either no more trains were expected or people know that Kiev railway station was not a good place to be tonight. And O'Reilly! Not a word since he had slipped away.

Time passed and Anna called to him to come in for a meal. Her face was glowing from the bath, but she told Armstrong she was tired of only one dress, and she hoped that if they were still in Kiev in the morning she would be able to buy more clothes. Armstrong grunted acknowledgement, and she said little during the meal, conscious of his mood and concern. He ate hurriedly, rising to his feet as soon as he finished. Before he went back to the platform, he took the precaution of changing his service holster for the western one his father had given him. With it fastened low on his hip, the leather ties crushing his baggy cavalry pants and the Colt slipped snugly into the supple leather, he felt ready for anyone. Standing, watching himself in the full length mirror of his compartment, he practiced his draw a couple of times until he was satisfied that he could gun down any European officer before the man had finished fumbling with his holster flap.

It is an uncomfortable experience for a soldier to be in a lighted area while all around is blackness so he had the acetylene lights on the front of the engine readied. When lit they would light up the track. He heard a challenge from one of the platform sentries, and dropped his hand to his gun, but relaxed when O'Reilly emerged from the darkness.

Seeing Armstrong he drew himself to his full five and a half feet and, with a very pukka military salute, said, "Acting temporary Sergeant O'Reily reporting back from patrol Sah!"

Armstrong groaned and said, "Cut the blarney you little mick and tell me what the hell is going on?"

O'Reilly grinned and said, "Just trying keep up the grand traditions of the British army amidst the toil and turmoil of a country that's going to the dogs."

"O'Reilly," growled Armstrong, menacingly.

"Ah yes melord. Well it's like this. The whole town is going to blow its top very shortly. There's Reds and Whites all over the place. Coming in quiet like, in small groups. And they're meeting up with each other and getting ready for a real donnybrook. This here station is surrounded by Bolshies, but I think they'll be too busy fighting each other to worry about us for a while."

"Have you seen anything of the Colonel and Lieutenant Hall?"

"No, squire. I found the allied mission HQ but it was surrounded by troops. Which didn't stop me from going inside of course. I talked to a fooking snooty redcap sergeant there, who wanted to have me put in cells as a deserter, but I persuaded him of the error of his ways, with the help of this here Webley, and he told me that the Colonel, Mr. Hall, and the Fount, had left some time earlier with one of the mission officers."

Armstrong cursed softly to himself. O'Reilly's report didn't help. "That's it eh?" he said, "Nothing more?"

O'Reilly shook his head. "That's it melord, except you should have seen that fooking redcap's face when I shoved me gun in his fat gut."

"Yeah, well there's enough revolutions going on here without you starting another. Get inside, get some food in you and then get back on patrol. In the meantime I'm going to move the train down track."

After telling the subalterns of his plans, he had the engineer ease open the throttle and the train moved to open ground away from the station buildings, leaving the platform in view so he could see when Boyle and Hall returned. Now they were away from the station lights, the blackness was not so menacing. Again the sentries were posted around the train, supplies of grenades were put ready to hand and the Hotchkiss was positioned on the tender with one of the sappers manning it.

The night was cold with intermittent flurries of snow gusting against the train. Armstrong paced the track between the train and the station, getting more worried as the hours passed. Midnight came, still the night was quiet. Sentries were changed. Men were fed. Anna appeared, a blanket on her shoulders, and gravely handed him a large mug of vodka-laced cocoa. She closed the door behind her and stood with him for a few minutes while he drank the warming concoction. After he had drained the mug, she took it from him, kissed him, shivered, and thankfully returned to the warmth of the car.

Across the rooftops he heard a church clock chime twice. As if it were a signal there came a brilliant flash that seemed to illuminate the whole city, followed seconds later by the thundering roar of the explosion that had caused it.

Startled he stared around as he roared out. "Stand to! Everyone on full alert."

With a rattle of equipment and the crunching of boots on gravel, the Rumanian soldiers leaped from their cars and took up positions under the wheels, ready for an assaulting force. Armstrong intended to fight as long as he could, but if the attacking force was too strong he meant to leave Boyle and Hall to their fate. Accordingly the footplate was manned and ready to roll on order.

The sky was red from the leaping flames of a burning building, visible just beyond the station. Now he could hear the pock, pock, pock, of rifle fire and the drumming of a heavy machine gun.

"Miles?" Anna's voice, with the hint of a quaver in it.

He turned. She was standing at the door, looking ephemeral in the flickering light of the fire. "It's all right, that's a few blocks over. Now you keep your head down. Remember the car's armor plated."

He could see her eyes flash and she said with some asperity. "I'm not worried about myself. It's you. You keep your own head down, you hear!"

With a clang and a whistle a bullet ricocheted off the engine and whined into space. "Hold your fire until we see them," bellowed Armstrong as he slammed the door on Anna. He dropped to a knee as he drew his Colt. Damn this, he thought. Where the hell was Boyle and Hall? O'Reilly too was out there somewhere.

A voice rang out form the darkness – a Russian speaking voice. "Hey you, Car-Nar-Dar. I want to talk to you."

Kaminski! Armstrong checked the train. His men were huddled close to the track making them difficult targets, but the flames were getting higher as the fire spread, and the train was clearly defined. "My Russian is not very good," he yelled back.

"Is all right, I do not want to talk much," replied Kaminski with a gutteral laugh.

"Wait," Armstrong yelled. Then, in English, "Who's on the Hotchkiss?"

"Brewer, sir," from the tender.

"You can handle that?"

"Damn right, sir," came a cheerful reply.

"Right then. I'm going to walk out a bit and get that bastard to meet me. Now if I drop to the ground you open up with that thing and nail Kaminski. Clear?"

"Yes, sir."

Armstrong bit his lip as he thought. "Streat," he yelled.

"Here, sir," came a reply from inside 451.

"If you see me fall to the ground, fire a flare over the Russians and open up with all guns. Understood?"

"Yes, sir."

Armstrong thought for a moment, then gave much the same orders to the subalterns in French, trusting that a Ukrainian ex-sergeant would not be as versed in that language as one of the officer class. He thought over his precautions, decided he couldn't do any more, so shrugged and called out,

"Kaminski!"

"Da."

"Meet me in the middle. Just you and me."

"All right Car-Nar-Dar."

Armstrong stood, eased his gun in its holster, squared his shoulders and, fully exposed in the glare from the fire, walked towards the sound of Kaminski's voice. His every sense was at maximum intensity. The taste of smoke from the fires, the hissing of steam from the engine, the crunch of his boots on the gravel, the exhilaratingly malevolent reek of detonated high explosives, the shadowy figure of Kaminski materializing into hard definition as he approached – all combined to pump his adrenalin to fever pitch so that he felt ready to handle any son-of-a-bitch that crossed him.

The two men stopped a yard apart from each other. The squat Ukrainian and the tall Canadian. Kaminski's face looked fiendish in the orange-red light of the flickering fires. The mouth and scar were blackly outlined. He carried no arms except for a ferociously long Russian bayonet in its scabbard.

"Why are you firing at a friendly ally?" asked Armstrong.

Kaminski ginned and spread his hand in a playful manner. "We just wanted to get your attention, Car-Nar-Dar. It was only a very little shot at a very big engine."

"Well I'm not amused. Firing on another country's property is an act of war, and if you want war you can have it."

Kaminski stiffened and his voice became menacing. "I would be more polite if I were you Car-Nar-Dar. I have fifty soldiers here. More than double yours and you are still very much in Russian territory."

Armstrong dropped his voice to match Kaminski's. "Just drop the bullshit and tell me what you want."

Kaminski's black eyes glittered and the scar seemed to pulsate. He leaned towards Armstrong, jabbing with a finger as words spilled out of him in a rush. "You listen to me Car-Nar-Dar. You have valuable Russian treasures on that train. Treasures that once belonged to the pig Tsar. Treasures that are now the property of the Workers and Peasants government, and you are committing a crime against the Russian people by trying to steal them."

Armstrong stared at the man.   So it was open knowledge that the train carried valuables. Which wasn't too surprising given the chaotic state of Rumanian and Russian administrations. "I don't know who told you that fairy story but I can tell you that the only things carried on that train are archives and artifacts belonging to the sovereign state of Rumania, which are being shipped according to the protocol of September 1917."

Kaminski sneered. "That too is "bullshit" I think. So I'm sure you have no objections to my men searching the train."

"I do, and you're not going to search the train."

Kaminski shrugged, "The blood of your men is on your head, Car-Nar-Dar. We have the track blocked both behind you and in front. A full scale civil war is being fought in the city. It is a pity that your little train was attacked by the savages that are loyal to the Kerensky pigs. You understand?"

Armstrong's hand flashed down to the Colt and in one smooth movement it was rammed into Kaminski's guy. "Now you listen to me!" he snarled. "This is a Colt 45 I've shoved in your belly and if I let this hammer fall it'll blow a bit hole in you. Now you tell your men to fall back."

Kaminski's eyes dropped to the gun then back up to Armstrong's face. "How did you do that so fast," he said, sounding mildly interested.

Armstrong grinned. "An old western trick," he said. "From Car-Nar-Dar."

Kaminski studied Armstrong with curiosity. "You shoot me, you die too. My men have rifles aimed at you. In fact I told them to shoot you if you reach for a gun. But I didn't know you are that fast."

"Yeah. Well I am, so tell your men to fall back." Armstrong held his Colt with the butt square in the center of his own belly. He had drawn it so fast, and with the gun being shielded by both their bodies, it was doubtful if either side knew it there.

Kaminski looked around as if thinking of a way out of the impasse, then his face split into his awful grin. "you had better let that hammer fall Car-Nar-Dar. Yes you shoot me, my men will shoot you. Then they blow up train, everybody will die. God Russian solution eh!"

Armstrong watched Kaminski, his thoughts racing. He felt and unwilling admiration for the tough soldier, but that didn't help the situation. With vicious and sudden swiftness he slammed his left fist into Kaminski's head and followed it by whipping the Colt across the other side of his head. Kaminski grunted with pain and surprise and he fell to the ground. Armstrong dropped beside him, yelling for his men to open fire. The Hotchkiss opened up immediately. The harsh clatter of its firing was joined by the whip-lash crack of rifle bullets whining over his head. Startled yells came from the Reds and some who had risen to their feet to aid Kaminski were hit and fell. Firing continued as Armstrong crawled back to the train, dragging Kaminski with him.

He cursed as the gravel bit into his knees and holstered the Colt, the better to get a grip on Kaminski. If he left him and ran for it he'd be shot for sure. His best chances were if he kept Kaminskit as a shield. Reaching another set of rails, he started to haul Kaminski over them when suddenly the man came to life. With a roar he butted his head full into the face of Armstrong, then leaped upon him, his hands going for the throat. Armstrong's head rang with pain and he saw a brilliant kaleidoscope of flashing lights. His nose felt broken and he couldn't breathe because Kaminski' large hands were crushing his windpipe. He desperately thrust both arms up through Kaminski's, breaking the man's stranglehold, then he smashed his cupped hands upon his ears. Kaminski howled in agony and staggered to his feet, uncaring of the bullets flashing by.

Armstrong got to his knees. His nose was streaming with blood, his head was ringing and his windpipe felt crushed. And Kaminski? He had taken both Armstrong's left hook and the pistol-whipping. His eardrums were probably broken, yet still he was on his feet – and he was coming back for more.

With blind fury he rushed Armstrong. Armstrong met him by rolling on his back and thrusting his legs full into his belly, tossing him over behind him so that he hit the ground with a thud. Both men rolled away from each other and ended on hands and knees, glaring at each other, eyes red with fury. Kaminski spat blood and whispered. "Tonight you die, Car-Nar-Dar."

"Bullshit." Croaked Armstrong and both men leaped again at each other to meet frame against frame like Greek wrestlers. Kaminski got his arms around Armstrong's waist and began squeezing in a bear hug. His powerful arms were like steel rods as they contracted, and Armstrong tried to throw himself backwards to break Kaminski's hold. But the stocky Ukrainian had his feet securely set and his head in Armstrong's chest as he slowly applied his immense strength to breaking his back. For long moments nothing happened as both men strained at each other. The firing continued, with

Brewer continually sending short, controlled bursts at the Reds, now clearly outlined against the background of the fires. No shots came their way from anyone, possibly because there was no way of separating between the pair.

Armstrong, mustering his last reserves of strength, suddenly felt a rail by his foot and, using it as a brace, he threw himself sideways, dragging Kaminski with him. Kaminski hit the ground with an animal grunt. His head smashed back against the rail and the pressure of his arms slackened. Armstrong smashed his head into Kaminski's and savagely bit his nose. His teeth met and he pulled back with half of Kaminski's nose in his mouth.

Kaminski screamed in pain and rose to his feet, staggering backwards until he fell against the side of 451. His hands went to his face and he felt the remnants of his nose. He looked at Armstrong who had shakily risen to his knees as he spat out flesh and blood. With a bellow of rage he pulled his bayonet from its scabbard and rushed at Armstrong.

Armstrong's hand flashed to his holster – the Colt was gone. He watched Kaminski charge, almost with detachment. The heat of the battle had drained him, and he watched Kaminski with clinical interest. He thought that the abnormally long Russian Bayonet, although fearsome to behold, was really too cumbersome for a knife fight. Armstrong's right hand went behind him, under his coat, to the haft of his buffalo knife. His foot was poised against the rail that had helped him before, like a sprinter using a foot block.

Kaminski's face was awesome to see. The red light from the flickering fires clearly showed the terrible destruction inflicted upon it as, with a howl of animal fury, he leapt at Armstrong.

Armstrong whipped his knife from its sheaf and, with every ounce of his sinewy strength, he propelled himself forward, almost horizontally, at the charging Russian. He never felt the bayonet pierce his back. He only felt fierce exultation as his wide blade sank inwards to the heart. Kaminski hung above him for a second, then crashed to the ground, his weight tearing the bayonet from Armstrong's flesh as he did so. Armstrong rolled over and lay beside him, conscious now of a searing pain between his shoulder blades. He looked at Kaminski feeling a sense of sorrow. As he watched, the man's eyes opened and his head turned to Armstrong as a huge gout of blood came from his mouth. His eyes fixed on Armstrong as he gasped, "Life is bullshit Car-Nar-Dar." Then the eyes went blank as the life force left.

Armstrong, senses reeling, vaguely wondered why he wasn't dead. He wondered why the Reds hadn't put a bullet into his exposed body. He wondered what the hell was all the noise. The explosions. The whooping! Surely that was O'Reilly's high-pitched Irish voice. He raised himself on his forearms and stared as he saw the Reds retreating in disorder as grenades exploded and the cool expert firing of the Hotchkiss created panic among them. He stared as he saw men coming towards him. Silhouetted against the still burning platform lights. Tolstoi. Hall. And between them, weakly hanging on to their shoulders, his once elegant uniform in tatters, the bloodied body of Boyle.

Armstrong's lips twisted in a grin, "Up the bloody Canadians," he murmured, just before the blackness came and his head fell forward into the gravel.

CHAPTER SEVENTEEN

Armstrong Groaned. His head felt like it was being squeezed under a steam hammer, his back was on fire and he was having trouble breathing through his nose – besides which he hurt like hell, everywhere! Above the noise of the steam hammer he thought he heard a distraught female voice calling his name. He opened his eyes and, through a red haze of, he saw the tearful face of Anna.

"Oh thank God, thank god," she cried as his eyes opened. "I thought he'd killed you." She raised his head and hugged it to her. Dimly he realized he was lying on a hard flinty surface and it was damn cold. Red fog? Why was the fog red? Was it blood in his eyes?

"Lieutenant Armstrong sir. Are ye all right sir?"

O'Reilly's voice? What the hell was the scrawny mick being so damn formal for. God, it hurt to think. Why didn't everyone go away and let him sleep.

"All right. Brewer take his feet. Let's get him inside right now. You two men help Brewer, stand back a moment, miss, until we get him inside."

Hall? Hall's voice…Good old Hall. Even if he did speak with that goddammed far-back limey accent.

Armstrong forced his eyes open as he felt himself being lifted. He saw Anna's concerned face looking at him. He saw it lit by the flickering red lights of a burning fire. Fire! Kaminski! The train! Recollection came flooding back, along with a shriek of pain from between his shoulders.

"Stop," he croaked. "Dammit. Stop, let me down."

His feet were lowered and shakily, his legs weak and rubbery, he stood upright. He looked around until he saw Kaminski's body, sprawled across a track. He looked at it for a long moment, impatiently shrugging off the efforts of people to get him to 451. He was aware of Anna anxiously watching him, as if afraid he would be too affected by the body.

"O'Reilly." God, it was painful to speak.

"Here, squire," subdued and attentive.

"Get my goddamned knife, and my gun's there somewhere."

"Aye, sir."

Armstrong turned away and, supported by men on either side of him, he climbed the steps to 451. "Boyle?" he said to Hall. "What happened? How bad is he?"

"Concussion of sorts I think," said Hall. "We were too close to that explosion when it occurred. Colonel Boyle was hit by flying debris. We were just leaving the headquarters of the local militia when the Reds blew it up. But enough of that. Lets get you fixed up."

"No.!" Armstrong ordered, clenching his teeth against the pain as feeling slowly returned "We haven't time. First thing first. Move this train. There's some dead men out there on the track and the Reds will be mad about it, se we don't want to be here when they return with reinforcements." He turned to one of the subalterns. "Your men. Casualty report."

The subaltern snapped to attention, his eyes wide with awe at the sight of Armstrong's bloody face. "Two dead, sir," he said, "and four others wounded. None of the wounds are serious."

"We got off light then," Armstrong grunted to Hall. "I saw at least three fall besides Kaminski." To the subaltern he said, "We'll take the bodies back to Jassy for burial. You get to your men and prepare them to move. George. Get this train moving. Oh, and Kaminski said he had the track blocked ahead. I don't know if he was bluffing or not, but keep an eye out. Maybe we can push it aside. O'Reilly, get up on the Hotchkiss in case there is a barricade and we have to fight through it."

He sagged into a chair as Anna appeared with a basin of hot water. "Oh, George," as Hall almost made it through the door. Hall stopped and raised an enquiring eyebrow. "Get the sappers to throw a line over the telephone wires that border the track. Let's drag them down as we move. That way they can't communicate ahead in a hurry." Hall nodded understanding and was gone.

"Now you stay still while I sort out this mess," said Anna, examining Armstrong's face.

"Boyle," winced Armstrong. "He's older than me, look after him first."

"Ivan's already doing that, so just let me get on with your wounds," said Anna.

She worked on his face gently but deftly, with no squeamishness, until all dirt was removed from cuts and bruises. She stood back for a moment and looked at him. "Hmm," she mused. "No irreparable damage there. I don't think your nose is broken but you'll have a lovely shiner for a while. I think I'll have to dally with one of those cute subalterns until you get your good looks back."

Armstrong made a playful grab at her, forgetting his back wound until the sudden movement caused him to grimace with pain. "You'd better see to my back," he muttered.

"Your back? What happened to your back," she said leaning over him to see.

"Yon Russky stuck his bayonet in me."

"Oh my God, so he did." Anna said with alarm. "You silly man, why didn't you say so first. Let's have that coat off now."

The train started to move as Armstrong stood upright and she gently pulled his overcoat and tunic off him to see the bloodstained torn shirt. "My God," she repeated as she ripped the shirt back in half and stared at his wound. "Come on, can you get to the table?"

Leaning on her, he staggered to Marie Feodorovna's highly polished and substantially built, dining table. He sprawled on top and she took a pillow from her room to support his battered head. She got the first-aid kit from Ivan and cut the rest of the shirt from him. Armstrong heard her suck her breath in as she bathed the wound. "How bad is it?" he said.

"Oh it's not bad at all, but you are one very lucky man, my darling. It's a surface wound across your right shoulder-blade, about six inches long. An inch deeper and you would be in deep trouble."

"An inch can make all the difference – as the Bishop said to the actress. Ouch, Shit!" His back flamed with agonizing fire as Anna dabbed iodine on the wound.

"Serves you right for making dirty jokes at a time like this," said Anna primly, suppressing a chuckle. "I really do think though that we should have a couple of stitches put in. What do you think?" to Ivan who had silently appeared.

Ivan peered at the wound, nodded his head and said to Armstrong. "We sew you up, eh?"

Armstrong groaned. "Do what you have to damn well do."

He gritted his teeth and endured as Ivan, with strong skillful fingers, put several stitches in the wound. Anna sat beside him, holding his hand while the operation was in progress and the train slowly rolled along.

"How's the Colonel?"

"Cleaned up and in bed," replied Ivan. "He has big bump on head. Maybe he will be better soon."

Before Armstrong could reply there came the whoop whoop of the train whistle and the train increased speed. Armstrong looked at Anna and said. "Sounds as if George..." There came a splintering crash and the clang of something hitting against the armored side of 451, "is going to ram the barricade," he finished.

The door opened and O'Reilly appeared, grinning all over his face. "Yon chappie is quite the impetuous one ain't he? Lieutenant Hall I mean. He took the fooking train, beg pardon miss, through that barricade full tilt. Mind you it was only built out of scrap lumber."

"Any men around it?"

"Didn't see any, melord." He stepped over and looked at Armstrong's back and whistled appreciatively. "Holy Mary and sweet Jasus. That's a hell of a nick, melord!"

"Looks bad, eh?"

"Well, I've seen worse on a Saturday night in Ballybunion but that was from a broken bottle. The poor lad fell on it, or so I told the constable."

Armstrong groaned, both from reaction to O'Reilly's blathering and from pain, as he eased himself off the table and stood upright. "Anna," he said. "Never believe anything this half-pint piece of Irish blarney tells you. Beware of him for he's a stranger to the truth."

Anna smiled at O'Reilly. "Sergeant O'Reilly and I have talked in the kitchen, and I'm sure you're exaggerating. He just possesses the Irish gift of colorful speech."

O'Reilly's eyes twinkled with mischief. "Tis wonderful how the Lieutenant manages to find people with the gift of blarney. Is it sure you are that you're not Irish?"

Armstrong grunted with pain as he headed for his room, unsteadily clutching at the wall as the train gathered more speed. "I'm going to bed. O'Reilly! If you can tear yourself away from Anna perhaps you can clean up my uniform. It looks as if I fought the entire war in it."

He entered his room, pulled off his trousers, gingerly eased himself onto the bed and rolled belly down. He thought it would be a good idea to get a slug of vodka to help forget the pain but, even as he thought of it, he fell asleep.

He slept for hours. He slept while the dawn eased its gray face over the eastern horizon, slept as the train, rattled its way across the southern steppes, slept while Anna came and gently bathed his face again, slept through the morning and afternoon, to finally waken as the train was bathed in the golden light of sunset.

He came slowly awake. The confused dreams that had disturbed him were forgotten as soon as his eyes opened. He watched the setting sun send long shafts of light across the room as he thought over the events of Kiev. Then he swung his feet to the floor, ignoring the pain as his movement strained the stitches on his back. He went to the door in his shorts and peered out. He could hear the murmur of voices from the kitchen but could see no one.

He opened the door wider and stuck his head out. The drawing room was empty except for Anna sitting in an armchair, her head turned to look out the window. She looked lovely sitting there in the twilight, the last rays of the sun creating an aura about her head.

"Psst," he hissed.

Soft as the sound was she heard it and her head swung to him. Her face lit up with pleasure as she stood up and came to him. He took her hand as she entered his room and pulled her into his arms. She felt wonderful there, her soft lips on his, the clean smell of her, the softness of her and his own body responded.

She murmured something and rotated her hips against him as they clung together. Then she pushed away and took a deep breath. "No my darling," she said. "It's the wrong place and time."

"Where is everybody?" he whispered.

"George has hardly left the footplate since we left Kiev, and Colonel Boyle is asleep. The other are on full alert in case of more trouble. Why do you ask, kind sir? Surely you're not going to take advantage of a poor weak maiden?"

He chuckled and said. ""Some maiden," then dodged as she swung a not so playful jab at him. "Careful," he said. "One mustn't strike at an invalid. Especially one who wants to give you something." She raised an eyebrow at him and he grinned at her as he let go of her. He went to his uniform, cleaned and neatly folded on a bedside chair. His sheathed knife lay on top of the clothes. He pulled the knife from the sheath and the dying rays of the sunset flashed off the bright steel. "I think it's time to give you the stone," he said.

She caught her breath and he whispered. "The stone! Just the biggest diamond you've ever seen. I think this is a good time to get it, don't you. The border's near and things could well hot up once we're over it, but you'll be safe."

Her eyes sparkled with excitement. "Yes, you're right. With everyone busy and Jassy so near." She cupped her hands to her face. "Oh me God. I'm actually going to see it."

Quickly pulling on a pair of trousers, Armstrong and Anna slipped out to her room. Telling her to keep watch, Armstrong took his knife, and inserted it in the crack in the paneling. Easing out the section of paneling, he reached behind it for the velvet pouch. He hefted it in his hand for a moment, feeling the weight of the massive rock. He tossed it to her, then carefully repositioned the panel, rubbing with his fingers to remove any traces of it being disturbed.

She let out a soft gasp of awe as she slipped the glittering stone from the bag and held it up, slowly spinning on its golden chain, its facets brilliantly scintillating as they cast racing flashes of light on the walls. "Oh my God," she breathed. "It's absolutely incredible. To think I've been sleeping here, just inches from it." She looked at him. "Do you really believe it's the Goliath Stone?" She bit her lip to hold back her tears.

Armstrong shrugged as he crossed and stood behind her. "Damned if I know," he said and cupped her breasts in his hands. "It should lie here, between these, and not in some bloody shrine."

She kissed him, then shook her head. "No, my darling. This is going to be displayed in much more splendor and for a whole nation to admire. I'd be much too afraid to keep it for myself. Look at it. Is it just a diamond, or does it really have the power of a seer stone?"

Armstrong watched it spin, and as he did so, the sun dipped below the horizon, sending one last ray through the window, which seemed to bathe the stone in an explosion of light. Armstrong gasped. For a moment he felt a thrill of awe and dread. Then the sun was gone and the stone was only a piece of crystallized carbon, dull and lifeless in the twilight.

Before he could answer, she heard Ivan walk along the passage outside and, looking at Armstrong, wearing just trousers and singlet, she said, "We'd better break this up. You standing there in your skivvies – what would people say? She patted his rear as she left the room.

Back in his own room he picked up his clothes. Someone, most likely Ivan, had carefully cleaned and sewn his tunic but it still showed signs of hard wear. He debated whether or not to dress in his best uniform but, deciding that they still may have some hard slogging to go, he dressed in the old clothes.

That evening they all met for dinner, including a pale and shaken Boyle and the two subalterns. They sat around the table as the train rattled through the night. Ivan made a great effort and presented a meal worthy of the occasion. The atmosphere was buoyant – partly because all felt this was the last night before Jassy, partly because of Anna's presence at the table, and partly because Kiev was behind them. As Boyle pointed out, with Kaminski dead and his men in disarray, the possibility of organized pursuit was remote. Hall seemed entranced by Anna. He sat beside her talking, his face flushed, whether from the icy winds of the footplate or from Anna's proximity, Armstrong wasn't sure. He felt a twinge of unease. Hall was no fool. Although his thin clever face appeared to be engrossed with Anna's charms, he could be probing her story.

The talk moved to the events of the previous night. Armstrong told them of his recognition of the countess' agent and said the fact that it had worried him enough to have all men ready for instant action had gone a long way towards giving them the edge when Kaminski attacked. Hall and Boyle told them about their involvement with the fighting. He, Hall and Tolstoi had been negotiating with the White commander of the district regarding their journey when his window had crashed in on them and a bomb landed on the floor – a primitive bomb in a tape wrapped tin about the size of a tea caddy, but with a very short fuse, hissing smoke and sparks into the air.

For one frantic moment they had all jammed in the door as they tried to get out of the room, then they were through and running for safety. Boyle, being the slowest was nearest to the bomb when it exploded and he had been battered by the blast. The building had filled with smoke and flames, and the uninjured Hall and Tolstoi decided to get Boyle back to the train, arriving in time to see the end of Kaminski's fighting with Armstrong.

The meal broke up. Hall took a reluctant leave of Anna and went on a tour of inspection. The subalterns went back to their car. Boyle went to bed and Armstrong, after talking for a while with Tolstoi and Anna, decided to do the same. Despite the soreness of his wounds he fell asleep almost immediately and slept deeply as the train labored through the night.

Dawn. The sun was a pallid imitation of the one that set in such splendor the previous night. Today it was a barely seen orb. The day was gray and cold with flurries of snow streaking past the train. The engine too was in trouble. It was rapidly becoming obvious that it was in need of a major overhaul. No matter what pressure the engineer was able to coax from the boiler, the engine could barely reach twenty miles per hour. Steam hissed from every joint and coupling as the train crawled across the land.

Armstrong and O'Reilly were on the footplate, both of them muffled up against the raw morning. He had taken over from Hall at six am, despite the man's protestations that he, Armstrong was not yet recovered enough to stand watch. Well, maybe he wasn't. But Hall had done enough. Someone had to be here, ready to sound the alarm. So Armstrong endured the twinges from his back, the icy wind across his bruised face, and thought of Anna and the future.

Jamerinka was the next town, about an hour ahead of them. The last town before the frontier. In fact, just forty kilometers from Rumania. Once through Jamerinka it would be less than two hours to the relative safety of that beleaguered nation.

O'Reilly left the footplate to return a few minutes later with a jug of Ivan's magnificent coffee. He poured it for Armstrong, himself and the two trainmen. The four men drank its welcome warmth in silence for a few moments, then the engineer nudged the fireman and indicated the falling pressure gauge. The fireman, with a shake of his head, again began to throw logs into the fire box.

Hall appeared after a while to allow Armstrong to go to breakfast, who thankfully sat at the table as Ivan – well educated by now to the appetites of his charges – placed a large, western style breakfast in front of him. Boyle was at the table, looking much stronger after a night's rest. Tolstoi was not to be seen, nor was Anna.

"Miss DeCourville still sleeping?" Armstrong queried.

Boyle shook his head. "No, I'm afraid not. One of the subalterns came through a while ago and it seems that one of the men who was wounded yesterday had taken a turn for the worse. She's gone there to nurse him, apparently she's had some nursing experience."

"Has she though?" said Armstrong, surprised. "I didn't know that."

Boyle leaned back in his chair and thoughtfully eyed Armstrong. "I think there's a lot we don't know about that young lady. But then, maybe it's none of our business." He took a slow sip at his coffee. "What are your plans when we get back to Jassy?"

Armstrong thought for a moment, then said, "I'm not sure. Be guided by circumstance I suppose. Theoretically I should wait there until the last minute in case her majesty decides to leave with me in the Bristol, but I don't think there's any chance of her changing her mind. Apart from that I'll see what orders are sent from London. How about you, sir?"

Boyle grunted. His face showed indecision for a second, then he masked it. "I shall return to Russia I suppose, if I can't stay in Rumania. I am still on the transport mission there and I'll be close if she needs me."

Both men were silent, thinking of the uncertain future, then the scream of the train whistle broke into their thoughts. Armstrong was on his feet immediately. "That'll be Jamerinka," he said. "Corporal!" and as Brewer came from the kitchen where he had been eating, "everyone on full alert, pass the word."

Brewer ran to the other cars to ensure the men were at readiness for action and Armstrong, after strapping on his gun, went to the footplate.

"Set up the Hotchkiss?" O'Reilly's voice.

"Yeah. You'd better do that," said Armstrong as he put field glasses to his eyes. Jamerinka! Right ahead where the two lives of track seemed to meet in a needle point. A cluster of low buildings and the inevitable onion-domed church.

Slowly, the engine wheezed its way the last few kilometers to the town. Armstrong bit his lip. Here was probably the last chance for the Reds to stop them. He had no doubt that they knew of the value of their cargo. That sort of thing was impossible to keep secret. Kaminski had known that the cargo was special and if he knew, then the whole of Moscow did too.

He tensed as he saw ahead an engine, standing on an adjacent track, steam lazily curling from its stack, with one car hitched to it.

"She's flying Rumanian colors," said Hall, his glasses glued on the other engine. Armstrong nodded agreement. He too could see the blue, yellow, red tricolor flag prominently displayed on the engine and painted on the car.

"Looks like an escort to take us to Jassy," he said and tugged the whistle cord a couple of times. He saw the white puffs of steam from the other engine before the answering whistles reached them. "I'd better report to Boyle," he said. "Looks like friendlies." He passed O'Reilly snugged down in the logs, the tip of the Hotchkiss pointing out at the other engine. "Keep that thing ready, but it looks as if we're among friends," he said. "Don't relax until I tell you."

"'Tis ready I am melord," said O'Reilly as Armstrong dropped down to the deck of 451 and entered the door.

"Looks like we have a welcoming committee," he said to Boyle and told him of the other train.

Boyle, looking pleased that the Rumanian authorities had arranged a welcome, began pulling on his overcoat, ready to meet the escort. Armstrong went back to the tender and stood up above O'Reilly watching the train as they neared it.

The soldiers in the waiting car and engine were leaning out the windows and cheering as Boyle's train drew alongside. Armstrong watched this with a frown. It seemed somewhat odd that the welcoming force had not been paraded for a formal military reception. Particularly with European soldiers being such sticklers for protocol.

Boyle's train drew level with the other and came to a halt as officers in the welcoming force stood at the salute. Armstrong returned the salute just as he caught sight of a whistle in one man's mouth. "I don't like this," he shouted to O'Reilly. "Stand by."

The whistle blew. With a roar, an explosion bucked Armstrong off his feet as it split open the engine with an astonishing, earsplitting gush of steam. The doors of the other train flung open and out poured soldiers – soldiers wearing the field gray of imperial Germany. Their rifles began firing as soon as they hit the track, and most of them stormed the third and last car. The one with the gold. The one Anna was nursing in.

O'Reilly needed no orders. Even as the doors of the other train burst open, he blazed away with the Hotchkiss. Above the roar of steam and the banging of his own revolver Armstrong could hear the man screaming curses as he hosed a stream of bullets at the enemy.

The Germans that had been detailed to attack the forward part of the train melted away under the intense fire of the Hotchkiss. On the German tender, soldiers had raised a heavy machine-gun but before they could bring it into action, O'Reilly's fire swept across and they were killed. Armstrong could see that fire was coming from both 451 and the other cars. At least the enemy hadn't achieved complete surprise.

The German train began to move even as the attacking force streamed across. With steam hissing from its cylinders it chugged backwards, away from the action and O'Reilly's fire.

"Keep firing, O'Reilly," yelled Armstrong. He scrambled to the front of the tender and took a quick glance at the footplate. The engineer and fireman were down, either dead or unconscious. Hall was standing in the corner of the footplate, revolver in hand, waiting for a target to present itself.

"George!" Armstrong roared. "Up here and back up O'Reilly.

Hall nodded, squeezed off a couple of shots and jumped up beside Armstrong.

"You stay here. I'm going to check the Colonel."

Hall got down beside O'Reilly in time to put another pannier on the gun. Armstrong dropped down to 451 just as a wild-eyed German came up the steps and lunged at him with his bayonet. Armstrong, without breaking stride, shot him then hammered on the armored door. "Open up," he hollered. Brewer's face appeared at the window and the door swung open.

Inside the car the two sappers were firing through partly opened windows. Boyle was on one knee, carefully triggering off shots from his Webley. From the kitchen came the boom of Ivan's antique rifle and the crack of Tolstoi's revolver. Armstrong squatted down beside Boyle and told him of the damage to the engine and what he had observed of the fight so far.

Boyle looked at him. His eyes were red with fury at being thwarted this close to Jassy. "Where the hell did these Germans come from, this deep inside Russia?"

"Probably rustled up by the countess," grunted Armstrong. "I knew damn well I'd recognized that bastard at Trubchevsk." He squeezed off a couple of shots at a running German and cursed when he missed. "He must have got a signal to her. And it's easy to get troops through the lines. Hell, what bloody lines."

The firing slackened because of an absence of targets as most of the attacking force was now out of sight at the rear of the train. "We can be glad that the Tsar had a tyrant's distrust of his subjects and built this car so strong," Boyle said. "At least the crown jewels are safe."

"I'm going to get Anna," said Armstrong.

Boyle swung his head to look at him. A flat refusal hovered on his lips, then his gazed softened and he said. "Good luck, keep your head down," then turned back to the window and squeezed off another shot.

Armstrong ran to the rear door, lifted the bar and cracked it open. The plate was empty, except for a dead German. He slipped out to the next car, the door of which was splintered and bullet pocked, and yelled a warning that he was coming in before he slammed it open with a kick. The firing had here stopped, as if the attack had been beaten off. But at a cost.

This was the car that held the actual state archives. The bulky volumes and boxes of documents had been stacked around the outside of the car, which fact had stopped a lot of the bullets. But not enough. The subaltern in charge of this car lay dead, his youthful eyes vacantly staring. The men in this car were now under the control of a veteran Sergeant.

"Have you heard from the others?" Armstrong asked.

The man shrugged. "No sir," he said.

Armstrong cursed and ran. The gold car had borne the brunt of the attack, as if the Germans had known of its contents.

Armstrong ran through the car, jumping over dead and wounded men to get to the next door. Before he reached it there was a shuddering crash and he lost his balance as the train shot backwards several feet. He scrambled to his feet again and realizing what had caused the shock, sprinted for the door, ice-cold fear in his guts.

This door had not been penetrated and was still barred. He wasted precious moments as he tore the bar out and flung it down. Pulling open the door, he rushed through, to see the third car already fifty feet away and gathering speed.

He leapt to the track and began frantically running after the car as the German manned engine pulled it faster and faster. But the gap increased. Through blood reddened eyes he saw the back door of the train flung open. He saw Anna appear. He saw her arm fling high. He saw something small and black come curving towards him. He saw a soldier, dressed in field gray fling his arms around her. He saw the German laugh at the sight of him running. Then his flying feet caught a sleeper and he fell as the train swept away from him. He fell flat on his stomach, sliding over the sleepers, fell so that his nose was scant inches from the object she had thrown. The black velvet bag that contained the Goliath Stone.

CHAPTER EIGHTEEN

Armstrong watched the train dwindle in the distance. He reached out and pulled the velvet pouch to him, feeling the hard rock within, as rage and fear churned within him. Running feet crunched the gravel behind him and he heard O'Reilly's voice shouting.

"Are ye all right, melord? Did yon buggers shoot ye?"

Armstrong shook his head as he got up. O'Reilly fussed over him, brushing the gravel off his overcoat and talking all the time. "I thought you'd gone fooking west when I saw you fall. I thought the bastards had shot ye. Thank the Jasus that you're not been hit. Now don't you worry about that Miss Anna too much, melord. She's a clever girl is that one and you can bet your life she'll be all right."

Armstrong looked at him with eyes so filled with fury that O'Reilly fell back a step.

"How the hell do I find them? How can I find where she'll be? The fucking Germans have raped half of Europe. Do you think they'll treat Anna differently? Those bastards shot Edith Cavell, remember."

"Ah yes, melord, but it don't do any good to think on that now. What we want to do is find them first. For sure they can't go far into Russia in those uniforms, so they must either come back this way or they've got lorries waiting somewhere."

Armstrong stood looking at the now empty tracks as they two lines melded into a single filament across the plain. "Yeah," he muttered. "So where the hell is somewhere?"

O'Reilly tugged at his sleeve. "Lieutenant Hall is coming," he whispered, a sly look in his eye. "You'd better put that little baggy in your pocket before he see's it, melord."

Armstrong grunted and stuffed the pouch in his pocket as Hall approached them.

"You all right, old boy?" Hall said, eyeing Armstrong with concern. "Such a damn stroke of ill luck with Anna being in that carriage just then."

"I feel like hell," Armstrong said bleakly. "But I'm going to find her and if they've harmed her, I'll kill every last mother's son of them."

Hall kicked at the gravel, his eyes not meeting Armstrong's "Yes, well. All we can do is hope and pray about her. But in the meantime we have to do something more pressing. We have to get moving. The Colonel wants a council of war, so let's get back to him."

Armstrong turned without a word and, blocking out all thoughts of Anna, walked back to the remains of their train. The pain from his wounds was forgotten, leaving him like an automaton. He was without feelings or cares beyond the one burning desire to kill as many Germans as he could if they harmed her.

Boyle was out on the track, giving orders to the remaining subaltern about care for the injured. He saw Armstrong and cocked an enquiring eyebrow. Hall shook his head and Boyle uttered a short barking expletive, then he turned to the cars and bellowed. "Every one out on the track! Fall in for orders."

Quickly the men fell in. Even the walking wounded came to listen. Boyle eyed them grimly as the subaltern and Hall reported to him.

"Casualties?" he queried.

Three dead, including the subaltern in the archive car, Hall reported. Six wounded, two seriously. Which left him with five fit men. The bullion car had contained twenty men, including the other subaltern, now they were all dead or captured. The engineer and fireman had been stunned by the explosion but were recovering. Of the others, none had been hurt, thanks to Marie Feodorovna's armor-plating and O'Reilly's enthusiastic use of the Hotchkiss.

"The Germans detonated a mine under our engine and it's a total wreck," Boyle said. "So we have to find transport. I want search parties to scour the area. George! You take O'Reilly and the Rumanian sergeant. The two sappers take a couple of the Rumanian's and form another search party. That leaves two men plus Lieutenant Armstrong, Ivan, and myself to keep the fort here."

Armstrong interrupted. "I want to take part in the search as well."

Boyle looked at him. "You look like hell son," he said. "You and I have been bashed about a bit. Let the fit men do the walking. It will be faster that way."

Armstrong grunted acknowledgement as Boyle continued giving orders. "Now it's mid-morning. That means there's about seven hours of daylight left. So talk to people, find out what's available and take it. If we have to use mules, sobeit. Take plenty of ammunition and don't let any one stop you. Keep an eye out this direction. If I have to recall you, I'll fire a verey flare."

The search parties left. Armstrong supervised the unhappy task of clearing up after the battle. Townspeople began to appear and Armstrong asked for their help to remove the dead to the local mortuary for burial as it was now impracticable to take the dead back to Jassy. Someone got the local undertaker and the bodies were taken, two at a time, Germans and Rumanian, on a plain handcart.

Armstrong examined the German dead to see if he recognized any, but they were all enlisted men – no officers among the dead. Their rifles and ammunition he collected to add to his arsenal. He checked the condition of the fireman and engineer. He found them sitting on a buckled footplate determinedly getting drunk from a bottle of vodka. For them the trip was over. The engine itself was tilted half off the tracks. The damp odor of steam mingled with the stench of high explosive. The mine had detonated right under the front wheels, separating them from their bogie and splitting open the boiler. The track was a mess of bent rails and broken ties around a deep crater. He thought it fortunate that they had almost stopped rolling when the mine went off, otherwise 451 could have rolled into the crater too.

And so the hours passed. Armstrong kept busy, refusing to rest and unwilling to take the time to eat when Ivan prepared a meal. The cars grew cold, there being no steam heat, so he had Ivan light the big stove in 451. He cleaned his Colt, wishing that it was pointing at the head of the bastard that had pulled Anna back into the car. Again he paced the track, careless of the burning pain from the wound in his back. And slowly the hours passed.

Brewer returned driving a small van, confiscated he said at rifle point. It would take very little of their cargo but it was a start. He said that if there had been any more transportation in Jamerinka it had been hidden when the townspeople realized that the aliens would be needing it.

Mid afternoon. Hall and the Rumanian sergeant returned empty handed saying that O'Reilly had disappeared and then was seen in the distance riding a horse in a southerly direction. In view of the fact that he had not informed them of his plans, they didn't have a clue as to his whereabouts.

Boyle walked the track with Armstrong. Both men were silent as they paced from the engine to the archive car and back again. Sixty paces and turn. Sixty paces back. Again and again they stepped the distance, each lost in his own bitter thoughts. Each thinking of the woman they had let down. Boyle, because of the gold he had wanted to return to his love, the queen. Armstrong because he blamed himself for not insisting that Anna stay in the safety of 451. Thirty minutes went by. They came to the end of the archive car and turned to come back again when a sound intruded in their silence. They stared at each other and, yes there it was again. A steam whistle. A train whistle.

Armstrong roared. "Stand to. Man your positions," as he ran towards the tender and the Hotchkiss. Boyle leaped up to the door of 451 like a young man, drawing his revolver as he did so. Rifles appeared at windows as the company prepared for battle.

Armstrong, gasping for breath, cocked the action of the Hotchkiss and then jumped to the roof of 451 the better to see. Again the whistle. Eerily, mournfully moaning across the plains. Then a series of short blasts. Armstrong, head craning in all directions, suddenly saw a whisp of vapor rise then fade away. From the south. Not the Germans returning. Binoculars to eyes he watched for a sight of a train. There! Just visible, coming out from a cutting, an engine. My God it was just an engine. No cars attached. From the south!

He looked at the south siding points through the glasses. They were closed. But the ones to the north were open because the German train had been able to come down and couple to the last car. That meant that the oncoming engine couldn't pass without stopping.

The engine was close enough now for him to see that it was a behemoth. It thundered along the track, its blue enamel paint glistening in the afternoon sun. Brass fittings gleamed, even the wheels were painted silver. And glittering on the front was the great golden two-headed eagle of imperial Russia. Again the whistle sounded in staccato blasts. Exhilaration rose in him as he saw a head sticking out the side of the cab. A narrow rat-faced head.

Protesting metal howled as brakes were applied when
the engine entered the siding and came to a halt opposite 451.
O'Reilly's face, ginning with devilish glee, looked at him, and
his screeching Irish voice yelled. "Ain't I the best fooking thief
in the whole British army then? You sent me fer something on
wheels and I've obliged ye. What do ye think of her, squire?"

Armstrong, grinning, looked at the engine in
admiration. O'Reilly's ebullience lifting his spirits despite his
troubles. "That has to be the most elegant engine I've ever
seen. How the hell did you find it?" As he spoke the engine
was surrounded by his own soldiers and Boyle, all loudly
cheering and yelling questions at O'Reilly. "Quiet!" Boyle
roared. "I want to hear O'Reilly."

"Tracked it down like a bird dog, melord." He turned
to the men in the cab with him. "All right you hairy sods. Get
yer fat arses out of here. Move it, move it, get down to the
ground before I belt ye another one."

Under O'Reilly's haranguing, the train engineers
dropped sullenly to the ground – one of them sporting a
swollen and partially closed eye. "Daren't leave 'em here,
guvner," he said. "They might take the engine away. Most
reluctant they were to come with me. I had to argue with one
of them." Armstrong and the rest gathered around the
Irishman and he preened himself under their attention. "Yer
see, gents, one of the things that me sainted father bequeathed
me was the sharpest set of ears in county Kerry. Which he had
to have on account of being a champeen poacher and yon lord
of the manor being a hard-hearted member of the fooking
aristocracy who had threatened to fire a shot-gun up his arse if
he caught him a-stealing of his game like."

Armstrong groaned. "Get to the point O'Reilly."

"Ah, yes. Well yer see, I was standing looking around
fer something that moved like, as was me orders, when I saw
this here old nag. Acting on me orders I appropriated it in the
name of Great Britain and the greater Irish people. Well, I'd
no sooner got on its back when me ears picked up this faint
sound. I recognized it straight away as a steam valve popping
off so I rides off in the direction of the sound and finds this pair
of diddicoys a-starting of their daily polishing of the
brightwork on the engine. So, I applied me well-known powers
of persuasion and they said they'd be glad to help us travelers
get to Jassy."

The engineers were closely questioned by Tolstoi and
Hall. Their sullen answers at first drew amazed exclamations
then gales of laughter. Even Armstrong with his limited

Russian understood enough to grin and shake his head in disbelief.

"What's the story? What's so funny?" asked Boyle.

Hall explained. "It seems the Tsar's train was once taking him the Black Sea for a holiday when his engine broke down. Ever since then at Vapnyarka, a few miles down line, there has been kept, by imperial decree, a spare engine, with steam up and manned day and night by shifts of men. And no one, Colonel, no one ever thought to rescind the order. This couple of scallywags have spent the war here boondogging. No wonder they objected to O'Reilly borrowing their engine."

The discovery of the engine was a great boost to the spirits of the party. After the other searchers had been recalled by the firing of a flare, the engine was manned by the Rumanian engineers, switched to the main line, coupled to the remaining coaches and then taken past the crater on the siding line. This engine to the old one was a prince to a pauper. It pushed the cars to Vapnyarka, then using the turntable there, it was coupled to the front of the cars to pull them the rest of the way.

The forty miles to the frontier flashed by as the big engine reached sixty miles per hour with contemptuous ease. O'Reilly, basking in the congratulations of the company, was at his most insufferable, crowing over his achievement until Armstrong groaned, "O'Reilly, I shall personally recommend you for the Imperial Train Stealing medal. Now enough," and he went to the footplate.

The miles melted away. The short winter daylight was fading as Armstrong finally saw the barrier across the track and the huts that marked the frontier. Rumania!

Goggle-eyed frontier guards stared at the imposing engine and car in awe. After presentation of credentials and frantic phone calls to Jassy they were allowed to proceed. The reception in Jassy was tumultuous. The platform was brightly lit with searchlights and flares. A band played. A guard presented arms. Government officials were there by the score. Curious spectators were lifted from their wartime apathy long enough to cheer and wave flags. A flamboyantly dressed aide to the king represented the royal family.

Boyle was whisked away in a car sent by Marie. Fresh guards were posted on the train and, after much hand shaking and cheek kissing, Armstrong and party were taken in cars to the allied mission headquarters. Rooms were found for Tolstoi and Ivan. Streat and Brewer were told they would be commended for a job well done, and finally the three, Armstrong, O'Reilly, and Hall, were alone in their rooms.

Armstrong walked to his bedside locker, took out the last of the whiskey he had brought from Stavros and poured equal measures into three glasses. He passed one each to O'Reilly and Hall, then raised the third glass to them and said. "Gentlemen, here's to you. Bottoms up!" He drained his glass in one gulp.

"Cheers," said Hall.

"God bless ye, squire," said O'Reilly.

The two drained their glasses and then looked at each other, the well-bred lieutenant and the impudent acting temporary-unpaid sergeant, and they grinned at each other with mutual respect. Then O'Reilly winked and nodded his head towards Armstrong. "And what are we to do with this boyo, Mr. Hall? Do ye think he'll be safe to leave on his own tonight?"

Armstrong, as if ignoring their attention, slowly poured himself another drink then sat on his bed and looked at them. "I know what my next step is," he said. "And I know when to do it. Tonight!" He took a slow meditative sip as they looked enquiringly at him. "The point is that what I am going to do is outside the scope of my orders, is most definitely illegal, and could cause one hell of an international incident. It could also result in a court-martial and a firing squad."

Hall grinned again. "Sounds like we're back to the normality then, so don't hog the whiskey old boy and tell us all about it."

Armstrong refilled their glasses as he talked. "The quickest way to find out where Anna is would be to find out where the gold is. And you can be sure that one person who knows the answer to that is the countess! Therefore I propose to kidnap her and force the facts from her."

Hall frowned. "Surely she'll be on her toes after such a coup. Might be impossible to get near her."

"That we'll have to find out," said Armstrong. "But I've had time to think about this and I'm sure that as far as she's concerned no one knows that she's involved. She doesn't know that I've recognized one of her men."

"O'Reilly slapped his leg and his eyes glittered with mischief. "That's right, melord, and tis a damned good idea, even if I didn't think of it first."

Armstrong looked at them. "I'd appreciate your help, but knowing the consequences of failure it's all right if you refuse. After all George, you're regular army. It doesn't matter a toot to me if I get cashiered, but to you it's a career.

Hall smiled sadly and said to O'Reilly. "Just listen to this man being so noble. One would hardly expect such from an ignorant colonial, would one." He looked at Armstrong. "My dear boy. I am in intelligence! Military intelligence. Now there are three ways of obtaining intelligence. One buys it. One steals it. Or one extorts it. Buying means you have to bribe someone. Stealing covers everything from theft to eavesdropping. And of course, extortion means blackmail." His eyes glinted with sardonic humor. "These things are hardly what one expects from a true blue pukka sahib who's been educated in all the best schools. Eh what? Therefore I'm already outside the pale, and if I'm caught people will say, 'That's what can be expected from one of those intelligence blighters.' So what have I to lose?"

The others were silent for a moment, then O'Reilly said, "What the fook did he say, melord?"

Armstrong threw back his head and laughed. "He said he's with us you, dumb mick."

"Ah," said O'Reilly, a wicked glint in his eye. "'Tis a fine thing indeed then to see such a grand Englishman has the proper contempt for law and order. Is it possible that ye might have some Irish blood in you, sir?"

"God forbid," shuddered Hall.

"The first thing to do is to check the whereabouts of the countess. O'Reilly! Get your working clothes on and see what you can find out. Scout her house and the queen's residence." Armstrong checked his watch. "It's seven o'clock. We eat here at eight, so you have an hour." He turned to Hall. "George. I think we have to put on a bit of a show here, returning heroes and all that, just in case there's some loose lips who'd go flapping to our enemies. So we'll be very much in evidence until after dinner. As soon as O'Reilly returns and has eaten we'll firm up plans. All clear?"

And so it was agreed. O'Reilly slipped away like a wraith. Armstrong and Hall, dressed in their best uniforms, presented themselves for dinner and suffered the interested remarks of the allied officers, all of whom had heard of the exotic train and its cargo of crown jewels. They fended off questions, politely accepted the congratulations, made excuses for Armstrong's battered face, and, pleading fatigue, went to their room as soon as possible.

They dressed in old clothes, Armstrong wearing the same boiler suit he had worn to break into the Kremlin, then sat in silence, awaiting O'Reilly's return. Armstrong smoked a cigar, his thoughts bleakly focused on the immediate problem of the countess. Was it possible that he had been mistaken connecting the man in Trubchevsk to her? But someone had tipped off the Germans to the value of the train, and who more likely than she.

The door opened and O'Reilly entered, his lank hair in disarray from the balaclava he had just pulled off.

"News, gentlemen. I have news. There appears to be a jolly old celebration going on at the countess's house. The place is full of men, an when I took a peek through a window they all had glasses in hand and were hoc-heiling each other like a bunch of Orangemen who had pee'd over the Popes picture. And, squire!" He paused for effect. "One of the laddo's I recognized from the men you pointed out to me in Moscow."

Armstrong's mouth twisted into a grin that had no humor in it. "So the bitch is involved as I thought. Let's go and wring her pretty neck."

"Steady on old boy," said Hall. "Let's be a little subtle about it. The more time we have to work on her the more we'll find out, and we won't have any time at all if we're pursued by the entire German and Rumanian armies." He turned to O'Reilly. "What else did you observe?"

"This here gathering is keeping everyone busy on the main floor. All the servants are running around like lost souls, trying to keep the glasses filled." He rubbed his nose thoughtfully. "I think it'll be easy to get up the back and go over the roof until we're above her room and then drop down to her window. There's two sentries at the front and one that circles the building, yer see. So we snatch her, take her over the roof and lower her down wid a rope."

"Yes," said Armstrong thoughtfully "That should work. George, if you'll get a car and wait for us to lower her to you, O'Reilly and I will do the breaking in."

"How are you going to keep her quiet?" asked Hall.

Armstrong shrugged. "Gag her, I guess."

O'Reilly shook his head and leered. "Oh no melord. I've something much better than that. I paid a little visit to the infirmary here and swiped some ether. A couple of drops of that and the woman will be as silent as the grave."

"For God's sake don't kill her, man," said Hall, alarmed by talk of the grave.

"No chance of that, squire," said O'Reilly. "I used it before, yer see. There was this horse at the Ballybunion races..."

"Enough jawing, said Armstrong, impatient to be off. "George, you get the car, and let's get moving."

Hall stood up and pulled on his uniform overcoat. "Should we perhaps wait until this celebration is over and all is quiet?" he said.

O'Reilly shook his head. "No gents, believe me, the best time to break into a house is when everyone's having a jolly time getting pissed. Nothing can happen, they think. It's when it's dark and quiet that sentries get nervous and sounds are heard."

Armstrong grunted agreement and Hall shrugged acceptance. Five minutes later they were rolling through the cobbled streets of Jassy in the landau.

"What do we do with her once we've got her?" queried Hall.

"Take he to the farm," said Armstrong, his thoughts ranging far ahead. "It's lonely there and with any luck we'll be uninterrupted."

Nothing more was said until they neared the house. The night was dark and the moon obscured. Street lighting was unknown in Jassy so they had only the lights of the car to show their way. They stopped in a street before the countess's house and Hall backed the car into a small lane between two buildings.

The three got out the car. O'Reilly hung a coil of rope around his shoulder, and they walked the rest of the way. Standing in shadows they looked at the house. It was ablaze with light and noise as O'Reilly had described. The entrance was flanked by civilian guards who periodically paced to the corner of the house and back again.

"Right, melords," said O'Reilly. "If Mr. Hall would stay in this general area, then you and me shall do a bit of climbing. We'll give an owl hoot when we're ready to be picked up in the car."

Nodding understanding, Hall remained in the shadows as Armstrong and O'Reilly disappeared into the murk of the side streets. Reaching the back of the house, they stood watching in a doorway across the street. The house was built close to the cobbled street with a tradesman door and much smaller window than at the front, as if the servants needed less light and air. The pair watched for a few minutes then O'Reilly nudged Armstrong as the door opened and a man appeared.

The man casually walked out to the street, looked all around, stamped his feet against the cold and went back inside.

"That's it," whispered O'Reilly. "Regular as clockwork. We've got about five minutes before he comes out again."

The two ran across to the house and Armstrong boosted O'Reilly up to a ledge where he caught hold of a drain pipe. Up he went, nimbly climbing hand over hand. Armstrong stood waiting, nervous taut, his thoughts focused on the operation. The rope snaked down. He tugged to make sure it was secure, then started to climb. Hand over hand he went up the two storied house, his feet scrambling for footholds. O'Reilly watched him, his white teeth visible in a grin against the blackness of his balaclava.

"To be sure 'tis a grand second-story man ye could be if ye were so inclined, melord," he whispered, as Armstrong rolled over the eave of the roof and knelt for a moment. His back hurt and it felt like he'd burst the stitching. Ignoring it, he stood up and looked around. The roof had an acute angle to it in the European style, but the front and sides had a low crenulated wall around, probably to make the building more imposing. It served to make their task easier.

Feeling their way on the icy tiles, they crept to the front of the house and looked over the edge. Two guards stood at the door and the murmur of their voices rose in the night air. O'Reilly, all silent efficiency now that the serious moment was here, hung the line until it reached just below the countess's bedroom, then secured it to a crenellation and swung himself over. Quickly he slipped down to the window. Armstrong watched as O'Reilly stood on the windowsill and appeared to struggle with the shutters. Minutes went by, minutes when it should have taken seconds to open the catch. Armstrong watched, biting his lip. He wanted to whisper a question but didn't. If he could hear the murmur of the guards they could hear him.

He heard the definite snick of a lock opening and he saw O'Reilly freeze as he watched the guards below for signs of alarm. None came. He looked at Armstrong, stuck up a triumphant thumb, opened the shutter and slipped inside. His head was back within seconds to give an all clear signal. Armstrong slid down the rope to him, and was pulled inside by O'Reilly.

They closed the shutters behind them before opening the curtains. The room was empty, lit by low gaslight. The bed was turned down and a nightdress had been placed ready for the countess. It was warm in the room with a banked up fire glowing in the grate. Armstrong decided that her maidservant had prepared for the countess retiring and likely would not be back. The bed was as high as he remembered. Kneeling he pulled the skirt aside. Plenty of room there he thought. One of them behind the curtains and the other under the bed. He whispered to O'Reilly. "You have trouble with the shutter?"

"Aye. I did that. The securing bar was stuck, and it aint easy lifting it off with one hand."

"I guess she must have missed the papers from her safe then."

"Maybe, Guvner, maybe. But I didn't take them all, yer know, and I left it tidy."

"Well check it now, while we're waiting. If you hear a noise, you get under the bed and I'll take the curtains. If she brings a man in with her we'll have to silence him too."

O'Reilly grinned, his eyes devilish in the flickering fire light. He put his hand to his hip and pulled a cudgel from his trouser pocket. "Brought me shillelagh."

Armstrong patted him on the back and crept to the door while O'Reilly busied himself with the safe. He cracked the door open and listened. The noise downstairs was high, but he heard her silvery, derisive laugh above it and he thought for a moment of the time he'd spent with her. He closed the door and went to O'Reilly. The safe door was already open so he sat by the firelight and read the papers from it. Time passed. O'Reilly stood by the door periodically opening it and checking on the party below. There were more letters from Ernst. Ernst, in spite of being besotted with his wife was, an exceedingly smart man. The tone of his letters had changed and were full of gloomy predictions now that the Americans were in the war. In one letter, Ernst told her that he approved of her plan, but that she was to be careful because of the danger of either side hearing of it.

Armstrong thought over the implications. It was now clear that the men on the train in Moscow must have communicated with her and told her that the third carriage contained the bulk of the treasure. The crown jewels, because they were hid in wicker baskets and disguised as red cross supplies, could not have aroused the interest that the heavy boxes in the third car did.

Impatiently he swept the papers back in the safe and closed it. He checked his watch. Ten pm. God. Poor old Hall had been standing on that corner for over an hour. His back was painful but Armstrong ignored it and stood by the door. Thoughts of Anna flashed across his mind and he dismissed

them. They were dangerous and distracting from the job in
hand. More time passed. He ached for a smoke, anything to
break the boredom of waiting.

   At eleven o'clock on the dot, as if the German passion
for order governed all aspects of life, he heard a hubbub of
noise as people began to leave. The front door opened and
closed several times. Boisterous voices shouted farewells and
the hum of motor cars came from outside. He looked at
O'Reilly, lifted an eyebrow, and continued to listen. Minutes
ticked by. There was still a faint murmur of voices from below,
as if someone was having a last nightcap before bed.   He
checked his watch again. Eleven thirty. What was that? The
faint creak of a stair? He hissed at O'Reilly as he rushed to the
window, closing the curtains behind him.

   The door opened and she entered, as lethally beautiful
as he remembered. Armstrong, peering through a gap in the
curtain silently cursed, because a maid followed her into the
room. He watched, as the maid unhooked her dress, helped
her out of it, then hung the dress in the wardrobe.   The
countess undressed to the skin and the maid helper her into
her nightdress. Armstrong saw the bed skirt crack open and a
bright eye watch the proceedings with interest. The skirt
opened wider and an eyebrow was raised in query. Armstrong
put his hand through the curtain to make a thumbs down
motion. He didn't want the complication of having to subdue
the maid as well.

   The countess sat at her vanity while the maid unpinned
her hair and then brushed it. He studied her face as she sat in
profile to him. She had a self-satisfied curl to her lips as if life
was good to her. Despite himself he stirred as he watched her
in the diaphanous nightdress. God, but she was a good-looking
woman. She reached up a hand to stop the maid's brushing,
spoke in a low voice and stood. She picked up a scent bottle
and sprayed once under each ear, then she crossed to the bed
and got in the open sheets. The maid turned out the light, said
"Goodnight madam," and left.

   O'Reilly head came out from under the bed and looked
to the curtains. Armstrong stuck his hand through with the fist
closed. One, two, three, four, his fingers sprang open. On the
fourth finger, O'Reilly slid from under the bed and was on top
of the countess.   The air filled with the reek of ether.
Armstrong left the curtains and was hurtling towards the bed
when from somewhere a stray thought connected perfume and
bed. He swung towards the door as fingers scratched it and a
male voice whispered "Marthe? Liebchen."

Armstrong flung open the door to reveal a man, wearing pajamas with a dressing gown over them. A man who stared with dumb-struck amazement as Armstrong gritted, "Come in, liebchen." And pulled him in with his left hand as his right fist landed on the man's face with a smack like a butcher pounding a steak with a mallet. The man collapsed with a groan, and Armstrong stuck his head out the door. Left. Right. All clear. He shut the door and turned the lock. He looked at the man on the floor. Well, dammit, he felt good. That was the bastard from Trubchesvk.

The countess was giving a final twitch as he looked at her. She must have struggled like a wildcat, for nothing could be seen of O'Reilly but a hand protruding from a tangle of satin sheets, clamped upon her mouth. Armstrong gave an insane giggle as he pulled the sheets off O'Reilly. This was real Biograph stuff.

"Jumping Jasus, suffering Mary, and all the martyrs. Yon woman just about killed me," O'Reilly gasped, his cheek bloodied from the scratching of the countess's fingernails. "The bitch fights worse than a couple of Kilkenny cats."

"She' out good," said Armstrong lifting her lid to see her eye rolled back. "Get the man tied up while I get clothes on her. Make sure he's gagged. I don't want any outcry until we're well clear."

"Fooking officers get all the good jobs," said O'Reilly as he wrapped the man's wrists with the dressing gown belt.

Armstrong searched the wardrobe and found a pair of riding breeches which he tried to pull on to the countess. But her body was so limp from the ether it was extremely difficult. He struggled until, with a snarl of exasperation, unwilling to spend more time in the house, he gave up and bundled her clothes in a blanket. Damn the woman, he thought. He slung her over his shoulder, just as she was, and went to the window. Opening it he looked out. The two guards were still there. He pulled the rope in and tied it around her. "I'm going up," he whispered to O'Reilly. "You tie her clothes on and then come up last. Make sure the shutters are closed. With any luck the alarm won't be given until morning. Shove that man under the bed."

He shinned up the rope, a fierce joy within him. He's hit that bastard so hard he doubted he'd ever wake up and he had the countess in his power. He reached the roof, and hauled her up. She came up like a corpse, so loose she almost slipped through the rope he had tied around her. He pulled her over the edge and laid her in the wet snow behind the crennelation. Next her clothes. One pull and they were up. Lastly came O'Reilly, swinging up like a monkey.

They gathered up the rope and ran to the back of the house. O'Reilly secured it while Armstrong went back to the countess. As he picked her up he heard the hoot hoot of O'Reilly's call to Hall. Armstrong had a sudden wild thought – he hoped the guards didn't know the difference between an Irish owl and a Rumanian one. He looked over the edge. All clear. Armstrong went down first. He watched the rope snake upwards then the countess was lifted by O'Reilly to the parapet and slowly lowered.

My God, a noise! Armstrong ran for the corner as the back door opened and a man stepped out. O'Reilly had heard him too, for he stopped lowering. Armstrong stared bugeyed at the spectacle of the man standing calmly sucking on a pipe while less than six feet above his head the almost naked body of the Countess Von Hess-Steiner slowly spun on the end of a line.

The man stood there, breathing in the cold night air. Minutes passed. A drop of melted snow from the countess's body splashed beside the man. Armstrong tensed, his knife in hand, ready to throw, but the man knocked out his pipe against the wall and went back inside. Armstrong ran forward as her ice-cold body was lowered into his arms. He felt a pang of conscience, but suppressed it as the rope end came snaking down. He stood for a moment watching O'Reilly come down the drain pipe like a human fly, then he ran for the cover of darkness.

He stood, with the woman slung across his shoulder, watching in a fever of impatience as O'Reilly coiled the rope, picked up the bundle of clothing and ran to him. "Where's Mr. Hall?" O'Reilly panted.

Armstrong looked around. "Probably frozen solid to the seat of the car. Goodammit, "I'm freezing myself. Here, roll the blanket around her while I hold her upright."

They had just completed this as Hall and the car arrived. The countess was soon stuffed in the back sear and they were speeding to the farm. Hall drove like a madman. He'd taken one horror-stricken look at the countess's bare legs and feet protruding from the blanket and he opened the throttle wide.

"How long is she out for?" he asked.

"I don't know," O'Reilly answered. "I've only given it to horses."

"Oh God," groaned Hall, and he drove even faster. They reached the farm house within fifteen minutes. Hall had already sent word by one of the sappers so that they would be expected. Armstrong picked up the countess and carried her to a main floor room that had been prepared.

He dropped her on the bed and looked at the others who had crowded in. "You men get out," he said. "I'm going to dress her. Alone. But throw some towels in the door."

O'Reilly and Hall left as Armstrong peeled the blanket from her. She uttered a small moan and her eyelids flickered, then she was still again. He ripped away the soaked nightdress, wincing at the bruises the rope had left on her skin. He picked up a towel that someone had thrown in, a rough gray peasant's towel and vigorously rubbed her body until the skin glowed. She moaned in protest a couple of times and her muscles, seemed to recover tone. At least it was easier now to pull on the riding breeches and a heavy sweater. O'Reilly poked his head in the door.

"I bought the rope melord, and also a bucket."

"What's the bucket for?"

O'Reilly rubbed his chin, "I've remembered that people throw up sometimes after ether so I thought we'd better have it."

Armstrong nodded acknowledgement as he tied her wrists and legs to the bedposts. He stood back and watched her. With her hair bedraggled, her face blotched, she looked a far cry from the elegant noblewoman he knew. He left the oil lamp burning and went to the other room.

He sat down with the others. One of the sappers that had been keeping guard on the Bristol came in and reported that all was well with the plane and no patrols had appeared. They sat around the kitchen table drinking coffee as they talked in low voices.

Presently a low moan was heard from the room and Armstrong stood up and went in. Her eyes were open and she was staring uncomprehendingly. Standing above her, he watched as her eyes focused upon him. She shook her head and closed her eyes. The head shaking caused a reaction for she jerked up, as far as the ropes would allow and looked frantically around. Armstrong picked up the bucket and held it for her as she vomited into it. When she had finished he wiped her lips with a towel as she sank back in the pillow.

She spoke, without opening her eyes. "Armstrong. You bastard. You'll die for this."

"Yeah," he answered her. "That's possible. But you'll be dead first."

She sneered. "So the brave aviator makes war on women now."

"Of course!" Armstrong said in a surprised tone. "Doesn't everyone?"

"What do you want? Why have you captured me?"

"I want information about the train attack. Why did you do it? What did you do with the boxes on the train? Where did they take them? What happened to the people on the train? Simple questions require simple answers. Give those answers and you will be released."

She affected a wide-eyed look of amazement. "What on earth are you talking about? Trains? Men? Boxes? You must be mad. Do you realize I am a personal friend of the King? You damned fool I'll have you shot for this insult."

Armstrong leaned over her and spoke in level tones. "Let me assure you, Countess, that we have read the contents of your safe. We have identified your men as being German agents, and we have further proof of your involvement with plots against the sovereign nation of Rumania. This country is in a state of war, and that's all the legality we need. We're entitled to shoot you now and report it later. In any case, no one knows where you are and no one is going to unless you answer my questions."

She looked around, taking in her surroundings. She looked at her clothing and became conscious of the rough material against her skin. "Who dressed me?"

"I did."

Her thin lips twisted in a sneer. "Did you enjoy yourself?"

"I've had more fun skinning rattlesnakes," he sneered back. "Now answer my questions."

"Go to hell."

Armstrong walked to the door. "Lieutenant Hall."

Hall appeared and made a great show of standing to attention before him. "Firing squad. Four men. Have them ready to parade at dawn. We'll shoot her then."

"Four men. Dawn sir. Yes sir," said Hall, all brisk efficiency.

Hall left him and he walked back to her bedside. "Have a good nights sleep, my dear Countess," he said. "I fear I shall sleep uneasily because the shooting of a woman is not a pleasant thing. But that is war, is it not? One must do unpleasant things."

Her face was white, ashen against the pillow. "If you shoot me, you'll never find out where the gold is."

"But we will," Armstrong said in a surprised voice. "Of course. I didn't tell you. We've also got the man who came to your room."

Her eyes opened wide and for a moment he saw real fear in them. "Werner?" she blurted out.

"The very man," said Armstrong cheerfully. "Werner. He will tell us what we want to know. He's out in the barn. Watching the irons heat up."

"What do you mean?"

"I mean we're going to burn him until he tells us all he knows, my dear Marthe."

She raised herself on an elbow and cursed him in several languages. Armstrong waited her out and when she paused for breath he said, as if he was talking to himself. "Of course. I might change my mind and do the same to you – before I shoot you."

She said nothing but turned her head away and looked at the wall. Armstrong left her and went to the barn, taking Hall and O'Reilly with him. He gathered them and the sappers around him and said.

"She's a tough nut to crack, but I'm going to do it. Who can give me a good scream." They looked at him as if he's gone crazy and he explained. "I've told her that we also captured the man who came to her bedroom and we are going to torture him with hot irons, so I need a nice loud scream with some real agony in it. Any volunteers?"

O'Reilly face split in a wide grin. "'Tis myself can screech better than a banshee, I bet."

Armstrong nodded, "You have the floor O'Reilly. Let her rip."

O'Reilly threw back his head and uttered a bloodcurdling scream that had the men holding their hands over their ears before it died away in a ghastly gurgle. Armstrong stopped him and waited until five minutes had passed then he told him once more. This time O'Reilly's scream was even more prolonged, quavering in and out like a soul in torment. Armstrong passed cigarettes around then and they all had a smoke. Ten minutes passed before he ground out the stub of his cigarette and said. "Let's see what she thinks now."

He went back into the farmhouse and entered the room. She lay flat on her back and tears had wet her face. She looked at him with total contempt.

He took a notebook from his pocket. "Now, "I'm going to ask you the same questions, and if you give me different answers to him I'm going to burn him some more, do you understand?"

Her eyes blazed hatred at him as he sat on the bed and looked fully at her. "Where was the gold taken to?"

She spat at him and cursed him for a cowardly depraved pig. Then she said. "I'll tell you. Oh yes, I'll tell you. I'll tell you because it won't do you any good to know, because there's nothing you can do about it. You don't have the time. That poor boy out there means nothing to me. Men like you mean nothing to me. Just toys I use and throw away. Yes I'll tell you, my gallant aviator pig. I'll tell you because then you'll know that I've won. Because you're too late. The gold is in Odessa. I sent it to Odessa. I have a shop there that's sailing for Istanbul. And you can't do anything about it because you can't get there in time." She broke into hysterical weeping.

Armstrong stood, his mind in a turmoil. What she said had the ring of truth to it. And it made sense. Instead of smuggling the gold through the lines to the Germans, it would be at sea, probably in a cargo that was marked for a Russian port. Once out to sea her men could take over the ship and head for Istanbul. Her sobs abated and he said, almost disinterestedly. "The men and the nurse in the carriage. What happened to them?"

She made an impatient movement of her head, as if the question was of no importance. "Oh, I don't know. Werner said something about handing them over to a battalion of Rumanians in Odessa who have joined the Bolsheviks. Why do you ask?"

"To check your story against Werner's, madam," said Armstrong. "The sentence of death against you is lifted until we find if you're telling the truth. What is the name of the ship?"

She shook her head. "I don't know. Werner arranged it, And as far as I was concerned my part in the mission was over."

Armstrong left her and went back to the others. "Odessa," he said. "Odessa is where they went. And they must be there by now. George, I want you to wait until morning. Then take the Countess, put a blindfold on her and let her loose in Jassy. She's told me all I want to know."

Hall studied him. "What are you going to do?"

Armstrong looked at him in surprise. "Do?" he said. "I'm flying the Bristol to Odessa, of course."

*   *   *   *

Armstrong lay asleep. After interrogating the countess, the
Bristol had been wheeled out and readied for flight. Jassy to
Odessa was only one hundred and fifty miles by air, and he
wanted to arrive in daylight, so it was necessary to wait for the
right time to take off. It was decided that Hall had to stay in
Jassy and he had gone back to the mission to arouse Ivan, it
being thought necessary to have someone fluent in Russian
with Armstrong. Ivan had eagerly accepted the chance to be of
service. Not only was he willing to help find the lovely Anna,
but he was prepared to be left behind in Russia. O'Reilly, of
course, had insisted he be included, it being possible to jam
two people in the observer's cockpit. When all preparations
had been made, the three men rested, while Hall filled the air
with radio messages to agents in Odessa.

Armstrong slept in the barn, the countess being on the
only bed in the house. Dressed ready for flight and wrapped in
a blanket, he had lain on the straw and fallen into an exhausted
sleep – six o'clock having been set for take-off, leaving about
four hours for him and the others to rest. His sleep had been
deep at first, but as time went by, shallow and disturbed. Then
his hand found the Goliath stone, wrapped in its velvet bag,
safe in his trouser pocket.

Immediately tension left him and he lay quietly on his
back. His face became serene and, in the moonlight shining
through the open door, it seemed to radiate an aura of light.

Armstrong dreamt. He watched a youth put his hands
into a stream and carefully pick out stones. He saw the youth
stand and purposely stride across a narrow valley. He saw that
the youth was handsome and strong, full of confidence, his face
lit with elation. He saw the youth stop and whirl a sling above
his head so fast the leather sang in the air. He saw the youth
release the sling and a blur of light shoot from it. He saw the
light smash into the head of a giant, who fell with a great
clanging of armor. He saw the youth take the giant's sword
and, with one swing of his arm, strike off the giant's head. He
saw the youth hold the head high, and heard a roar of approval
from a host, watching from the valley's crest.

Scene followed scene in Armstrong's dream. Scenes
passed through his mind so fast it was as if he was in a
biograph theatre and the film had been sped up. He saw
armies wreak destruction upon large cities. He saw massacres
and triumphs. He saw great civilizations. He saw appalling
ignorance. He saw armies locked in battles, one after another,
the only difference being that weapons and costumes changed

with each battle. He saw his own war and watched thousands of men wallow like pigs in mud. And then he saw machines he didn't recognize. He saw planes. Not the flimsy, fabric covered planes he knew, but metal covered, sleek deadly machines that howled through the sky at amazing speeds without propellers. He saw railway engines pulling box-cars, and here the dream slowed its passage, as if to impress upon him the importance of what he was seeing. He saw the box-cars jammed with people who wore crudely shaped yellow stars sewn on their clothing. He saw the trains stop at an immense camp that seemed to stretch forever across a plain. He saw the passengers herded from the train, stripped naked and pushed into large chambers. He saw and heard their screams as they died. He saw large tractor-like machines with heavy blades in front, pushing the dead into mass graves. The scene changed. He saw ships wallowing with the weight of people in them. He saw the ships approach a shore at night and the people land and flee into the darkness. He saw the people become strong and vigorous as a new nation arose. He saw the new nation at war with its neighbors. He saw the people, young and old, soldiers and business men, Rabbi's and farmers, men, women, children, shouting, weeping, and praying with joy, as they fell to their knees before the temple wall in old Jerusalem. Then the dream changed, the visions faded but he felt warm and comfortable, and he sensed that he lay bathed in a pool of golden light. And the light took away his wounds and pains and, before it faded, he heard a voice, calm, measured, a voice that he heard, not with his ears but with his while being. A voice that said, "My people shall come home!"

Armstrong then lay in a sleep so deep it was close to death. Dreamless, peaceful sleep. Sleep that wiped away the bruises and wounds until they were no more. The wound on his back lost its angry fire and the bruises on his face were as they had never been. He slept, until Hall's hand shook him awake and Hall's voice quietly said. "It's time to go, Miles."

CHAPTER NINETEEN

Armstrong leaned forward, flexing his back muscles to relieve stiffness. He marveled that he no longer felt the pain of his wounds. In front of him the Falcon III engine roared with a self-satisfied bellow, as if pleased to be working after such a long rest. Off to his right the winter sun was thrusting its rays over the eastern horizon. Dawn! He wondered how many dawns he had watched from ten thousand feet since this war began. Dawn! Military planners were mesmerized by the tactical advantages of attacking at dawn. The hour when men's reflexes were supposedly at the slowest. The hour when an attacking force could begin an assault in darkness and reach the enemy when it was light enough to fight. The hour when the enemy's morale was at a low ebb. Or so the brass-hats thought.

The morning's dream stayed in his thoughts. He'd tried to dismiss it as fancy, brought on by his struggles since Kiev, but he knew that wasn't right. He thought about it as he flew. He didn't understand why he had been selected for this vision. Did all who had the stone see things? Or was he unique?

He looked back and got a wide open grin from Ivan. The big Russian was enjoying his first flight. Somewhere behind his bulk, jammed into the observer's cockpit with him, was O'Reilly. The original plan had been to take O'Reilly alone but, on Hall's suggestion, Ivan had been hauled from his bed and pressed into service.

Armstrong checked his watch. It was just over an hour since he left the farm. He thought about Odessa. The Landau carried a Baedeker in its glove compartment and he had skimmed through it. Odessa was the chief port for the Ukraine and ice-free year round. It was a large city, sitting on bluffs above its harbor, the most important on the Black sea. Its half million population was, at one time, a third Jewish. But, since the Potemkin incident, when the battleship had supported the workers revolution in 1905, pogroms had been vicious and extensive. The Tsar found the Jews to be very convenient when it was necessary to find people to blame for the uprising. As a consequence, large scale emigration to the New World had decimated the Jewish population.

Armstrong decided that if Hall's contacts drew a blank he would seek out the remaining Jewish leaders and try for their help. But Hall had sent a signal to his agent in Odessa, so with any luck, he was already digging out information.

The engine droned steadily, eating up the miles in a manner undreamed of by the Countess. Now, ahead he could see the buildings of a large city and the shining expanse of the Black sea. Odessa!

He studied his map. Off to the right, towards the Dniester, was a military airfield. He sideslipped the plane lower. He saw the field and flew low over it, hoping that the chaotic conditions in Russia wouldn't prompt some trigger-happy gunner to blaze away at him. No response, so he leveled out, checked the windsock and landed.

He taxied over to some huts, looking around as the plane rolled across the field. He thought the field reflected Russia's turmoil. There were no planes, unless one counted a couple of cannibalized air frames sitting disconsolately under the trees, and no soldiers or other personnel. Except, as he cut the ignition and the Falcon clattered to a halt, a man stepped out of one of the buildings. A man wearing the British Warm overcoat common to officers.

Armstrong pulled off his goggles and climbed out, dropping to the ground as the man neared him.

"Armstrong?" the man said. "I'm Captain Buchanan. Lieutenant Hall in Jassy signaled me to meet you. I'm with the Allied mission here."

Armstrong saluted, then shook Buchanan's hand.

"Very good of you, sir," he said. "We're going to need as much information as you can give us."

Buchanan was a spare, tall man with a world-weary face and bleary bloodhound eyes. He regarded Armstrong with interest. "American? Canadian?"

Armstrong grinned. "Both, in a manner of speaking." He turned as Ivan climbed down, followed by squashed and silent O'Reilly. "These are my men, Sergeant O'Reilly and Mr. Ivan, a Russian citizen."

Buchanan looked around. "Yes, well we'd better get
the plane under cover in the hanger – don't want everybody to
see it. This field is deserted since the revolution, you see. If
you can get your men to do that while we have a talk?"

Armstrong pulled off his flying gear and tossed it into
the cockpit, then he and Buchanan paced while the others
pushed the Bristol into an empty hanger.

"Hall tells me that you will brief me fully on the
problem but he asked me to do some preliminary digging,
which I've done." Buchanan patted his pockets and pulled out
a packet of cigarettes. He offered one to Armstrong and lit it
from a battered lighter made from an empty cannon cartridge.
He saw Armstrong looking at it and smiled sadly, "From my
trench time in '15. Copped a 'Blighty' there and have been out
of active service since."

Armstrong noticed that the man walked with a limp.
"Yes," he said. "I did some time there too before I transferred
to the Flying Corps."

"Ah," Buchanan nodded. "Well to business. I've
checked the harbor-master's list and the only ship scheduled to
sail today is a small tramp vessel named "Narva". Her
manifest says she's taking general cargo to Sevastopol. If
you're looking for a ship she's the one. Don't get too many
sailing these days you know."

"When does she sail, what time?"

"Oh it won't be until after dark. Germans have a couple
of small surface raiders operating out of Constanta, so the
Russians don't take any chances."

"So I've got about ten hours to carry out my
assignment," said Armstrong. He walked for a moment in
silence as he pondered how much to tell Buchanan. "You see,"
he went on. "We were bringing back to Rumania some highly
sensitive papers, along with her archives and various other
artifacts, and I guess the Germans got wind of it. They attacked
us and got away with the rail-car that had the most stuff in it,
and obviously want to embarrass the Allies by letting the world
know of their coup. My orders are to destroy the cargo before
that can happen."

Buchanan thoughtfully rubbed his nose. "Lot of fuss
over a few papers!" he observed.

"Apparently very embarrassing to HMG if published,"
said Armstrong.

"Ah yes," said Buchanan dryly. "His Majesty's
Government must never be embarrassed, eh? How do you
propose to destroy this cargo? Fire? Explosion?"

"I thought that if we could get some kind of time-bomb on board so that the vessel sinks at sea, it would be satisfactory to all concerned."

"An infernal device, eh? As Sherlock would describe it. And how do you propose to obtain such a device?"

"I was rather hoping you could help me with that."

They turned as O'Reilly and Ivan closed the hangar doors and came towards them. Buchanan said. "I can get hold of some explosive for you all right, but the technical aspect of putting it together is a bit beyond me. Always left that kind of thing to the sappers, you know."

Armstrong grinned. "Don't worry about it. Between O'Reilly and myself we have enough expertise to handle it."

Buchanan beamed at them all. "Ah. Well. That's all right then. Let's get on the old bus and I'll take you down into Odessa."

The old bus turned out to be a battered Peugot sedan which showed a marked reluctance to get going. After O'Reilly had unsuccessfully cranked it several times, Ivan applied his massive arm to the task and whirled the engine with ease while Buchanan fiddled with the controls. It spluttered reluctantly into life and, sagging on its springs under their combined weight, it took them into Odessa.

"I think we'll spy out the land first," said Buchanan as the Peugot ran down the hills to the harbor. "Odessa's an interesting old place, you know. Local legend has it that it got its name from Odysseus. Supposed to have stopped here during his wanderings. Center part is built up on the bluffs, and the commercial industrial section is on the lower level, near the harbor."

He stopped the car on top of a low bluff in the shadow of a factory building. The men walked to the edge of the bluff, and Buchanan studied the scene below with binoculars. He lowered them with a satisfied grunt and gave them to Armstrong. "There she is," he said. "Got steam up too. If you'll follow the harbor wall left to the coaling jetty, you'll see her just left of the overhead chutes. That's where ships wait when they've finished loading and are ready to ship."

Armstrong took the glasses and found the ship. She lay against the jetty, singled up to breast ropes and springs. She was typical of her breed. A square superstructure proclaimed her Clydebank heritage, and her black sides were so streaked with rust she looked as if she hadn't had a coat of paint since she had slipped into the waters of the Clyde some quarter-century earlier. Battered, worn-out, sold and resold so many times it would be almost impossible to trace her history. Now a Russian ensign drooped over her poop.

Armstrong looked long and hard at her decks. Except for a man leaning on a guardrail, smoking there was no other sign of life. He bit his lip as he watched. This had to be it. The only ship scheduled to leave tonight. But it looked very peaceful – a typical merchantman. Then a man came out of the old-fashioned high forecastle and strode amidships. Armstrong watched him as he climbed the ladder to the bridge, opened the door, saluted and entered. Armstrong lowered the glasses and a warm feeling of fulfillment came over him. That was the ship. Goddammed Huns! Always so rigidly Prussian. One thing for sure, no merchant seaman ever saluted like that, particularly on a rust old tramp streamer.

He swung to Buchanan and the others. "This dockyard illuminated at night?" he asked.

"Not really, said Buchanan. "There's little work being done since the revolt broke out. Just a few jetty lamps here and there."

Armstrong gave the glasses to O'Reilly. "Can you get us a small rowboat?" he asked Buchanan

"I expect so," he said. "What's the plan?"

O'Reilly answered as he intently studied the ship through the glasses. "We're going to climb up the side like the Pirates of Penzance and make yon sods walk the plank. Ain't that so, melord?"

Armstrong ignored him. "Get on. Get in. Place the charge and get out is the plan."

O'Reilly spun around, eyes shining with excitement. "Is it blowing yon ship up we are?"

"That's the idea," said Armstrong.

"Holy saints alive," said O'Reilly. "What a wonderful job this is. I haven't had so much fun since the convent of the Sisters of Mercy burnt down one night and all the nuns came out in their underwear."

"Ha humph," grunted Buchanan, a stunned look in his eyes. "Er, he isn't regular army is he?" nodding his head at O'Reilly.

Armstrong shook his head sadly. "Alas, no," he lied. "Otherwise I would have had him shot by now."

They got back into the car and drove down a steep slope towards the commercial section of the town. They stopped outside a private house, guarded by poilu. From the roof of the house fluttered the flags of the Allies. "You'll be hungry," said

Buchanan. "I've told the cook to have breakfast ready for you. Your men can eat in the other rank's mess."

While Armstrong ate he gave Buchanan a list of articles he would need to make the bomb. Fortunately, there was a Lieutenant of engineers attached to the mission. He was called into conference and assured Armstrong that everything he needed would be ready for him early in the afternoon.

Armstrong finished eating and sat back with a sigh. "That was good, he said. "Nothing like a dawn flight to give a man an appetite. He looked at Buchanan, the engineer having left to get the supplies. "Now," he said casually. "Also with the train the Germans took prisoners, one of them a woman, a nurse. Have you heard anything of them?"

Buchanan shook his head, then frowned thoughtfully. "Well," he began hesitatingly. "One of my sources told me that some men were taken aboard another ship. I didn't pay too much attention because people are always being taken aboard this ship. She's in the hands of the so-called Death Brigade. They are a bunch of renegade Rumanian soldiers who have thrown in their lot with the Bolsheviks and apparently they're a damn sight worse than the Russians."

"Death Brigade!" said Armstrong alarmed. "My God, that sounds ominous."

"Yes it is rather. They've rounded up all the local Rumanians and have them locked aboard this hell-ship. Hope your boys aren't amongst them."

"I'm not worried about the men," said Armstrong. "They're soldiers and can take care of themselves. But the woman is the niece of the Baron Barreroth, and if these Reds find out they'll probably execute her. Hell, they've killed enough of their own aristocrats."

"That's serious," said a concerned Buchanan. "Do we try for her first?"

Armstrong slowly shook his head. "No, the Narva is more important. I'm afraid she'll have to wait her turn." He dismissed Anna from his thoughts. "I've been thinking about the Narva. I would like her to sink well out to sea, away from any possibility of easy salvage. We'll have to wait until dark to do the job, so I might need more time to get on and set a charge. If she sails at nightfall before we've set the charge it will be too soon. Is there any chance of delaying her sailing for a few hours?"

Buchanan grinned. "If sovereigns are still made of gold there's every chance. The harbor-master has a passion for good old English sovereigns. I'm sure a few of them jangled in front of him will result a problem on the harbor boom or suchlike that will take several hours to clear."

"That'll do it," agreed Armstrong. "Will you look after that then and also get us a boat. I am going to take a look at this hell-ship. Let's meet back here early this afternoon and see about making the bomb."

"Well be careful – they're a trigger-happy bunch of sods. The ship is called the Imperator Trajan and she's in the inner harbor. Good luck."

They separated, and Armstrong, after gathering up Ivan and O'Reilly, left the mission and walked through the streets until they were at the harbor again. Finding the Imperator Trajan was easy enough. She lay alongside a jetty flying red flags from every conceivable staff and mast. On her decks were throngs of soldiers wearing the red arm-band of revolution. They were all listening to a speech being given by someone standing on the capstan. Of prisoners there was no sign.

Armstrong sent O'Reilly off to get to the ship to observe. He himself examined every inch of her through the binoculars. After an hour O'Reilly returned, shaking his head.

"Nothing to report, Guvner," he morosely said. "They've got her sealed up tighter than a pig's arse. I hung around the dock long enough for one of them to tell me to shove off, or that's what I think he said, me Rumanian not being as good as me Russian. But not a sign or anything of the prisoners."

"Yes," agreed Armstrong. "I haven't seen anything either, and I've watched every porthole for a sign of life. They've probably got them locked up in the hold." He looked at his watch. "Well. Enough of this! Let's see if we can make this bomb."

Buchanan and the sapper officer were waiting for them as they entered the building. They were ushered into a basement room where the materials were to hand. A couple of army haversacks and a plain wooden box about twelve inches square.

The sapper was a thin Lieutenant with a nervous stammer that disappeared as he spoke with enthusiasm. "Now," the sapper began. "I've put about forty pounds of amatol in each of these haversacks, and the box contains the priming charge." He opened the box with a proud flourish to show the contents. "I've used dynamite sticks in here, as you can see, and a dry cell connected to the electric detonator. The timing mechanism is this alarm clock," he looked at

Armstrong. "I thought of using an acid timer, but we don't have one that will give you the time interval you asked for, the maximum we have here will only give you two hours. With this clock, of course, you can get twelve hours."

Armstrong leaned over to examine the lethal package. Four sticks of dynamite were in the box, with a detonator taped to them. Wires ran from the detonator taped to them. Wires ran from the detonator to the clock, which was nestled on its back in a bed of cotton wool. The clock was an expensive looking piece of equipment with a large brass bell on top.

"Nice clock," he observed.

"Yes," stammered the sapper. "Aaaactually my mother gave it to me on my last leave, said something about it being better then those ssssilly bugles to wake up to."

Armstrong looked at him. "I'm sorry. Don't you have another you could use?"

"Oh tttthink nothing of it. Mmmmother will be delighted when I tell her her gift blew up some of these ddddamn Bolsheviks – Tory to the bbbone is mother. In any case it's a damn sight more reliable than anything I could pick up here. Don't want you bbbblowing yourself up you know when you switch it on. Looks bad for us engineers."

Armstrong smiled. "How do I operate it," he said.

"As you can see, we've got a wire from the positive to the metal case of the clock and we've soldered it there. Now, my men have carefully insulted the bell from the clock and the other wire is soldered to that. As soon as the alarm is actuated and the clapper touches it will detonate. We tested it and it cracked a detonator most satisfactorily." He pointed out every component with pride. Obviously, Armstrong thought, a man in love with his job. "The clock needs winding and the alarm spring too. Set the time that you want, then pull out this button and she's ready to blow. Except for one thing. This little knife switch here." He indicated a small switch near the cell. "That's your safety. Close that last of all. So start the clock, pull the alarm button, and if it doesn't start ringing you're safe to close the switch. All clear?"

Armstrong nodded. "Yes, that should do the job just fine."

The sapper beamed at him "Jolly ggggood then. Oh, one little thing. Do set the box so that the cccclock is upright. Runs better that way."

Buchanan said, "So he has to find a spot in the bilges. Set the primer. Pack the amatol on top and get the hell out."

"In a nutshell, yes," agreed the sapper.

"Eighty pounds enough to sink the ship?" queried Buchanan.

"Oh yes," said the sapper. "Old rust bucket like that, probably break her back. Oh yes, she'll ssssink all right. Provided the charge is in the right place. Of course, if you can find a mmmmagazine to set the charge against, so much the better."

Buchanan looked at Armstrong. "That's all there is to it. I have a rowboat ready for you. The harbor-master has already informed the Narva that there's trouble with the boom and told them they have to wait 'til midnight. That'll give you another five hours after dark."

          *   *   *   *

Ivan rowed slowly, but every stroke had his full weight behind it, and the boat slid gurgling through the black waters of the harbor. Armstrong sat at the tiller, steering the boat so that it never left the shadow of the jetty. He and O'Reilly had blackened faces, and had amatol packed haversacks strapped to their backs. His eyes were fixed upon the Narva ahead of him, watching for signs of life and danger. The ship had been under observation all day and even now, scant hours before sailing, the Narva looked like any other superannuated old tramp in its last years. The only suspicious thing Armstrong had seen was the flourishing salute.

If the men who had attacked the train were aboard they were very discreet. Armstrong doubted that all of those in the attacking force had made the journey. Probably the actual soldiers had been sent back across the lines to their unit, while the Countess's strike force had remained with the gold. As chaotic as Russia was with the revolution, he doubted that the presence of uniformed German soldiers would have been tolerated.

"Oars," he hissed at Ivan as the blunt bow of the Narva loomed over them. Ivan slid the oars inboard as O'Reilly, looking like a dark evil imp in his burglary black, stood up in the bows and caught hold of the rough plating of the ship. Hand over hand he pulled along the side, needing only an occasional stroke from Ivan to keep the boat against the ship.

"Give me a cigarette, Rolf." The voice came through an open scuttle above their heads – and the voice spoke in German! The men in the boat tensed as a mumbled reply was heard. Then there came a hoarse laugh, and the blackness of the porthole was disturbed by the reflected flare of a match.

Another voice was heard. Different from the first, also in
German. "Damn this wait. Suppose I run aft to our supplies
and get some more cigarettes?" A third voice, harsh and
authoritive, said. "Orders are clear and explicit. We are not to
leave here under any pretext until the ship had left harbor. So
control yourselves. Anyone attempting to leave will feel my
boot up his arse. Erwin! Break that cigarette in half and give
half to me."

Armstrong smiled with satisfaction, and nodded to
O'Reilly who began pulling the boat ahead again. This was it.
The bastards were on board and lying low.

In discussing where to put the charge, it had been
decided that the best place would be in the bottom of the fore-
hold, against the boiler room bulkhead. An explosion there
should open both the hold and the boiler room to the sea. With
two main compartments flooded the Narva had to sink.

Armstrong wrinkled his nose as the boat slid
amidships, towards the stubby old-fashioned bridge, the
Narva's bottom was foul with weed that streamed out from its
sides and stank of age. The cooling water discharge from the
boiler room was narrowly avoided, then they were in position.

Armstrong stood up as Ivan and O'Reilly clung with
their fingertips to the plating and tossed a small grapnel over
the bulwark above him. It hit with a soft clunk, for he had
wrapped rages around its arms, and he pulled the rope taut to
make sure it had a good hold. It was firm. He looked at the
others, nodded and stepped off, his rubber-shod feet
scrambling for footholds as he pulled himself arm over arm up
the rope.

He rolled over the bulwark, and squatted down, alert
for danger, knife in hand as he waited for O'Reilly. The deck
was empty, gloomily lit from the jetty lamps. The old fashioned
foc'sle deck was silent. If there was a sentry there, he was
asleep. O'Reilly slid over the bulwark and squatted down
beside him.

Armstrong motioned to Ivan to lay off, then he jerked
his head to O'Reilly and went to the deckhouse. He stopped by
a screen door, gingerly eased off the clips securing it, and
cautiously looked inside. A passage ran the length of the
deckhouse and just about mid-ship a ladder went upwards.
Below it a hatchway and another ladder went down. The
passage looked like the rest of the ship. Rusty, uncared for
paint-work and peeling, splitting woodwork.

"Jasus," whispered O'Reilly. "It smells worse than a
Turkish whore-house."

Armstrong hardly heard him. He listened to a murmur of voice that came down the ladder. Up there would be cabins and the bridge. To his right, running athwart ships was another passage, and half way along that was a small hatch in an alcove. That looked promising. He made a chopping motion of his hand to O'Reilly, who nodded and pulled his shillelagh from his trousers. They entered the deckhouse, closed the screen door behind them and went to the thwart ship hatchway.

The hatch was secured by wing-nuts and they began to unscrew them. The threads were like the rest of the ship – rusty! But O'Reilly, with a wink, pulled a can from a pocket and Armstrong smelt the odor of penetrating oil. The alcove sheltered them to an extent from anyone passing through the fore and aft flats, so they huddled as close as they could. Finally the last clip fell off and they were ready. O'Reilly squirted the rest of the oil on the hinges and they swung up the hatch, securing it to its clip on the bulkhead. Armstrong hung over the edge and shoe his torch through the blackness of a cavernous hold. His nose twitched in distaste, the hold smelled as if it normally carried guanu. He played the beam over the extent of the hold, noting that the cargo consisted of a few boxes and canvas covered pallets in the center of the hold. A ladder led vertically down.

"Let's go," he said to O'Reilly.

"What shall we do about the hatch," O'Reilly whispered.

Armstrong looked at it for a moment, then shook his head. It was tempting to leave it open ready for a quick exit but too risky. If anyone passed and it was open they would be sure to see it; closed, maybe they wouldn't notice that the clips were off. Motioning for O'Reilly to go first, he waited until he was clear then stepped on the ladder himself, lowering the cover to its seat as he went down.

Reaching the bottom they stood for a moment playing their torches around and getting their bearings. The hold smelt of bilge water, rotten vegetables, diseased meat, animal fertilizer and whatever other cargos it had held in the past quarter century. Armstrong walked to the forward bulkhead, and studied the area. Beneath his feet was a section of grating and he knelt down to look through it. The smell of bilge was stronger here and he could see the gleam of water, but he could also see there was a horizontal frame. And the frame was large enough to stack the charge.

"Over here," he called to O'Reilly, who was snooping around the cargo. O'Reilly came and they lifted out the grating. Armstrong lowered himself on to the frame and eased the haversack off his back.   O'Reilly took his off as well and emptied out the oil-cloth wrapped squares of amatol, stacking them neatly, ready for Armstrong to reach for.   Armstrong began stacking his squares along the frame.   Eight squares, each five pounds in weight, innocent looking squares.   He put the priming charge in the middle and stacked the forty pounds from O'Reilly on either side of it.   He checked his watch – ten p.m.   He carefully wound both the mainspring and the alarm then set the alarm for eleven hours ahead.   Scarcely breathing, he activated the alarm button.   The clock ticked, a healthy confident tick.   He checked the alarm button, the soldered connections, the set time; then, with sweat cold on his forehead, he closed the knife switch.   God help us he thought.

He checked his watch again.   They'd only been inboard a half hour.   Where the hell was O'Reilly?   He swung himself up out of the bilge and hissed for the man.   O'Reilly came running, his torch flicking all over the hold.

"Let's get this grating back," Armstrong brusquely ordered.   "Less chance of the charge being discovered."

They dragged the grating back into position and settled it in its frame.   It slipped in with a dull clang and Armstrong froze for a moment, wondering if the sound would carry, then he muttered to O'Reilly.   "We've been here long enough.   Let's go."

"Take your haversack then, melord," said O'Reilly in a very chirpy voice.

"What the hell for," grunted Armstrong.   "Lose them in the crates there."

"Ooh but that wouldn't be such a grand idea would it, melord?   If they find them and start to wondering, maybe they'll search the ship."

"Yeah," Armstrong said.   "I suppose we should have thrown them in the bilges while we had the grating off.   Okay give me it."

"It's at your feet, Guvner," said O'Reilly, again in that strange voice.

Armstrong looked at him suspiciously, reached down to pick up his haversack and almost fell on top of it, being unprepared for the weight of it.   "What the hell have you put in here, man?" he asked.

O'Reilly snickered.   "Gold, melord.   Bars of yellow gold."

Armstrong was startled. "You mean it's here? Our gold!"

"Aye, that it is. All bundled up nicely on those pallets there."

"Great God Almighty," breathed Armstrong. "I would have thought that they'd have it locked away in a strong room somewhere, not in a cargo hold." He made to go to the pallets but O'Reilly caught his arm.

"Begging yer pardon, melord but it wouldn't be such a grand idea to do any more rooting around there. I've covered our traces ready good and if we get out now they won't notice it too soon. I've put enough gold in the haversacks for two strong men to carry and that's all we can do."

Armstrong looked at the Irishman, thought for a moment, then shrugged his shoulders into the haversack straps. "You're right of course. I suppose they think they're pretty safe. They don't know yet that we've taken the countess."

Armstrong led the way up the ladder and cracked the hatch open. He hung from the top and cautiously peered out. He looked to the left, clear. To the right? Damn! Someone wearing scuffed seaboots came clomping towards him. He froze, not daring to lower the hatch in case the man detected the movement. The boots shuffled by and he heard the atonal humming of a tune. He waited. All was quiet. All was clear. He swung the hatch up and climbed up the last few feet. He stood in the passage, knife in hand, as O'Reilly came through the hatch, puffing with the weight of his haversack.

Quickly they screwed shut the wingnuts, not daring to leave any of the eight off. Then they sprinted for the end of the passage. Seconds later they were hanging over the bulwarks while Armstrong flashed his torch twice. They waited, then the shape of the boat loomed out of the darkness and Ivan was here.

Armstrong whispered to O'Reilly. "I want you to lay off and wait for me. I'm going to see if I can look at the charts."

O'Reilly's head jerked around as if he had been mortally insulted. "Melord," he protested. "That's not safe on your own. Let me do that. I've got the experience."

Armstrong shook his head. "No," he said. "You wouldn't know what to look for." Cutting short further protestations, he ordered the man over the side. He lowered his haversack down to him, then crept up the outside ladder from the well-deck to the deckhouse.

The ladder led to a passage above the one he had reached from the well-deck, except this one had the outboard side open to the sea. Here the deck was unscrubbed wood. To his right were the portholes of cabins, all darkened but for the most forward one. In the center of the flat was the ladder that he had seen from below and from which he had heard the murmur of voice. Now all was silent. The only illumination came from the porthole.

Armstrong, soundless in his plimsols, crept to the midship ladder and climbed up it. This would be, he realized, the self-same ladder he had seen the man climb up who had given the show away by saluting. He reached the door of the bridge, blessed the fact that it was all dark and entered. The bridge was as dirty as the rest of the ship. It also stank. Apparently its master favored a particularly rank brand of Turkish tobacco. Light filtered through years of dirt and tobacco stain on the big square windows. It was enough to see that the starboard corner was a table littered with papers. He crossed to the table and risked switching on his torch. One chart sat among the papers.

The chart was filthy and ringed with coffee mug stains, dog-eared at the corners and streaked with countless pencil marks. It was of the northern part of the Black Sea, probably the only chart the ship possessed or needed. Armstrong examined it carefully. It looked as if the Narva had spend the entire war sailing between Odessa and Sevastopol. Except! One thinly drawn line ran from Odessa in a dog-leg course to the Bulgarian coast. Armstrong smiled to himself as he looked at it. Interesting! It looked as if the countess had not been entirely truthful. The destination was not Istanbul but Varna, Bulgaria. And there? The kaisers's coffers? Not likely. If he had judged his woman correctly, the gold would end up in a numbered account in a Swiss bank.

He tensed as he heard a laugh, and the murmur of voices again from the deck below. He crept from the bridge and down the ladder to the main deck. The voices were from the cabin at the forward part of the superstructure. Armstrong hesitated for a moment, unwilling to increase the chances of being seen, but some inner sense urge him on. He slipped to the open port and squatted below it, listening.

A burst of laughter came then a voice spoke – a cultured aristocratic voice. "This voyage will pass as if we traveled on Mercury's wings, my friends. For me at least. As soon as we clear the harbor I am going to teach that Hebe bitch some manners. She will learn that it is not acceptable for a Jew to spit at a German officer eh!"

Armstrong's guts tightened as there came a burst of laughter and a sycophantic voice said, "And what kind of lesson will the Herr Count be teaching?"

Anna? She was in this ship and not the Imperator Trajan?

The Count's answer to the question must have been physical not verbal because another gale of laughter came through the porthole, and a third voice said.

"Perhaps, when the Count has finished with her, I could take over the lessons. After all, it was I who captured her."

The Count – it had to be Ernst – snorted and said. "When I have finished with her anyone can have her, not that she will be any good to them. As long as she goes over the side before Varna. I don't want my Marthe to know we took her with us. Women are best kept in ignorance, eh? Now pass the bottle again. God damn this waiting. Stupid Russian bastards can not run a naval base."

Armstrong heard a murmured question and Ernst said. "Yes, the master tells me he has received permission to sail at midnight. So just over an hour and we move."

Armstrong crawled away from the porthole and stood up. Anna was on board. Where? For the first time since he had watched her disappearing on the train he loosed his tight control of his emotions, and allowed himself to hope. He looked at the three other darkened portholes. Cabins? She could be in any one of them. And there should be a like number on the port side. He went to the stern portion of the flat and there was an athwartship walk to the port side and half way along the walk, a door. He cautiously opened the door and slipped through.

Before him was a mid-ship passage with four cabins on either side. The forward starboard on held Ernst and company. The port forward one was probably the master's. The rest, no doubt, were for mates and the occasional passenger. Armstrong thought that the cabins furthest aft from the bridge would be the most likely. He tried the door on his right. It was unlocked. He slid inside and risked a flash from his torch. Empty! The next one to the right. Unlocked. He stuck his head in and saw a bulk lying on the bunk. He went towards it, hardly daring to breathe. He stopped, a sick feeling of disappointment in his stomach. This wasn't Anna. Too big, and whoever it was stank of stale sweat and garlic.

The other cabins except one were unlocked. As he looked around them he realized that the ship was under-manned, for these were empty of possessions or bedding. That left the locked one. He stood outside it, wished for a moment he had brought O'Reilly to pick the lock, then inserted his knife into the door jam and levered. The wood was rotten as the rest of the ship. With a dry snap the lock broke away from the door and Armstrong froze, his heart pounding. Had the noises been heard? Nothing happened and he slipped inside.

He played the torch over the contents and realized why the cabin had been locked. There was a small arsenal in it; side-arms, rifles, the distinctive stick grenades used by the Germans, and ammunition. He checked his watch. Just over a hour to mid-night. This ship would be bustling with activity in less than thirty minutes as if prepared to get under way. Swiftly he thought over his options. Getting O'Reilly on board to help search would take too long. And the more men on board the more chance of getting caught. Anna's dark eyes swam into his thoughts and he cursed. Time for action the Armstrong way.

He opened the cabin door and looked out. The passage was still deserted. He slipped into the cabin that held the sleeping man and drew his knife. The man had rolled onto his back and was emitting garlic impregnated snores into the ripe atmosphere. Armstrong put his knife between his teeth and clapped a large hand over the man's mouth and nose, effectively cutting off all air. The man started to gag and, in the dim light coming through the porthole, Armstrong saw his eyes flick open.

He swung his right fist full force down into the huge gut and air left the man in a whoosh that splattered spit and snot out past Armstrong's hand. The man's eyes bugged out with fear and panic as his chest heaved for breath. His hands tried to reach for Armstrong but he took the knife from his teeth and held it, without speaking, at the man's throat. The man saw and felt the great shining knife, his eyes rolled up and his body lost all control as he slumped in a faint.

Armstrong cursed. He played the torch beam around the cabin and saw a sink, a typical cabin sink, miniscule, in a wooden stand. He saw a glass there, unwashed and stained. He filled the glass with water and dashed it into the man's face. The man spluttered, opened his eyes and Armstrong again placed his hand over his mouth as he waggled the knife under his nose. The man's eyes, bulging with fear, followed the knife as it moved.

"I'm going to take my hand away," said Armstrong in his careful Russian. "If you call out it will be the last sound you ever make. Nod your head."

The man did so and Armstrong slowly removed his hand.

"Now listen. You have a lady on board. A prisoner. Where is she?"

The man wiped the streaming water from his face. "A lady, sir," he stammered.

Armstrong's patience snapped. "Yes a lady," he said, putting the knife on the tip of the man's nose. "Where is she? Where? Where?

The man gulped. "I think there is someone in the cable locker sir," he said. "The captain doesn't tell me. Just says to keep out of there until we sail."

"Can you open it?"

The man looked terrified. "The captain will kill me. He's got lot of money from these men who have come on board and he told me he'd shoot anyone who snooped there or in the holds."

Armstrong hauled the man upright, the blade never moving from the man's face. "I will kill you here and now unless you lead me there," he said. He grinned, deliberately showing his teeth in a sadistic leer. "Make up your mind. Me or the captain."

The man decided in a hurry that the captain was the less immediate evil and he heaved himself out of the bunk, pulling on his trousers while Armstrong kept the knife poised.

"Is it locked?"

"Yes sir, but I have a key. I'm the mate."

Armstrong pulled open the door and checked outside. All quiet. He pulled the mate by his vest towards him. "Okay, outside and to the cable locker."

The mate whimpered, "It's cold sir, can I put on my coat."

"No dammit," Armstrong snarled. "Move your fat body now, before I slice you up."

They left the cabin and, rather than pass by the cabin that held the count, Armstrong made the mate go down the after ladder and through the main deck flat to the forward cargo deck. Keeping tight hold of the mate's belt he followed him to the blunt bow. A door from the cargo deck was opened and they went into a passage that led further for'ard.

In the middle of the passage was a hatch in the deck and up through it came the murmur of voices. The same voices he had heard when he was in the boat. They skirted the hatch and went to a door at the end of the passage. The steel door was clipped shut and a shiny new padlock was hanging on it. The mate took keys from his pocket and removed the padlock.

Armstrong jabbed him with the knife. "Open the clips quietly," he hissed, apprehensive over the nearness of the crew hatch. The mate heaved at a clip but couldn't move it. Clips generally require a sharp blow to force them off their seat, Armstrong realized, and the mate didn't have enough strength to move them slowly. With an impatient curse he pushed the man aside and heaved at a clip. "You move and I'll bury this knife in you," he whispered to the mate. His muscles tensed and the veins in his arms stood out like cords as he exerted his full strength on each clip. Slowly they came. One to six. Each one carefully pulled off its seat and laid back without knocking. As the last one was pulled off he looked suspiciously at the mate and motioned him to open the door. With a creaking noise that set his teeth on edge it swung open and, pushing the mate ahead of him, he entered.

Closing the door behind him and setting one clip lightly to hold it closed, he switched on his torch. He didn't see her at first because all of his attention was taken up by the stench of the locker. All cable lockers smell of the stink of the sea bottom that sticks to an anchor cable, no matter how carefully it is hosed off when winched in. But this locker smelled as if no one had ever bothered with a hose. It stank of rank mud, dead fish, raw sewage and seaweed from every ocean bottom of the seven seas. The deck was slimy with mould, and gobs of mud were petrified to the chain as it hung from the navel pipe overhead.

Armstrong shuddered at the stink and flashed the beam from the torch around, but the mate reached out to push an electric switch. A feeble light came on from a bare bulb and Armstrong saw a heap of canvas and on it Anna, who stared up at him with eyes that softened in relief when she recognized him. She was bound at hands and feet and a filthy gag was across her mouth.

Armstrong cut through her bonds, then holstered his knife and pulled the gag away. Her face was gaunt with privation and her huge dark eyes stared at him. "I knew you'd come," she said. "I knew." Tears welled in her eyes and slipped down her face.

Armstrong picked her up and held her to him. He was incapable, momentarily, of speech. He hugged her and felt her body shaking as she sobbed against him. She still wore the same dress as on the morning of the raid, now foul with muddy slime. "I'm taking you out of here, my darling," Armstrong said and stopped talking. The door swung open and a man stood there. A man with a Luger parabellum in his hand.

He entered, eyes flicking unbelievingly from the mate to Armstrong and back again. "What have we here?" he said in German. "Treachery? Betrayal? A rescue? My God. What will the count say to this?" He walked towards Armstrong. He was a big man wearing a fisherman's sweater over seaman's trousers. He looked a sailor, until one realized that his boots weren't seaboots but jackboots. He stared at Armstrong and recognition flickered in his eyes. "You," he said. "I know you. You are the man we chased from the Countess's house in Jassy. The night you raped her!" With a sudden movement he swung the gun against the side of Armstrong's head. Armstrong staggered back to the anchor cable, his head a flaming ball of pain. He sensed Anna falling away from him. He also sensed a tug at his waistband.

"The count will be delighted to meet you," said the man. His eyes flicking from Anna, crouched apparently terrified on the canvas, and back to Armstrong. "He has a special place in his heart for you. Of course, no one wanted to tell him the full details, you understand. One doesn't directly tell a senior officer that his wife has been raped, but we found a way." He sniggered, as if the memory amused him. "How glad I am that I persuaded him to allow me to inspect the prisoner one more time before we sailed. Now I will move to the side. You will move ahead and I will follow. The woman can stay here until we sail." He waved the pistol, a cocky grin on his face. "If you make a suspicious move I will shoot you. Do you understand?"

He moved aside to let them pass, confident of his mastery, but Anna suddenly screamed a curse, and hurled the knife she had taken from Armstrong's waist at the German. The knife flashed by his head and clanged against the steel side of the ship. The German, shaken, swung his gun to her but, as he did so, Armstrong hit him in a hurling charge. The German hit the door, it crashed shut, the gun flew from his hand and Anna dived for it while Armstrong and the German struggled.

The pair rolled over and over on the slimy floor, punching and kicking. Anna found the gun but was afraid to use it, as a shot would alarm the rest of the Germans. Armstrong felt his strength waning. It had been only a couple of days since his fight with Kaminski and the German was in superb shape, big, muscular and fit.

They rolled once more, Armstrong was underneath and the rim of the cable locker was under his neck. The German's hand was on his chin, forcing it back over the rim. Through a blur of pain he sensed Anna struggling with the mate. Armstrong had a hand around the German's wrist, trying to force it away from his throat and with the other he was swinging heavy punches into his opponent's side. Then a voice spoke from inside his head. Clearly it said. "Show him the stone!"

Armstrong's hand went to his pocket and the stone slipped from the bag into his palm. He pulled it from his pocket and held it high, swinging from its chain. The German's eyes opened wide, he reached for it and his grip on Armstrong's throat eased. He never reached the stone. As his hand opened to grasp it a beam of light, brilliant and narrow flashed from the stone to his eyes. He screamed with pain, both hands went to his eyes, and Armstrong butted his head into the man's face.

The man staggered to his feet and Armstrong rolled clear and stood upright, watching in awed silence as the man staggered back to the door with blood spurting out form beneath the hands he kept so tightly pressed to his eyes. And as Armstrong watched, the door opened and two huge hairy hands appeared, one each side of the German's head and, almost casually, twisted it until the neck snapped. Armstrong looked up at Ivan, whose big tombstone teeth were bared in a grin.

"We thought you needed help," he growled. "We saw man go forward."

"Yeah," said O'Reilly, who had one arm around the neck of the mate in a sleeper hold. "That's the last fooking time I'm letting you go on your own. You're not safe to be out." He smiled at Anna as he released the mate who crumbled to the floor. "How are you doing miss? Lovely to see you again, though I must say I've seen you looking better."

Armstrong went to Anna, put his arm around her, then said. "Let's get the hell off this ship."

Ivan looked at Anna, hissed in dismay, and effortlessly picked her up. Armstrong grinned at O'Reilly and said. "What do you say to carrying me?" O'Reilly rolled his eyes and shook his head as they left the cable locker.

They crept past the open hatch. All was quiet now, as if the men below were sleeping, and they came to the blessed open air of the cargo deck. O'Reilly whispered to Armstrong.

"Does yourself know that he stinks worse than a Frenchman with dysentery."

Armstrong held up his fist and O'Reilly lapsed into silence as they reached the boat. O'Reilly pulled the boat in on its line and slipped down. Ivan, with Anna clinging to his back, went next. Armstrong, as he waited for them to get safely down, marveled that the fight had disturbed none of the crew. But at any moment now the ship would be stirring as they prepared to leave harbor. Beneath his feet he could feel the trembling of the deck as the boilers built up pressure. He took one last look around and swung himself over. As he did so he heard the clang of the bridge door. He slide down the rope so fast he landed in a heap in the boat bottom. O'Reilly pulled in the rope as Ivan pushed away from the Narva, then Ivan rowed while O'Reilly steered and Anna sat huddled in Armstrong's arms.

As they cleared the bows Armstrong saw lights come on in the wheel house and a couple of men appeared on deck and stood by the wires. He wondered what action Ernst would take when he found Anna gone and one of his men dead.

CHAPTER TWENTY

A nna sat in the Peugeot, wrapped in a blanket, while Buchanan and Armstrong stood, binoculars to their eyes, watching the Narva ease away from the jetty. She pulled the blanket tighter around her and huddled in its warmth. Her body craved a bath and she could smell the stink of mud in her hair but she felt lightheaded with joy at her release. She looked at Armstrong and again remembered the rush of excitement and shock she experienced when she had seen it was him in that awful cable locker. She knew she loved him more than she had ever thought it possible to love anyone.

"Hah," said Buchanan pointing, as a man ran from the bows to the bridge. "There goes a greek bearing messages."

Armstrong grunted as he watched the man enter the bridgehouse – this time without saluting – "He's committed now. He can't stop and search for Anna. The cargo is more important to him than any woman."

Anna snorted at this from the car. Armstrong turned and smiled at her. "Not in my opinion of course."

"Do you think he'll search the ship?" queried Buchanan.

"I doubt it," said Armstrong. "Oh, I'm sure he'll inspect the cargo, but why would he think someone's mined the ship? No, I'm confident about that. He'll think we wanted only to free Anna and are planning to grab him and the ship in Sevastopol. He doesn't know we know he's sailing to Bulgaria."

Buchanan lowered his glasses and looked at Armstrong. "I see that you took some samples of the cargo," he said, his voice and manner inquisitive. "Those haversacks your man stowed in the car looked heavy."

Armstrong watched the Narva as she stood out to sea. He saw her head turn to the east before she disappeared into the dark night. "There she goes," he said. "Trying to fox us that she's heading south-easterly to Sevastopol. As soon as she's out of sight she'll be hauling around to the west." He turned to Buchanan. "The cargo samples you mentioned." He made his voice heavy with meaning. "Afraid I can't discuss them, old man. Classified you see. Need to know and all that."

O'Reilly, standing nearby with Ivan, grinned to himself as he heard Armstrong, and muttered himself. "Sure and 'tis a grand larcenous laddy yon fellow is becoming."

Armstrong looked at his watch then said to Buchanan. "Let's go to the mission. We all have to clean up, snatch a few hours sleep, and be off at first light."

The five of them got in the car and Buchanan drove them to the mission headquarters. Anna sat in the back with Armstrong and huddled close to him for comfort and protection against the night air.

At the mission, Ivan picked up Anna, still wrapped in the blanket, and carried her past the sentries. Buchanan told them all was in order, and the party went to his room, with Armstrong and O'Reilly carrying the loaded haversacks.

Buchanan yawned. "If I'm to get you to the plane by sunup I'd better get some shuteye. Your men know where they can sleep and I suggest Miss DeCourville use my room tonight. I'll use a couch in the lounge." He looked at her and gave an embarrassed cough. "I'm afraid the baths are at the end of the corridor and this is a men-only establishment. But I'm sure everyone's asleep, so if Lieutenant Armstrong keeps watch you can use them. In the meantime I'll try and find some fresh clothes for you."

"Trousers and tunic, anything like that will be suitable," said Armstrong. "She's flying back with me. I have a spare sidcot she can wear as a topcoat."

O'Reilly and Ivan left for their quarters, and Buchanan went to find clothes. Armstrong told him to leave them in his room and he would see that Anna got them.

The bathroom was furnished in the ornate Russian style. A huge tub sat high off the floor on claw-footed legs, decorative tiles lined the walls and floor and on claw-footed legs, decorative tiles lined the walls and floor and well-polished brass fittings shone in the light of a hissing gas lamp. Armstrong turned the taps and steamy water gushed out in a roar. He looked at Anna, standing with her arms tightly crossed as if she was finding the situation hard to believe and said, "I think I'll wait outside while you bathe. This is a little public, and I don't want to give Buchanan ideas."

Anna gave a wan smile, and Armstrong left her and went to Buchanan's room, just as the man returned.

"I opened up the quartermaster's store," Buchanan said. Here's the smallest uniform I could find, and a sweater."

"That should do it all right," said Armstrong. "I'll see she gets it."

Buchanan looked at him, and his bloodhound eyes blinked uncertainly. "Er, you know where the lounge is," he said. "There's another couch there for you, if you need it."

Armstrong grinned at him, amused by the man's manner. "Thank you," he said. "I'll be there as soon as I've seen Miss DeCourville settled and after I've bathed the stink of that cable locker off myself."

Buchanan left and Armstrong returned to the bathroom and tapped on the door. "It's Miles," he called. "I have some clothes for you."

The door latch clicked, he waited a moment then turned the handle and entered. Anna walked away from him towards the tub. She had undressed to a floor length shift of white cotton that clung to her body in the moist air. She stopped by the bath and looked at him.

"I've brought you some clothes," he said, holding up the drab khaki. "Not quite Bond street but I'm sure ma'aselle will be able to give that certain touch which will lift them from the ordinary."

She turned off the taps and in the sudden silence she said, "Put the clothes down and talk to me."

Armstrong hung the clothes on wall hooks, then looked at her. He wanted to hold her but he was uncertain of her emotions after her expectations of the last few days. She felt the water, turned on the cold tap to cool it and said, "All I had to hold on to when I was taken was the thought that you would come for me. I can't begin to tell you how I felt when I realized it was you in that awful place." She bent to turn off the tap, then she straightened and looked at him. Her dark eyes were shining through tears that rolled down her dirty face, leaving white streaks.

Her lips quivered in a tremulous smile as she saw his filthy, slime smeared, overalls and his blackened hands and face. Her hands moved and the shift slipped from her shoulders and fell to the floor. Naked, she stepped into the bath and sank down in its water. In a low husky voice she said, "this bath is big enough for two. Put the catch on the door and come tell me I'm not dreaming."

Armstrong pulled off his clothes in a blur of movement. He stepped into the bath, gasping at the hot water and slid down behind her. Displaced water splashed to the floor and ran gurgling down the drain. She leaned her head back against him and said, "Please, oh please, wash my hair."

He got to his knees and picked up the soap – Pears translucent soap, officers for the use of – and begun to lather her hair. He massaged her head with the rich foam, washing away all traces of the filthy cable locker. Her head was tilted back, her eyes closed against the lather and she made small murmurs of pleasure as he rubbed. He saw a galvanized bucket under the sink and he got out the bath and filled it with hot water. Anna sat in the bath, eyes still tightly closed, her head tilted back. Armstrong grinned to himself, put the bucket down, picked up his trousers and removed the velvet bag. Carefully he slipped out the Goliath Stone, then lifted the bucket and poured clean water over her head. She put her arms up to wring the water from her hair and he stopped her.

"One more bucket, my love," he said.

Refilling the bucket, he again poured it over her and, as the water cascaded down her body, he slipped the stone over her head, so that it lay glittering between her breasts.

She opened her eyes and gasped as her hands flew to the stone. She whirled around in the bath and reached for him pulling him into the water in a great splash. "Oh darling, darling, darling," she cried, kissing and pulling at him until he lay in the bath with her on top, her legs straddling him. He reached to hold her but she stopped him and put his hands on the sides of the bath. "Wait!" she said. She carefully removed the stone from her neck and laid it on her clothes. "I'm a hardheaded cynic usually, but I don't think we should be doing what we're going to do, while that stone is around my neck. It seems irreverent." She washed the traces of blacking from his face with a sponge. "First I want you to tell me how you found me. I'd almost given you up you know. I felt I was going to disappear forever on that ship." She winced at the bruises from his fight with the German. "My God, darling, next time shoot the bastards, it's much easier on your poor face."

"Ain't going to be a next time," said Armstrong huskily, wondering how long he was expected to control himself with this wonderful, slippery, silk-smooth body hanging over him.

"Close your eyes, you'll get soap in them."

Armstrong closed his eyes as he told her about the Narva and his discovery of her. Anna listened gravely as she pulled his head into her breasts and washed his hair. He

gasped in the steam-laden atmosphere and kissed her nipples –
nipples that hardened in an unmistakable invitation.

She laid his head back and slid herself downward until
he was able to enter her. Her eyes closed as she reared
backwards, forcing him deeper inside her. He watch her, awed
as always by her beauty, seeing tears slide down her face and
mingling wit her perspiration. His hands found her buttocks
and held their soft roundness. She made love with tenderness,
slowly moving her body on his until they both reached a peak
of shuddering passion. Afterwards she clung to him, her lips
locked on his until the water cooled, then they got out and
dried themselves. Anna reverently placed the stone in its
pouch and bundled it in her dirty clothes.   She wrapped a
towel around herself and rubbed her hair with another.
Armstrong stood with a towel around his waist, waiting. She
suddenly stopped rubbing and looked at him. "So you're
letting them get away with the gold?"

Armstrong shrugged. "There's too much of it to steal,
and I can't have the ship arrested and have the gold removed
without telling the Russians about it, and they'd just keep it, so
a pox on both their houses."

"What do you mean?"

"I mean that at nine a.m. the ship is going to sink. I've
mined it."

"Oh my God," said Anna, her eyes huge. "All that gold
at the bottom of the sea."

"Better there than feathering the countess' nest," said
Armstrong. "But enough talk. Morning will be here soon."

Armstrong opened the door and checked the passage –
all was clear.   With towels around them they went to
Buchanan's room and Armstrong showed her the narrow army
cot. Gathering up his clean clothes he leaned over and kissed
her. "Til morning," he said and left.

      *   *   *   *

Armstrong banked the Bristol and flew, once more, over the
field and the two waving figures below. It had been difficult
saying goodbye to Ivan. He had been a true friend to them all.
O'Reilly for once had been almost speechless as he rung Ivan's
hand and now he glumly sat in the rear cockpit with Anna and
watched as Buchanan and Ivan dwindled in the distance.
Armstrong had quietly handed Ivan one of the gold bars when
he had said goodbye and the big Russian's bearded face had
split in a wide grin as he had crushed Armstrong in a bear-hug.

Whatever the future held for Ivan he would have enough money to face it.

Armstrong flew south until he was over the sea, then he banked around to the south-west. He cursed the weather. It had changed from yesterday. Today a half gale was blowing from the west and rain periodically splattered against the windscreen. The cloud base was low, about a thousand feet, with a consequent reduction in visibility and he kept the Bristol just below it. The return to Jassy might be hazardous if this weather continued inland. He checked his watch – five after eight. The Narva had been at sea for almost eight hours. She would have turned as soon as possible to her westerly heading. Give her eight knots maximum. He was sure that there would be no worries about conserving fuel or overheating machinery. What was in the hold would buy the master a fleet of Narva's – providing the count let him live long enough to enjoy his bribe. But eight knots meant sixty odd sea miles. And that was quite a distance to have to find a small ship in.

Onward droned the plane. He looked back to Anna and her teeth flashed a smile. That was all he could see of her, muffled as she was in a big leather coat that Ivan had worn, a flying helmet on her head and goggles over her eyes. O'Reilly hung over the side watching the sea below – a rough sea that was a mass of whitecaps. The wind was westerly, and Armstrong wondered how many knots it was deducting from their speed. He was thankful that both tanks were topped up at Odessa. Today he was going to need all the fuel they could carry – of course, the same headwinds would be slowing the Narva too.

Time passed. Forty-five minutes past eight. Armstrong throttled back a little, unwilling to overheat the engine. Death would be swift if the engine failed over these waters. O'Reilly's head swung around as he heard the different engine note and he cocked an enquiring eyebrow, as if indignant that Armstrong should worry about his engine.

Armstrong kept the image of that thin pencil line in his mind as he flew on. He looked to the right, to the coast line of Rumania, barely visible about twenty miles away. As far as he could judge he was following the same course as the penciled one.

Minutes ticked by. Armstrong flew a weaving course, either side of the mean. He checked his watch again – five to nine- almost an hour since takeoff and five minutes to the explosion. He reckoned the head-wind to be about forty knots.

They had probably covered about sixty miles over the ground by now.

At two minutes to nine Anna reached forward and rapped on Armstrong's head. He turned to look and her eyes were huge under the goggles. "The Stone," she screamed, the words just audible to him. She clutched her Sidcot jacket between her breasts. "It's hot!" She fumbled her hand inside the jacket to pull the stone away from her skin. Armstrong, stared at her uncomprehendingly for a moment, then, realizing what it meant, he rolled the Bristol and dived almost straight down. He pulled her level a couple of hundred feet above the water and there she was – the Narva, her tall thin funnel belching black smoke as her stokers fed the boilers and her blunt bows battered into the waves as white water spumed over her, almost obscuring her from sight. Armstrong yelled with relief. He was right. The stone was right. He throttled back and flew low over the ship, uncaring if they saw the plane. All looked intact and the Narva's single screw, at times buried deep and then fully out the water, as the vessel pitched, kept churning the Narva closer to its destination.

He throttled back and slowly circled, intently watching the bows of the Narva rise and fall. Every now and then an extra large wave – sailor's swore it was every seventh wave – would burst clean over the ship, forcing her bows deep into the mountainous seas.

He looked at his watch. It was five after nine, and he felt that his guts had turned to ice. Had they found the explosive? At five minutes and thirty two seconds past nine the Narva's bows lifted to a seventh wave and, as she reached the crest of the wave, her fore-hatch cover blew off in a flaming explosion, leaving a great gaping hole. The bows dipped and buried themselves deep into the wave. This time there was no hatchcover to shed the tons of water. This time the ship did not rise to meet the next wave. This time the ship, dealt a death blow by the tons of water pouring into her hold, continued her plunge. The seventh wave roared on, triumphant over an empty sea.

Armstrong, shaken by the sudden end, stared at O'Reilly and Anna. One ship. Three tons of gold, and God knew how many men, gone in seconds. He flew in a circle, scanning the sea below. Then he marked the position on his map and mentally shrugged off the image of the men he had drowned. He'd recovered the Irish jewels, won the Goliath Stone and saved Anna. Three out of four wasn't so bad. And those gold bars under the observer's cockpit were a very nice bonus.

He turned to look at Anna. Her face was calm, and she had pulled the Goliath Stone out through her jacket and was holding it for him to see. It swung on its chain, glittering brilliantly. She gripped it in her palm as she looked at him and shrugged, indicating that the stone was now cold. Armstrong nodded his understanding. He thought that a little of that stone went a long way, and the sooner they got it into the hands of the Baron Barreroth the better.

He shoved the throttles forward and took the Bristol in a gentle climb through the cloud and into bright sunshine. Next stop Jassy.

The End.

Printed in the United States
By Bookmasters